WWW.PREHISTORICMAGAZINE.COM

PRIMAL

Michael Esola

CRANE CANYON PUBLISHING

Library of Congress Control Number: 2015951907
Crane Canyon Publishing
Pittsburg, Ca.

Cover design copyright © 2019 by Michael Esola

Book layout by ebooklaunch.com

Printed in the United States of America

Visit Michael Esola on the world wide web at:
www.PrehistoricMagazine.com

To my children, Ethan and Adelaide, who were born during the writing of this novel. I love you both very much and can't wait till you're old enough to read one of these books.

"May a never-ending flow of energy forever be granted to those who continue to seek the impossible."

—Bick Downs

PROLOGUE

Vietnam, 10,000 Years Ago

The young hunter stood absolutely still just at the edge of the dark and entangled forest. His ears took in the familiar sounds from the limbs and branches behind him. Before him lay a long grassy expanse, a break from the dense and dark world of tall, towering, green bamboo trees from where he had just emerged. Materializing silently from the heavy growth was yet another hunter. This one though was much older, stronger, wiser, and he had the deep and gouging scars across his body to prove it.

The man that stood next to the young hunter was in fact the boy's father. His muscles were taut and muscular, his body the direct result of a lifetime of a brutally hard existence. Not an ounce of fat was on him; it was nothing but lean, taut muscle. Together, father and son stood mired deep in silence, their bodies all but naked except for a small loin cloth around their waist covering their mid-region.

The older man stepped forward and raised his bow, but today was not about him as the young hunter pushed past his father. Today was about the young boy, about his attempt to prove himself as both a man and a hunter to their people. This was a big occasion, a rite of passage if you will, and both men knew it.

Stepping up on a large boulder, the boy scanned their prehistoric world. Before him lay a field full of long grass, an area roughly the same size as that of a football field. Here the thick bamboo forest let up for a moment and gave way to a gentle, sloping grassland. The boy watched as the top of the long grass blew back and forth in the early morning wind. The field for the most part was a light yellow and brown in coloration.

The father continued to watch from a distance. Slowly the boy edged himself forward and lowered his body down into the long grass. Concealing himself as best he could, he began moving forward now at a silent yet brisk pace. A look of determination and resolve was plastered squarely across his face. Suddenly though, the boy paused, listened, and waited. He both felt and heard the long grass around him as it blew back and forth. It was everything his father had taught him: learn by what your surroundings tell you, root yourself firmly in the moment. And that's exactly what he was doing now. He listened for a few more seconds before continuing on. He would be triumphant in the hunt. This would be his day. He was certain of both of these.

• • •

Meanwhile back at the forest's edge, the proud father continued to watch his son for as long as he could. He was no longer able to see the boy as the young hunter had disappeared down and into the long grass, but the older man's eyes could just barely make out the top of the grass that was being pressed down as his son continued making his way silently through the field. A slight smile crept across the older man's face. But that was it. He would not let his emotions go any further than that. Age and the difficulty of life itself had hardened his emotions and if he allowed his mind to roam back to the past, he could remember when he was the young hunter and his father had taken him to this very same grassy expanse.

Suddenly, his eyes shifted back toward the grass field. His momentary distraction had caused him to lose sight of the general area where his son lay crouched in hiding. Quickly, his eyes darted back and forth. He could no longer see the long grass being pressed and matted down. He had no clue as to his son's whereabouts.

The boy was on his own now. But the same could essentially be said for all of them that happened to be living in this part of the world at this particular moment in time. Here life was tough, raw, and savage. These conditions caused early man to grow up at a young age. At the ripe old age of twenty-five, the man was already well into his prime, with the average life expectancy here coming at thirty-five years of age. Here life was both brutal and harsh. It was like a candle that burned fast from both ends.

Suddenly, the man heard noise from behind him. It had come from deep within the confines of the bamboo forest, back where the shadows were long, and where the forest was perpetually bathed in a dim grey lighting. Immediately, he felt his taut muscles ripple as he spun around and stared at the swaying stands of bamboo. The wood from the bamboo trees creaked and groaned as the bases of the trees rubbed against one another. The entire forest was slowly coming to life. He listened with his honed hearing and again he heard the sound. It sounded like something very large was moving through the brush. Slowly, the man took several steps back, his thoughts no longer with himself, but with that of his young son. Fearing for his own well-being as well as that of his son, the older hunter immediately took off sprinting back toward where he believed the boy to be.

● ● ●

The young hunter had been paused in absolute silence for going on close to a minute now. Doing his best to slow his breathing as well as his nerves, he had firmly rooted himself in this moment. This had been something his father had communicated to him time and time again. And now he was employing this idea to the fullest.

He steadied his body, adjusted his positioning, and studied his intended target. A short ways away, the young animal he had come all this way for stood grazing silently on all fours. The boy took another few seconds before quickly realizing this was his moment. Carefully, he drew an arrow from the small leather pouch slung across his back. Setting the arrow into position, he raised the bow in front of him. Letting out a quiet breath through his mouth, he took another few seconds to calm his nerves. His heart was beating hard against his ribcage. Finally he let the arrow fly. It made a soft whooshing sound as it sailed through the air, pinning the intended target somewhere on its thick and muscular neck. The result was instantaneous.

Immediate pain. The young hunter could now see the brightly colored tail of the arrow protruding from the creature's neck as it reared up onto his back two legs and let loose a blood-curdling cry of pain.

Suddenly though, the young boy heard movement from elsewhere. Something was quickly moving toward him. The young hunter hardly had time to even raise his weapon before he was competely engulfed. In one swift move, the boy's father swept him off his feet and lifted him high into the air. Now the two were moving quickly through the field, the dry long grass brushing by them on both sides as the sounds of the wounded animal from behind continued to bellow out across the clearing.

As the two continued to make their way, tall stands of swaying bamboo bordered them tightly on both sides. Suddenly from somewhere off to their right, they heard cracking and snapping sounds from deep within the dense bamboo. The trees were really swaying back and forth now, coming to life as if they themselves were a living, breathing monstrosity.

They kept running though, kept moving fast through the long grass. The man's eyes spotted the far end of the grassland, an area still populated with the bamboo forests that still remained in this region, but hopefully free of what it was he knew was responsible for the sounds. The noise however did not stop, and now deep cracking sounds of bamboo being broken and splintered rang out from all sides. The older hunter quickened his pace. Now they were truly moving as fast as they could through the long grass.

Meanwhile, the eyes of the young hunter still cradled in his arms began to dart back and forth and all around. The cracking sounds of bamboo continued to ring out. The boy's father ran a few more frantic paces before finally coming to a stop. For a minute he just stood there, his chest heaving in and out while still cradling his young son in his arms.

With no other option, he gently set the boy down in the grass. And there the two stood. The breaking and cracking of bamboo was now accompanied by deep, immense, bellowing roars. As the two continued to stand there, it was becoming clearer with the passing of each second that things were rapidly moving toward them.

Looking down, the older hunter and father made eye contact with his son. Not a word was said between the two, only direct eye contact. Both men drew an arrow and raised their bows out in front of them. And together, the pair stood strong and faced the deep and unnerving sounds as huge hulking forms slowly emerged from the trees and began converging on them from all sides.

1

Lang Son Province, Northern Vietnam: Present Day

John Corstine carefully whisked away at the surface with his brush while blowing ever so gently toward the area that he had been working on. Corstine was sixty-one years old, Caucasian, average height and build, and had a salt and pepper beard to go along with his gray hair up top. Slowly, little by little, the real-estate entrepreneur and President of The Society of Cryptozoological Agents was working to uncover what lay just beneath the surface. He paused for a moment, still laying flat on his stomach as he whipped his leather hat off and wiped the sweat from his head with the side of his long-sleeved Patagonia dry-fit shirt. This blisteringly hot and humid region of Vietnam was already taking its toll on his aging body. As they continued to work well into the latter hours of the day, the sun high above had been beating down mercilessly all day on them. Such was the relentless nature of life in this part of the world.

Despite this though, Corstine continued brushing for a few more seconds before finally setting the brush down and forcing his old body to sit upright. Looking over at the young man who had accompanied him to this isolated and remote part of the world, he knew what lay delicately atop the old blue blanket before them was enough to potentially set the scientific world ablaze, or at least give it one good swift kick in the ass.

Corstine's assistant and acting guide this very late afternoon was a twenty-six year old kid by the name of Diego Rivera, a first-year paleontology student at the University of Madrid who was being paid rather handsomely by Corstine for his services today. Diego was being paid for two reasons. First, to show John Corstine where the recently uncovered remains of a Gigantopithecus blacki specimen were located, and second and most importantly, to keep his academic mouth shut. The second part of the deal was nearly almost as important as the first part. You could say that the two parts of the deal worked in a tight, symbiotic relationship with one another.

Corstine continued to brush away gently at the surface, exposing more and more of the bone that lay beneath the surface. A few more whisking motions with the brush and then Corstine knew that was it for the day. Sixty-one years on this planet had more than taught him when it was officially time to call it quits. And as Corstine sat upright and stared at the long shadows cast around him, it was most definitely time to pack it in and call it a day. The heat and humidity had finally won out. That he knew with certainty. With a slight grunt and a bit of a struggle, he managed to stand to his feet, wincing in pain as he now stood fully upright. Corstine also knew that sixty-one years on this earth had left him with bad knees, knees that hurt and swelled on occasion, but he was still walking and upright, still traveling to the far-flung and remote corners of the world, so he had that much to be grateful for at least.

Corstine looked over at Diego. The young paleontology student sat neatly at the edge of the blanket carefully assembling the various array of bones, teeth, and ribs that had just been uncovered from the dusty hillside earlier this morning. Of course, this hadn't happened over night. They had been at it for nearly two weeks now, and the way that Diego saw it was that the money that Corstine was paying him would either go in the bank or fund his first full-fledged dig once he in fact became a legitimate paleontologist. Whichever route he decided to take, one fact remained: he was eternally grateful for both John Corstine as well as the man's deep pockets.

Quietly, Corstine began moving toward Diego, but more importantly toward where their treasure trove lay. Lowering his left hand, Corstine scooped up his pick out of the dirt and continued on his way. For a moment he thought about paleontological dig sites, particularly toward the late 1800's, early 1900's when the hunt for dinosaurs and other forms of prehistoric life would have been as wild and ruthless as the wild west itself. It would have been quite the scene, not to mention the inherent dangers involved. He continued to ponder what that must have been like as he continued walking.

Corstine finally arrived at the blue blanket. Carefully, the President of The Society of Cryptozoological Agents set his equipment down next to his day pack. Rather than squat as Diego was doing, Corstine pulled up his tiny folding chair that he had dragged with them out here to the middle of goddamn nowhere. But it was necessary as his aging knees would not allow him to stand for prolonged periods of time anymore. Right now, the chair was most definitely worth its weight in gold.

Corstine scooted his chair toward the far left corner of the blanket, toward where Diego was squatting and examining things.

"Señor Corstine," Diego spoke as he pointed.

Corstine nodded and looked down at the various array of teeth. Some were the teeth of humans from ten thousand years ago, but that was not what had caught Corstine's eye this late afternoon. Hunching over in his seat, he carefully examined a set of three teeth, each equally enormous in their own right.

"Very good specimens," Diego said proudly, the twenty-six year old motioning with his hands. "Quality excellent."

"Sí," Corstine said nodding his head. "Sí, mi amigo."

The teeth belonged to none other than Gigantopithecus blacki, the largest ape that the world has ever known.

Corstine sat back in the chair for a moment and pulled his leather hat down over his head as far as it would go, giving his face as much shade as possible in this land of eternal heat, humidity, and persistent sunshine. He thought to himself for a second how large and powerful an adult male silverback gorilla is. With adult males standing close to six feet in height, weighing around four hundred pounds, and with an armspan stretching from seven foot seven inches to eight feet six inches, Corstine was well aware of their physical attributes. He had seen their terrifying territorial displays of aggression up close and personal on safari in the Congo region of Africa. The brute displays of power mixed with grace were unlike anything he had ever seen before. It was truly something to behold. But what about the beast that lay scattered in bits and pieces on the blanket before them? That question had been swirling in Corstine's head all day now. What type of awe-inspiring power had this animal possessed when it was alive? Surely the sense of raw brute power would have been difficult to comprehend, difficult to wrap one's head around, difficult to fully understand.

Corstine and Diego had been mired in silence for going on a solid minute now, and as John Corstine sat back in his chair, he felt no need to clutter the moment with unnecessary conversation. As Diego sat there, the young paleontology student seemed to also be exhibiting the same need for silence as well. The wind whipping up the dirt around them and the blistering sun still high above provided the only forms of life at the current moment.

Suddenly, Corstine's eyes caught movement just to the left of them. He watched as a lizard wiggled and then buried itself in the sloping dirt hillside adjacent to where they had been working all morning. Corstine's eyes followed the tail before it burrowed its way and disappeared out of view. And then his thoughts began to consume him. He looked down toward the bones atop the blanket and let his mind wander. Gigantopithecus was thought to have gone extinct some one hundred thousand years ago, yet what lay before them was the bones from a member of the Gigantopithecus species, and it had been uncovered from rock and sediment that dated back to as recent as ten thousand years ago. As both Corstine and Diego sat exposed to the elements and working diligently, it seemed hard to contain oneself.

"Truly fascinating stuff," Diego remarked. "Magnífico."

Corstine nodded but did not reply.

"Ten thousand years ago, Señor Corstine, ten thousand years. Freaking unbelievable."

Again Corstine nodded his head. This time he managed a slight smile as he folded his arms.

"Señor Corstine," Diego said.

Corstine looked up at him. "Give me a minute, my boy."

Diego nodded, placed his hands behind his back, and stood there in silence.

"Ten thousand years ago," Corstine mumbled to himself.

It was the blip of an eye in terms of geologic time. Nothing. Absolutely pittance in the four plus billion years since life had originated on this planet. And it was hard to imagine, hard to comprehend, that it was a mere ten feet away from both of them.

"Señor Corstine," Diego said as he sat down in the dirt in front of the sixty-one year old man. "We both know what this means."

"Indeed," Corstine replied. "That the species survived to far more recent times than previously thought."

"Si," Diego said staring off into the distance. "Sí, Señor. Much, much more recent."

With a look of determination on his face, Corstine grabbed his chair and was once again on the move. His eyes were unwavering, his resolve unbreakable. Corstine continued carrying the chair until he was at the area that his eyes had been so transfixed upon. He placed the chair down in the dirt and had a seat. Once again, Diego joined him, the young student wondering why he hadn't lugged a chair all the way out here as well.

From a paleontological, hands-on point of view, Diego Rivera had very little experience out in the field. In fact, nearly all of his time had been spent in the laboratory back at the university either looking at things under a microscope or working to clean off fossils that had come in from the far corners of the globe. But this moment, this moment in a remote corner of Vietnam standing next to none other than John Corstine was proving so far to the be the single greatest moment of his short-lived career in paleontology. Nothing had even come close. And he couldn't say a damn thing about what both of them had uncovered. That's why he was being paid so handsomely, to keep his mouth shut, and to both aid and assist John Corstine in any way possible to uncover the remains of what they now had excavated out of the ground.

"Man and Gigantopithecus living as recent as ten thousand years ago. Absolutely fascinating," Corstine breathed. "Truly breathtaking stuff. A person could work a whole lifetime and never uncover something half this spectacular."

Diego nodded his head. "Indeed, Señor Corstine. The find of a lifetime."

But Corstine knew that what he was saying was only half the story. In fact, none of this compared to what lay at the bottom of Corstine's pocket, neatly packed away in a small leather pouch.

Already as Corstine thought further about it, he was set to deploy a small team to go in search of what they had uncovered the past few weeks. What they had uncovered was a bunch of fossils, stale old and dusty fossils, yet what Corstine's team would be doing out in the field was as real as it gets. The real deal, if you will.

It was a scientific revelation to in fact find out that it appeared as though Gigantopithecus blacki had lived much later than scientists previously thought. Ninety thousand years was the blip of an eye in terms of deep geologic time, but still to the average human with an approximate life expectancy of eighty odd years or so, ninety thousand years was still a giant chunk of time.

Man and Gigantopithecus blacki, Corstine thought quietly to himself, *living as recently as ten thousand years ago.*

It was an intriguing possibility, enough to send his pulse through the roof, and enough to keep him up literally all night for going on the past two weeks with little to no sleep. But as Corstine once again plunged his hand back into his pocket, gently placing his fingers atop the small leather-bound pouch, he wondered two things to himself. Could Gigantopithecus have managed to survive in isolation into current times, but more importantly, if this revelation in fact proved true, just what exactly had the animal evolved into?

"Eternal flame of motivation, may you always burn brightest for those in need."

—Bick Downs

2

Namibia, Africa Somewhere in the Namib Desert

Standing atop one of the massive towering sand dunes of the region, Bick Downs craned his neck up and gazed out toward the horizon for a brief moment. Stretching out before him was quite a magnificent sight to behold. He was gazing out at the Namib Desert on the southern coast of Africa.

Bick Downs was thirty-one years of age. He was fit, trim, and sported what most would consider to be a muscular and very athletic body. He was Italian and Serbian, and at 6'3" inches in height, he came in at two hundred pounds. Downs had broad shoulders, well-sculpted arms, and strong muscular legs. He sported a buzz cut up top and had a good week's worth of beard growth going on.

For the moment, Downs lay completely enamored and lost with the beauty of where they were. The sweeping sea of red sand ran as far as the eye could see in all directions, the blisteringly hot sun high above, and the dry desert air was already cracking and drying out his skin as well as his lips. And as he thought about it even further, he realized he was absolutely loving every second of it.

Downs stared for a few seconds longer before returning his eyes to the book that he had been reading. He was seated atop a flimsy rectangular piece of cardboard and it wasn't the most comfortable, but it sure as hell beat sitting on the scorching hot sand atop this most massive sand dune. He was reading a paperback book. The book had been written by his fellow colleague and teammate Tori Nguyen, and it was her debut book as a published writer. As he turned the paperback book over in his hands, he was amazed at just how fast she had gotten the damn thing written and published. It was most definitely an act of sheer will, not to mention dogged persistence. And he had nothing but the utmost respect for what she had been able to achieve in that short period of time.

Downs flipped the book over and looked at her picture on the back. Then he returned to the very pages of the book itself. The book was about man's attempt to resurrect the woolly mammoth, and so far Downs had been really enjoying it. And judging by Tori's recent email to him in regards to her sales numbers, so too had the rest of the world. She had sent him an email several weeks ago with the ecstatic news that the book had managed to sell just north of ten thousand copies in the last three months. That was a massive number, an inconceivable amount of books sold given the fact that she had self-published the book herself and had spent zero dollars on marketing and advertising. Tori had managed to get word out via her author website, YouTube channel, Twitter account, Instagram,

Facebook, and various other social media sites. She had even found a way to harness the power of LinkedIn to her advantage. And it had all worked beautifully.

As Downs continued reading, he knew that with sales numbers like that, she stood a good chance of attracting the attention of a traditional publisher. He couldn't have been happier for her. Downs was estactic for Tori in that she had achieved her lifelong goal of becoming a published author, and now she was quietly kicking ass and taking names.

Downs pulled his hat down lower and readjusted his sunglasses, damn thankful that he had made the decision to bring both. To say that it was extremely glary up here was quite the understatement. From the height of some 1,256 feet, both Downs and his good friend Josiah Young were situated atop one of the largest sand dunes in the world. And they had come to the Namib Desert for one purpose and one purpose only. They were going to snowboard down a few of these magnificent and massive sand dunes, some of the largest sand dunes on earth.

"Jesus, man," Josiah Young said as he came plowing through the sand holding his snowboard. "You still readin' that damn book?"

Downs nodded. "Yup. Good stuff."

"Not nearly as good as this view," Josiah replied as he put his hand over his eyes to shield the sun while continuing to breathe in the majesty that was the Namib Desert.

Josiah Young was thirty-three and about to finish his doctorate in vertebrae paleontology at UC Berkeley. Roughly six feet in height, Josiah was strongly built with shoulder-length dreadlocks and a neatly trimmed beard. With his African American and Irish heritages, Josiah Young had striking good looks.

Downs set the book down atop the hot sand. "Yeah, no kiddin'. You glad we came?"

Josiah laughed. "I shouldn't even have to answer that shit. Fuck yeah, I'm glad we came. Now you ready to get to why they hauled our asses all the way up here in the first place?"

Downs and Josiah had been dropped off via helicopter just a little over an hour ago. Both men now held snowboards in each hand, and right about now those snowboards were going to be put to good use. Downs placed his board down in the sand and began the process of clipping both feet in. Josiah was already busy doing the same.

"You seen Tori since the last mission?" Josiah asked, clipping his right foot into place.

Downs shook his head. "Nah. Just talked a few times back and forth by email. That's it."

Josiah stood up and straightened himself. "Why not? Not even a text?"

Downs scanned the horizon, the beautiful colors of the desert melding to form an endless sea of sand, the sand stretching out as far as the eye could see in all directions. Downs felt like he was staring out onto an alien landscape. "Just haven't had the time to talk to her. Been busy with my store and a few other side projects."

"Yeah, yeah, yeah," Josiah said. "You know what my baseball coach used to say. Excuses are like assholes, we all have 'em and they all stink. How're sales goin' back at the store though?"

Downs smiled. "Crept into the black last quarter and we're finally showin' a profit."

Josiah breathed in a big lungful of desert air. "Nice. And what about now, man? Who's back home watching the shop?"

"A friend," Downs replied.

Josiah grinned at him. "No shit. Didn't know you had friends other than me."

Downs gave his good friend the middle finger.

"But seriously, what's up with you and Tori?" Josiah asked again.

Downs stared straight ahead. "Nothin'. We're just friends. That's it."

Josiah nodded to himself and smiled. "Friends for now. We'll see about that."

Both of them looked at one another.

"Now," Downs said. "Let's do this."

"Hell yeah, man, that's what I like to hear," Josiah said as he let out a scream. "Top o' the world up here!"

Wasting no more time, Downs watched as Josiah pushed off from the top of the sand dune and immediately began the sharp descent downward toward the flat desert stretched out a long, long way below them. At first, the sand was deep and thick, but in no time Josiah's board began to pick up speed as he disappeared around a bend.

Before Downs pushed off, he stuffed Tori's paperback book into his backpack. Then he looped the light pack around his arms. This was going to be one helluva ride. But Downs knew something. Before they had strapped into their snowboards, he had managed to sneak a peek to his cell phone, back to the real world for a moment. There was a new mission quickly brewing. The minute they hit the bottom of this thousand foot plus dune, the trip would officially be over. But Downs didn't want to ruin Josiah's harrowing trip down this most massive sand dune. He'd tell him at the bottom, after they had successfully boarded down the 1,256 feet of pure awesomeness. Now Downs put his attention back to the task at hand. Slowly, he shifted his weight forward on the snowboard and began the downward descent.

3

San Francisco Zoo, Zoology Department

Thirty-year old Max Caldwell tapped his pencil lightly on the side of his desk and let out a sigh of frustration. He was having a hard time concentrating. Actually as he thought more about it, he was having a hard time doing anything as of late. Seated in one of eight desks in the open work space, Caldwell was at work in the San Francisco Zoo's Zoology Department. He had already seen the hours of the day tick by and he hadn't gotten a damn thing done yet.

Slowly, he raised his head up from his desk and had a good look around. There was no one in the office. All was quiet. As discretely as he could, Max wheeled back in the chair and slid the lower drawer of the desk open. Again his head scanned back and forth around the office. Not a soul in sight.

Reaching down with his left hand, he grabbed hold of a rather large object that was wrapped in a cloth and placed it gently down atop the desk. Wheeling his chair back in tightly so that the bulk of his body hovered closely to the desk, Max used his body to conceal the object as his hands slowly began unwrapping the cloth.

Despite the fact that he knew the contents of what was inside, he still felt his stomach jittery and brimming with excitement. Before him was by anyone's estimates a very large tooth. It was splayed out across the desk. Max's eyes gazed from one end of it to the other. It was quite a piece of dentition to say the least. But what was more important to Max was that he wasn't staring at a fossil, he was looking at an actual tooth. The tooth had been sent to him by none other than John Corstine, the President of the Society of Cryptozoological Agents. It had arrived by mail earlier in the week.

Rather abruptly, the door into the zoology department suddenly swung open. Max found himself completely caught off guard. Now he could do nothing except pull the tooth still neatly displayed atop the cloth as closely as he could toward his chest. And there the zoologist sat, hovering over the desk, hot and flustered as Jimmy Sternberg stood before him with a confused look on his face.

"Jesus, Caldwell, you look like you seen a ghost or something," Jimmy said as he crossed his arms. "Catch ya at a bad time?"

Max swallowed the saliva that had built up in the back of his throat. All of a sudden he felt hot and flustered. He had also broken out into a cold sweat.

Slowly, Max found the courage to speak. "No, um, y-you just startled me. That's all."

"I just s-s-startled you," Jimmy Sternberg said, mocking Max's occassional stuttering problem.

Jimmy continued to stare a hole through Max. "We only all work together for the past year or so. C'mon Caldwell. You should know this isn't your office.

Maybe one day you'll work your way up to tenure at some university, but till then, be on guard."

Max decided it best not to speak; rather he just nodded politely to this prick of an asshole that stood before him. Jimmy Sternberg seemed to be enjoying this, enjoying seeing Max squirm in his chair like a kid that had just been caught red-handed cheating on a test.

Suddenly though, Jimmy's eyes went from making direct eye contact with Max to the desk area that the zoologist had been so fiercely guarding. "What ya got there, Caldwell?"

This time, Max spoke quickly. "Just some work. That's it."

Jimmy returned his arms to a folded position once more and tried to peek with his head around Max's body. "Oh, really? Let's see it then."

Although Max may not have been aware of this subtle movement forward, whether subconsciously or out of fear, he had edged his body another inch or so more over the tooth. The tooth for the most part now remained concealed under the bulk of his chest.

Jimmy crept forward slowly. "Cough it up, Caldwell. There's no company secrets in a setting like this. You should know that by now. Company protocol."

Max could say nothing in return. Jimmy was right. Every employee signed a non-disclosure agreement stating that any inventions or ideas on company time would revert back to the San Francisco Zoo. Jimmy Sternberg was absolutely one hundred percent acting like the prick he was day in and day out, but the asshole was still right.

Oh shit, Max thought to himself, as a wave of panic suddenly washed over him.

Although he couldn't be certain if Jimmy would in fact put two and two together with regards to the enormous tooth lying atop his desk, he couldn't chance it. He had to protect the anonymity of the tooth at all costs. Max cursed himself for having been so stupid as to pull the tooth out in such an open setting, especially at work of all places. But even Max had to admit that he was totally enraptured with the tooth. The mere thought of it sent the scientific academic part of his brain into complete overdrive. But therein lay the problem. Others would no doubt be as enamored by the tooth as he was of it.

"Okay," Jimmy said moving forward. "Enough of this nonsense. Cough it up, Caldwell. Time's up."

With no plan whatsoever in regards to how to get out of this one, all Max could do was hold his ground. Refusing to budge, he remained hovered over the desk, his chest and shoulders still covering the very existence of the tooth.

Now Jimmy had a very sinister look plastered squarely across his face as he continued inching ever so closer. He was within an arm's length of the tooth when suddenly a loud and authoritative voice crackled over the speakers mounted in the office.

"Will Jimmy Sternberg please report to the ARC immediately, I repeat will Jimmy Sternberg please report to the ARC. We have volunteers that need training ASAP in the Animal Resource Center."

And then just like that, the room fell silent. Max forced himself to take a much needed breath.

Shaking his head and cursing silently to himself, Jimmy returned an angry look to Max. "Next time, Caldwell. Next time."

And with that, Jimmy Sternberg turned and headed for the door. Max followed the man with his eyes until he pushed through the door and disappeared out of view. The door fell back into place with a heavy thud. Max stared intensely for a few seconds before quietly letting out a deep sigh of relief while staring up at the ceiling.

The zoologist took in another breath of air. He was still quite hot and flustered to say the least, but Max knew one thing with absolute certainty: he had really dodged a bullet with that one.

4

Maui, Hawaii

Thirty-six year old Jeremiah Corstine stood on the first tee at the Kaanapali Golf Course and took his practice swings. What a beautiful morning it was. But weren't all the mornings, afternoons, and evenings pristine and picturesque on the islands? Focusing on keeping his head down through impact, Jeremiah had managed to work his way down to a seven handicap. He was a pretty good golfer compared to your average hack that went out a half a dozen or so times a year for a round with the boys and some beers.

Jeremiah had maintained the same routine for years now while managing his father John Corstine's vast real-estate empire on the islands. On Monday through Friday he went to bed around ten and woke at five in the morning. From his two bed, two bath ocean side condo, it was only a ten minute drive to the golf course. He would tee off five days a week at six in the morning, and would be done with his round of golf sometime around 9:30 a.m. This left plenty of time to head back home, take a nice shower, and have a quick breakfast before finally sitting down in his back office by 10:30 a.m. This had been his routine for going on two years now, and he had loved every minute of it.

His back office overlooked the Pacific Ocean and the way he had his desk positioned meant that he could take in the beautiful waters and light blue horizon for as long as he desired. From his condominium, Jeremiah was responsible for managing the real estate that his father John Corstine had accumulated over the last thirty years. His father had begun his maniacal quest to be one of the largest property owners in the state of Hawaii back in the late eighties. It began with the simple acquisition of three small condos, each with their own magnificent views of both the beach as well as the blue waters of the Pacific Ocean. Eventually, Corstine traded those three condos in and purchased a small, five-unit apartment building. That apartment building was sold in the early nineties and from there John Corstine was off to the races. He began gobbling up as much Hawaiian real estate as he could, and this meant apartment buildings—the bigger the better. The strategy from the get-go had been simple: purchase small multi-family unit apartment buildings, hold for a period of three to five years while collecting the rents, and then sell and trade up for bigger apartment buildings down the line. And the strategy had worked. All in all, John Corstine's company controlled and owned thirty apartment buildings scattered throughout Maui, Kauai, and the Big Island. These thirty buildings equated to nearly one thousand individual apartment units. What this meant was that when Jeremiah Corstine happened to find himself in this particular part of the world, it left him a very, very busy man. But still, he found time to play his beloved golf.

Jeremiah took another practice swing with the driver and then decided to put the club back in the bag. He didn't need it. Instead, he pulled a five iron from his Taylor Made golf bag and took a few more practice swings with the iron. He would be opting for accuracy instead of distance on this hole.

As Jeremiah approached the ball which was already tee'd up, he heard a vibrating sound from inside his golf bag. It must have been a text message. He continued to stare at the pocket where the phone was stored before finally proceeding toward the ball. He was going to enjoy this round of golf. He would be heading to the airport later this afternoon. His days of golfing and overseeing his father's empire were over for a short period of time. Business called, and that business came in the form of the Society of Cryptozoological Agents. But that was for later in the day. Right now he was golfing. That was all he was concentrating on at the moment. He took one last practice swing, stepped up to the ball, and then proceeded to blast the small white dimpled golf ball right down the middle of the fairway.

• • •

Thirty-two year old Vietnamese-American Tori Nguyen finished typing the last sentence of her email before finally looking up for a quick breather. Actually, it was more like her eyes needed to take a short refresher from all that forced screen time. Letting out a sigh, she recognized for the first time in months just how tired she in fact was. She had been running on adrenaline for far too long now, and she felt as though she could literally lie right down on the floor in her office and fall into a deep sleep. But she wasn't going to get a rest now. In about an hour or so she was due to report into work to assist her parents with the lunch hour at their Vietnamese restaurant in Concord, California. It was by far the busiest time of the day for the small, family-owned restaurant, and therefore the most demanding and stressful as well. But it was when they made all their money, so it was an important time nonetheless.

For a moment she looked down at the rather large sleeve tattoo on her right arm. The artwork ran from her shoulder all the way down to just above her elbow. She had gotten the ink done three years ago and it was literally an honor to her families' Vietnamese heritage. On the top by the shoulder was a picture of her grandparents now in their nineties who still lived in Vietnam. Moving down were several cousins also from Vietnam. But in the middle of it all was the main centerpiece, the reason why she had gotten the extensive and painful work done in the first place. It was a large image of her parents on their wedding day from the early 1980's. Both were young and full of life and in their early twenties. Letting out a sigh to herself, she knew she'd do absolutely anything for her parents. They had given her everything and she owed them the world.

Slowly, her eyes glanced to the far right corner of her desk. Perched neatly one atop the other was a stack of ten paperback books. But they weren't just any books. They were her books, her debut book on man's attempt to resurrect the woolly mammoth. And as she reclined further in her seat and closed her eyes, she allowed herself to breathe a momentary sigh of relief.

It was hard to imagine that over the past three months, her little book had managed to sell just north of ten thousand copies. It was truly an astonishing number, bigger than she could have ever hoped for or imagined. If you had asked her just a little over a year ago when she was waist deep in what was essentially an unfinished manuscript what a fantastic number of books sold would have been to her, she would have pegged that number at somewhere around one thousand books.

Ten thousand books, she let that swirl around in her head for a few seconds. *Ten thousand freaking books. Unreal.*

The number was ten times what she could have ever dreamed possible. A small smile crept across her face. It was an enormous number, an enormous number that had happened in a relatively short period of time. The growth of her debut book had been explosive to say the least. And what made it all the more impressive was that Tori had self-published the book and had spent zero dollars on marketing, relying solely on her ability to utilize all her social media platforms to their fullest. Ten thousand books had put close to thirty thousand dollars in her pocket. Nearly all of her book sales had come from e-book, but that didn't mean she still didn't enjoy looking at the physical paperback version of it. A very influential Chinese blogger had gotten wind of her book chronicling the various bio-tech companies existing in South Korea and their obsessive quest to bring back the woolly mammoth. She had reached out to the blog owner and sent her a paperback copy of the book. A week or so later, the blogger had published a very positive review on her site. That was all it took as sales started to take off from there. That blogger had literally made Tori's full profit. Tori felt a nice box of chocolates was in order. She had left a yellow sticky note on her desk, reminding herself to get that box of chocolates off to that blogger once this expedition to Vietnam was over.

Tori scooted forward in her chair and began proofreading the email that she had been diligently working on for going on twenty minutes now. The email was being sent back to an acquisitions manager at Random House. The large publishing house had reached out to her once word had gotten out about not only her book's explosive growth, but also about its enormous potential. There was talk of a big advance in terms of a dollar amount. If this deal was to officially go through, Tori would be selling the hardcover rights to her book to Random House and seeing it available in a year or so in brick and mortar book stores, grocery stores, and airports. It was an enormous opportunity, and if this truly was her fifteen minutes of fame, then she needed to capitalize on it to the fullest.

As Tori continued proofreading the email, making damn sure there were no grammatical errors, she finally had one last look at it before hitting the send button.

"There," she mumbled to herself. "That's done for now at least."

She'd have to wait to see what the terms of the deal would be, meaning how big of an advance, how many copies they'd be printing up in the first run, and how early she could expect to see her book available in bookstores. There was still a mountain of questions as well as unfinished business, but that would have to wait until after she returned home.

For a moment, Tori thought about opening another window on the computer and beginning to take up work on her new book project. She quickly scratched that idea though. She closed her laptop down. She stood to her feet and looked over at her bed. She was going to take a quick power nap. It was going to be a long day. Actually, it was going to be a ridiculously long day. Tori was going to work the afternoon shift at her aging parents' restaurant, and then after that she had a red-eye flight out of the San Francisco International Airport all the way to the rural jungles of Vietnam, halfway around the world. Looking over toward the door, she could see her packed luggage. This time tomorrow, she would be arriving in Vietnam. With those dizzying thoughts in mind, as well as the publishing advance she had dreamed of nearly all of her adult life, she flopped down onto the bed. Her eyes closed the minute her head hit the pillow.

• • •

Fifty-eight year old Burr Wellington paused for a moment and reached into his backpack. He pulled out his canteen and drank thirstily from it. Stuffing it back into his bag, he looked straight up. His eyes locked in on the top of the forest canopy as the trees swayed back and forth in the wind. It was late in the afternoon and the wind was really starting to pick up now. He listened for a moment now as the wind made a low moaning sound as it whipped through the forest.

Burr once again reached into his backpack and pulled out his iPhone. Out here he didn't have cell phone connection or the internet for that matter, but he had already downloaded an aerial map of the part of the mountain where he was currently situated. Clicking on the aerial image, he zoomed in with his finger and did his best to guesstimate the distance between where he was and where he needed to get to. It was getting late in the afternoon and he had already been gone from his cabin for nearly the entire day now. This was far longer than he had originally anticipated.

Suddenly, he heard the noise of a branch cracking from somewhere close by. It sounded like something had been stepped on. Immediately, Burr froze in place. The only sound his ears registered was the wind as it continued to whip its way through the forest, rustling the leaves, swaying the limbs and branches and downright chilling the Washington forest.

Burr Wellington was standing smack dab in the middle of a pine forest on the eastern side of the state of Washington. He had traversed this forest dozens if not hundreds of times before. The last time he had come here, he had come to an abandoned settlement where drug dealers had unfortunately taken up residence. They had been growing fields full of marijuana. But Burr had not come for the drugs. He never touched the stuff. What he had come for was an abandoned potbelly wood-burning stove. He smiled at the thought of his two hundred and fifty pound frame hauling the potbelly stove back to his truck via the aid of a wheelbarrow. It had been hell, but most importantly it had been worth it. The stove still sat proudly in Burr's family room and had heated the house magnificently over the last few cold winters. The thing continued to work like a charm, heating the house from room to room. It had been one of his better acquisitions over the years.

But today, Burr had not come in search of a stove. Nor had he come to merely take a hike in the woods in all its scenic and natural beauty. Several days prior, a good buddy of his back in town had gotten word from a close contact of his that there were several trees that had been all marked and scratched up. They appeared not to have come from a bear, but rather from something else entirely. One fact remained consistent—whatever the scratch marks had come from, they had come at the hands of something very, very large.

Burr had come in search of potential evidence of Sasquatch in these lone and isolated Washington forests. For the past fifteen years of his retired life, he had been in search of the mysterious animal, and after the unfortunate passing of his wife several years ago, he had hunkered down even more into the secret world of cryptozoology. The fact that there could be long thought to be extinct creatures still roaming our planet was something that kept him getting up day after day. It had given him purpose and drive in his life.

Pulling out his canteen once more from his backpack, Burr drank thirstily from it as another late afternoon cold breeze rippled through the forest. He stuffed the bottle back into the bag and glanced down at his watch.

"Shit," he cursed silently to himself. It was much later than he had thought.

Putting his large hands on his hips and scanning the forest, he both watched and listened as the trees creaked, groaned, and swayed in the wind. He heard branches high above rubbing against one another and the sound of leaves rustling from somewhere close by. And at that exact moment, Burr Wellington realized two things. The first being that fall was now in full swing, and second, and most importantly, he realized that he had missed his opportunity today. He had missed his window. It was getting late, and whether out of sheer old age or just the mismanagement of time, Burr realized he should have already been to the scratched up tree by now. With a heavy sigh, he turned and faced in the direction back down the mountain. As he began the slow and arduous hike back to his pickup truck, he realized it was okay. Things would work out. He needed to save both himself as well as his energy. After all, he had a flight out of Washington later tonight.

Good morning Vietnam, he thought to himself with a smile.

5

Ha Giang Province, Vietnam

"Let's set up and be sure we film this," Stacey Winston muttered to himself as he placed the legs of the tripod down into the wet mud for a moment and stopped to take a breather.

The hot and humid conditions really did take quite a toll on the human body, seeming to strip the vital elements of life right out of you. Perched precariously on the side of a rather steep sloping jungle hillside, this was going harder than previously expected. Everything was soaking wet—every leaf, branch, and tree in sight was absolutely dripping and teeming with water on account of the hard rain that had just pounded down on the area a short while ago.

Stacey Winston was a thirty-five year old freelance video documentary filmmaker looking to make a name for himself with the goal of ultimately one day directing big budget Hollywood blockbuster films. He was six feet tall, Caucasian, and built wiry thin. He had short, cropped red hair, a pale complexion, and hailed from the great state of Tennessee. Having worked as both an editor and videographer for Discovery Channel, Stacey had broken away several years ago to do his own thing:

to start his own small production company. At least that's the story that he had told his parents and close friends. But in actuality, Stacey had gotten laid off due to company downsizing. Either way, it had freed him to do what he had always set out to do, which was to start his own small production company with the hopes of one day breaking into the world of directing huge blockbuster films. It was something he had been yearning to do for quite some time now. And yet as he was here in Vietnam essentially out and about doing his own thing, he was finding it to be so much harder than he had ever fully anticipated. Way out here, life did not cooperate. Things were wet, muddy, slippery, and prickly. The jungle itself seemed to constantly be working against you. They were here in the rainy season, which only served to make matters worse, make things more challenging.

Oh, this bastard jungle, Stacey thought to himself with a momentary sigh of frustration.

This bamboo forest didn't care that you needed to get a particular shot a certain way with the light filtering down from an opening in the canopy high above. It didn't preoccupy itself with such matters. Rather, it simply did what it did best—rain; get hot, steamy, and humid; rain some more; get absolutely pitch black when night falls, and then repeat the same process all over again the next day.

There had been a time when Stacey had officially come to terms with the fact that he would forever be a company man, taking the steady paycheck and good benefits that ultimately entailed working for the so-called "man". He had achieved minor successes during his time at Discovery, having both filmed, written, and edited short, five-minute long documentary films about the supernatural, haunted houses, and many types of other paranormal activities.

Stacey's brief fifteen minutes of fame came when he both directed and filmed a short documentary film for the Discovery Channel about an abandoned mental institution that was supposedly haunted. He had gone there with a small team of four to stay the night in the abandoned building on the outskirts of Dallas, Texas. The content that they came away with from their short stay within the creepy confines of the mental institution was enough to warrant one million or so views on the official Discovery YouTube channel. One million people had viewed the short film, with over forty-two thousand likes and garnering an impressive nineteen thousand comments. At that exact moment in time, Stacey Winston could officially say he had produced something that had gone viral. Even if it was only over the course of a month or so, the short video had been viewed by people from all over the globe. But despite the relatively short-lived success that Stacey had achieved, eventually he watched those around him in the media department lose their jobs and be laid off. These company reorganizations lasted for nearly one year, and Stacey had weathered them all. But after twelve months of dodging bullets, eventually his number was up.

Nearly three years to the date since being hired, Stacey's position was officially eliminated from Discovery Channel. The layoff had come rather abruptly, but it was not a shocker. After all, Stacey had watched all those around him lose their positions for going on over a year, so he had ample amount of time to prepare himself mentally and financially for what was to come. But week after week, month after month, instead of looking for a new place to work, Stacey found himself working on many short video projects. These projects were entirely his own. So when the time came for him to be officially laid off, for the first time since turning eighteen and graduating high school, he found himself completely one hundred percent unemployed and without a job. Stacey wasn't one to panic though. It wasn't in his laid back Southern Tennessee nature. He was, however, forced to move back in with his parents. The move back home had been a tough one. He had been forced to tuck his tail between his legs and accept the humility of the situation. Eventually he was able to move in with a friend in a tiny apartment in downtown Seattle. Stacey stayed in a tight and crowded back bedroom as he began the grueling task of setting up his small freelance production company.

It was hard to imagine that all that had been a little over a year ago, and now here he found himself halfway up a remote jungle hillside in rural Vietnam searching for something that by all accounts wasn't supposed to exist. Stacey propped himself up momentarily on the heavy legs of the tripod and drank thirstily from his water bottle. He inhaled the water in big aggressive gulps. Just the hike up this goddamn hillside was enough to tire out even the heartiest of individuals. The area was ripe with vegetation as tall and slender stalks of green bamboo trees crowded in everywhere there was room to grow. It was a goddamn clusterfuck of vegetation, a Garden of Eden on the other side of the globe. But most importantly, it harbored the potential to hide a great secret. And they had come all this way to see if the secret was true or not.

Quickly, he stuffed his canteen away. Stacey was waiting for the rest of his small film crew to arrive. As he continued to wait, his mind started to roam, started to wander on him. He found it perplexing that all documented accounts of Bigfoot that had come out of the forests of the Pacific Northwest of the United States have chronicled a large animal that walks upright and is both swift and agile. Stacey grabbed at his water bottle once again and gulped a few more mouthfuls of water. It was unbelievable just how dehydrated he felt. What they were after was essentially a 1,200 pound lumbering quadruped. It was hard to imagine, hard to comprehend, even otherworldly, but that's what they had come all this way for. A huge furry mountain of an animal that walked on four limbs.

But if such a magnificently powerful and enormous creature did in fact actually exist, what would the mobility of such a beast be? And would it pose a direct threat to them?

Stacey suddenly shrieked as something touched him hard on the shoulder. He spun around to see Bob Hohrman standing in front of him with a wide grin from ear to ear.

"What's the matter?" Bob joked. "Seen a ghost or something?"

Stacey quickly composed himself. Bob had literally scared the living shit out of him. "Nah, I'm good. Just trying to get some air into the old lungs. This jungle's just about done me in, ya know."

Bob put his own hands on his hips and let out a sigh of his own. "Tell me about it."

Bob Hohrman was fifty-two years old. Six feet tall with an average build, he was Caucasian and sported a cleanly shaven bald head. Bob was a former cancer survivor who had lost his hair due to radiation and chemotherapy treatment. Over the years, he had simply kept the bald look for convenience purposes. He liked the idea of getting out of the shower in the morning and drying his head simply by toweling off quickly. Bob could be best described by his friends as a happy-go-lucky guy who was always smiling, an eternal optimist, and a true kid at heart.

Bob looked down at the now collapsed tripod in Stacey's hands and then to the lightweight backpack that the director of this small film project was carrying. Then Bob's hands touched his own pack. Slung across both his shoulders was an enormous backpack that was as large as one could expect people on an entire day's hike up to Half Dome in Yosemite National Park to be carrying.

"Try luggin' this seventy-five pound behemoth around," Bob said as he readjusted the enormous pack.

Bob turned in Stacey's direction as the director spoke to him. Stacey didn't make eye contact with the man as he spoke. "How far back are the others?"

"Clark is down the hill recording a few things here and there, and Diane is working on taking some stock footage of this forest," Bob replied.

Stacey cleared his throat. Still, he didn't make eye contact with Bob as the man continued to scan the hillside. He felt slightly bad for the fact that Bob was carrying such an enormous pack, but most certainly wanted no part in carrying all that weight. His back wanted no part in that whatsoever. Such a burden he also felt would hinder his creative juices, and at this stage of the game that would ultimately be a disaster. "Well they better hurry their asses up."

Already, Stacey was starting to feel the pressure with regards to this documentary. As the director, he knew it would all be falling squarely atop his shoulders. If it was to be a success, all praise would go to him, and if they fell flat on their faces, he knew where the shitstorm would be headed. They had been given $100,000 to finance and make this project. It wasn't chump change but it certainly wasn't a $150 million Hollywood blockbuster budget either. It was, however, a start—a start that Stacey desperately wanted to build upon to parlay into something greater. If all went according to plan, he figured that by the end of the next decade, he'd either be in pre-production or involved with the principal photography of what he would hope would be his directorial debut on a full-length feature film. And Stacey was hoping, even praying, that there'd be a big budget attached to the film as well. He had been dreaming of that moment for longer than he could remember now. And he was hellbent on doing all in his power to make that a reality. He remembered telling his friends a few years ago that he'd dial Satan if he had a direct line to him. He was scrappy, motivated, and beyond driven to get to his dreams in life. He was willing to do absolutely whatever it took to get there.

Bob suddenly sneezed, bringing Stacey back to the present. That was the pipe dream, the top of the mountain if you will, but for now all Stacey knew was that he was caught on a steep muddy jungle hillside in the remotest corners of Vietnam searching for something of both myth and folklore. Before he could even set foot, or allow his mind to wander any further with regards to him being in the director's seat of a big budget Hollywood film, he had to first turn this current project into a success.

Stacey quickly turned his head and looked over at Bob, this time making direct eye contact with the man. "Hey. What's takin' the others so long?"

6

The sun beamed brightly as the humidity was slowly on the rise. Meanwhile down below, the dense green leafy canopy stretched for miles in all directions, an endless sea of green that grew and thrived in this tropical part of the world. In the distance however, dark storm clouds stacked menacingly one atop the other. It looked as though rain was in the forecast for later on in the day.

Continuing further down from the lush green canopy, in the dark and shadowy world that was the bamboo forest, life thrived from every inch and corner down here. Here the shadows were long, and the entire forest was constantly bathed in a dim grey lighting, the direct result of the near impenetrable canopy that existed way up top. Life was very much flourishing on the forest floor, with trees spawning new trees, low-growing vegetation clinging tightly to the ground, and the ever-present tall and slender bamboo trees dotting every inch of this massive labyrinth of an ecosystem. One could easily be placed here and lose one's sense of direction in a matter of minutes. The sheer density of the growth here was something not to be taken lightly.

Suddenly though, the life that was inside this thriving lush forest came to an abrupt halt. The sounds of buzzing and chirping were now gone as a gentle breeze blew in and out of the foliage. In the parts of the forest that were packed tighter with bamboo growth, several stands of tall and slender bamboo rubbed, creaked, and groaned against one another on account of the wind. The overall effect was that of a gentle rhythmic sound, almost like wind chimes on the far corner of one's porch. It had a very soothing, almost meditative quality about it as the trees continued to knock back and forth against one another.

Suddenly that all changed though. Out of nowhere, an overwhelming and immense shape materialized out of the shadows and lifted itself from the ground. Slowly, the enormous being stood to its full height. Reaching out with an equally enormous limb, it plucked the fruit from some fourteen feet up high in the tree. And there the animal remained perched for a moment as the limb recoiled and brought the fruit back toward the big head. A gaping black hole opened wide and dropped the fruit down and into the cavernous darkness that was the opening.

Meanwhile, the forest had most definitely taken notice to the enormous creature's presence as it remained in a deep silence. Once more the huge limb extended itself outward toward the plentiful array of fruit. Slowly, the fruit was reeled in toward the enormous head and again the equally enormous mouth opened wide, exposing an impressive array of teeth. Within a matter of seconds, half a dozen or so pieces of fruit had disappeared down and into the gaping black hole.

Standing back up to its full height of just slightly taller than a ten foot tall basketball hoop, the creature took a moment to scan the sloping jungle hillside that lay at its back. Then it looked back up and into the tree. There was a lot more fruit up there, but the ripe and succulent pieces were higher up, away from the pieces that had just been plucked from the fourteen foot tall range.

The creature lowered its head and scanned the forest for a moment. Then the big head swung upward once again and peered up into the tree. It could see the fruit. Problem was, despite the enormous height that it had attained in life, even it could not reach the places where the majority of the fruit was congregated. The creature stopped reaching and slowly lowered itself to all fours. There it remained for a few quiet seconds. And then in one final act of aggression, it lifted its immense bulk off the ground and reared onto its back two legs. The creature beat loudly on its wide chest with the flat palms of its hands before letting out an ear-splitting cry.

The enormous bellowing roar could be heard as it reverberated through the bamboo forest.

7

Noi Bai International Airport, Vietnam

B ick Downs stood with two feet firmly planted on
the tarmac as he squinted against the harsh glare
of the early morning sun. The sun had a faint, red tint
about it. Standing next to Downs was Josiah Young.
Just seventeen hours ago, both of them had been hiking
up and surfing down some of the biggest sand dunes in
the world back in the Namib Desert on the eastern part
of the African continent. Now, they found themselves
in the Noi Bai International Airport, the largest airport
in all of Vietnam and the second busiest just behind the
Tan Son Nhat International Airport.

As Downs looked around and saw the sheer hustle
and bustle of the airport, he realized quickly why it was
the second busiest airport in all of Vietnam. Josiah
stepped forward and began massaging both his back and
neck. "We gotta talk to John about using his private jet
next time, man. This commercial shit is crazy."

Downs nodded as put his shades on. "Tell me
about it. Back feels like hell right now."

Josiah was referring to none other than John
Corstine, the President of the Society of Cryptozoological Agents. Corstine, a real-estate entrepreneur

47

whose portfolio was valued in the hundreds of millions had summoned Downs and his team. Even though the summoning happened to coincide with both Josiah's and Downs' week long excursion in Namibia, they had no choice. This was part of the job as well as the expectations, that no matter what, at the drop of a hat, they had to answer the call of duty. This was what the Society of Cryptozoological Agents was about in a nutshell, an organization dedicated to keeping the prehistoric wonders of the world secret at all costs. When duty was called, it needed to be answered.

Downs now had his Nike golf hat and sunglasses on and therefore didn't need to strain so much against the harsh early morning glare. He allowed the muscles in his face to relax as he took a moment to get his bearings straight. Meanwhile, Josiah was still busy working on unkinking his neck as well as his back. These seemed to be the all-too-common problems of flying commercial, a nightmare by anyone's assessment.

Downs smiled and began massaging his own neck. "I'll talk to Corstine next time about using the ol' private plane."

"Where're the others?" Josiah asked.

"We're meetin' at a hotel downtown," Downs replied.

Downs looked around and then glanced down at his Nike wristwatch. Their ride should have been here by now. No sooner than he looked up, a middle-aged bald Vietnamese man approached them from behind in an electric golf cart.

"Mr. Downs, Mr. Young?" the man asked with a rather thick Vietnamese accent.

"Are you Bao?" Downs asked as he turned around.

"Yes," the man replied. "Please hop in. Very strict orders. Get you to where you are going. Must hurry. Must go fast."

Bao greeted both men as he took Downs' and Josiah's bags and stowed them at the back. He hooked them in where the golf clubs would go.

"Please, please," Bao reiterated. "Must move fast now."

They watched as the small yet agile man made his way around to the driver's seat and plopped down. Josiah squished in next to him, which left Downs seated on the far edge. Wedged in tightly in the two-person golf cart, the electric motor quickly moved them forward.

"Must make two seats three today," Bao spoke as he continued to drive with two hands firmly atop the wheel. The man gripped the wheel and drove with the intensity of someone driving in full on commute rush hour traffic.

Now as the golf cart got up to its full speed, both Josiah and Downs were able to get their first full view of the Noi Bai International Airport as it opened up. Beyond the airport and in the surrounding hills hung a thick grey haze. It was pure smog—nothing more, nothing less. They were now both seeing and experiencing firsthand the problems surrounding pollution currently plaguing Vietnam. With a population of over ninety-five million people and growing, the thick smog that they were now witnessing was a combination of rapid development mixed with deforestation. Also, a short list of the contributing factors include literally non-existent vehicle emission standards, pollution from motorbikes, and overall poor urban planning.

As the electric golf cart continued to make its way down the tarmac, Downs found it hard to believe that people could live and operate like this on a day-to-day basis in such bad breathing conditions. After all, this was just another ordinary day. For a moment, he recalled back to the horrific Northern California Napa fires from October 2017 in which the fires grew to such a level and magnitude that smoke eventually poured into San Francisco, essentially creating air quality the likes of which Northern California residents had never experienced before. Unfortunately, those breathing conditions seemed to be an everyday occurrence here.

Jeez, give me a cool, refreshing San Francisco breeze any day of the week, Downs thought to himself as the humidity had now reached what most would consider to be an oppressively uncomfortable level.

Out of the corner of his left eye, he saw Josiah sneeze loudly as he covered his mouth.

"You okay?" Downs asked.

Josiah nodded. "Crap air. All good though."

"Well," Downs replied as his eyes scanned the busy airport. "Where we're going, should be plenty of fresh air. Humid and suffocating air, but fresh nonetheless."

"Let's freakin' hope so, man," Josiah said as he sneezed again. "Lookin' forward to that."

Downs continued to take in the airport as Josiah suddenly angled himself toward the driver. "Good day for a drive. Nice weather, huh?"

What had once appeared to be a friendly and outgoing middle-aged man picking them up in an electric golf cart had now melded to be one with a solid look of determination plastered squarely across his face. Bao was a man on a mission, and that mission was to get the two men in the cart to their intended location. As the sun continued to rise higher into the sky, the small electric golf cart continued onward.

· · ·

Some seven minutes after being officially introduced to this Vietnamese man by the name of Bao, Bick Downs and Josiah Young parted ways and were dropped off. Now they found themselves seated in plush leather seats at the very back of a black stretch limo as the air conditioner bathed them in its cool embrace.

"Okay," Josiah said as he put his hands behind his head and sank back into the leather seat. "John's service is slowly startin' to get better. I'm likin' this, this is good shit."

"Agreed," Downs replied as he leaned forward and opened the mini fridge.

"Feels like we're goin' to the prom or something," Downs joked.

Josiah laughed. "Yeah, no kiddin'."

Downs swung the door to the mini fridge open. There was no alcohol inside, but one thing was for certain. It was absolutely stocked full of sodas, energy drinks, candy bars, and most importantly, his all-time favorite drink, ginger beer. And it was his favorite kind—Bundaberg to be exact.

"Shall we," Downs asked.

"Never gotta tell me twice, man," Josiah said as he lifted himself from the seat and extended his arms toward the tiny refrigerator.

Downs grabbed one of the cold glass bottled ginger beers, and so did Josiah. The two looked at one another with a smile as they went to work ripping the tops off.

"Well," Downs said. "Here's to another successful mission."

Both men clinked bottles with one another and then proceeded to drink thirstily from them. Josiah set the ginger beer down in the cup holder next to him. "Wonder if the others are getting the same type of star power treatment?"

Downs shrugged his shoulders. "Hard to say. I'd hope so. J.C. supposedly has all the money in the world."

Josiah looked up at Downs. "Speakin' of money, thanks for spottin' me the last few months while I get my financial act together."

"Hey man, what are friends for?" Downs replied. "Besides, raising money on the GoFundMe site ain't the prettiest of things."

Josiah nodded. "For sure. You got that spot on."

The driver suddenly turned abruptly and both men were momentarily lifted from their seats.

For going on the past three months, Downs had been diverting a small portion of the rent from his apartment units above his small-action sports store to fund part of Josiah's research at UC Berkeley. Josiah had originally applied for a federal grant to study dinosaur bones in the Sahara desert in order to finish up his doctoral work in vertebrae paleontology. When the grant fell through and the metaphorical shit essentially hit the ceiling, Downs decided he would step in and help. After all, things had been going well for the last several months in terms of sales at his sports store that he owned and operated in the Potrero Hill neighborhood of San Francisco.

Josiah took a few more gulps. "Thanks again, and the money will be repaid to you."

Downs sipped at his ginger beer and waved Josiah off with his hand. "Don't worry about repaying. My gift to you. No worries on that."

"Well, we'll see about that," Josiah said as he looked out the back window of the limo. The airport was now long gone, but they found themselves in wall-to-wall gridlock traffic.

"Shit," Josiah cursed. "We're not moving at all."

"Fuck. Worse than Bay Area traffic," Downs fired back.

"You come to a far flung corner of the world like this, and your ass is still caught in wall-to-wall traffic. We could have done this shit at home," Josiah said leaning back into his seat.

Downs suddenly looked over at Josiah. "Promise me one thing."

"What's up," Josiah said looking up.

"First dinosaur you discover is named after me."

Josiah laughed. "Will do. You got it man. First dino shall be the Downsosaurus. Got a nice ring to it."

Downs shook his head back and forth as he laughed. "Sounds like shit. Gonna be hard to get the academic world to peer review your paper with a god-awful name like that."

Josiah laughed. "Ah, screw 'em. Bunch of stiff academics. If that name doesn't work, we'll go with a more traditional Latin sounding name."

Downs took another sip of gingerbeer. "Better go with the Latin name. Just play the game, man. Get where you need to get to, until you're finally in a position where you can call the shots. Know what I mean?"

"Agreed," Josiah replied as he raised his drink in salute. "Gonna fake it till I make it."

Suddenly, Downs' phone began to vibrate several times from inside his backpack. They were text messages, and he had a good feeling he knew exactly just who they had come from. Josiah looked over as Downs pulled his phone out. Swiping the screen, he could see he had seven new text messages.

"What's up?" Josiah said, polishing off the last of the ginger beer. "Good till the last friggin' drop."

Downs looked over at his buddy. "The others are already here."

8

Tori Nguyen scrolled quickly through her email on her laptop while sipping at the tall glass of ice cold water that had just been handed to her. She rattled the ice cubes around at the bottom of the glass for a bit before finally setting it down. The flight to Vietnam had been a bastard. The forced long hours up in the air had thoroughly dehydrated her, not to mention dried out her sinuses as well as her skin beyond belief. Her eyes looked over at the nightstand where a small bottle of moisturizer and sinus rinse lay. She'd be fully employing the services of both in just a little while. Flying had never really been her thing, but unfortunately it was a necessity.

Still no reply back, she thought to herself. She was referring to the email that she was expecting back from Random House. If all went as planned, her agent had told her she could expect a book advance somewhere in the mid to low six figures. And she had some big plans for the money. If it was truly a sizable amount, then it was going to allow her parents to retire from running their restaurant once and for all. But she'd believe it when she saw it deposited into her bank account. Things had been going well for her since she made the jump into the publishing world, and hopefully in time they'd continue to get even better. There appeared to be many bright things on the horizon for her to look forward to including a large advance from one of the big four publishers, the chance to see her book in hardcover format in book stores, the current book she was working on, and lastly, her future projects and endeavors.

For now though, she sunk herself back into the present. Looking around the hotel suite, she found Jeremiah Corstine seated atop the nearby bed at the end of the room flipping through the endless supply of T.V. channels that all hotel rooms came equipped with. Seated in the small little living room of sorts, Max Caldwell sat in a stiff yet elegant upright chair reading the latest edition of Science Magazine. Burr Wellington was in the adjacent room taking a quick power nap. They were awaiting the arrival of Downs and Josiah. And as Tori continued to look down at the small clock on her laptop, she knew they should be arriving any minute now.

The team was situated in a plush hotel room at the very top of the Hilton Hotel in Hanoi, the capital of Vietnam. From way up top here, the large glass-paned windows looked out over the whole city. From this bird's eye view, one could see the magnificently constructed skyscrapers which rose out from the ground, the commotion of the small markets below, and the overall feel of a busy, chaotic, and thriving city.

Jeremiah looked over to Max. "Anything good in that issue?"

Max Caldwell took another moment while adjusting his glasses. "Um, a few good ones, just skimming the last pages of the magazine now."

"Well, toss it my way when you're done," Jeremiah said as he went back to channel surfing before finally settling on CNBC. He figured he'd see how the markets had closed for the day.

"Sure thing," Max said as he continued flipping through the magazine.

Meanwhile, Tori took one last look at her laptop as she hit the refresh button. Still no email from Random House.

Patience, she reminded herself. *Patience. All good things take time.*

Just about ready to close her laptop down for good, she looked to the upper right of her screen. In big and bold lettering the file read:

NEXT BOOK PROJECT.

She clicked on it. In the file was essentially her next book. She only had eleven pages, but hey, it was a start. These things were tough, writing and publishing books that is, one page at a time, one day at a time, one word at a time, one royalty payment at a time. Such was the plight of the writer. While the success of her debut book had caught her completely by surprise, she realized that the only thing she could control now was getting to work on her next book. Whatever type of book advance from Random House that awaited her now lay completely out of her hands. The ball was in their court. She had more than done her part. For a brief moment, she allowed herself to daydream about a mid six figure book advance. If she found herself lucky enough to receive such a sudden windfall of cash, then she most surely was going to give the majority of it to her parents. They had been running their Vietnamese restaurant for over thirty years now, and had it not been for their help, she would have never been able to afford tuition at the University of California, Davis. The money from the book advance was going to allow them to retire once and for all. And what a gift that would be for them. If all of this worked out and the planets truly did align for her, then the next order of business would be what to do with the family restaurant business?

Her parents had truly worked their asses off to build a profitable family-run business for all of them. They had worked diligently to build up a reputation in the small East Bay suburb of Concord, California. The idea was not to sell the restaurant. Rather than sell the business, the idea was for Tori to one day take it over. But running a restaurant that was open for both lunch and dinner was a full-time endeavor. And with something that had a very minimal and at times non-existent staff, this would all fall on her shoulders. She wasn't certain whether or not she was up to the challenge. How did being a small business owner fit in with her new and emerging writing career? How did all of this also fit in with the Society of Cryptozoological Agents? She didn't know the answers to the questions currently plaguing her, but hoped in time that they would come.

Quickly, a knock came at their hotel door. Tori looked up and immediately closed her laptop. The others had finally arrived.

9

Josiah Young rapped his knuckles hard against the hotel door as he straightened his body. Behind him, Bick Downs glanced at his Nike wristwatch. They were right on time, right on schedule.

The door opened slowly and the two men immediately recognized a familiar face. Jeremiah Corstine stood before them with a big grin from ear to ear.

"C'mon in, guys," Jeremiah said as he greeted Josiah with a handshake. "Party's just getting started."

Downs patted Jeremiah on the shoulder as he walked past the thirty-six year old man. Meanwhile, Tori got up from her seat and Max Caldwell set his magazine down. Burr Wellington came out of the back room and patted both men on the shoulder with two equally enormous hands. For several minutes, idle chit chat had completely engulfed the group. It had been roughly three months since they had officially last been together as a team, capturing a rogue prehistoric creature in San Francisco and then successfully sedating and transporting a terrifying hybrid creature up north in the small agricultural town of Santa Rosa, California.

As the team settled back in to one another's company, getting used to each other once again, catching up, having a few laughs here and there, Downs made his way over to Tori.

"Great to see you," he said.

Tori took a moment to brush her hair away from her face. "Likewise. How've you been? How's the store?"

Downs nodded. "Store's good. Knock on wood, everything else has been going good. Can't complain."

Downs looked over toward the others. The group was slowly making their way into the small living room. Any minute now, they were supposed to jump on a quick Facetime call with John Corstine in order to get the rundown for their current mission.

Suddenly, Downs remembered what he had in his bag, what he had been carrying with him since the Namib Desert. Quickly, he set his bag down on the ground and unzipped it. "Almost forgot what I've been luggin' around with me."

Downs stood before Tori Nguyen with a big smile on his face. In his hand, he held a paperback copy of her debut book, the one that she felt so much of her future was riding on.

"Damn," Tori said. "I'd have been happy to get you a free copy."

"Nope," Downs said with a shake of the head. "I'm a paying customer. Happy as hell to do that for ya."

Tori laughed. "Well, thanks for that. That's another dollar something in my pocket."

"Hey, every bit helps. How're book sales?" Downs asked.

"Waiting to hear back from Random House on a hardcover deal," she replied as she folded her arms, her face and posture having now taken on a more serious demeanor to it.

Downs' eyes bulged a bit. "Damn. Goin' straight for the jugular. Kickin' ass and takin' names."

Tori let out a slight sigh as she looked down at the ground. "That's the plan. We'll see if it actually works out that way."

"And your family restaurant, how's that goin'?"

"Busy," Tori said with a smile. "Just plain busy. But I guess that's a good thing."

"I'll bet," Downs said as he folded his arms and quickly glanced back toward the others.

The group was quickly settling into their seats. The Facetime call was about to begin.

"Well, I guess we better," Downs said motioning with his hands.

Tori was already busy moving in that direction. Downs followed suit.

The group was seated in the small living room of the hotel room. In the middle of them, Jeremiah had secured his iPad onto a small tripod stand for the Facetime call.

Downs squished himself in between Max and Josiah. The Facetime call rang for a few more seconds before it was finally answered. Seated before them was John Corstine. The real-estate entrepreneur and President of The Society of Cryptozoological Agents sat with his hands neatly clasped atop his desk in his San Francisco Victorian mini-mansion.

"Nice to see all of you," Corstine spoke as he cleared his throat and drank momentarily from a tall glass of water. The team watched as he placed it neatly atop his desk, noting the meticulous manner in which the man moved.

"Dad, we're all here," Jeremiah said as he scooted forward in his chair.

"Very well then," Corstine replied. "Let's begin. Last we spoke, I had informed all of you of the growing situation at hand."

To Downs, it was already hard to imagine that they were back at it again. The Northern California mission seemed like it had just happened yesterday. And yet that was over three months ago. Insane how fast time went, absolutely insane.

"As I was saying," Corstine continued. "We've long since suspected the possible existence of one of the great ape species from our prehistoric past. And our organization has been following this particular case with increasing interest for the past couple months, as my son Jeremiah can attest."

Jeremiah nodded toward the screen as Downs adjusted his positioning on the couch. Downs looked to his right as Max extended an arm and handed him a Gatorade. Downs smiled as he began to screw the top off.

"So flat out, we're talking about Bigfoot, right?" Burr Wellington asked as he stood up and began pacing back and forth nervously.

Downs watched the big man for a moment. The fifty-eight year old Washington native was still sporting his hat which read: BIGFOOT LIVES. Accompanying this was a flannel shirt with a t-shirt underneath that read "UFO'S: I BELIEVE."

Glad to see some things never change, Downs thought to himself as he took a swig of the energy drink, replenishing what electrolytes had been lost on the trip over here.

"Not necessarily, Burr," John Corstine said as he shuffled through a stack of neatly piled papers at the corner of his desk.

"But it is undoubtedly true that many legends are in fact based on some type of historical scientific facts," Josiah said.

"Right you are," Corstine replied. Now, the President of the Society of Cryptozoological Agents appeared to not be paying attention to them as he swiped at his iPhone.

Jeremiah sat forward in the chair. "Dad?"

A second or two passed before Corstine looked back up.

Jeremiah spoke up once again. "Dad, are you with us?"

"Indeed," Corstine replied. "Business never sleeps, and it seems as though the minute you put out one fire, there is another one that needs tending to."

"Tell me about it," Jeremiah said as he rolled his eyes sarcastically.

Downs glanced over at Jeremiah. Living with such a powerful entrepreneur and visionary must have been a difficult thing to do as a child.

"Where were we then?" Corstine said.

"Sasquatch," Burr replied, still pacing back and forth like a caged lion.

"Extinct species," Corstine continued. "We believe with relative certainty that we are in the presence of another species thought to have died out some one hundred thousand years ago."

Corstine paused for a moment, letting his last words sink in.

Meanwhile, Downs took another sip of Gatorade. He knew what they would essentially be hunting for once they officially stepped foot in that deep and isolated bamboo forest in a remote and rural part of Vietnam. It would be like stepping back in time.

John Corstine cleared his throat. "Gigantopithecus blacki, a genus of extinct ape that lived as long as nine million years ago and died out as recently as one hundred thousand years ago. From what the fossil record tell us, the species is the largest known ape to have ever walked the earth. Standing at nearly ten feet in height, and tipping the scales at over one thousand three hundred pounds in weight, this was most definitely a formidable beast. An absolute brute in every sense of the word. A beautiful and majestic creature of prehistory."

Downs looked over to Jeremiah who was nodding his head slowly.

"Like many things with the S.C.A," Corstine continued. "We monitored this current case, watching and waiting to see if other parties eventually took notice, meanwhile allowing the animal to live in peace. And when finally over the last month or so, another active party did start to take notice, we made the decision it was time to act."

Corstine took another moment as he gathered a stack of loose papers from the far corner side of his desk. "A rather small fledgling film company is currently navigating the very spot where you will be dropped, trying to get video footage and pictures of the largest ape that has ever existed and expose it for all the world to see. From what I gather, they are trying to create a documentary, get rich, famous, and exploit the existence of the animal to the fullest. The very existence of our organization is predicated on the fact that situations like these will no doubt arise and continue to occur, and when they do, we must do all in our power to squash them. We must take swift action and we must not act with hesitation."

"I've been after such a beast for the last twenty-five years or so," Burr said as he stretched out his back. "Bloody quarter of a century."

"Well, you're finally going to get your chance," Corstine said. "This will no doubt be a very dangerous mission. But just know we will take every precaution to get you all in and out safely. Most importantly, take every advantage at our disposal to make the overall mission objective a success."

Downs stood up. "When do we head out?"

"Early in the afternoon," Corstine replied. "You will be dropped in via helicopter to a rather remote and lush track of bamboo forest in the northern part of Vietnam. The mission is as always: locate, sedate, and prepare the animal for transport. From there you all should know how the rest of the story goes. Call in the air team and they will take care of the rest. We must also make sure that all evidence via cameras, phones, tablets, and any other forms documenting the existence of the animal are confiscated and ultimately destroyed.

Then spic and span you're done and back off to live your lives."

"Oh, is that all?" Josiah said as he stood and laughed. "Sounds like a walk in the park."

Downs was beginning to get the hang of how the Society of Cryptozoological Agents in fact worked. They were essentially the ground team, the hired muscle, the grunt work, responsible for locating, tracking down, and sedating these long thought extinct creatures. Then from there they would call in the air team who was responsible for coming in via helicopter and preparing the animal or animals for transport to a remote outpost in the wilds of Siberia, owned and operated in secrecy by the Society of Cryptozoological Agents. Sounded simple enough, but nothing in this life ever was.

"Okay then," Downs said as he stood to his feet and polished off the last of the Gatorade.

This prompted the others to stand as well.

Jeremiah took hold of the iPad, holding it up to his face as the rest of the team gathered around him. "Okay, Dad. What time are we looking at here?"

Corstine replied. "We ship out in three hours. Get as much rest as you can. You're all going to need it."

10

S tacey Winston stood next to his filming partner Bob Hohrman. He wondered just what in the hell was taking the others so damn long? Just about ready to reach to his side pouch of his backpack for his phone, he quickly scratched that idea. Amidst the endless sea of green canopy high above them, there was no cell phone service. Out here they were essentially cut off from the world, completely on their own. Suddenly, noise stirred from somewhere down the hillside.

"There they are," Bob said as his body listed forward.

Clark Geiger abandoned his camera equipment momentarily as he raced out to reach the others.

Bob headed down the hillside to greet his fellow teammate. "What took you guys so long?"

"Go easy on us," Clark replied as he struggled to catch his breath. "We filmed some amazing background stock footage. If it's not used for this current project, we can definitely use this stuff for the next project and so on and so on. Good quality footage."

Twenty-nine year old Clark Geiger was of average height and build, Caucasian, and with thinning dark brown hair up top. He was by no means fat, but he definitely could stand to lose a few. He knew it, and getting his ass in the gym was something that was on his radar once they in fact got home to the states.

Bob smiled as he looked back to Stacey. "Sounds great. Look forward to seein' it."

"Yeah Clark, bite me," Diane fired back in a feisty and fiery tone. "You fucktards just make sure you stay on assignment."

Diane Clor was hauling herself as well as her heavy daypack up the steep jungle hillside toward the two men. She was in her early fifties, Caucasian, and with dark blonde hair. Back in her early twenties, the bouncers at her local bar used to solicit her services in breaking up fights. She had broken up many a bar fight in her day, and at 5'5 inches in height, she packed quite a punch.

"Okie dokie," Clark said eyeing the approaching lady "But the boss isn't too happy. Need to keep closer together."

By now, Stacey Winston had ventured a ways down the hillside to join them. "Listen, y'all need to keep closer to one another. Not mad, just sayin' we need to keep a tighter watch on one another, watch each other's back. Know what I mean?"

Diane put her hands on her hips and forced a smile. Although she probably didn't always mean to, often times to the outside world her tone of voice came off very standoffish and intense. "We're doin' the best we can. This jungle is already beatin' the livin shit outta me."

She raised her arms, exposing a myriad of cuts, scrapes, and gashes. It wasn't a pretty sight. "By hook or crook, we will get this documentary done. That I can assure you."

Stacey forced a smile. He was trying his best to work with her, but for some odd reason the woman simply rubbed him the wrong way. But he was working hard to get along, trying to press forward with the greater goal of creating one hell of a documentary. "I like the spirit."

"Well, you better," Diane fired back. "Cuz it's the only type of attitude that will lead us to success in a place like this, especially with the type of budget we're working with here."

Stacey merely nodded and smiled, removed his baseball cap, and toweled his sweaty head off. In this sweltering jungle, it seemed as though one was always bathed in a constant layer of grime and sweat.

Clark suppressed whatever urge he had to say something and simply stared down at the ground. He had never been one for confrontations, and quite frankly Diane Clor intimidated him. But nonetheless, he had to get along with her; they all had to get along for that matter.

Out of nowhere, Stacey suddenly felt a rumbling sensation from deep inside his stomach. "Let's hike to the top of this hillside and get ourselves back into the open clearing. From there we can break for lunch for the next hour or so, y'all. The stomach's hungry."

"Can't complain with that," Clark said with a smile.

• • •

Ten minutes or so later the small documentary film team had managed to scramble their way up the hillside and back out into a rather large sunlit clearing. The clearing itself was completely surrounded on all sides by tall swaying stands of bamboo and was a far cry from the dark and, more often than not, dimly lit forest.

Clark unhooked his pack from his shoulders and carefully placed the camera equipment down on top of it. Next, he sat down Indian style right there in the middle of the clearing, prompting the others to do the same as well.

Diane looked down at the man now seated on the ground with a bit of a scowl. That scowl of hers seemed to be her natural disposition. Whether that's how she intended to portray herself toward the outside world or not, that's how it came off.

Clark reached for the bag that held the food. With a bit of a struggle, he hauled it closer to them and began to unzip it. Premade sandwiches and four bags of lunch-sized chips would have to suffice. Dessert would come in the form of four bright and shiny red apples.

The team quickly went to town devouring the sandwiches. They were hungry and had been hiking nonstop for several hours now, hacking their way through the dense foliage and at times uneven terrain.

"Okay y'all, let's go over some of the game plans," Stacey said in between a mouthful of sandwich.

The others were busy chowing down on their sandwiches as well.

"Let's break for the next thirty odd minutes or so, and then get back to it," Stacey said as he took another bite of his sandwich.

Stacey Winston possessed the energy of a jack-rabbit, and seemingly never ate, drank liquids, or slept for that matter. But today, because of the difficulty in acquiring their morning footage, hiking up and down steep and unforgiving hillsides all day, he felt it necessary for the food consumption. Other than that, he seemed to be in a constant state of motion, and his wirey thin frame supported such a lifestyle.

Really got some great footage a ways back," Clark reiterated as he reached for the bag of chips.

"Yeah," Stacey replied. "In a bit, let's sit down and have a further look"

The comment drew an immediate response from Diane. "Bad timing. Let's finish out filming for the day while we still have light, then let's have a look later tonight."

Stacey smiled to himself as he polished off another bite from the deli sandwich. "Let's have a look now. See what's up with the footage you took. See if we're heading in the right direction that we ultimately aim to take this documentary."

Diane shook her head as she set her sandwich down on the ground, not seeming to give a damn about cleanliness in the least bit. Even though Stacey was the director of this documentary, and essentially the one in charge, Diane was nearly twenty years older than him, and it showed. It seemed as though the executive producer was having none of what the director of this documentary was asking for.

Clark adjusted himself where he was seated as the tension continued to build around him.

"We're losing daylight," Diane said in an aggressive tone. "Let's get the shots we need now, rendezvous at night, plug it into the computers, and see what we've got. Simple as that."

Stacey wasn't backing down either. "And if the shots aren't correct, we run the risk of moving on without addressing the issue of getting new footage, correct footage that can shape the whole tone of this documentary."

"I took the goddamn footage myself," Diane said in a fiery tone. "It'll work."

Slowly, Diane sighed to herself and let out a deep breath. Things were starting to get ugly.

"Okay Diane, I know you mean well and all, but first things first, this is my project," Stacey said as he stood up. "This is my first time in the director's seat. Know what I mean?"

Diane stood to her feet as well. "Yeah but don't fuck up a good thing. If this animal really exists, then we have a once in a lifetime opportunity to get some never-before-seen footage. To document. To understand. To share. Comprende?"

Stacey just stood there, placed his hands atop his hips, and once again removed his baseball cap. For what seemed like the tenth time today, he began toweling the sweat from his head. This terrain reminded him of being in a sauna. To Stacey, it felt like he had been breathing through a sponge since they arrived.

An uncomfortable few seconds of silence passed as Stacey continued to wipe the beads of sweat from his head. Meanwhile, Diane sat back down and continued chomping aggressively at her sandwich while staring off into the distance. That left Bob Hohrman and Clark Geiger in somewhat of an awkward position as they looked at one another, each with blank expressions on their face. Bob smiled and looked down at the ground as he continued working on polishing off his own sandwich.

And then without warning, Clark suddenly stood to his feet. With his sandwich still in hand, he brushed himself off and quietly began moving away from the group. Never having been one to be an active participant in physical confrontations of any sort, he slowly found himself feeling uncomfortable with regards to how the whole situation was playing out. So Clark just continued taking steps backward, slowly getting closer and closer to a thick stand of bamboo trees. As he continued moving away from the group, he began to hear the bantering between Stacey and Diane pick back up once again. But now Clark was merely focused on putting as much separation between himself and the others as possible, so the heated words that were being thrown back and forth quickly fell into the background.

Now the sounds of the forest came back into focus as Clark continued moving himself backward. He heard birds chirping back and forth to one another from high atop the outstretched limbs that formed the canopy. He heard the persistent drone from the myriad of insects down at the ground level. Clark eventually came to a stop when the back of his shirt touched some outstretched limbs from the thick vegetation that grew close to the edges of the clearing. He now stood about a good one hundred feet away from the others. As he stared back toward the group, he could see that the bantering back and forth from the director and executive producer was still going strong.

He watched for a few more seconds taking it all in. And then oddly, something strange happened. From somewhere behind him, deep within the brush, his ears suddenly picked up on something. It sounded like either a branch or a twig snapping. He didn't know which one it was; all he knew was that it was there. The sound had taken him by surprise. Immediately he felt the hairs on his arm stand up. Something didn't feel right about the situation.

Clark listened further as he turned himself around. He was greeted with solid bamboo growth. It resembled a damn near impenetrable wall of green vegetation. The growth here was so thick that he could only see a dozen or so feet back into the forest. But again, he heard the sound.

Snap.

"What the fuck," he mumbled quietly to himself.

Turning his neck at a rather awkward angle, his eyes quickly shifted back toward the group. Now he saw nothing but arms flailing back and forth and people up in each other's faces, but there was no sound. Clark Geiger heard nothing now but the sounds of the dense forest all around him. For a moment, things felt tight and constricting, like the forest was slowly starting to close in on him from all angles. Maybe it was, or maybe he was losing his grip on things. Either way, his senses were tripping out on him.

Now his ears picked up on a heavy and intense scratching sound. It sounded like something large was rubbing itself up against one of the bamboo trees. But again, he really couldn't see much of anything.

Clark turned back around and saw the others. Bob Hohrman too had stood to his feet as Stacey and Diane continued going at it. A quick turn back around to the trees and the sound of something rubbing itself up against one of the trees could once again be heard. But this time the sound had come from much closer. Clark felt like he was having a mini panic attack, and no one, absolutely no one, was taking notice. When he felt he could absolutely take no more of it, his lungs let loose a damp and wet gurgled scream.

"Quiet!" Clark blasted at the top of his lungs.

It had been a monstrous sound, and for a moment Clark stood there absolutely stunned at what his lungs and vocal chords had managed to pull off. He had always had what most would consider to be a rather weak and unassuming voice. But nonetheless, the monstrous roar had done just what it had intended to do: get the attention of the squabbling twosome.

Now the entire group stared back at Clark. Clark said nothing though as all eyes continued to be on him. And he didn't have to. Everyone quickly picked up on what he had noticed only moments prior. Movement was stirring from somewhere out there in the deep brush. Now they knew with certainty that something heavy was making its way slowly through the forest. And as they continued to listen and take it all in, it also sounded like something was being dragged. The dragging sound continued until finally it came to a stop.

Clark looked up toward the top of the canopy. Now only the wind blowing softly through the trees could be heard as the bamboo gently rattled and scraped against one another. The entire forest seemed to have pushed the pause button. Everything for the most part was silent.

Clark was just about to step forward a few steps, to put a bit of distance between his body and the edge of the foliage, when suddenly the dragging sound picked up once again. Clark paused mid-step right where he was. Quietly, he set his right foot down. It was close now.

Clark shot a quick stare toward Stacey, the director busy reaching for what looked like his camera. Despite being frightened, Clark gave him the thumbs up. Maybe if they couldn't actually get footage of whatever was causing the noise, at the bare minimum they'd be able to get some great audio.

Clark continued to watch Stacey from where he stood. He saw the director quickly extend the legs of the tripod and then go about securing the camera to the top of it. Now he was ready to begin filming with the thirty thousand dollar camera.

More noise shot out from behind Clark. Branches and twigs were now breaking and snapping. Whatever it was appeared to be moving quicker through the forest now. Slowly, Clark started to move away from the bamboo. As he continued doing so, he saw the others materialize next to him. Bob Hohrman had the boom mic extended outward toward the bamboo.

Clark turned to his right and saw Stacey. Without putting any more thought into it, Clark watched as Stacey went plunging head first into the vegetation. The director showed little regard for his own well-being as limbs and branches scratched and clawed at him from wherever they could. But as he had conveyed to them time and time again, "We directors are desperate people who will do anything to get the right shot." Stacey was doing just that, being completely at the mercy of the shot. That's all that mattered now, getting the much-needed footage, the footage they had come all this way for.

"Stacey!" Clark called out as he moved forward several feet.

Bob reached out with his left arm and stopped Clark from moving forward. In his right hand, he still held the boom mic. Both men could now hear the director as he continued plowing his way through the dense brush. Stacey Winston had disappeared completelely. The forest had literally swallowed him up.

With his heart pounding, Clark reached out and pushed Bob's hand away. Clark suddenly looked to his left. In all the commotion, he had lost track of where Diane was. And then without giving it any further thought, Clark moved forward and entered the forest.

He kept pushing forward for a dozen feet or so until finally he came to a stop and tried to get his bearings. Quickly, he scanned. No sign of Stacey. All was silent as well. The familiar birds calling out from high atop the canopy had died down. Even the constant drone of the insects could no longer be heard. The forest had grown deathly still. Clark was once again on the move though, but in doing so had failed to realize that his pants had become entangled in the thorns of several vines. The forest now seemed to be clawing and reaching out at him from all angles. This bastard place had that quality about it.

With a quick tug and a pull, his clothing tore away from the thorny overgrowth. He had managed to free himself, but the minute he went to push off with his right foot, he found himself caught once again. This time, sharp thorns scraped along his forearms and the back of his neck. The pain only continued to intensify. Now he was entangled in thick vegetation.

The sounds of panic and commotion rang out from what seemed like all corners of the forest now. Quickly, his eyes darted back and forth as he attempted to move forward.

Where's Stacey?

Somewhere down below him and off to the left, he again heard the dragging sound. For a second, the dragging sound came to a complete stop. And then it picked up right where it left off. Now Clark found himself really starting to panic. He should have followed Bob's advice. He shouldn't have entered the forest. It was far denser in here than he could have ever imagined. He literally felt as though he couldn't even fucking move.

"Guys!" he shouted at the top of his lungs. "Hey, guys! I'm trapped over here!"

With his heart beating against his ribcage, Clark managed to turn himself around. It did little good though. He was really jammed in here now.

"Jesus fucking Christ," he muttered as he tried to extricate himself from the dense underbrush.

And then suddenly, he heard something come up from behind him. He went to spin around but it was too late. Out of nowhere, an enormous bellowing roar rang out. It had come from an insanely close distance.

Now Clark felt his blood run cold on him. He listened and waited. It was all he could do.

Thirty seconds stretched into a minute. More silence followed.

Clark was just about ready to try to turn and make his way back up the hillside toward the clearing when suddenly something came up quickly from behind him.

11

Bick Downs eyed his teammates as the B14 helicopter banked hard to its right. Out in front of the flying aircraft stretched for the most part a beautiful, sun-drenched sky. And down below, a vast and silent world of green bamboo trees stretched as far as the eye could see in all directions. Despite the bright and beaming sun, there were still thin wispy trails of fog that clung low to the forest canopy below. Also from time to time, the team found themselves staring down at muddy brown rivers which snaked back and forth between the trees. It was a sea of green of immense proportions and it had an untouched and rugged nature about it. To Downs it seemed very primal and raw in both its nature and overall appearance. He absolutely loved that quality about it. It felt like they were stepping back in time.

As the helicopter continued to soar high above all of it, it was also hard to imagine that such remote places still existed on planet Earth, but they did. The team was being dropped into a rugged part of untouched forest in the northern side of the country in the Ha Giang Province of Vietnam.

It was late in the afternoon now as the B14 made a hard bank to its left. The helicopter was now heading straight toward the sun as the beautiful sunset continued to light up the late afternoon sky in radiant oranges and yellows.

Downs looked over at the rest of his team. Everyone was wearing noise-cancelling headphones accompanied by a mic to make communication easier. The Society of Cryptozoological Agents was going to be dropped off. Downs adjusted his headphones and spoke through the mic to the others.

"Gonna be a quick one. The minute we touch down, grab your gear and we're out," Downs said.

Downs made eye contact with each member of the team as he nodded to himself. All in all, this was their second mission together.

For a moment, Downs fidgeted in his seat. There was no doubt he was nervous, but he was also antsy, jittery, and thankfully excited for what was to come. The team, albeit new and still learning, formed a small wing of a much greater part of a secret organization known only to insiders as The Society of Crypto-zoological Agents. Headed by the president and real-estate mogul John Corstine, the team had been sent halfway around the world to look for a myth, a legend that had its roots in a half or so dozen different cultures scattered throughout time.

To the majority of the world, the term Bigfoot means an animal that walks upright on two legs and is something that holds its roots and origin in both myth and folklore. The fact that humans had always attributed its ability to walk on two legs had given it more monster characteristics than actual animal traits over the years. But as Downs let out a deep breath, he knew better. They weren't dealing with a monster. They were dealing with a living, breathing creature, something that had supposedly died out some one hundred thousand years ago. He thought about that chunk of time for a moment.

The chopper banked hard right once more, and in doing so, Downs watched as their equipment which was stowed under Jeremiah's feet went sliding along the ground. Downs pointed toward the sliding gear. Jeremiah quickly reeled the equipment back in. It was the bag that contained their radios, their means of communication to one another once out in the field. It wouldn't be long now. They were almost there.

Time to sink or swim, Downs thought.

Looking over one last time at his teammates, he saw Josiah Young give him the thumbs up. Downs felt good about the team they had assembled. They had already achieved quite a bit, and in time, hopefully they would continue to keep quantum-leaping their efforts, capitalizing on their successes, learning from their failures, and simply becoming a better, more efficient and cohesive unit.

From inside the cabin, the helicopter shuddered as it quickly started to descend from the sky. The chopper began to fall at a rather fast rate now. Downs felt an increase in his heart rate as he looked out the window. They were dropping fast now as the tree line below quickly came into focus. The rotor wash from the helicopter was now beating back the surrounding limbs and branches from the trees below. As the helicopter continued its sharp descent, Downs watched as the blades nearly missed the surrounding foliage. For a second, Downs thought that the blades might actually hit, but to his surprise, they didn't. The pilot kept bringing the aircraft down with the steady hand of a surgeon, taking them lower and lower into this world of green bamboo trees. Their mission was about to officially begin. For a moment, Downs thought back to his action sports store in San Francisco. He wondered how it was going and if everything was okay. Quickly though, he shrugged that thought off. Shit was about to get real now. They were being dropped off in what appeared to be a small clearing of sorts, an area of open ground that saw a break in the trees.

Quickly, the others began scrambling to gather their belongings as the chopper continued its sharp descent. Things were getting a bit more turbulent than expected. The aircraft suddenly dropped unexpectedly before finally stabilizing. Downs quickly began doing his last-minute checks as the helicopter momentarily hovered some fifty feet above the ground.

His overnight bag was stowed at his feet. Check. Each member of the team was dressed in head-to-toe camo gear. Check. They had enough food and water to last up to three days. Check. Downs looked over to Burr Wellington. The big man adjusted himself in his seat as he slung his overnight bag over one shoulder. Next, he quickly opened the large duffle bag at his feet. As Downs watched the large man unzip the hefty bag, his eyes locked in on the air rifles and tranquilizer guns. These were essentially the non-lethals that the team would be using to take the creature down with. There was also more though.

As Downs slung his overnight bag over his own shoulder, he looked down at the small case stowed at his feet. Inside were two Astra .357 revolvers. This had been a recent issue of contention amongst the Society of Cryptozoological Agents, the issue of lethal weapons versus non-lethal weapons. It was most definitely a fact that the S.C.A worked primarily with non-lethals, tracking down, capturing, sedating, and relocating creatures long thought extinct to their remote outpost in the wilds of Siberia. And if all went according to plan, they would be doing so once again.

But there was also the growing and burdensome issue surrounding confronting others who weren't in the same business as they were. These were individuals and organizations that had an interest in the wonders from the prehistoric past, but who wished to capitalize financially on these ancient wonders. And encountering such individuals out in the wild was both a tricky and dangerous task all in one. On the last mission to San Francisco and the farming suburb of Santa Rosa, Downs and his team had been outfitted with an Astra .357 revolver, a gun only to be used in the most dire of circumstances. The team had been outfitted again with the weapon by John Corstine. The gun itself was capable of stopping a charging rhino. But this time, instead of one gun, the team had been granted two. Downs had a revolver as did Burr Wellington. Both weapons were only to be used as a last resort. The S.C.A. prided itself on stealth over brawn. It wasn't that the organization was against using excessive force; it was simply that force was only to be used when all other options had been fully exhausted. But all in all, both revolvers had been added to their arsenal simply as a means to better protect themselves, to better ensure that they returned homed safely. Downs felt somewhat grateful for that.

The helicopter dropped sharply, causing Downs and the others to be momentarily lifted from their seats. Downs looked out to the left. Now they were close. He could see the canopy on one side of them being beaten back by the rotor wash. Down along the side of the hill, they had come to a small clearing of sorts. He watched as the long grass continued to be beaten back and flattened as the skids of the chopper neared. They touched down on the sloping hillside as everything within a short radius was beaten back and flattened by the merciless rotor wash.

Suddenly the hatch opened. "Let's go," Downs yelled.

One by one the team began filing out. Downs was the last one to leave. He did his best to give the inside of the chopper a quick glance. The pilot turned around in his seat and gave him a thumbs-up. Downs returned a thumbs-up to the pilot as he exited the helicopter and hopped down and into the long grass. Once outside, he was instantly bathed in the deafening and constant thumping of the rotors. Quickly, Downs hurried on over toward the others.

Loaded heavily with gear, Downs turned and craned his neck just as the helicopter began to slowly lift up and into the sky. Now he had reached the others, and together the team watched as the pilot with his dark aviator sunglasses gave them all one last, final thumbs-up.

The chopper rose higher and higher into the sky until finally the aircraft edged its way forward and headed off in the opposite direction. The team remained in silence for a moment as they watched the chopper before it finally disappeared off into the distance.

The sounds of the surrounding forest took a moment to return before Downs entered the middle of the group and pulled out his iPad. Before they had left, he downloaded a bunch of maps of just where they were. Bringing up the aerial image of their current location, Downs zoomed in on the screen with a tap of his finger. He had just begun to zoom in further on the screen when suddenly Max Caldwell began to back away from the group. Slowly, the zoologist extended his hand outward and looked up toward the sky with a worried look on his face.

"Ah, guys," Max said while still looking up.

But Downs was busy showing the others where they had been dropped off via several more taps of his iPad.

"Um, guys," Max said once more, the palm of his hand still flat and outstretched.

This time though, Downs had heard him. Downs pulled back from the group, unaware that Max had separated from them in the first place. Immediately, Downs craned his neck back toward the sky. The others followed suit as well.

"Well, I'll be damned," Burr Wellington said as he took off his hunting hat. "Son of a bitch. Damn storm literally blew in outta nowhere."

"Typical in this part of the world," Jeremiah replied. "And we're here in the rainy season."

"Well," Burr said as he zipped up his jacket and put his hat back on. "Looks like we're gonna need to take shelter, and quick."

No sooner than Burr had spoken those very words, fat raindrops began to fall from the sky. It started slowly, but within thirty seconds things had materialized into an all-out deluge. These were the monsoon rains that the team had been warned of. And now they were experiencing the wrath of those rains firsthand.

12

San Francisco, California

Sixty-one year old John Corstine lifted the piping hot mug of coffee gingerly from the corner of his desk and brought it carefully toward his mouth. The Colombian blend was his absolute favorite, and as Corstine brought it once again toward his mouth and blew ever so gently on it, he realized the drink was far too hot.

Better safe than sorry, he thought to himself as he set it back down.

There was nothing worse that Corstine hated than burning his mouth. As wispy strands of steam continued to rise from the hot coffee mug, Corstine cracked open his laptop and brought it closer toward him. Opening up another browser window, he logged into his emails and quickly began scrolling. There were dozens upon dozens of emails pertaining to the many businesses that he owned and operated. Despite the sizable amount of unread emails, they only accounted for a small fraction of his vast empire. But that's not what had Corstine's interest this morning. He'd deal with the emails later.

Corstine hovered the cursor over one of the emails, just about to open it up to have a read when suddenly he pulled back for a moment. One of the successes that Corstine had attributed to his monumental growth was the discipline to not embark upon a certain task unless fully committed. And as silly as this strategy sounded, it pertained to email.

"Never open an email unless you're one hundred percent committed and ready to dig in," Corstine muttered to himself. "Never."

The last thing he wanted to do was to begin clicking on emails that he wasn't fully commited to handling at the moment. He would wait and open the emails up later when he had a clear mind. As he closed the browser, he knew they'd be waiting for him the minute he decided it was once again time to run his empire. Everything would be there the minute he was ready to pick back up. That fact always remained consistent.

Corstine reclined back in his chair for a moment, let out a sigh, and looked out the window to his left. Such a lovely view of the tall, towering eucalyptus trees that made up the neighboring Julius Kahn Park just across the street.

Coffee.

Like a light bulb going off in his head, Corstine reached for the coffee mug. This time it had cooled off considerably and Corstine had himself a nice and relaxing sip. Setting the mug down meticulously on the desk, he could already feel its effects warming his insides. He had always found the cool and at times drab San Francisco weather to be the perfect mix for drinking coffee literally at all times of the year. It was one of the things that made him love the city so much.

Next, he opened another window on the computer and logged into a separate email account. But this account was not linked to any of his businesses. This account was strictly for matters pertaining to the Society of Cryptozoological Agents (S.C.A.). Quickly Corstine began scrolling down. There was a long list of unread emails in this account as well.

Pulling back from the chair for a moment, Corstine again stared briefly out the window. His thoughts now began to consume him. Plain and simple, he missed his son, Jeremiah Corstine.

Corstine returned his gaze to a sign that hung just above the door into his office. In big and bold lettering it read: **PROGRESS NEVER SLEEPS.**

Corstine reached for the mug and took another sip of the smooth blend of coffee. He remained entranced in his thoughts. On the one hand, that sign and the message that it so boldly displayed had literally allowed himself to build an empire, both in the world of real estate as well as the rest of the businesses that he owned. The same type of monumental success could also be said for the S.C.A. and the many secret agents and strategic alliances that they had built up in all the corners of the globe. But all of it, the business success, the S.C.A., it had all come at a huge cost. John Corstine had not been the most attentive father and husband at times over the years. It wasn't that he wanted to neglect his son and wife; he loved them both to pieces. It was that just like so many entrepreneurs before him, building empires from the ground up had been a very selfish and time-consuming endeavor. The world of entrepreneurialism had been one big great time suck, and his family had suffered as a direct result.

The balance between entrepreneurialism and fatherhood was more often than not tipped heavily in the direction of business and forward-moving progress. Corstine's eyes shifted again toward the sign that had hung so proudly above his doorway for so long now. It was almost an epiphany of sorts. For over three decades now, Corstine had worked diligently building himself an empire, looking up to that sign as if it were a beacon of sorts, his motivation night after night to keep grinding and chipping away. But now as Corstine sat all alone in his leather chair surrounded by books and beautifully handcrafted furniture, he saw the sign for what it truly was. The sign had shown, like so many other highly successful business men and women, that he had let his family down. Corstine's wife had sadly passed away years ago, but what was left from that family lived on through his only child Jeremiah.

And now Corstine had sent his son, his only son, to a far-flung and remote corner of the world and potentially put him in harm's way. Corstine thought about that for a moment as he drew in another sip of his coffee. He had sent the entire team to that remote corner of the world for that matter. He wondered how it was going for them? He could only hope and pray that everything would be okay.

13

F at, heavy raindrops splatted down noisily all around the team as the ground was quickly turning to mud. The thick layering of bamboo trees that rimmed the clearing were now swaying back and forth on account of the powerful wind gusts. The team had been somewhat caught off guard by the sudden torrential downpour.

Downs eyed the trees as they continued to knock back and forth against one another. It was really coming down hard now. Downs couldn't remember the last time he'd seen rain like this. It might have been on one of his trips to Florida but he wasn't quite certain.

Downs was forced to shout now on account of the rain. "We need to get outta this stuff!"

Burr yelled back and pointed with his large hand. "Need to set up our makeshift camp in there."

Burr was pointing toward the thick stands of bamboo, where the clearing transitioned into dense forest.

The trees were beating and back and forth aggressively now, creaking and groaning as their bases knocked back and forth against one another. Despite the pounding of the rain and battering wind gusts,

Downs thought he heard something for a moment. With his heavy daypack still on his back, he had a waterproof bag slung over his right shoulder that held the tranquilizer guns, air rifles, two flare guns, and two Astra .357 revolvers. Downs edged forward. From deep within the foliage, he could have sworn he had heard something moving.

He took another step forward and tried to listen as best as he could. It was hard to decipher much of anything though. And then a hand suddenly touched him on the shoulder. It was Josiah.

"You okay?"

Downs nodded. "Yeah, just thought I heard something in there."

Through the unrelenting sheets of rain, Josiah had himself a good look as well. By now, the others had gathered around the two men.

"Well," Burr Wellington said as he slapped a large, wet hand atop Downs' back. "No time like the present. Let's get our asses in there."

Their mission had officially begun.

14

Stacey Winston found himself soaking wet, bleeding, and absolutely miserable in every sense of the word. Now was most definitely when the going had gotten difficult. It was no longer pouring, the rain having instead been replaced with a thick mist that bathed the forest in its cool embrace. He looked down at his arms and felt around on his neck with his fingers. This bamboo forest was slowly cutting the living shit out of him. He was bleeding pretty good and from multiple areas, but still he dragged both himself as well as his tripod and camera through the dense foliage. It was fucking ridiculous just how thick and overgrown this place truly was in certain spots.

Vegetation on steroids in the absolute middle of nowhere, he thought to himself.

He paused right in front of a thick gathering of wet ferns, the outstretched fronds absolutely teeming with water. For a moment, he watched as water dripped from the ferns and onto the mud of the jungle floor. Slowly, Stacey pulled the rest of his body through the growth and peeked his head out. He was perched halfway up this jungle hillside, and by the looks of it, he felt as though things had reached their saturation point.

It appeared as though at any given second, this hillside potentially had the ability to turn into a slick mudslide. That would be a living nightmare. Meanwhile, down below about a hundred feet or so, life slowly stirred to life in the lower parts of the forest.

Stacey pushed several of the fronds from the fern aside and set the tripod down in the mud. Everything was soaking wet in this damn jungle now; literally every inch of this place was wet, muddy, and dripping with water. But it would be worth it in the end. At least that's what he kept telling himself. Get through all this shit, the deplorable conditions, the lackluster film team that had been assembled, and the relatively small budget that the studio had shelled out to fund this mediocre documentary.

"Just get through all of this," he reiterated to himself as he took in a deep breath and winced through the pain currently shooting through his body. "It will all be worth it in the end."

Stacey was hoping that with the success of this project, there would hopefully be bigger things on the horizon. And by bigger things he was hoping that this meant the chance to direct his first full-length feature film. He hoped like hell that this was the start of something big for him. He really had been at it for what felt like a short eternity, and he felt like he was due for a good opportunity to come his way. It was just a matter of time. Luck is where preparation meets opportunity.

With a quick flick of his hand, he slapped at his neck. "Fuckin' mosquitoes."

That was yet another bug bite to add to the long list of bites currently plaguing him. Slowly, he moved his body forward through the foliage and turned the camera on. The light blinked red, signaling it was on and ready to capture high quality HD footage. Now Stacey returned his eyes to where he had been previously staring. About one hundred feet down the jungle hillside, Stacey could see one of the members of his team. At first he couldn't tell who he was staring at, but as he kept watching, he could see that it was Clark Geiger.

Stacey watched Clark for a moment, the man stumbling awkwardly through the jungle as if it were his first time using his legs. Clark Geiger was in his late twenties and was someone who had done whatever it took to get into this crazy film and television business in the same relentless manner as Stacey had done, the only difference being that one was in the director's seat while the other was not.

The fact that this was a four-man operation still did not change the fact that Clark was a lowly person in this production and Stacey knew that given how many strings he had to pull not to mention asses he had to kiss, there was very little chance the kid would ever work his way up the ladder. Hell, maybe it was possible, but it certainly seemed an impossible industry to break into. But still, he commended Clark for even trying. That was the simple fact of how things worked. To Stacey, just landing this directing gig of this short documentary was a success in its own right. Sometimes it felt like he had hit the small-time lottery.

But as Stacey readjusted himself from inside the ferns, he found it odd to be watching Clark from such a close, yet at the same time concealed, vantage point.

The denseness of the jungle was so thick and encompassing that it would be difficult for Clark way down at the bottom to see all the way back up to where Stacey was currently crouched and hiding. Slowly, Stacey brought the camera and the tripod around in front of him. He stared for a moment and zoomed in on the man below. Surprisingly, he had a good angle down toward Clark. Suddenly, he felt an odd sensation tingling through him. He had the urge to film. He thought about the fact that often times directors were desperate people, completely at the mercy of their next shot. And right now he was desperately at the mercy of making this documentary a success. He needed it to be a success, big time, both for his career as well as his own mental sanity. Rather than fight it, he did just that. Quietly, Stacey began to film Clark. He figured it could be used as good initial footage chronicling their trek through the bamboo in their ultimate quest to find the elusive.

As Stacey continued to both watch and film, it soon became apparent that Clark was injured. Perhaps that's why the man had been moving so gingerly, so awkwardly through the forest. Stacey continued to watch in silence, his feet squishing down in the mud, his arms and neck constantly brushing against the fronds of the ferns. Just how bad were the man's injuries? Clark suddenly changed positions, allowing Stacey for a new and unobstructed view. From the way that Clark's left arm hung limply at his side, Stacey estimated it to be dislocated if not broken. Again not a major problem in a city, but way out here, in the middle of nowhere, it could indeed turn itself into a much larger problem. Jungles had that ability about them, the ability to compound one problem on top of the other. Injury leads to infection which can often lead to death.

Stacey looked back to the camera and checked on the positioning of things. He focused his eyes through the lens for a moment. All looked good. The director of the documentary had just repositioned the legs of the tripod in the thick mud when suddenly noise from somewhere deep in the trees caught his attention. Stacey Winston settled himself back into the foliage as the scene below him continued to play out.

• • •

Clark Geiger came to a complete stop. He keeled over in agony once more from the splitting pain to both his ribcage as well as his arm. He drew in several deep and ragged breaths. The sheer humidity of this place wasn't helping either. But the pain that he felt in his rib cage paled in comparison to the blinding, searing pain that he was currently experiencing in his left arm. It had been nearly twenty years, but when he was ten, he had broken his right arm in a fall during P.E. class. It had hurt worse than he could have ever imagined, and now here he stood, at the ripe old age of twenty-nine, in the middle of this steamy and humid bamboo forest in Vietnam having appeared to now have broken the other arm—the only difference now being the lack of medical attention. To Clark, things had already started to feel rather surreal and detached, like they were happening to someone else. It didn't seem real being here, stumbling around way down here, lost, injured, and scared out of his mind. To make matters worse, it felt as though his mind was slowly failing him.

Summoning the strength to straighten himself, Clark did just that, but then immediately found himself again hunched over in pain. This was not looking good. There was a considerable amount of pain to his rib cage, and it had him wondering if he had also broken a rib or two during his fall down the steep hillside.

Leaning over to his left, he fought off the urge to vomit. Suddenly, he found himself feeling hot and clammy all over. A hot flash suddenly washed over him and Clark threw up all over the rain-soaked vegetation. Ferns and bamboo stalks were spared no mercy in the wake of his mouth as he continued to wretch. Spitting and struggling to regain himself, he found little relief in throwing up. Now as stringy spit and vomit clung and dripped from the foliage, Clark's body felt as though he was dying, literally racked in more agonizing, gut-wrenching pain than he knew how to comprehend. For a second, his thoughts ran with that idea. They were out in the middle of nowhere, and his fall down the mud hillside had severely injured his body. Is this how he would meet his end? He hadn't even reached his thirtieth birthday yet.

Just then, he heard something. It had come from somewhere close by, but he couldn't quite place exactly where. The foliage off to his left was simply too dense to afford any type of glimpse back into it. It was amazing just how tightly-packed together things were at the bottom of the hillside. Here at the bottom of the bamboo forest, life seemed to be flourishing, literally exploding from every corner and inch where there was soil and space upon which to take up root. Even if there was not room to lay down one's roots, the plants took other measures to survive. New trees took up root at the base of existing trees and flowers shot out and grew from other flowers. Life was most definitely thriving here. It didn't take a degree in botany to make this simple observation.

Again, noise stirred in the brush off to his left. He couldn't turn to look though. His body and his neck for that matter wouldn't let him. Suddenly, Clark threw up again all over the vegetation. For a moment, he remained hunched over right where he was. Now he saw strings of pink vomit dripping from the fronds of a tall fern that grew next to him as he wiped his mouth.

With his lips coated with vomit and saliva, Clark somehow managed to straighten himself and turn his body. His left arm hung limply at his side as he stared out and into the deep vegetation wondering just what in the hell was down here with him?

· · ·

From up above, still perched in the mud and hemmed in closely by vegetation, Stacey Winston stared through the camera and continued filming the scene unfolding below. All appeared to be in nice working order. The camera was rolling and he felt he already had some good footage so far.

Almost out of nowhere, a strange question popped into his head. Why hadn't he gone to help his fellow colleague? He pondered that for a moment. He honestly didn't know the answer. And then he shook his head. This was ridiculous; he had watched the man stumble down there for far too long. He needed to go help him. Stacey was just about to shut the camera off and collapse the legs of the tripod when suddenly an enormous, dripping wet, shadowy figure emerged from the thick foliage. Just as Stacey darted back to the camera to zoom in and have a better look, the enormous figure sprung to life.

• • •

Clark had no time to react as the forest crackled and exploded with life just to his left. He forced his body around to have a better look, but as he did so he was lifted up and off the ground. Something gripped him tightly and immediately began plowing through the vegetation with him.

Clark went to scream, but before he could produce any vocalization whatsoever, he was suddenly thrown through the air.

• • •

Stacey Winston stood both stunned and tongue-tied behind the lens of his Canon EOS C700 Full-Frame Cinema Camera. The thirty-three thousand dollar camera was capable of capturing images with up to 5.9k resolution and it had just captured everything down below, and with stunning clarity. Standing in thick mud and still surrounded on all sides by a mixture of dense bamboo and heavy fern growth, if he had wanted to scream at what he was seeing, he would have been incapable of doing so. He was stunned, actually horrified was more like it, but despite the sheer terror of it all, he felt he had to keep going, had to keep rolling with his footage. The show must go on. It was a simple adage, but it was so true. As a filmmaker, he often felt a slave to the camera, doing all in his power to get the so-called "money shot," the footage that would officially put him on the map once and for all.

Quickly, he panned the camera to the right. He had momentarily lost sight of what was taking place below. Now he felt like a movie-going patron, glued to what was taking place at the bottom of the jungle hillside. As Stacey continued panning to his right, he still had no clue as to Clark's whereabouts. He scanned for a few more seconds back and forth before he eventually caught back up with the action.

• • •

Clark felt his body racked in unbearable pain as his eyes slowly flickered open. He was bleeding and slumped in an awkward position at the base of an enormous tree. All around him, thick vines and thorny leaves crowded closely to where he lay. It felt as though the forest was closing in on him, trying to literally swallow him whole, tear him limb from limb. And for all intents and purposes, it was.

His back felt as though it were broken in multiple places. His two front ribs felt more than likely broken as well, and in the madness of it all, he had lost his front tooth. He laid over onto his side and spat thick blood. His hand reached up and felt the hole where the tooth had previously been. It was an odd sensation and for a moment, his eyes scanned the ground for the tooth. The search turned up nothing.

He was now bleeding from his mouth as well as more locations than he could count. Gritting his teeth together and writhing in agony, he did his best to sort of snake-crawl himself out and away from the base of the tree.

And then suddenly, Clark heard a deep wheezing sound. The noise stopped him dead in his tracks. He felt his blood go icy cold on him as his heart rate accelerated and all other sounds of the forest died down. Now there was only silence as he lay there, heart racing like mad, racked in unbearable pain, completely helpless in every sense of the word. And to make matters worse, he was lying face down on his stomach. His positioning couldn't be worse.

Next, Clark heard movement. Painfully, he lifted his head up as the forest once again came alive. Something big was moving through the bamboo. There was also the ever-present sound of heavy crunching on the forest floor, littered with decaying leaves, branches, vines, and a host of other jungle flora. At this point, Clark honestly had no clue where the noise was coming from. All he knew with certainty was that his body was telling him he couldn't simply just lie here helplessly. So Clark began pulling himself forward as fast as he could.

Whatever pain he had felt was momentarily pushed aside by his sudden rush of adrenaline. Now, sheer terror gripped him. Clark was in the process of pulling himself to the side of a rotted-out tree stump with ferns growing out either side of it when suddenly he saw a long shadow materialize and cast itself over him. Something had momentarily blocked what little sunlight there was filtering down through the canopy high above. But still, he continued onward, not stopping, not knowing where he was trying to get to or what exactly it was that he was trying to achieve. All he knew was that he needed to keep moving forward, keep moving away from whatever it was that was behind him. Anything was better than just laying on the ground a sitting duck.

And that's when the smell hit him full on. An immense reeking odor suddenly filled the air. It was a musty and rank odor and smelled like a combination of blood and meat. The smell reminded him of being up against an enclosure near one of the big animals at the city zoo or something. It had that same type of pungent aroma to it.

Clark kept pulling himself forward. He looked to his left and suddenly saw a brightly colored green snake. The reptile was coiled tightly and appeared ready to strike. The snake hissed at him as it reared back with its mouth agape, fangs ready to strike, poised in a very aggressive manner. Having no clue what species it was, he knew one thing for certain, and that was that nearly everything in this godforsaken jungle was more than likely poisonous. He wasn't stopping though, couldn't afford to. For a few seconds he lost track of everything around him, his body, primarily that of his elbows, becoming attuned to the duty of pulling the rest of himself forward across the forest floor as he continued to snake-crawl his way. Beneath the mass of his body, he could hear the sound of dead leaves and twigs crunching and snapping as he continued pulling himself forward. The forest floor was essentially one great big recycling process, with everything eventually returning back to the forest in one way or another. Life always found a way.

"Oh shit," Clark blurted out. Suddenly, he felt things starting to crawl atop his neck.

Immediately, his eyes darted to the right. He must have dragged himself right through an ant colony as large ants passed by the leaves in dense and furious trails. He had gone from feeling a tickling sensation atop his neck to that of being completely inundated. In a matter of seconds, the ants swarmed him in their thick black masses. Ants traveled along his arms, some crawled down his shirt, others up his pant legs, while some made their way into his mouth, nostrils, and even his eyelids. No orifice was spared the fury of their wrath.

And in a moment of sheer terror, Clark had completely lost track of where he was as he did his best to roll over onto his other side. In doing so, he caught a glimpse back up toward what had initially cast the shadow above him in the first place. Suddenly, he saw a huge hulking figure looking down at him. The giant mountain of fur rested on all fours and stood as still as a statue. Meanwhile, two large eyes continued to watch the struggling man covered in a thick, black writhing mass of ants.

And then that calm and placid nature lashed out at him. The huge hulking figure burst forward. In a blinding flash, the creature tossed him to the side as if he weighed but a mere few pounds. His body landed on something hard, possibly a large rock or tree stump, although he wasn't certain. All he was certain of was that whatever it was had shaken free the swarming mass of ants.

Quickly, the swarm of ants scattered back across the forest floor in all directions before eventually returning to what they had been preoccupied with moments prior. It was only another matter of seconds before Clark again heard the distinct thud of heavy footsteps from behind him.

He managed to turn himself around. At first he saw nothing, only a solid wall of brown intermixed with shades of black and grey here and there. And then his eyes locked in on an enormous, dome-shaped head. Eyes like black holes stared down at him. He saw the teeth as the gums rippled back into a menacing grin.

Before Clark could process things any further, the enormous shape came rampaging forward. He instantly felt the hot breath from the animal upon his skin and smelled the creature's musty stench. And then he saw a massive leathery hand open wide as it reached out for him. For a second, he saw nothing but the huge palm of the hand as the five thick fingers spread wide. Next he felt the enormous fingers on top of his face. It was as if a small weight had suddenly been placed squarely atop his head.

With little effort, the hand pushed his face back a bit. And then Clark saw the hand pull away from his face. Again, his eyes registered nothing but the huge leathery web of the palm of the creature's massive hand. Then suddenly, the hand emerged and five enormous fingers spread wide and gripped his head as if it were a basketball. Clark felt an immense pressure as the fingers gripped his skull tighter. All at once, he felt the enormous pressure pushing at his skull from all sides. Pressure followed more pressure and then once again the huge hand released itself.

This time, however, the hand hadn't gone very far. The massive leathery fingers pulled back several inches and then Clark saw two fingers stab quickly over his eyes. Clark felt the two fingers plunge deeply into his eyelids. He felt an enormous explosion of pain as they dug into his eyes like two fiery knives. The thick and muscular fingers plunged deeper and deeper, the pain building and building until suddenly there was only darkness.

A few more seconds passed by before it all came rushing to him. It hit him hard, hit him like a ton of bricks. He had been blinded. The creature had gouged both his eyes out.

Almost immediately, Clark began flailing wildly with both arms. Several moaning gasps escaped his lips. Now true terror was coursing through him. He was lying in the mud, blinded, bleeding, and with an absolute monstrosity of a creature hovering over him.

With his ears he did his best to take it all in. He heard a soft wheezing sound. And then he heard movement. The creature had shifted its weight. Silence followed.

And then suddenly an enormous and rumbling roar rang out. A blood-curdling cry of sheer terror escaped Clark Geiger's mouth as the creature lunged toward him.

• • •

A few seconds of silence passed before Stacey heard a blood-curdling scream cut off abruptly. Pausing for a moment, Stacey's head shot straight up as he stood still as a statue. There was no doubt that had been Clark. He shuddered just thinking about having to go toe to toe with such a colossal beast.

Stacey Winston stood frozen in place, absolutely frozen behind the camera, his heart pounding fiercely against his ribcage, his breathing coming in short, intense, ragged breaths. He was absolutely stunned at what he had just seen, witnessed, and filmed. It was beyond words, beyond comprehension. And beyond the breathtaking, terrifying wonder of uncovering such an animal was the horrifying reality that Stacey had just sat back and let it happen, let his colleague get swept off into the deep foliage like that.

"Breathe," he muttered to himself. "Breathe."

Stacey convinced himself that he was too far up on the hillside to have actually helped Clark, that because of his awkward positioning there was nothing he could have done for the man. It was amazing just how fast he had convinced himself of that. They had all known the inherent risks coming out here. Stacey's mind was working on overdrive right now, trying to convince himself that it was not his fault, that what had happened couldn't have been prevented. But somewhere deep in the subconscious, he must have known that was a lie, but for the moment he was doing all in his power to convince himself otherwise. Still though, he shuddered quietly to himself with the thought of what was happening to Clark way out there in the deep vegetation. By now, the creature must have been having its way with him.

Stacey peered through the camera once more and then pulled back. Quickly retrieving a small set of binoculars from inside his backpack, he put them up to his eyes and stared through them down the hillside toward the area where he had just filmed. It took a few seconds but eventually he picked up on lots of blood. Through the binoculars, he could see that bits and pieces of the limbs and vegetation were covered in blood. It was Clark's blood, and it was everywhere.

Continuing to peer through the binoculars, Stacey was still busy convincing himself that there was nothing he could have done for Clark. Now the guilt for what he had just allowed to happen was running at an all-time high. He forced himself to take in several deep breaths. He knew that continually telling himself he had been in too awkward of a position to in fact help was one hundred percent a bold-faced lie, but this was going to be his story from here on out. He had made his decision and there was no turning back now. Stacey Winston now had to live and die with the decisions that had been made while he had been perched precariously on this muddy hillside.

He stepped carefully away from the tripod for a moment, tugging his feet free from mud. The bottoms of his shoes were now caked thickly with the stuff. Slowly, he began to stretch out his back as well as his neck. He took a few more seconds before finally returning back to the camera.

The footage that he had acquired was downright incredible, almost beyond words. And they wouldn't stop there, they wouldn't rest on their laurels. They would pursue the creature, but most importantly, they would pursue more breathtaking footage. He just needed to get back to the others. Quickly, he found himself already working out the details in his head. Still reeling from what he had both seen and filmed, he wasn't certain what the correct answer or approach was. Should he just tell them what had happened straight up, that he had witnessed a potential firsthand encounter with the long thought to be extinct Gigantopithecus blacki? If he did, questions would arise, and they would no doubt be directed solely at him. Or should he merely tell them that in his mad scramble through the jungle in pursuit of getting footage of the creature he had lost track of everyone, literally lost track of himself for that matter? He did have that going for him. This jungle was dense, and even stepping a dozen or so feet away from one's neighbor could increase the chances of completely disappearing into this web of vegetation. It was most definitely a believable excuse.

Stacey shook his head to himself, as if the simple act itself would bring some clarity to the situation. The answer was he really didn't know. Moving over toward the tripod, he started to pick it up. He always wanted it out and ready to film, to film the perfect shot at a moment's notice. That's the way he had operated time and time again throughout his short, yet intense, film career.

And then quickly, he collapsed the legs of the tripod in his left hand while grabbing his backpack in his right. Quietly, Stacey Winston began pushing his way through the rain-soaked vegetation and back toward the others.

15

Downs had never actually seen a bamboo forest before in the flesh. What he saw before him appeared to be a confusing array of vegetation, a labyrinth of tall slender bamboo trees. And as he stepped a few feet even closer, he realized the bamboo trees weren't entirely green as he might have expected. Now from a closer distance, Downs could see that the tall thin trees came in different shades. Some were a consistent tone of green, while others had portions of them that were tinted a yellowish in color. Downs kept moving forward. He could hear the bamboo trees swaying and groaning as they knocked against one another. Each tree was sectioned off with what appeared to be a banded solid white line every eight inches or so. The forest was already proving to be more spectacular than he could have ever imagined. Downs stopped right where he was, craned his neck back up and looked to the tops of the trees. He was looking up toward the top of the canopy now. It was probably a good ninety feet until you reached the top. Slowly, he looked back down at the thick almost impenetrable wall of trees that marked the transition from the clearing into the forest. It appeared quite the daunting task to enter what was essentially one great big tight and constricting environment.

Downs set the large duffle bag still slung across his right shoulder down on the ground. Quickly, he unzipped it and began passing out the air rifles and the tranquilizer pistols.

Each team member wore a belt with a holster. The tranquilizer pistols were to be holstered at their sides at all times. A tranquilizer air rifle would also be slung across each of their shoulders. Downs and Burr would be in charge of handling the lethal force—the two .357 Astras. Lastly, there were also two flare guns to be used for either signaling or as a means of a last line of defense. Burr held one and Downs held the other. Hopefully all of this would be enough to allow them to meet the mission's objective and to most importantly return home safely.

"Lotta stuff," Downs said as he handed the last tranquilizer rifle to Burr. "Easy to get weighed down a bit, but it's the nature of this business."

"Hey, man," Josiah said. "Better safe than sorry."

"He's right," Burr replied. "Can't be taking no chances out here."

Downs motioned with his head toward where the forest began. "You mean in there?"

Burr smiled. "Yep."

Handing one of the .357 Astra handguns Burr's way, Downs took possession of the other Astra and holstered it at his left hip. Then setting the small carrying case down in the mud, he made eye contact with the team. "If no one objects, Burr and I will carry the lethals."

Burr had just clipped the handgun into his holster at his left hip as he looked up. Not a word was said amongst the team.

"Good," Downs said as he clapped his hands together.

Meanwhile up high in the sky, thunder rumbled from off in the distance as dark and formidable clouds had already begun to stack themselves one atop the other.

Downs nodded and pointed toward the tall stands of green bamboo. As everyone quickly gathered themselves as well as their gear and began trudging forward toward the thick wall of trees, Downs could only wonder what truly awaited them once inside.

16

Downs and the team quietly pushed through the thick, entangled layer of foliage and into the forest. They had left the grass hillside that made up the small clearing behind and officially entered the confines of the bamboo forest. Moving forward slowly several dozen feet or so with their gear loaded heavily atop their backs, now they got a true scope and scale for just how impenetrable things were here. The going was slow at first, the ground underfoot was damp and spongy, and the air itself was incredibly hot and heavy. Everything appeared to be held in and trapped tightly beneath the dense forest canopy high above. Moisture and water dripped from the leaves and branches and puddled wherever there was a flat surface upon which to do so. It was a steamy hothouse, a green Garden of Eden, and looming high and tall above this sprawling green world were the tall yet eloquently thin bamboo trees.

Downs found himself taken aback by the sheer scope and density of this place. He was somewhat unprepared for the tight and at times claustrophobic feeling that went along with being in these lone and isolated bamboo forests. It was incredible the way that each and every bamboo tree shot up at a ridiculously straight angle toward the canopy high above, the tight and narrow passageways existed at the ground level below, and most light was blocked out by the density of the crisscrossing and entangled leaves and branches that melded together to form the dense canopy high above. It was a spectacular place, but it was a place for the most part that was continually bathed in a dark and perpetual gloom.

The team now found themselves immersed in a world filled with different shades of green. The tall, thin bamboo trees which grew everywhere there was space absolutely dominated every corner of the forest.

The ground beneath their feet was littered with a solid layering of yellow, brown, and withered bamboo leaves. As Downs looked around, it was easy to see how an environment like this was essentially one big recycling process. Soon the leaves themselves would fully return to the soil and the cycle of growth, flourishing, and death would once again be in full swing. Here nothing went to waste.

As the sounds of the forest slowly began to come into focus, the team could hear several bamboo trees that grew in tightly packed formations knocking back and forth against one another. Downs craned his neck up and he could both hear and see that the canopy high above was alive and rustling with movement as well. Moving his head lower, he could see the bases of several bamboo trees continuing to knock back and forth against one another. This lasted for a few more seconds before finally a deep silence embraced the forest. For the moment at least, all was relatively quiet. Max Caldwell took the opportunity to say a few words. "The, uh, climate mixed with the high humidity and temperature here in Vietnam is very advantageous for bamboo growth."

You can say that again, Downs thought to himself as he looked around at the sheer density of this place. *Growth on steroids.*

Max pointed upward toward some of the tall, thin, towering trees. "Bamboo is considered to be an evergreen perennial flowering plant. They are in the subfamily Bambusoideae of the grass family Poaceae."

Max walked up to one of the trees and placed his hand on its slender base. "Here's where things get real interesting. Much like grasses, the internodal regions of the bamboo stem are more often than not hollow. The vascular bundles that comprise the cross section are scattered throughout the stem. Also absent is the dicotyledonous woody xyem. Resulting from all of this is the fact that the absence of secondary growth wood causes the stems of flowering plants, palms, and most importantly the large bamboos we see here to take on a columnar appearance instead of one that's tapering."

Max cleared his throat, adjusted his glasses, and continued on. "Bamboos are some of the fastest growing plants in the world. Certain species have been known to grow at the mind-boggling rate of thirty-six inches within a twenty-four hour time period. Truly incredible stuff. And, um, according to one of the forest inventory reports I had a chance to peruse just before we left, bamboo forests account for roughly eleven percent of total forest area in this country. There are also currently about twenty species of bamboo found here in Vietnam, but some speculate that if more detailed survey were to be conducted, the number of bamboo species might jump anywhere from one hundred and fifty to two hundred."

"Love all this academic talk, really, good to know, but right now let's keep moving forward," Burr grumbled from behind. "This shit is thick."

When the team had trudged probably a good hundred feet or so more, they came to a stop. Now backpacks were taken off and water bottles were pulled out. The hot and humid conditions were only amplified by the thick and entangled canopy above which seemed to trap all heat in. Already this place was starting to take its toll on the body. As the team stood there and worked on rehydrating themselves via their canteens, the sounds of the forest once again returned to their usual audible levels.

Water dripped all around them. The stalks of bamboo creaked and groaned as they gently knocked against one another, creating a rather soothing sound. It sounded like wind chimes on the corner of someone's porch.

"Now what?" Josiah asked as he looked around.

As far as the eye could see in all directions, the team was surrounded by tall green stalks of thin bamboo trees. The trees shot up and grew everywhere. Some of the trees were wiry thin, while others were a foot or so in diameter. The majority of the bamboo trees grew to towering heights of one hundred plus feet, the canopy high above melding into a jumbled mess of explosive growth. The canopy blocked out most of the available light.

Things scurried about on all sides of them now. There was even noise of scuttling and movement from up high in the trees. Life flourished from every corner of this living and breathing green world.

Downs gazed up, his eyes following a thin green stalk of bamboo as it shot up at a precisely straight angle toward the canopy high above. The tree literally appeared as though it was making a beeline straight for the sky. He continued to take it in for a moment before eventually stepping in front of the team. "We need to set up camp, get some type of protective perimeter around us. Gettin' late."

Jeremiah cleared his throat. "And after that, brings us to our next pressing issue. Nighttime."

Downs swallowed what saliva had built up in the back of his throat. Now's when the shit was about to get real. Things like the common cold always had that knack of flaring up the most at night, and if you happen to find yourself to be in one of the deep dark jungles of the world, that's when the place truly came alive as well. Nighttime is when things truly flourish.

Suddenly, each team member's head shot around as the sound of something cracking nearby caught their attention. Downs turned just in time to watch as a rather spectacular, brightly colored bird pushed off from halfway up a bamboo tree and made its way up and into the canopy. Squawking loudly, the bird seemed to have caused quite the disturbance. Soon other birds began calling out from all corners of the forest, and for a moment the team was caught in a cacophony of rising bird sounds of varying pitch.

The bamboo forest had suddenly come alive. Squawks, screeches, and low rumbling cooing sounds cried out from everywhere. Downs and the team meanwhile had dropped their gear in the middle of them and formed a formation where they each had their backs pressed up against one another in what could best be described as a defensive circle. Each of them stood staring out at the surrounding forest, air rifles pressed forward, while scanning diligently with their eyes.

Downs heard the last of the bird sounds as they slowly faded off into the distance, the remaining faint bird calls from the outer edges of the forest dying down like a song that slowly fades to black. And then just like that, the impressive display of bird vocalizations came to a complete stop. The forest was once again silent.

Downs' ears picked up on the soft gurgle of water from somewhere close by. Although he couldn't see it, the leader of the team knew there must have been a small stream nearby. No one said a word.

And then suddenly from out about a hundred feet or so, the sound of wood breaking and splintering rang out. Something appeared to be moving out there.

"Anyone have eyes on that?" Burr said through gritted teeth.

Downs felt he had a good idea of where the sound had originated from. Despite the urge for all of them to look collectively as a group, he barked out the next orders. "Hold your position out in front of you, I got eyes on it."

"Roger that," Josiah said. The paleontologist was on the opposite side of the circle and had his back to Downs.

"He's right," Burr said, "Hold your intended positions. Often the attack comes from behind, when you least expect it."

And Burr Wellington had been correct. This time though, it was Max Caldwell who caught sight of the visual before any other member of the team could.

Out about a good forty feet from where the zoologist stood on guard shot an explosion of both sound and color. Mostly, it was sound as a dissonance of different varying pitches of noise scurried quickly through the undergrowth toward them with frightening speed.

Downs tried to make out what it was from where he stood but instead shouted out the orders once more. "Just stay put. Keep your eyes peeled in front of you."

"We got it covered!" Tori yelled back.

As Max watched whatever it was that was quickly racing through the low-lying vegetation toward them, he felt his trigger finger twitch in the direction of firing a shot. Thankfully though, he didn't. Somewhere in the back of Max's brain, he could only think that was the true definition of trigger happy.

Out of nowhere, Downs heard another loud explosion of noise from somewhere off to his left. While still maintaining his grip on the air rifle in his right hand he quietly unclipped the Astra from its holster. On the last mission up in Northern California he had felt they had taken risks, calculated risks at that, but risks nonetheless. Here in the middle of an isolated and remote area in rural Vietnam, he didn't want to take those same risks this time. Now he held both the revolver as well as the air rifle in both hands.

"Bloody hell!" Burr cried out as sounds now rang out all around the group's tightly-formed circle.

The entire forest appeared to be scurrying, scuddling, and rushing its way toward them. Something had scared the inhabitants of this bamboo forest, and now it appeared as though everything was fleeing, trying to get to a safer, more isolated, corner of the forest. Downs braced himself as did the others. Now shrieking and panic-shrilled cries also rang out from the canopy high above. The team found themselves suddenly thrust into a forest that was in all-out turmoil. They heard heavy and intense cracking sounds from somewhere way out in the deep foliage. These sounds continued until finally the chaos around them suddenly came to an abrupt stop. Now all that remained were the sounds of cracking and the breaking of bamboo from way out in the foliage.

It wasn't just the team that was experiencing the cracking sounds; the entire forest had suddenly taken notice as well, as once again the forest had been plunged into a deep silence.

17

Downs held firm, both the revolver and air rifle pressed out in front of him. For the next fifteen minutes or so not a word was said amongst the team. They stood in stone silence, their backs pressed up tightly against one another in a tight circular formation while diligently scanning the forest around them.

Again Downs heard the soft gurgle of water from somewhere close by. There was no doubt that the water was hidden by the density of growth that this forest had produced over time, hidden beneath the leafy and organic matter that covered the bamboo forest's floor.

After another five minutes or so of intense silence, Downs stepped forward, his boots crunching down on the small leaves and twigs beneath him.

"That's enough for now," Downs said.

Burr let out a big sigh. "Sweet Mary, Joseph, and Jesus, the old back's about to give out."

"Yeah, for real man," Jeremiah replied.

It appeared that the aging yet hulking man that was Burr Wellington wasn't the only one feeling the effects. Standing in a tight configuration with a tranquilizer rifle pointed out in front of oneself surely wasn't the easiest of tasks to pull off. Now it was time to rest for a brief moment, to give the body a short yet necessary reprieve. As each member of the team put their air rifles down, only Downs remained with his raised. Having holstered the Astra at his side, he now had two hands squarely on the air rifle.

Tori came around to where he stood. "You should take a break for a little bit as well."

Downs took a few more seconds before finally setting the air rifle down. "Guess you're right."

"Yeah c'mon," Tori said. "Any more tensing up and our limbs are gonna fall off. Not to mention our backs. For a second I thought I was back working at my parents' restaurant."

Tori had a playful smile on her face. Downs nodded and smiled back at her. He knew how hard she worked in that restaurant and would do anything for her parents. He respected the hell out of her for that. Tori's smile was a warm and receptive one, and for a brief yet spectacular moment he found himself completely lost in the genuine warmth of that smile. He quickly shook it off though. Now was neither the time nor place for such matters. They had serious matters to attend to.

The team's reprieve was short-lived as noise stirred from back in the group. Downs' and Tori's eyes shot back to the others. It appeared as though Max had found something. Quickly, the two made their way back to the zoologist. When they got there they found Max down on his hands and knees in the mud pulling back the vegetation.

"Uh, Max," Jeremiah said. "Please be careful what you're touching and pulling back. Lotta poisonous things in this forest."

Max simply nodded though. As a zoologist, he knew better than any of them the types of creepy crawly things that called this place home. Max was well attuned to the fact that Vietnam is home to thirty-seven different types of venomous snakes. Not to mention the Vietnamese Giant Centipede, a fast-moving one hundred legged terror feeding on everything from bats to wolf spiders. Despite knowing all of this, none of it seemed to slow the man one bit.

"Max, what's up?" Downs asked as he finally reached where the zoologist was crouched, diligently pulling back the vegetation.

Josiah followed Max as he kept moving forward. "Yeah, Max be ultra careful in there man, shit ton of poisonous things in this fuckin' jungle."

"Ah hah," Max said as he finally stood to his feet and brushed himself off. "Small water source."

By now the team had gathered around the zoologist. Max had found the source of the gurgling water that Downs had noticed a short while ago.

"Um, you guys know the routine. We follow this. Animals need water, and if this is a small tributary, it will connect to a much bigger water source."

"Done," Downs said picking up his stuff off the wet ground. "Let's move out."

For a moment, the team just stood there, the soft sound of rushing water in the backdrop, before Burr spoke up. "Y'all heard the order. Now let's move out."

"Uh, guys," Tori said motioning with her hands to their soaked clothes. "Perhaps we should get outta this wet stuff and into something dry before we go trekking off."

Burr glanced over at Downs. Downs looked up to the canopy for a second. It was unbelievable just how tangled and dense it was way up there. "We're here in the rainy season, this heavy rain issue's gonna be a continual problem for us. But I agree. For now, let's get outta this wet stuff, into some drier clothes.

• • •

Minutes later the team found themselves in dry clothing. It may have been temporary, but for now at least they were completely dry. Each member of the team quickly gathered their belongings, took one last look around, and then proceeded to move out. With Max Caldwell out ahead leading the way, they were now following the small stream as it snaked and meandered its way deeper into the forest.

18

Stacey Winston fell flat on his face in the mud. It was the third time he had done so, and this time the camera and the tripod clunked him hard in the back of the head as he went down awkwardly onto his stomach. For a moment, he simply lay there, the front half of him covered in thick and gooey mud.

With a bit of a struggle and a grunt, he planted both hands down in the mud and pushed himself back up to his feet.

"Fuck," he cursed to himself as he wiped the thick mud from the palms of his hands off on his pants.

The front half of him was now an absolute mess, and he used the bottom of his wet shirt to towel off the caked mud from his chin. A dejected sigh of frustration washed over him as he looked at the camera and the tripod just lying there in the mud. Quickly, he picked it up and began to towel off the legs of the tripod with that same wet part of his shirt. Moving upward, he was thankful to see that the camera for the most part had stayed relatively clean.

Now with the tripod back in his hands, he looked up. He wasn't certain how much further he had until he reached the end of this bastard jungle hillside. His goal was to push out of the bamboo trees and emerge into the small clearing that he and the team had gathered in for lunch a short while ago.

As Stacey thought about it, that lunch time break had felt like hours ago, a mini lifetime if you will. Never having been one to wear a watch, and with his phone tucked away safely inside his backpack still looped around his shoulders, he wasn't exactly certain what time it was. While the phone offered no internet or phone access for that matter out here, it did at least offer up a clock. There seemed to be no sense of time in this world of tall growing bamboo trees perpetually bathed in a dim grey lighting. The entire place always seemed to be in a constant state of shade, no matter what time of day. But Stacey had a good sense that if the sun were in fact to be shining on this particular muddy hillside, then there would have been long shadows cast by now. The internal clock in his body told him that it was getting late, and that he really needed to get back to the others. He hoped like hell that they were still located where it was that he was aiming for.

Setting the tripod down carefully this time, he bent momentarily to tie his shoes. Meanwhile, all around him the forest had taken on a serene and peaceful feel to it. But beyond the peaceful serenity of it all, there existed a savage and primal monstrosity, a monstrosity that lurked in the shadows and the dark places and corners of the forest. It was a terrifying thought.

Stacey thought about the creature for a moment before eventually shaking his head, essentially bringing himself back to the present. He stooped one more time to tie his other shoe. Grabbing hold of the tripod and camera, he quietly began pushing his way up the hillside once again.

Continuing to slog his way up the completely saturated hillside, and with the front half of him still covered in a solid slathering of mud, all his mind could process at this point in time was the idea of him being on the set of his first full-length feature film. Oh, it would be a great sight to behold if it one day in fact actually came true. The chance to work on and direct a big budget Hollywood movie, work with cinemotographers, writers, co-producers, executive producers, financiers, screenwriters, and the list went on and on. But the one constant that motivated him beyond anything in this world was the idea of being on the set of his very own movie, with him at the helm. The chance to direct a big budget Hollywood film was about as intoxicating a thought as he could conjure up. He could think of nothing else in this world that could give him such a high. No drug, no alcoholic beverage, simply nothing could take the place. It would be a feeling like no other, and he desperately wanted to make it happen.

That thought alone put an added pep in his step as he started trekking faster up the hillside now. Continuing to move through the trees and surrounding foliage with a new and renewed vigor, his mind suddenly registered the next problem currently plaguing him. What would he tell the rest of the team regarding Clark Geiger?

Stacey shook his head to himself as he plowed through a gathering of waist-high ferns and then stepped over several fallen bamboo trees that lay in his way. What in the hell was he going to tell the others? Would he just tell them straight up that he had actually seen the poor man's demise and because of his awkward positioning atop the hillside he couldn't get down in time to help him, or would he say that he had gone in search of the man but instead came up empty-handed?

Or maybe? Stacey thought to himself.

Maybe the director of this documentary wouldn't have to say anything at all. Maybe he would let the rest of the team tell him what had happened. He nodded his head to himself. Yeah that was it. Stacey looked up and thought he could see the top of the hillside now. He knew that he was nearing the end of this bastard trek up this godforsaken muddy slope. Once he exited the bamboo trees, he should spill out into that open clearing that they had been in earlier in the day. And then hopefully he would let the rest of the scene play itself out. He would let the others do the talking first.

As he continued to plow further and further up the hillside, he knew that one journey was now shortly coming to an end, while another one was freshly brewing. Stacey had never considered himself to be much of an actor. Behind the camera had always been where he felt most at home, or at the very minimum, behind the computer working on either a book or a new screenplay, but an actor, no way. He wasn't one of those delusional directors that continually gave themselves small cameos in their own movies, nor did he plan on doing so in the future. That most definitely wasn't his cup of tea, wasn't his forte. He would leave the acting to the professionals. But now as he made his final push to the top, he knew he would need to put his best acting skills on if he was to truly convince the others.

Stacey Winston let out a deep breath of tension as he neared the top of the hillside.

19

The creature readjusted itself, hunkering its mass down and into the surrounding foliage. The slender and tall green bamboo trees that made up the forest did little to conceal its huge hulking form, so it sunk itself further down and into its current concealment. Four fallen bamboo trees lay propped up against one another, lying at a slight angle against another more solid bamboo tree that shot one hundred feet up to the top of the canopy. Beneath the bamboo trees grew a densely packed gathering of lush ferns.

From beneath the fallen bamboo trees and just behind the heavy fern growth, the creature crouched low to the ground in hiding. Now the animal stood there in silence as it gazed out onto the forest. Two enormous eyes stared out from the darkness at the small band of humans continuing to make their way along the winding stream that for the most part lay enshrouded beneath thick clumps of vegetation.

Shifting its enormous bulk, it did its best to follow the humans for as long as it could. When it could barely make out the last of them, it shifted its mass once more. But this time, its enormous size proved too great for its small and dark concealed hiding place. Its heavily muscled right shoulder gently grazed one of the bamboo trees that rested just above it. That was all it took as the impact from its huge shoulder sent the slender green shoot tumbling down and onto the forest floor. The disturbance hadn't gone unnoticed.

• • •

Downs' head shot up as he held up his right hand in a closed fist. Immediately the team came to a stop. They had been busy following the small, three foot wide meandering stream when out of nowhere the sound of something crashing down hard jolted them.

"What in Sam Hell?" Burr said from behind, his big arms flexing as he held the air rifle with two hands out in front of him.

Meanwhile, Downs quickly stepped forward a few paces toward Max. The zoologist had been busy poking and prodding his way through the dense leafy vegetation and grass that suffocated and hid the existence of the small stream at times. Max had been leading the way, literally uncovering the stream as it continued to snake its way through the trees when suddenly the sound of something crashing down halted their progress forward.

"Get the feeling we're being watched?" Tori asked from behind.

"Most definitely," Jeremiah said as he came around to where Downs and Max stood at the front of the line.

At the very back of the line, Burr was sweeping back and forth with both the air rifle and now the Astra leveled out in front of him. Downs turned and faced in the same direction as Burr for a moment. It also became apparent that the usual insect chatter from the forest had died down as well. All was quiet.

Josiah stood next to Burr and together the two men watched as the others converged up at the front of the line.

"What'll we do now?" Tori asked.

"Well," Downs said as he wiped the sweat dripping down the side of his head with his shirt. "We follow this water source till it opens up into something bigger."

Max had been preoccupied with bending down, pulling back the thick shrubbery in order to figure out where the small stream snaked its way to next. The stream for the most part was still covered beneath dense vegetation that clung tightly to the ground.

Max stood to his feet. "Um, i-i-it's where we stand our best chance of making contact with this creature, at a much bigger water source."

Meanwhile, Tori's eyes continued scanning and twitching back and forth. Here, surrounded by tall green shoots of bamboo, nowhere felt safe. It was a maze of trees, a clusterfuck of overgrown vegetation deep in the remote parts of Vietnam. And for the most part, it seemed as though something could literally be hiding anywhere.

"Let's keep moving," Downs ordered.

The team quickly assembled back into a straight line and continued onward.

• • •

Having caused a slight disturbance on account of its overwhelmingly large bulk, the creature lifted itself from its dark hiding place and now stood crouched low to the ground. Its large eyes continued to follow the small team. With secrecy no longer an issue, the animal slowly came out of hiding. And there, from the edge of the fallen bamboo trees and the lush fern growth, the animal resurrected to its full towering height.

As the small band of humans continued to snake their way through the labyrinth of bamboo trees, the creature took several steps forward. Now the animal rested on all fours. And there it remained, listening, waiting, but most importantly watching. When the humans who were so preoccupied with following the small water source could no longer be seen, the huge animal quietly disappeared back into the brush.

20

The team had been moving about in stone silence for what had to be going on twenty minutes now, following the tiny stream as it snaked its way back and forth through the trees. After some time, Max relinquished the lead out in front and Downs took his place as they pushed deeper and deeper into the forest.

The team had also been diligently watching the ground with each step taken. The jungle had more than its fair share of poisonous things to put even the heartiest of souls on edge. They needed to exercise caution.

Suddenly, Jeremiah spoke. "There it is."

What was probably no more than a hundred feet or so at best past the endless rows of bamboo existed a clearing, a break in the monotonous cycle of one green bamboo tree after another. A beautiful cascading and shimmering waterfall emptied down into a small lagoon which fanned out below.

"Whoa," Max remarked from just behind Downs.

Downs gave the high sign for them to continue forward. "Let's watch our step. All animals need water, including predators."

As the team pushed forward, Downs felt his mind starting to wander on him. On the inaugural mission together back in California, they had been after a small thought to be extinct predator by the name of Eusmilus, and shortly after that they went in search of a large carnivorous hybrid animal called a Eusmiger. Both animals were formidable predators, but the one constant was that they knew what they were up against, but more importantly what they were getting themselves into.

Here in these relatively isolated bamboo forests of rural Vietnam, they had absolutely no clue what to expect, or just what in the hell they had fully gotten themselves into for that matter.

Suddenly, the sound of something breaking caught their attention. Downs' head shot around, and so too did the others. Downs turned and leveled both the air rifle as well as the Astra out in front of him, and then he heard Burr Wellington's deep and booming voice barking out commands from the back.

"Bloody, move!"

"Make for the clearing!" Downs shouted.

And with that the team took off running, dodging the thin bamboo trees left and right. They were no longer following the small concealed stream. Now the forest had truly come alive as the sound of breaking and crackling continued to ring out.

Downs was out in front leading the way. Now he ran with both weapons pressed out in front of him. Moving at high speed like this, it quickly became abundantly clear just how difficult it was to move in this type of terrain. Tall, wiry, thin bamboo trees grew every four to five feet or so, but still the group pressed on, moving as fast as they could toward the waterfall that lay just beyond the confines of the trees.

Downs was moving fast now. His body, however, was unfortunately taking the beating that came from being torn up by the thick vegetation. Despite this, he continued to plow his way through it. Out of the corner of his left eye, he was barely able to make out a long and slender shape that unfurled itself from a fallen bamboo tree that lay propped up against another bamboo tree.

"Oh, fuck!" Downs shouted as he ducked at the last second, narrowly avoiding the blurry shape that hung downward like a vine from the bamboo.

Not knowing which type of snake it in fact was, all he could do was get out of the way as the snake hissed and then lashed out at him, mouth open wide, fangs ready to inject. Managing to avoid this imminent threat, at the last second he watched as the mouth closed down onto nothing but air. As soon as Downs had navigated the threat, he immediately flung himself around in an attempt to warn the others.

Meanwhile, the neon green snake in all the commotion had unfurled more than three quarters of its body toward the ground. It could now easily strike anyone unfortunate enough to get in its way.

"Go around," Downs shouted. "Snake!"

The team did just that as they peeled off to the side and went their own respective routes. Just as Downs was about to turn himself around, again he heard deep and immense cracking sounds.

Downs turned and began to take up chase once again. Now they were close. But the problem was the forest was being beaten, battered, broken, and most importantly it was all coming their way, steamrolling toward them like an out-of-control freight train.

Downs looked back to Burr. The big man appeared to be having a hard go at it. And then some twenty feet behind where Burr was so diligently making his way, Downs watched as an enormous shape materialized out of the trees and rose up on its back two legs. From the height of a regulation ten foot tall basketball hoop, the gigantopithecus beat aggressively with its two pillar-like forearms across a ridiculously wide, muscular, and powerfully-built chest. The result was a distinct and aggressive thumping sound. It was a terrifying sound, like nothing he had ever experienced before.

Downs felt his eyes go wide on him. And then he watched as the immense creature suddenly dropped to all fours and immediately began charging forward in Burr's direction. Downs pushed off with his legs and sprung himself forward and into position.

Now Downs was yelling and waving with both weapons. "Burr, look out! Look out!"

Burr must have known what was close on his heels. Without turning around, the big man upped his speed as he jumped over a fallen bamboo shoot, his two hundred and fifty pound frame landing solidly in the mud as he continued to navigate the dense passages of the forest.

Downs meanwhile continued coming forward until he had gotten himself into a reasonable position. Taking a split second to gather himself, he raised the air rifle, took aim, and squeezed the trigger. The gigantopithecus noticed immediately what was taking place. The creature roared as it shot off to the right, tearing a wake of destruction upon a dense gathering of bamboo trees that grew in a tight formation. The bellowing monstrosity of an animal could be heard as it tore and broke off any and all vegetation that stood in its way.

"C'mon!" Downs shouted to not only Burr, but the rest of the team as well.

When Downs had a solid visual of all of them quickly converging upon where he stood, he finally turned and took up running once again. Now they were close. Downs could hear the waterfall as it plunged down and into the lagoon below. Finally, Downs navigated through the last of the trees and shot out into the open clearing. The rest of the team was close behind him.

Instantly, Downs felt the burning hot sensation of the sun beating down hard on him. After all that rain just a short while ago, the sun had once again broken through the cloud cover and now shined brightly on the clearing. Downs spun around and waited for the others.

It wasn't more than ten seconds before the rest of the team came exploding out of the vegetation and into the sun-drenched clearing that lined the small lagoon. Downs heard shouting from a myriad of voices, and then finally one voice in particular rang louder than all the others.

"Keep moving!" Burr's voice boomed as he finally had caught up with the rest of the team. "Keep bloody moving!"

"Where to, though?" Jeremiah replied, John Corstine's son breathing hard as he struggled to recapture his breath.

Downs took a moment to take in the whole picture. The entire clearing was ringed with a thick layering of bamboo, the forest itself encroached right out onto this small open area. And in the middle of it all lay a lagoon probably the size of two basketball courts. On top of the lagoon sat a beautiful waterfall that continually dumped tropical water down into the lagoon. Downs continued surveying until he saw where they needed to go. He pointed. "There."

On the opposite side of the clearing from where they stood flowed the waterfall. And behind the waterfall, there was a small ledge . It appeared fairly secluded amongst the vegetation and therefore offered up the best chance to conceal themselves.

Meanwhile back in the forest, things were snapping and breaking at a frantic pace now. The destruction continued moving toward them like a tidal wave about to make landfall. They needed to get out of the open, and quickly.

Downs pointed with the butt of the air rifle toward the tiny ledge that sat behind the waterfall. The others took notice immediately. Quickly, they shot off. The team traversed through the dirt and low-lying vegetation and made their way toward the waterfall.

In order to get to the waterfall, they had momentarily been plunged back into the vegetation that hung and draped itself over the edges and outward toward the lagoon. For a brief moment, they found themselves back amongst the bamboo trees moving quickly. As they ran, the denser parts of the forest that lay off to their right lay quiet for the most part.

The thick growth of the forest eventually gave way to slippery rock, large rocky boulders that were constantly bathed in a thick and cool mist produced by the waterfall. Moss grew on the boulders in the wetter areas, forming slick dark patches. The boulders led upwards now at a sloped incline. Downs and Burr hung back as they helped everyone off the jungle floor and up onto the rocky surfaces.

"Go," Downs said. "Just go."

He helped Tori up and then watched as Burr gave Jeremiah a hand as well. And then Burr Wellington looked at Downs.

Downs quickly motioned with his hands. "Go, big guy."

And Burr did just that as Downs aided the two hundred and fifty pound, fifty-eight year old Washington native. Downs felt the strain and struggle for a moment in his lower back as well as his legs. When Burr was finally scurrying his way across the rock toward the others, Downs quickly picked up both weapons off the ground and followed.

Downs found the rocky surface to be quite slippery, the overhanging vegetation still dripping with water, the mist from the waterfall constantly bathing the large boulders in a cool embrace. They were now moving through a solid layer of mist as if they were traversing through a cloud. And there was moss, lots of it, and it was slippery as hell. Carefully, he managed to find his footing as he hurried onward toward the others. The bamboo forest grew right up to the edge of the large boulders that bordered the small lagoon.

Downs found himself hiking upward now at a slight angle through low fern growth mixed with a type of creeping vine growth that he couldn't identify. The waterfall was just to the left, probably no more than twenty feet away from him now. As he drew nearer, the roar from the waterfall intensified and grew louder.

Downs pulled his body through the wet, waist-high vegetation and joined the others behind the waterfall. The team was instantly engulfed in a moist and wet dampness. The smell of moist earth dominated the air now. Water dripped from the cave-like ceiling above, small ferns grew on the dirt hillside at their backs, and they were each standing in what had to be a good two to three inches of water. In the areas where little or no fern growth existed, a thick covering of moss grew heavily over the rocky ground.

Out in front of them, a thin broken sheet of water fell down to the lagoon below. The waterfall was no more than ten feet in width. In certain spots, they were able to see back to the lagoon and surrounding bamboo trees. Now everyone was busy catching their breath, chests heaving back and forth, open mouths breathing in the damp warm jungle air.

"Ladies and gentlemen, you are now seeing the backside of water," Josiah joked.

"Just like the, uh, jungle cruise at Disneyland," Max fired back. "Haven't been on that ride in ages."

Downs allowed himself to crack a quick smile. But as he glanced over at Burr and then toward Jeremiah, he could see that both men had stern looks plastered squarely across their faces as they stared out across the lagoon. Downs looked back out toward the lagoon.

"Over there," Downs breathed.

Now looking out across the shimmering green lagoon, Downs pointed high up. Heads turned toward the top of the canopy and together they watched as the tops of the bamboo trees shook back and forth. Something was moving about on the jungle floor below, tearing a path of destruction straight for the edge of the lagoon.

Downs watched as the sounds of snapping and cracking continued to ring out just on the opposite side of the lagoon. The tops of the bamboo were really knocking back and forth now. And then suddenly everything came to a stop. All was still. For a moment, the tops of the trees still swayed gently back and forth. Downs felt his muscles tense and tighten up on him as he watched a pair of tropical birds flying low to the canopy and squawking lightly to one another. The two birds flew for a short distance longer before finally fading off into the canopy. Now there was only the sound of the waterfall.

Downs edged himself forward a few inches, his two feet still firmly planted in a shallow puddle of murky water. And then suddenly out of nowhere, the cracking in the bamboo forest returned and the trees started up swaying back and forth. Downs' eyes shot up toward the top of the canopy. Several trees had been broken in the wake of destruction. Downs watched as they toppled and fell to their sides, quickly disappearing out of view.

A long and heavy silence passed for what must have been a minute or so, and then just like that, an enormous shape came barreling through the bamboo and emerged out and into the light. Wasting no time, the gigantopithecus let out a monstrous roar as it bellowed in the open clearing on the dirt. It charged forward aggressively toward the water, stopping just short of it, and lifted itself onto its back two legs. It beat several times on its huge chest while letting out another ungodly roar. The deep rumbling sound filled the clearing.

"Jesus, Mary, and Joseph," Burr breathed as he stumbled forward and scratched his head, setting his air rifle down for a moment.

Tori moved closer to Downs and whispered. "Do you think it knows we're in here?"

Max spoke up. "Yes. Definitely. But the water from the falls should keep it at bay."

Downs felt himself having difficulty breathing on account of what they were seeing. Once again, even for an organization dedicated to finding, sedating, and transporting long thought to be extinct creatures, it was still difficult to comprehend what their eyes were taking in. The animal had supposedly died out some one hundred thousand years ago, yet here was a member of the species standing right before them in the direct sunlight.

They watched as the huge animal knuckled its way forward. It walked on four enormous limbs. The gigantopithecus was now moving along the edge of the water.

Sporting a long, flowing, dark brown coat of fur, the gigantopithecus also possessed stripes of black and a gray coloration on its front side. Downs saw heavily muscled shoulders, big eyes, a huge dome-shaped head, and large leathery fingers to go along with its back two massive legs. The huge back legs were shorter than the creature's longer two front legs. The beast's limbs were as big as small tree trunks. Jutting out on either side of the creature's face and hidden beneath the skin that made up that huge face was the saggital crest, a ridge of bone that ran lengthwise along the midline of the top of the skull. Such a crest is also present in the skulls of many mammals and reptiles. The presence of the huge ridge of bone indicated enormous strength in the jaw muscles. All of this combined together to give the massive animal that stood before them just at the water's edge its crushing bite.

Downs looked back at the huge animal. The face and overall appearance most definitely resembled a modern-day orangutan. Yet despite the familiar aspect of some parts of the giant creature, there was still a very raw and primal nature about this beast. It stood close to ten feet in height when standing on its back legs, weighed in at a hefty twelve hundred pounds in weight, and had a monstrous wingspan of some fourteen feet. The animal that stood before them in the clearing was as spectacular as it was frightening, something that a wise and sane individual would want absolutely no part of. Downs watched as the big head suddenly swung in their direction.

"Everyone, back up," Downs said as he held out his outstretched arm.

The team moved themselves back up until their behinds were resting gently against the damp earth.

"It knows we're in here," Downs said.

"What about smell?" Jeremiah asked.

145

Max took the question. "Gorillas in general are known for having a good sense of smell. They can even pick up on the musk of an unknown gorilla and are surprisingly able to detect strong odors in their environment such as human sweat."

Burr Wellington snorted quietly to himself. "Good thing I put on my antiperspirant this morning."

Suddenly, the team watched as the huge creature raised its two front limbs high into the air and sent them slamming down hard into the dirt, sending up a small plume of dirt. The huge mouth opened wide and the gigantopithecus blasted another bellowing roar that moaned out across the landscape. Once again the huge mountain of fur was announcing its presence to any and all willing to listen.

And then suddenly the gigantopithecus began racing toward where the team stood crouched in hiding behind the shimmering waterfall. The animal stopped short of a large gathering of ferns that grew just at the water's edge. Again, the huge animal sent its two limbs slamming down into the earth as it roared. Then it reared up onto its back two legs and thumped aggressively on its wide chest with the flat palms of its hands. It then lowered itself onto all fours, seemingly staring a hole through the waterfall.

"Arm yourselves," Downs quietly whispered as he raised both the air rifle and the Astra.

The others followed suit.

But then suddenly, out in front of them, just at the part of the lagoon closest to them where the water from the waterfall was gently rippling its way toward the far edge where land started, an animal quietly lifted itself from the shallow reeds.

It was a Vietnamese sika deer, one of the main sub species of the sika deer. The animal couldn't have weighed more than a hundred pounds at best and sported a light brown hide with white spots down its sides and back. Downs watched as the animal raised its head and the antlers suddenly came into view. The deer immediately froze in place at the sight of the huge hulking creature resting on all fours just at the water's edge. There the two animals remained, eyes locked in on one another, uncertain as to what the next move should be. The Vietnamese sika deer looked pitifully small in the presence of such a powerfully-built creature.

A few more seconds passed.

And then just like that, the small animal burst forward through the shallow water. The sika deer was headed for the protection of the tall bamboo trees that ringed the water's edge as water now splashed on all sides of it.

The gigantopithecus, seeming stunned by the small animal's brazen attempt, sprung to life as well. The huge creature lurched forward and was upon the terrified animal in a matter of seconds.

There was a loud crunch followed by the sound of bones being snapped and broken. Downs and his team both heard and witnessed the small animal's neck and spine meet its end as the gigantopithecus scooped it off the ground. Both hands crushed down on the terrified animal as the huge mouth opened wide, fangs bared, and in an act of pure savagery, the mouth closed down around the head of the animal and tore away.

Pinning the decapitated body down with its enormous right forearm, its eyes now flaring wide with rage, the animal's bellowing roar could be heard as it dominated the area.

Quickly, the gigantopithecus went to work on the deer. Pulling the body apart as if it were a ragdoll, the creature sunk its teeth down into the warm flesh as blood ran down both sides of its jaw. With its mouth and teeth now reddened, the animal secured the deer in its grasp, let out one final immense roar, and went bounding off. The huge creature quietly disappeared back into the forest.

21

A very tired, winded, and bloodied Stacey Winston pushed through the last layer of bamboo before finally emerging out into the open clearing. It was late in the afternoon now and the shadows had grown long. The sun shined on the tall stands of bamboo that grew on the opposite side of the clearing from where Stacey stood. But still it felt good, felt liberating to be out of the dark and gray confines that was the forest. At least out here in the open, one felt as though one could actually take a breath and not have to look over one's shoulder constantly.

It took the director a moment to get his bearings straight. But when he did, he found himself noticing the part of the clearing where they had broken for lunch just a few short hours ago before all this madness had gone down. Heading off in that direction, at first he thought he was seeing a mirage.

Moving rapidly now through the clearing, his first instinct was to scream and shout at the rest of the team. He quickly put that idea to rest though. As he continued moving with the tripod and camera clutched tightly in his right hand, a sudden chill washed over him as he remembered the creature, but more importantly, what it had done to Clark Geiger. The gigantopithecus had manhandled the poor assistant producer as if he weighed but a mere few pounds. It gave him chills just thinking about the idea of being in the terrifying clutches of such an immensely powerful beast. And for a further moment, he thought about what must have transpired after Clark had been dragged off into the deep vegetation. What had happened to the man? What type of horrifying reality had he met? For a moment he recalled the terrifying scream that suddenly cut off abruptly. Surely that had signaled the man's death. He shook his head. Enough. He didn't want to stretch that thought any further.

"Stick to the script," he muttered to himself as he continued hurrying through the middle part of the clearing now. "Just stick to the script. Don't stray."

Halfway toward the rest of the team, it was an odd sight to see them just sitting there Indian style across from each other, talking and laughing, waving their hands in the air as if nothing at all had happened. Oddly, it reminded him of the time he had gone with some friends on a trip to Australia. They had visited the small town of Alice Springs, the dead center of Australia, a brutally hot and desolate town by any stretch of the imagination. Upon arriving in the town, he and his friends found the Aboriginal Indians to be seated at the bottom of dried-up river beds sitting in small groups conversing with one another Indian style. It was the oddest of sights, and here once again in Vietnam, his small team reminded him of that.

"Stick to the script," Stacey mumbled once again to himself. "Just stick to the fucking script."

Now he was damn close. He had rehearsed several times just what he was going to say to the others. Actually, it was more like what he wasn't going to say. He was going to let them do the talking, let them ask the important questions, let them dictate where things went. After that, Stacey would just be reacting to the barrage of questions that would most definitely be coming his way. He knew it would be a shit storm and he now felt he was prepared for it.

Stacey waved to the small group as he neared closer to them. The team appeared excited at his arrival and each of them stood, shouting out words, but Stacey was still a bit of a ways away to actually make out what was being said. He hurried quicker now, his heart beating hard, his mind racing at a million miles an hour.

As Stacey neared to within twenty-five feet of what had now been reduced to a three man team including himself, Diane Clor stood to her feet and dusted herself off. "What took you so long? We were worried."

Stacey immediately found it odd that Diane didn't have her usual snippy tone to her voice. She had spoken to him normally and generally seemed concerned for him. It took a few more steps to process the question, to ready his mind as well as his body. He didn't answer the question until he stood with the others at the small little area just at the edge of the clearing near a tall and thick stand of bamboo trees that marked the beginning of the forest on the other side.

Sticking to his game plan, Stacey did just as he had rehearsed in his mind. Time and time again on nature documentaries on T.V. he would see the host pause, look square into the camera, and pretend to be winded or out of breath. Stacey wasn't certain why such a tactic worked in front of the camera, just that it did, the idea that an individual could be hiding in secrecy near a pride of lions on the Serengeti of Africa while whispering and breathing heavy in front of the camera seemed to always do the trick.

"Got some incredible footage," Stacey said in between breaths as he made his chest go up and down, making himself appear out of breath as if he had just run a marathon. He tapped the legs of the tripod, focused his eyes on the camera.

Bob came round to where he was, looked at the director and then up to the heaving man's chest. "Must be some amazing footage."

Stacey was still breathing heavily, having to take big gasping breaths in between words, trying his hardest to sell this as best as he could. "Oh it is. Can't wait to get back to the studio. Already have the perfect guy to do the soundtrack for us. Gonna be riveting stuff when it's all edited together. This stuff is gonna make us famous, put us all on the map."

Suddenly though, Diane came round to where Stacey was standing, looked around briefly, and then looked back to the director. Whatever playful and light-hearted tone she had exhibited just a few seconds ago was gone. Now she spoke bluntly and to the point. "Just where in the hell is Clark?"

The minute the question had been asked, Stacey felt his heart rate accelerate. He felt he had already sold it for all it was worth. Taking in several more huge breaths, he tried his best to answer the question.

Again the words came in between gasping breaths here and there. "Thought…he…was…with you."

Diane shook her head, staring Stacey straight in the eyes. "We all thought he was with you. Been waitin' here for both of you this whole damn time."

Now Stacey really felt his pulse starting to thump, his heart pounding against his ribcage. Obviously, the breathing-hard, seeming-winded thing didn't appear to be working, so he decided it was time to wind that down and try to execute another strategy. Rather quickly, he spun himself around and had a good look at the clearing. The clearing was large, about as big as a football field. He saw nothing, only the tall stands of bamboo that ringed the clearing.

"I-I, uh, thought he was with y'all?" Stacey managed to say.

Now that the breathing hard strategy was over, it was time to play dumb, to play as if he didn't quite have all the necessary pieces of the puzzle together.

Stacey frowned and crossed his arms. "Y'all sure you guys didn't see him? I was off pursuing the perfect shot. You guys know how it is with us directors, we're desperate people."

Stacey cracked a smile, but in the heat of the moment he absolutely had no clue how it had come off.

Somewhere in this whole encounter, Stacey had failed to realize that Bob had gone back to sitting Indian style on the ground. "So you didn't see Clark at all, not even a glimpse of the man? He literally was following right behind you when you entered into the trees."

Stacey managed to swallow what saliva had built up in the back of his throat, praying to God that he didn't look nervous and skittish, praying to God that he didn't look guilty.

"No," Stacey said. "I didn't see him. Remember my top priority when all this went down was to get the footage, the footage that we've come all this way for. I felt it was imperative to do whatever it took to get the proper shot."

Stacey cleared his throat and set his arms on his hips. He felt good about how those last words had come out. The business of making movies and films for that matter hinged entirely on the ability to get the right shot, to get the actor to move or behave in a certain manner, to get the setting sun or the fog rolling in, to do whatever it took to get the perfect shot to move the production forward. It didn't matter the hour or the time of day. Surely, his small makeshift film team had to at least understand that much.

"Shit, Stacey," Diane said as she began to wander away from the two men and set her eyes toward the top of the canopy.

Stacey now turned and faced in the direction of Bob Hohrman. And for a moment, it appeared to be working. Bob pulled out a pair of binoculars from his backpack. He fidgeted with them for a moment before finally bringing them up to his face and staring through the lens in an attempt to look for Clark.

The clearing was a rather open space, but to step into any part of the forest from where they stood meant entering a lush and crowded crisscrossing world where the plants and vegetation reigned surpreme. As Stacey watched the two attempt to scan every inch of the clearing with their eyes, he quickly glanced back to the camera and the tripod. He knew that the footage he had already managed to capture was absolutely incredible. It was also downright terrifying, breathtakingly horrifying cinematic footage. He believed the footage when edited and packaged together correctly would play out like a movie. But more importantly, it was something that had the potential to officially put him on the map, to make this short documentary a one hundred percent success. But the one problem that remained was how would he deal with the issue of the fact that it showcased a man essentially being dragged off and killed?

Stacey thought about that for a moment, let out a quiet sigh to himself, and looked up to the blue sky high above. These were enormous monumental problems, but the good thing was that these were great problems to have. He would worry about them later. For now, he had the footage that they had come all this way for. The incredible, good-as-gold million dollar footage that he felt he had waited a lifetime for.

It was at that moment that Stacey also made a secret pact with himself. Clark's death wouldn't go in vain. It would be for something, and that something would be the ultimate success of the documentary. Perhaps when things got rolling and money started to come his way, he'd even donate a portion to Clark's family. He thought about that for a few seconds longer before finally grabbing the camera and tripod and heading off to join the others.

22

For a brief moment, not a word was said amongst the team as they continued to stare out from the small cavern tucked just behind the waterfall. A look of stunned silence was freshly plastered across each of their faces. Now only the cascading water falling down into the brackish colored lagoon could be heard. The jungle had fallen for the most part silent. Even the bamboo trees had ceased swaying back and forth in the gentle breeze. All was still. All was quiet as the late afternoon sun continued to shine down upon both the water and the clearing.

Max cleared his throat and addressed the team. "Gigantopithecus blacki. The largest known primate species ever to inhabit the planet. Um, however, what we, ah, just saw, most definitely defies what is written in the fossil record about Gigantopithecus. It appears we witnessed some type of upgraded version of it."

"Upgraded or altered," Josiah replied back.

Max cleared his throat again. "Both. For some reason or another, time has seemed to stand still in this part of the world."

Downs looked over to Max and nodded at his good buddy.

Max continued on. "That Vietnamese Sika Deer is now considered extinct in the wild. Yet for some reason or another, it has managed to stay intact here in this part of Northern Vietnam."

"Where there's prey, there's no doubt predators," Downs said.

Burr stretched his back. "That poor deer, that poor thing. Sasquatch in the flesh. The thing's a bloody predator for cryin' out loud. Been searching the second third of my life for this big boy."

"Or girl," Tori added.

Burr shrugged his shoulders as Max nodded his head and gazed out at the waterfall. All was still quiet. No visual sign of the creature.

"Hard to say if what we're dealin' with here is new to the fossil record or not. The evolution of a species can be a very complex thing comprising many different factors. I believe with certainty this is still Gigantopithecus, it's just an evolved version of the animal." Downs said as he stroked his chin.

"Yeah, into a blood-thirsty monster," Josiah said stretching his back out. "This shit is crazy man. Bat shit fuckin' crazy if ya ask me."

Max cleared his throat. "Downs is right. The evolution of a species can be a very complex and lengthy process. Can literally take up to one million years for a new species to evolve, and comes about because of a change to an organism's environment. The organism must ultimately change to fit and adapt into its new environment."

Downs let out a breath and stared behind himself for a moment at the low growing ferns that grew in the damp soil. Then he looked back out toward the stand of trees where the gigantopithecus had disappeared. "So Gigantopithecus faced the issue of slowly going extinct in the bamboo forests it called home, or coming out onto the grasslands to hunt. As its habitat shrank, it was forced to adapt and change."

Max nodded to him. "So it seems."

The thought itself had just popped into Downs' head. Perhaps this giant ape had evaded extinction, had cheated death by adapting and changing into something that nature never originally intended it to be.

Downs once again look back toward Max.

"It's possible the creature could be an omnivore as well." Max said. "We can't rule that possibility out either at this point."

Josiah adjusted himself. "Always a possibility but we need to remember front and center what we're up against now."

Suddenly Tori looked at both Downs and Burr. "You two hold tight to those two handguns of yours, will ya?"

Downs nodded as did Burr.

This time it was Jeremiah that let out a sigh. "How do we even begin to tackle such an animal?"

Downs shot John Corstine's son a serious glare. "Very carefully."

Burr snorted with laughter. "Easier said than done, boys. Often times the real world isn't so cookie cutter and things more often than not don't go as planned. Shit hits the ceiling pretty quickly when you're out and about in the wild."

Downs agreed with Burr's statement completely. More often than not in Downs' thirty-one years on this planet, things usually didn't go as planned in real time. It was just the way things were, and as Downs stood with the others behind the waterfall amidst the damp and spongy, moss-laden wall of dirt and rock that lay at their backs, he knew this expedition would more than likely be no different.

"It's hard to fully wrap our heads around what we just saw," Downs said folding his arms. "But it seems this animal is still here because it took on more of a predatory role in life. At least that's what it looks like to me."

Tori looked at him and nodded. "Definitely."

"Well, um, like it or not, it appears to be true," Max said. "My general guess is, ah, that in order for the animal to have made this evolutionary leap would have entailed most certainly an increase in size to the canine teeth at the front of the mouth. The molars in the back of the mouth most certainly grew larger as well, possibly resembling modern-day gorillas, just much, much larger in overall size."

"This is incredible" Burr remarked. "Absolutely incredible."

"Indeed," Max continued. "For starters we know that Gigantopithecus supposedly disappeared completely from the fossil record some one hundred thousand years ago. The animal was a ground dweller, with deep and strong jaws. It needed to have huge teeth that were broad and flat in order to feed on the tough fibrous plants, bamboo, seeds, and fruit that made up its environment. And we also know from the fossil record that this great ape lived in what scientists call a mosaic habitat, meaning a combination of forest and grassland. But it appears that this great ape also preferred to live under the dense forest canopy and therefore would have very rarely strayed out into the warm grasslands, if ever. It would have fed exclusively in the cool, humid forests. The animal would have been very similar to modern-day orangutans and mountain gorillas."

"It led a specialist lifestyle," Tori said. "Generalist animals are known for their ability to thrive in a wide variety of environments and possess the ability to make use of different resources. A specialist animal for example can really only thrive in a narrow range of environmental conditions as well as a limited diet. Gigantopithecus would have probably assumed this specialist lifestyle. For quite some time it would have worked, been an okay strategy. It would have found the right combo of food and habitat to suit its massive needs. But its specialist habits made it very vulnerable to a constantly changing world."

Max nodded and continued on. "Precisely. From the fossil record, we know that Gigantopithecus blacki existed in the forests of Southeast Asia for a few million years. The animal lived during the Pleistocene and this time is known notoriously for the glaciers that were continually ebbing and flowing across the land. This constant ebbing and flowing of glaciers meant that the habitats way back then were constantly in a state of flux, which in turn exerted pressure and stresses on creatures such as Gigantopithecus. There were periods of long prolonged warmth which in turn allowed forests to both grow and survive, but then just like that there could be cold spells lasting tens of thousands of years. The result from this was that grasslands would have spread. For a while, Gigantopithecus managed to survive these cold spells but that all changed a hundred thousand years ago during another cold spell. As the ice expanded during this time, so too did the grasslands, and consequently the forests that were home to Gigantopithecus began to shrink."

"And it supposedly went extinct," Josiah said. "Vanishing from the fossil record altogether."

Max snapped his fingers. "Or so we thought at least."

"So for all these years, we've believed the notion that the species wasn't able to adapt to a changing world, that its refusal to leave the bamboo forests ultimately led to its extinction," Downs said as he glanced out toward the open clearing.

A gentle breeze had once again returned to the area, which in turn caused the tall bamboo trees to sway back and forth. It was quite the peaceful scene.

"That's correct," Max said with a nod. "For all this time, we've believed that."

"Its specialist lifestyle made it vulnerable to major climatic changes," Tori said.

Suddenly, cutting through the noise created by the waterfall, an immense bellowing roar rumbled out across the landscape. Downs felt his muscles tighten up on him as he stepped closer toward the falling water. But this time, the roar had not come from inside the dense bamboo forest. It appeared to have come from atop the waterfall.

23

The deep cavernous roar that rang out from above them lasted just a few seconds before finally dying down. Now the sound of the waterfall out in front of them came back into focus. Quietly, everyone looked up, but they couldn't see anything, only the rocky ceiling above them.

And then suddenly, the sound of bamboo trees being bent and pushed back could be heard from back inside the trees. Downs' eyes shot back across the lagoon. It took a moment but the sound of more bamboo being broken and splintered from inside the forest could be heard. Downs looked up to the top of the forest and could see the trees swaying back and forth. Once again, something was tearing its way through the forest toward the water.

And then in a stunning display of aggression, the gigantopithecus burst through the trees and emerged out into the open. The huge animal charged forward as it roared. The animal rose up onto its back two legs and beat several times on its wide chest. Meanwhile, the last of the day's sun continued to shine down brightly on the animal.

The gigantopithecus let out another deep and throaty roar. But the animal was no longer looking at the small band of humans huddled tightly behind the waterfall. Rather, its large dome-shaped head was staring upward toward the top of the waterfall where the other immense noise had come from.

Downs scooted himself forward. But just as he did so, an enormous bellowing roar could be heard from above them.

"Jesus Christ," Burr muttered quietly as he pulled his hat off and scratched his head.

"Well, we knew there couldn't be just one of these things runnin' around," Josiah said.

"Wouldn't be much of a population with just one," Downs replied.

Meanwhile, the lone gigantopithecus maintained its position, resting on all fours just at the water's edge. As Downs continued to watch it, he suddenly found himself wondering if it had the same natural aversion to water that modern-day gorillas did. The thought had come quickly to him. Seeing the monstrous animal just standing there resting on all fours, Downs pulled out his small monocular and peered through the lens. It took a moment to focus in but eventually he got it. Through the monocular he saw the large broad shoulders of the animal, the equally large domed-shaped head, and the thick coat of fur adorning the towering animal's body. Now with the aid of the small lens, Downs could see for the first time just how truly spectacular the creature's coat of fur was. The base of the animal was a solid brown, the chest melded into a sort of dark black, and forming the underbelly was a grayish color. To Downs, the animal's physical attributes reminded him of its close relationship to modern-day orangutans. For a moment, Downs lost himself completely in the moment, gazing at and admiring the huge beast that supposedly had died out some one hundred thousand years ago. It was a spectacular, awe-inspiring scene to be witnessing the animal in the flesh.

Suddenly, Josiah tapped him on the shoulders. "Anything up?"

Downs shook his head and handed the monocular to Josiah. "Here, have a look."

The creature let out a distinct grunting sound. And then the animal let out another distinct grunt. It appeared as though the two grunts were directed solely toward the other creature perched high atop the waterfall. It had not been a loud sound at all, rather merely what seemed to be an inquisitive grunt. It appeared as though the two creatures were communicating to one another.

Downs looked over to Max quickly. The zoologist, however, was lost deep in thought as he continued to watch and examine the unfolding scene. Again, another grunt came from the lone gigantopithecus' mouth just at the water's edge. Although this time it had been a bit louder with a bit more guttural force.

This was followed by an equally similar sound that called out from high atop the waterfall.

"They're communicating," Max whispered as he staggered forward, water still dripping continually on all of them from atop the ceiling of the overhang.

Meanwhile, just at the water's edge the lone giganto-pithecus moved out and away from where it had been so diligently resting on all fours. It moved quickly now through the thick mud. The team watched as the large creature knuckled its way forward a few steps. And there the gigantopithecus reared up on its back two legs and roared triumphantly.

The large animal quickly dropped to all fours. And there it remained. The silence lasted all but a few seconds before an immense and monstrous roar rang out from high atop the waterfall. The team still could not see the animal responsible for the savage cry, but whatever it was, it appeared to be larger and more domineering than the gigantopithecus at the water's edge.

And then just like that, the gigantopithecus took off galloping. Now the animal raced in the opposite direction of the waterfall, seeming to purposefully be steering clear of the water. And then the animal lowered an enormous right limb as it continued to race near the water and began tearing away at the vegetation that grew just at the water's edge. It tore, discarded, tore, discarded, and tore all vegetation in sight. Any vegetation that grew in close proximity to the water's edge wasn't spared in the animal's aggression. The gigantopithecus continued to tear vegetation wherever there was vegetation to be torn. Then suddenly the animal came to a stop, breathing hard, dirt and leaves raining down on both sides of its body, still clinging tightly to a large heap of ferns with their roots exposed.

Downs and the team continued to watch as the giant creature dropped the vegetation into the water and began moving sideways across the ground in front of the water. The gigantopithecus was now moving sideways in continuous, strange, crab-like movements. Suddenly, the animal began slapping the ground aggressively while making as much noise as possible. The gigantopithecus still moving in this strange crablike manner now began slapping at an area of lush foliage. This display lasted for about another minute or so before the animal rose up onto its back two legs in one final display of aggression and beat several times on its wide and imposing chest.

And then just like that, the lone gigantopithecus dropped to all fours, knuckled its way through a fresh patch of dense ferns, and disappeared quietly once again back into the forest.

24

San Francisco, California

The sound of the coffee pot going off broke John Corstine from his thoughts. The real-estate entrepreneur and president of The Society of Cryptozoological Agents quietly made his way through the kitchen and toward the freshly brewing pot of coffee. Corstine was dressed in a robe with slippers on as he crossed through the newly renovated kitchen and reached into the cabinet high above for a coffee mug.

Setting the mug down, he proceeded to pour himself a piping hot cup of coffee. Corstine watched as the tendrils of heat rose in twisting formations from the mug.

Corstine stood with his arms folded, leaning against the new marble counter tops that were installed less than half a year ago. There was a beautiful island in the middle of the kitchen with a glass bowl that held a neatly stacked pile of freshly washed fruit. Corstine stared at the bowl of fruit for a moment and smiled to himself. All was good with the house and all was perfect with both his personal finances as well as his businesses. He had finally gotten both of them in good working order, just the way he wanted it, and he couldn't be happier about that. Like most high net worth individuals, John Corstine was essentially a control freak when it came to issues of money and finances.

Corstine reached with his right hand and gently blew at the hot coffee mug. Blowing on it several more times, he finally worked up the courage to take a sip. Instantly, the coffee was already starting to have a warming effect on his body.

Corstine's eyes went from the island in the middle of the kitchen to the newly-furnished family room that sat just off to the side of the kitchen. In one corner of the living room, there was a state-of-the-art entertainment system, complete with a seventy inch flat screen television mounted on the wall and Bose speakers hung from each of the four corners up near the top of the ceiling. But as Corstine took another sip, he realized that all was not right. In fact, there was quite a bit wrong by his own admission.

Corstine took another sip of coffee as his thoughts slowly began to consume him. Instantly, his mind gravitated toward his son Jeremiah. He wondered how it was going for them? Most importantly, he feared for their safety. These types of issues always kept him up late into the night, worrying for not only his son's well-being, but for the other members of the team as well.

Next, Corstine's thoughts gravitated toward his late wife, having lost her battle to cancer ten years prior. It had been a hard and lonely ten years for him, but Corstine had forged on, gripping down tightly on his businesses and not letting go until they were running like the finely-tuned machines he had always believed they could be. That was always how John Corstine handled stress and the pressures of the world, by bearing down tightly on each and every one of the businesses that he owned. Corstine knew that in a sense it was his way of hiding from the world, avoiding the inevitable pain that existed, but it was how he had always operated and probably would until his last dying day.

For a moment, Corstine thought about his late Uncle Howard and suddenly felt a twinge of sadness wash over him. The man had never married, never had children, never purchased his own home. Uncle Howard had spent the better part of his adult life serving as a Vice President for an office supplies chain, investing his large salary, and living what most would consider to be an extremely frugal and meager existence. When the man died he had an estate worth in excess of five million dollars, an incredible amount of money for any one single individual to amass. Corstine remembered vividly one day thirty years ago when he asked him why he had never married and never settled down. His uncle replied by saying that he had hid away in his brother's house the last ten years of his life, just hid not wanting to face the harsh realities of life. That was something that John Corstine had never forgotten, the idea of hiding from one's problems. Had he himself been hiding out in the same manner that his Uncle Howard had done decades prior? Now the realization was coming full circle to him as he continued to sip gingerly at his coffee.

His mind focused back on the current mission, and then it gravitated toward the find that he and the young paleontologist Diego Rivera had uncovered on a desolate hillside in rural Vietnam a short while ago. If announced, it would most definitely set the scientific world ablaze. Corstine could already envision the latest issue to National Geographic announcing the major find. There would be a firestorm around the uncovered fossil and both he and Diego would become scientific rock stars. The flame would burn hard and fast, but it would most definitely burn.

Corstine took another sip of coffee and then set the mug down on the counter top and wandered his way over to the island in the middle of the kitchen. It was funny. Here he was a real-estate entrepreneur with a net worth valued in the hundreds of millions and the President of The Society of Cryptozoological Agents, and he was daydreaming about the attention and publicity that he would ultimately receive for announcing the gigantopithecus find. For starters, the animal was thought to have died out some one hundred thousand years ago, yet he and Diego found the remains of one that appeared to have existed as recently as ten thousand years ago. It was truly remarkable stuff. But that wasn't the kicker. The kicker came from the fact that the animal had adapted, had changed in order to survive. What Corstine and Diego had found was not the gentle giant that supposedly lived in the bamboo forests of Southeast Asia, an animal that supposedly preferred the protection of those dense prehistoric bamboo forests to that of the open grasslands. What Diego and Corstine had uncovered were the remains of an animal that leaned heavily toward the side of predation.

Corstine took another sip of coffee and pondered what he had just thought. It was a head trip. Over the last three decades that he had served as President of The Society of Cryptozoological Agents, the name Gigantopithecus had always been something on his radar. After all, how could it not? From the fossil record, Gigantopithecus was the largest ape that has ever existed.

Corstine let out a sigh as he stared up at the ceiling. To encounter a silverback gorilla in the wild was a visual sight he had never forgotten. He had done so on safari in the Congo of Africa some twenty-five years ago with the accompaniment of a guide and game warden. It had been a spectacular, breathtaking experience to be in the presence of something so effortlessly powerful. But what would it be like to encounter a full grown Gigantopithecus?

Terrifying, Corstine thought to himself. *Utterly terrifying*.

Again he took another sip of coffee. Encountering a creature that would have neared ten feet in height and tipped the scales at some thirteen hundred pounds would no doubt have been frightening. Corstine knew one thing for certain—before one could even begin to hypothesize how immensely powerful a full-grown Gigantopithecus would have been, you first have to understand the power of a silverback gorilla, with a gorilla being four to nine times as strong as an adult male.

Corstine looked over at the pot of coffee and then back toward the family room. The plush couch did look awfully warm and inviting. He could actually sit down for once and enjoy himself, turn on Netflix and watch a movie, or there was always option two. Corstine thought about it for another moment and then decided he would pour himself that second cup of coffee. As he poured the coffee and the steam from the mug continued to waft up toward his face, he knew just what he was going to do. Corstine would retreat quietly to his office where he would do what he had always done time and time again during times of stress and uncertainty. He would sink himself back into his businesses. Old habits die hard.

25

The big male gigantopithecus stood with its four massive pillar-sized limbs planted firmly on a huge boulder atop the flowing waterfall. Standing close to eleven feet in height when resting on its back two legs and weighing in at a crushing sixteen hundred pounds in weight, it was every bit the terrifying creature that its female counterpart was and then some. With a total wingspan of nearly fifteen feet, it was also a dark brown in coloration. It had large patches of orange to reddish-brown on the front part of its body. The orange in certain areas gave way to bright and spectacular streaks of red, splashed and mixed with streaks of brown across the chest and underbelly. The huge male had dark black, oversized, flappy cheek pads known as flanges on both sides of its face. The females were particularly fond of this characteristic. Lastly, the big male had a huge, dark, black throat sac that hung below its jaw. The throat sac could produce a loud and throaty call that would echo through the forest. Known as the "Long Call," it was used to signal a male's presence to females and as a warning to other males to keep away.

The features of this massive beast were more distinguished and pronounced than that of the female.

Its huge, dome-shaped head was slightly larger, as was the wide chest, broad shoulders, and the hands and limbs. The saggital crest, a ridge of bone that ran lengthwise along the midline of the top of the skull, was also larger and more pronounced than that of the female. The increased size in the saggital crest gave the big male a more powerful bite than that of the female in terms of overall force. All of this added up to the fact that the huge animal perched precariously atop the large boulder was a true force to be reckoned with, a prehistoric nightmare that had evolved over time into its current form.

The big male was a massive and ancient relic of the past, but something that was still very much alive. It had survived into current times by making its way out of the bamboo forests and being forced to hunt on the much warmer grasslands. This animal was not the docile creature that once existed as the enormous animal opened its mouth, exposing a gaping black hole that housed an impressive array of dentition. The edges of its mouth were stained red with blood and the fur on its two front limbs also bore the same blood-stained coloration.

Suddenly, the creature lurched forward ever so slightly. It hung its mass over the edge of the boulder and peered down toward the lagoon below. Meanwhile, back in the forest that surrounded the edges of this small water source, several birds called out to one another at the top of the forest canopy. Trees blew lazily back and forth in the wind and the lagoon water shimmered with tints of green and brown as the late afternoon sun continued to set.

The big head shot upward and glared out at the birds. The gigantopithecus watched as more birds flew in, quietly landing on the surrounding limbs as they joined the rest of their kind. Big and beautiful tropical birds landed nosily atop the tall bamboo trees, the slender stalks swaying ever so gently on account of the arrival of new weight at the top of the canopy. Now half a dozen or so birds squawked noisily to one another while bobbing their heads up and down.

Slowly, the big male lowered its head once again and stared at the water below. And then the creature leaned its mass over the edge of the boulder and blasted a monstrous roar. The forest had no doubt taken notice.

The result was instantaneous. The birds in the neighboring trees ceased their activity at once. Not a sound was made by the flock still resting gently in the limbs and branches at the top of the canopy. The air was both still and quiet.

• • •

The team of six that made up a small wing of the much larger Society of Cryptozoological Agents had heard every bit of the roar that had just rung out from atop the falls. It stopped them all dead in their tracks. After an unnerving minute of sheer silence tucked behind the small waterfall, life began to slowly stir once again.

"How many of them could there be?" Josiah muttered to no one in particular.

Max took the question as he readjusted his glasses. "A small enough population to still be in existence all these years, but I'd say one that is very much teetering on the edge. Hard to say exactly, but whatever that number is, it most definitely is small."

Burr Wellington straightened himself, his aging back proving to be a minor disturbance to his still-hulking form. "I must say, this organization never fails to amaze me."

Burr tipped his hat in the direction of Jeremiah, John Corstine's son still managing to keep a bit of separation between himself and the others. Now that all eyes were suddenly on him, Jeremiah started to come forward toward the group.

"Like so many expeditions before," Jeremiah began.

Downs stared at the ceiling from the overhang above them.

Max looked over toward his good friend. "I think it's fair to say it's gone now."

"As I was saying," Jeremiah continued. "As we mounted and started to put together the beginning seeds to this mission, Dad was here in Vietnam on a remote dirt hillside accompanied only by a young paleontologist."

"What'd they find?" Josiah asked impatiently.

Jeremiah cleared his throat. "I'll spare you guys the details and get right to the point. They found the teeth and mouth of what one would hypothesize to be that of a predator. Or at least an omnivore at the very least."

"Makes perfect sense," Downs said as he nodded to himself and motioned with his head back out to the lagoon.

Almost in unison, all eyes made their way back out across the water toward where the original giganto-pithecus had disappeared back into the forest.

Jeremiah continued. "Dad and his paleontologist-for-hire found the remains of a ten thousand year old gigantopithecus-"

Josiah cut him off. "That means the species lived on for another ninety-thousand years further than what was previously thought."

Downs nodded his head, and as he looked around, he could see the others doing the same as well.

"Ten thousand years ago is a long time," Burr said as he cleared his throat. "Blip of an eye though in terms of deep geologic time, but to us humans it's still a large chunk of time."

Jeremiah nodded. "Indeed."

"But obviously the animal has made it into current times," Max said, "so we can scratch that whole ten thousand year ago thing."

Josiah shot him a playful look as he saluted him. "Thanks, Captain Obvious."

Downs grinned. "But the animal that officially went extinct a hundred thousand years ago is somewhat different from what we just saw."

Max Caldwell adjusted his glasses once more and began to stroke his chin. The gears were most definitely churning inside the zoologist's head. "Can you imagine what type of attention such a find would garner?"

"I can," Downs replied. "And that's why we need to achieve what we've set out to do here, keep these things a secret no matter what the cost."

Max nodded to him.

Again Burr Wellington went to work straightening his back as he grumbled out his words. "Well, now what'll we do?"

Downs motioned with a quick flick of his eyes back toward the bamboo forest. "We go in there. Track one of these creatures down."

26

The last of the day's sunshine quickly faded as the team quietly emerged out from behind the waterfall. It was hard to tell how long they had in fact been in there, but when they finally emerged out into the fading afternoon light, they found that the lone gigantopithecus atop the waterfall was nowhere to be seen. It had blended back into the trees and vegetation that surrounded the upper part of the waterfall.

Now the team was carefully making their way along the narrow dirt trail that lined the water's edge. Stepping over ferns and other vegetation that grew in close proximity to the water, the bamboo forest that lay to their left was quiet. Even the usual chatter from the resident bird life had died down. Now only the constant and heavy drone of insects could be heard.

Downs looked around. He saw the large heaping piles of uprooted vegetation that lay strewn about on the ground and floating about on the surface of the lagoon. To his left, back in the bamboo forest he could see just how dark it had already gotten in there. While there was still dim lighting around the open clearing where the lagoon lay, night was fast approaching back in the trees.

Downs quickly hurried past the others and made his way up to Max.

The zoologist seemed startled by Downs' sudden arrival. "Hey, what's up?"

The rest of the group came to a stop and huddled closely around Max as Burr stood watch. The big man had the air rifle stowed at his side while he scanned with his eyes.

"We need to set up a small camp, establish a perimeter," Downs announced.

"Um, good idea," Max said. "That'll be a nice start."

"We can take turns keeping watch when night falls," Jeremiah said.

Downs turned and looked back into the bamboo.

"We need to get further in there, and quickly," Burr said. "Getting darker by the second and we need to set things up while we still can."

The group nodded. A rather heavy bag was slung around Jeremiah Corstine's right shoulder. Inside the bag included the night vision goggles. Jeremiah tapped on the bag. "These babies will most definitely come in handy in a little while."

The team was just about to leave the small path next to the lagoon behind when Downs quickly spoke up. "I got a plan, and it involves the perimeter around our camp."

Burr Wellington snorted with laughter. "Boy, do I hate last-minute plans."

27

As darkness slowly began to creep in on the small clearing that the documentary film team found themselves in, the overall attitude of the group had gone from worried and concerned about their fellow team member, to one of anger and doubt. And that anger and doubt was directed solely at Stacey Winston. For going on twenty minutes now, he had been subject to a barrage of questions. Actually, they felt more like accusations instead of questions, and the hardest of the questions had come from Diane Clor. She had held nothing back, left no stone unturned.

Stacey had stepped several feet away from the group. The director was literally feeling the heat now as he tugged on his collar and dabbed with his shirt at the beads of sweat that had built up around his forehead. Whether he wanted to admit it or not, Stacey was not the greatest of liars. Quickly, he wiped away at the constant layer of perspiration that seemed to always be building up. As he did so, he could see the others slowly working their way toward him once again out of the corner of his eye. He needed to get it together and fast.

Diane approached quickly. Her arms were folded, her face was scrunched up into a tight ball of concentration. "So you're tellin' me that after you ran off in hot pursuit of potential footage, you eventually took up looking for him and then lost track of him entirely. That's it. That's the whole story."

Stacey nodded. "I was pretty preoccupied trying to get the footage. I took a few sweeps, tried to locate him, but then he disappeared, and so too did I. Got entangled in the denseness of the terrain and vegetation. Literally got swallowed up by the place. Y'all know what we're dealing with here."

Bob Hohrman shook his head back and forth, not necessarily looking mad or suspicious. Rather Bob's look was simply one of sheer concern. "When did you last see him?"

This time it was Stacey who shook his head. "Not sure. Hard to say. Once I got completely turned around in there, I shifted my attention on getting the shot as well as some nice audio. That's been the goal since the start."

Stacey knew those words had been a lie though. Once he was out and about moving through the jungle, he never did in fact go after Clark. He had run in there to get footage, amazing footage, terrifying footage, footage that once and for all was going to change his life and put him on the map. Diane suddenly looked down at her watch and then back up to the sky. Even standing in the open clearing where they were, things had grown quite dark. "Jesus, Stacey. We're talkin' about a lost man here, who's now facing the real possibility of spending the night in the forest alone. Completely fuckin' alone."

"Shit," Stacey said as he kicked at the dirt.

Once again, Bob Hohrman crossed his arms. "Stacey, are you positive you didn't see anything else? You're one hundred percent positive of this?"

Stacey nodded several times. "The vegetation eventually obscured my view entirely of him. You guys know as well as I do how thick it can get in there."

Diane came around to Stacey's side. Her arms were folded in a threatening manner. Stacey felt as though the two were ganging up on him, like they were confronting him in a dark alley and were about to beat the crap out of him.

"What is this?" Stacey said in frustration as he threw his hands up in the air. He finally felt as though he had reached his limits. "Instead of working together as a team to try and find him, here we are self destructing on one another. C'mon y'all, we're better than this."

Bob shook his head back and forth slowly. "Stacey, no one's self destructing, just trying to get to the bottom of this. That's it. It's getting real late, and we got a serious situation on our hands now."

Stacey wiped at the side of his face. He felt like these two individuals were coming after him, pointing the finger, placing the blame.

"Okay," Diane finally said. "Let's gather our belongings. Maybe we can go in search of him while we still have some light."

Doing his best to fully conceal it, Stacey breathed a momentary sigh of relief.

Praise the Lord, he thought to himself. *Praise the freaking Lord.*

Finally, at long last, it appeared as though Diane Clor and Bob Hohrman were momentarily off his back, and for that he was grateful.

Stacey looked over at Bob; the fifty-two year old sound engineer was busy strapping on his headlamp. Stacey then watched as Diane quickly began shuffling around in her bag as well.

Stacey snapped his fingers together. "Good idea. We'll be needin' to use those in a little bit of time now."

Quickly, the director set the tripod down in the dirt and began rummaging through his own bag. Stacey found his headlamp. Then he put it around his forehead, picked up the tripod, slung his pack over his left shoulder, and then hurried off toward the others.

28

Bick Downs continued scraping and digging with his hands before finally lifting back up and watching the small man-made moat as it slowly flooded into action. Little by little, the team had managed to dig a makeshift moat in the dirt, a small perimeter in the shape of a rectangle that outlined the tiny camp that they had resurrected in the middle of the bamboo forest. These were the last-minute preparations that were being made before nightfall.

The team stood back and watched as the water that they had managed to divert from the stream now began to fill the rectangular-shaped moat. They watched as the water trickled in from the creek until finally it had filled the moat on all four sides. They now had a small boundary around their camp separating themselves from the rest of the forest.

Josiah came over to where Downs was standing and rested his hand atop Downs' shoulder. "Hey man, you think this Mickey Mouse stuff'll work?"

Downs looked at the small moat. It couldn't have been more than three inches in depth and six inches in width. "She's not much but it's at least something."

"Bick's right," Max said as he came round to join the two men. "Gorillas have a natural aversion to water. They have been known to travel for miles in a certain direction simply to avoid stepping over a small creek. They steer clear of it at all costs."

Burr's head popped up. "Yeah, but who says we're dealin' with your average run-of-the-mill gorilla here?"

Downs shrugged his shoulders. "You're right, but it seemed as though the gigantopithecus steered clear of the water back there as well as the waterfall. At least that's what I saw."

Burr smiled. "Yeah, just before it sank its teeth into that poor deer and snapped its spinal cord. Man, oh man."

Max came around and set the piece of bamboo down that he had so diligently been digging his portion of the moat with. "We, um, have to trust what research tells us, and the current research of the day tells us that gorillas in the wild seem to have a natural fear of water. There have, however, been a few reported citings of gorillas swimming, but those are rare. Now, in a zoo setting, they've been known to play in the water, but for the most part in the wild this appears to not be true. They seem to steer clear of water at all costs. Now in regards to the gigantopithecus, I guess we'll just have to wait and see. Only time will tell."

"Let's hope," Tori said. "Let's freaking hope so."

Jeremiah was the last one to come around as the team officially took a look at what they had created. They were now just barely able to make out the moat that surrounded their makeshift camp on all four corners. Nightime was quickly approaching.

"Gives us just enough time to fire up the barbecue, Burr said.

Josiah shot him a ridiculous glare. "Man, could I go for a well-cooked steak right about now. Goddamn."

"Burr's right though," Downs said as he folded his arms and let out a deep sigh. "Let's get some food in us. Then begin to make preparations."

"By preparations I'm assuming you mean—" Tori motioned with her hand to the forest.

Downs nodded. "Let's get ready for nighttime."

29

Night came quickly. Once the sun had officially gone done, the forest was immediately plunged into a steady chorus of hoots, chirps, buzzing, and the ever-present vibrant chattering of countless species of insects, many of them probably undocumented to the world of science. The forest had truly come alive as Downs stood guard. Holstered at his side was the Astra should the situation call for it.

Meanwhile, leveled out in front of him, he held the air rifle firmly in two hands. The forest was bathed in a phosphorescent green glow from the aid of the night vision goggles. Black jungle surrounded them fiercely on all sides. He stared out into the dark and deep passages of thick and entangled trees. The darkness seemed to be pressing on their small camp from all sides now.

Josiah stood just off to Downs' right side. The young paleontologist stood with his own air rifle leveled out in front of him. And lastly, on Josiah's right side loomed the huge hulking figure that was Burr Wellington. The overwhelmingly large two hundred and fifty pound Washington native stood guard in the same manner as the other two men, eyes peeled staring through the night vision goggles, air rifle secured firmly in his huge hands. Together, the three men stood watch.

Resurrected in the middle of the camp were two small tents. Jeremiah and Max were quietly asleep in one while Tori was holed up in the other. This mission was going to require every ounce of strength they could muster, so any time to squeeze in some much-needed sleep had to be taken full advantage of.

Downs lowered his head toward his feet. Through the night vision goggles, he could see the small moat that they had dug out of the dirt a short while ago. The shallow water bordered their camp on all four sides. To his left, Downs could hear the soft gurgle of water from the hidden stream that lay twisting and clumped in amongst the tangled vegetation.

Downs had read about the gorillas' aversion to water himself in books as a kid. But as he looked down at the small moat no more than three inches in depth, he wondered if this would prevent something from wandering into their camp? Especially considering what he knew was moving about in the deeper less navigable parts of the forest.

Suddenly there was a noise. It had come from way out in the deep foliage. It sounded like something was moving about, moving through an area loaded with dense leafy vegetation. Downs swung the air rifle around in the direction of the noise. Whatever was out there now had come to a complete stop. Not a word was said among the three men. They had all heard it, and as the three of them stood with their air rifles faced in that direction, now there was only the gentle gurgle of water from the stream nearby.

The air was still quite humid and heavy. Nighttime brought little relief in the way of the suffocating embrace that the humidity had on everything in this part of the world. The three men stood in a rectangular formation with the tiny makeshift camp in the middle of them. Suddenly though, noise began to pick up once again. Downs continued to stare straight ahead toward where he pegged the sound to have come from. The goggles bathed the entire forest in a faint, neon green lighting, and as Downs looked out even further into the foliage, he could see just how dense the bamboo growth was out there. To put it in the simplest of terms, the forest appeared to be one immense labyrinth comprised entirely of tall, thin bamboo trees. The trees grew everywhere.

More cracking sounds ensued. The noise appeared to be coming just to the right of where Burr was situated.

Downs and Josiah were just about ready to swing their air rifles in that direction when Burr quickly waved them off. "I've got it. Hold your positions."

Downs remained with his eyes transfixed on a specific patch of vegetation. Out of the corner of his right eye, he could see that Josiah was doing exactly the same. More cracking sounds could be heard from the part of the forest where Burr was positioned toward, but as Downs continued to stare straight ahead, he also sensed that something was out there as well.

"Oh, fuck," Downs mumbled quietly to himself.

Shit was about to go down.

Were they surrounded on all sides? Perhaps now would be a good time to wake the others. But no further thought could be put into this as noise quickly began crashing loudly through the forest. The sound of foliage and brush being trampled and bent back could be heard. Something was making a beeline straight for them.

"Son of a bitch," Burr yelled as a large shape went scurrying right on past him.

Whatever it was had completely disregarded the man-made moat and had now crashed into the first of the two tents. Downs spun around just as the first tent twisted and collapsed inward. The animal tore through the side of the tent with a loud growl. He then saw the large figure emerge suddenly with something in its mouth. It was a bag. It took Downs a moment, but eventually he realized it appeared to be the bag that contained their radios. With a sudden burst of adrenaline, the large figure shot off into the trees.

"What the," a voice shouted from inside the tent as a shape suddenly took form and sat up inside the nylon mesh.

Downs could see that it was Jeremiah. John Corstine's son was now twisted and turned around inside the tent as both he and Max attempted to extricate themselves.

But Downs could pay no attention to the struggle back at the tents. He and Josiah now had their own problems to deal with. Whatever was responsible for this sudden disturbance, was now rampaging and crashing hard through the surrounding trees and heavy brush.

"Keep your eyes peeled," Downs yelled as Josiah stepped to his right side.

The sound of bamboo breaking and splintering rang loudly now. Whatever it was sounded quite large and powerful. Downs and Josiah held their ground though. At their backs they could now hear the ruckus from where the two tents lay.

Now the scrambling noise from the trees in front of them was practically upon Downs and Josiah. Through the night vision goggles, Downs still had a hard time seeing much of anything, just dense bamboo growth. Slowly, Downs unclipped the Astra from his side. Now, he had both the lethal and non-lethal weapon leveled out in front of him as the forest continued to come alive.

Not takin' any chances, he thought to himself.

From somewhere behind him, Downs heard a scramble of different voices. But above it all, he heard indecipherable word's coming from Burr's deep booming voice radiating through the madness. Through the night vision goggles, Downs squinted as a medium-sized shape emerged from the bamboo trees. The image came barreling forward. Downs flung himself to the right, narrowly avoiding the blur of a shape that had quickly overtaken their camp.

Before Downs could do anything, let alone even make sense of whatever it was that had just come barreling right through their small moat, Josiah had fired a dart. Suddenly, a squealing howl of pain filled their camp.

Next, Downs saw a rather large head swing in his direction. A mouth full of powerful teeth opened wide and the creature blared a roar of hot breath in his direction. Downs squeezed the trigger and fired a dart with the air rifle just as he heard Max Caldwell's voice cut loudly above it all.

"Sun bear!" the zoologist screamed at the top of his lungs. "Sun bear!"

Downs' shot had been an accurate one, pinning the small yet powerful bear on its distinctive yellow crescent-shaped patch on its chest. Again, the bear growled a fierce and commanding roar, this time swinging in the direction of Josiah. With two feathered darts now protruding out of its body, the small yet fierce creature was enraged.

Downs was able to get his first good look at the assailant. He had never actually seen one up close and personal, but Max's observations had indeed been correct. It was a sun bear, or known more affectionately as a honey bear. At a maximum length of roughly five feet, they are among the smallest known bears throughout the world.

But Downs knew better than to judge this small yet aggressive creature solely by its size. With another deep and throaty roar, the sun bear turned and began bounding toward Josiah.

"She wants the infant!" Burr cried out. "The infant!"

Downs turned and watched as Burr dove toward one of the tents. Meanwhile inside, a small furry object appeared as though it had gotten entangled in the mesh fabric of the tent. Now Max was also down on his hands and knees working furiously to locate the small furry animal.

Downs turned in horror and watched as the adult sun bear opened its mouth, roared, and began moving swiftly toward Max. Downs sprung forward and butted the end of the air rifle square into the side of the honey bear's jaw. There was a sickening thud as the butt of the rifle collided with bone that made up the jaw muscles. The animal spun around, now a small fiery ball of rage and teeth. The sun bear blasted another roar Downs' way.

Meanwhile, Tori had come up from behind the small mother and surprised it. Wasting no time, she fired a third and remaining dart into the bear. But this time, it had been an errant shot as the dart bounced off the sun bear and disappeared out into the dark jungle.

For a fleeting moment, the honey bear spun around. It appeared unsure of itself, possibly confused or disoriented, or a little of both. Then the animal let out another roar.

Meanwhile, Burr and Max had finally managed to find the juvenile sun bear. Downs spun around and saw the large Washington native hunched over trying desperately to scoot the youngster toward its mother.

Downs turned and watched as the mother sun bear suddenly took off bounding straight for Max and Burr. The bear may have been one of the smallest bear species in the world, but the aggression and ferocity the small animal possessed was a sight to behold.

"She's comin' your way," Josiah yelled, pointing toward Max and Burr.

The sun bear roared as it planted its foot down into the small moat and knocked the sleeping tent over in its frantic pursuit to get to its infant. Now Downs found himself chasing after the small bear.

Again the sun bear roared as it continued onward. The animal was now a small and tightly wound ball of aggression. Bellowing what appeared to be another moaning roar of agony, the animal continued onward, stumbling, yet persistently making its way toward its infant.

And then suddenly, the animal's back right leg gave out from underneath it and Downs watched as the bear, still refusing to give up pursuit of its infant, now dragged the back half of its body through the mud.

Now the sun bear was howling in agonizing, course, ragged gasps. This display continued onward for about another minute or so as the bear did its best to move itself forward via its two powerful front limbs. But the liquid contents inside the darts now protruding out of the animal had already managed to work their way into its bloodstream. Ten seconds later, the bear collapsed right there in the mud.

There was no time to spare. The juvenile sun bear was still loose in the camp, still running rampant.

"Help me get it," Burr yelled again. He spun around as he followed the noise.

Now the team went to town trying to locate the small animal.

Downs pointed to Josiah and Tori. "You two stay watch."

Both nodded back to him and did exactly as told.

"I gotcha," Burr said as he had finally caught the youngster by one of its back limbs. "Gimme a hand."

Downs was on it quickly. The juvenile sun bear had worked its way into one of the fallen sleeping tents, and the team was now trying to remove the small yet powerful burrowing animal. Somehow, someway, the little creature had managed to get its body fully twisted up in the mesh fabric. Burr was trying to pull the animal out via its back legs. Downs got down on all fours and so did Max as they attempted to aid the big man.

"Careful," Max said, "they can deliver quite a powerful bite."

The two could hear Burr grumbling as he began sliding his way out of the tent with both hands around the two back legs of the infant sun bear. "No different than my two dogs at home. C'mon little one. You can do it. C'mon."

"Okay," Max said, "just be careful."

Burr didn't reply. At this point Downs and Max really weren't doing much of anything. Downs' eyes shifted around their tiny campsite. He saw Tori and Josiah located on the perimeter, standing guard just behind the small moat. And then Downs' eyes shifted once more, and through the night vision goggles, he saw Jeremiah.

"Oh shit," Downs blurted out.

Tori turned and faced in the same direction. The two saw Jeremiah as he now stood at the far corner of their camp. The man was dragging something. Downs could see what looked to be the adult sun bear. Jeremiah was dragging all one hundred pounds of its dead weight through the mud.

Downs pointed to Tori. "I got it, stay put."

"Roger that," she said back.

Quickly, Downs hurried his way on over to Jeremiah.

"I got you, man," Downs said to Jeremiah as he arrived at the man's side.

Jeremiah set the sun bear down for a moment. He had been dragging the thing through the mud and dirt by the animal's front two limbs. Now it simply laid there with the soft gurgle of water from the moat just to its left.

By now, Max had come scurrying on over to join them. Following close behind the zoologist was Burr, but the big man miraculously had something in his arms.

"Kinda cute and cuddly," Burr said petting the infant's head as it playfully slobbered its mouth and teeth all over his chest. "Might think about takin' it back to Washington with me."

Downs looked at the small, playful animal. "Get rid of that immediately."

Max nodded his head. "Yeah, uh, have to side with Downs. Burr, we must insist that you let the animal go at once."

Burr smiled as he continued to pet the small sun bear. "You boys are a bunch of pussies, but on this one, I have to agree with ya."

Burr looked down at the young bear still cradled gently in his arms. "Sorry, little fella. Woulda been fun, woulda been epic, but it's not meant to be."

And with that, Burr carefully set the bear down right next to the small moat. It sniffed around the water's edge for a few seconds before finally making its way over to its mother. It sniffed her too, sniffing around the stomach region before eventually scrambling up and onto her back. And there it remained perched as it tilted its head back to the humans and proceeded to let out small yapping cries.

"Poor thing," Max said. "It's probably wondering why she's not getting up."

All of a sudden, the sounds of things breaking and snapping rang out from the deeper parts of the forest. Downs' eyes shot back toward Josiah and Tori; the two of them were still standing guard. Next, Downs looked back out toward the darkened forest.

Jeremiah set his hands at his hips. "Was trying to get her as far away from camp as possible so when she wakes up…"

Jeremiah was cut off mid-sentence by more cracking sounds from way out in the deep foliage. Whatever it was was moving about through the bamboo trees.

"Let's move it outta here quickly," Downs whispered.

"Roger that," Jeremiah said as he once again picked the front limbs of the bear up. Downs picked up the back half of the creature. With two fully capable men now working in coordinated efforts, they quickly made short work of getting the bear a good ways out to an area probably some one hundred yards from their camp. Burr and Max stood guard on both sides of the party as they moved deeper into the foliage. Tall, green, straighter-than-an-arrow bamboo trees passed by on both sides. When the team felt as though they had worked there way deep enough into the forest, they carefully laid the sun bear down in and amongst a dense clustering of ferns. Throughout the entire time that they'd been making their way, the infant sun bear had repeatedly been yapping and dancing around their ankles as they walked. Now that the mother sun bear lay nestled in and amongst the ferns, the infant yapped loudly as it nuzzled its face into the side of its mother.

"She'll hopefully wake up soon enough," Max said.

Downs took one last look around. And then just like that they turned around and quickly headed back toward camp.

• • •

Several minutes later the team arrived back at camp to find Tori and Josiah not standing guard. Rather the two were moving about quickly through camp. Their heads were lowered as they continued to scour the ground.

"How'd it go, man?" Josiah asked from his position at the far corner of the camp as his head popped up.

Burr wiped both hands together. "Got the bear a good ways out there. Let's hope the two of 'em move on to greener pastures when she wakes."

"We did our best," Downs said. "If the thing hadn't come at us like a bat outta hell, we wouldn't have had to do what we did."

"Yeah but I'm glad we did. I fear the two of 'em woke up the rest of the forest though," Jeremiah said looking around.

Wasting no time, Tori walked right up to Downs. "The bag with the radios is gone. Nowhere to be seen," she said breathing hard. "We searched the entire camp and even a ways out into the surrounding brush. No sign of it. Nothing."

Tori's words confirmed what Downs suspected he had seen a short while ago when their camp had been abruptly overtaken by the sun bear. The team looked down at their trampled and crumpled tents which now lay in ruins.

Downs looked Tori in the eyes. "You sure of this? When the attack happened, I did see the bear with somethin' in its mouth. Was too chaotic at the moment to be absolutely sure though."

Tori nodded back to him. "We scoured every inch of camp and even into the surrounding foliage and trees."

"Damn, man," Josiah said as he looked down at the ground. "Shit just got a lot more real."

"You better believe it," Burr snorted aggressively. "Things often don't go as planned out in the field."

Downs looked around momentarily. The moat that made a rectangle around their camp was still filled with water. That much he could see at least.

Downs looked up and gazed in Jeremiah's direction. John Corstine's son was staring toward the area from where they had just come.

"Jeremiah, what's up?" Downs asked.

Jeremiah turned and faced the group. "Appears we got a lot goin' on right now, but I really think we need to see if she's up and awake, the bear that is. Maybe she needs our assistance."

Downs let out a sigh as he turned and looked at Max who simply shrugged his shoulders.

"No way," Burr interjected. "She may be small, but that bear packs quite a wallop when rampaging like that. Like a tightly coiled spring or something, that animal."

Again Downs looked back toward Jeremiah.

"Then I'm going on my own to check on her," Jeremiah announced. "I think we owe her and her cub that much decency at least."

Inhaling a big breath of air, Downs finally responded. "Okay, I got your back. Let's go."

Downs quickly looked back to Tori.

She nodded to him. "We'll do our best to retrace our steps again, scour every inch and into the surrounding trees."

Downs managed a smile. "I know you will."

It was settled then. Downs was going to escort Jeremiah back to the part of the forest where they had carried the sun bear, and that was that.

"This'll be quick," Downs said. "Should be gone ten minutes, twenty tops."

Josiah smiled to his good buddy. "Famous last words."

• • •

Jeremiah and Downs had managed to work their way back to the small gathering of ferns, repeatedly pushing their way through dense and at times waist-high growth. Doing their best to follow the same route as they had done before, they snaked their way through the dark maze of towering bamboo trees guided only by their night vision goggles and basic intuition regarding the lay of the land. Although it was hard to imagine, they felt as though they had somewhat of an idea of where they were in this forest. The entire time, Downs' eyes twitched back and forth, watching the tall slender bamboo trees as they passed by on both sides of them.

The two of them held their air rifles pressed out in front of them.

When they finally got back to the area where they had left the sun bear not more than twenty minutes ago, they found that area of the forest to be completely devoid of life.

"Well," Jeremiah said nervously as he looked around.

But Downs hadn't heard a word that John Corstine's son had just spoken. Slowly, Downs continued moving forward. When he finally got to the general vicinity of where they had laid the sun bear down just a short while ago, he found that several of the ferns were flattened and bent back. Upon first glance it appeared as though they had been trampled and pushed down by something large.

Jeremiah quickly made his way to where Downs was standing. Looking down at the ferns while pointing, Jeremiah carefully took a few steps, trying to retrace the steps of the sun bear. Downs meanwhile strained with his ears to listen. Was the infant sun bear close by? Downs shook his head. No. Both the infant and adult sun bear appeared to be long gone by now. His senses told him that much at least.

All of a sudden something caught Downs' eyes. From where he stood, he couldn't quite make it out though. Bending down, he set the butt of the rifle down in the mud and reached out with his right hand. Jeremiah crouched alongside of him. And together both men took in the gruesome scene.

Splattered across half a dozen or so outstretched limbs of vegetation, the two men saw lots of blood. And as they looked around even further, the blood was smeared across the vegetation in thick globs everywhere. And it wasn't just the ferns in this particular part of the forest that were covered in blood. Everything within a ten foot radius had been doused with a solid slathering of it. There were slick patches of blood everywhere.

Downs shifted his eyes to the mud. Gently tracing his hand through the soft and squishy terrain, he was slowly starting to get the sense that something had been dragged off through the vegetation against its will. Downs turned. Again, he saw more blood smeared across the surrounding foliage. Both men looked at one another. As they continued to hover over the scene, one constant seemed to be true. It appeared that a struggle had ensued after they laid the bear down to rest. But most importantly, the bear had been dragged off into the forest.

30

The helicopter hovered low as the dark canopy lay stretched out below, the thick rotor wash beating back the tops of the bamboo trees as the first man approached the open hatch. There was no trepidation in his step, no hesitation, only sheer determination mixed with that of self-confidence and one hundred percent belief in both himself as well as his abilities. Orders were being shouted out from behind him, but at this point the ex Special Forces soldier was already ready and committed. Putting no further thought into this, he stepped out into the warm humid air and began to fall.

Decker Johnson descended quickly down the thick black rope that extended all the way to the forest floor below. Despite the best efforts by the pilot to put the small covert team in the path of least resistance, meaning minimal extending branches and other sharp things of the jungle, Decker Johnson still felt himself getting cut and scraped as he continued to slide down the rope. Using his feet intertwined below him for stability and the thick gloves that he had on, Decker slid ever faster. Now he was plummeting toward the jungle floor below at a sickening speed. He needed to slow down.

Using his feet for friction, Decker quickly began putting the brakes on. Judging from the trees around him, he knew he was getting close. Now he was slowing down, gliding gently down the thick rope. The forest around him slowly started to come into focus. It was as if he had literally been dropped into a buzzing and vibrant world, a far cry from the open hatch of the chopper just a few short seconds ago.

Now Decker could actually see the forest floor below. Squeezing the rope tightly with his hands, at long last his boots touched down on terra firma. Quickly he went to work unclipping himself as he spoke into his radio.

"Send down the next one," Decker said.

Now fully unhitched from the rope, he stepped aside, brushed himself off, and waited for the next teammate to arrive. Meanwhile all around him, the forest continued to buzz, humm, vibrate, thump, and chatter with life. Now that he was all alone down here, he was amazed at just how noisy the forest in fact was. That had been something he had not been prepared for. At 6'2 inches and two hundred and twenty pounds, Decker Johnson was a solid and well put together individual. In his early thirties and of English descent, he had spent his early to mid to late twenties playing professional rugby in Europe before a persistent lower back injury forced him to give up the game for good. Through the night vision goggles, Decker looked back up the rope and toward the chopper.

Craning his neck back he stared straight up as best as he could. He had always had what one would consider to be a problematic neck. The canopy above him was dense and he couldn't exactly see back to the chopper, but he could most definitely hear it. The loud rotor wash was still very noticeable. He could see the thick rope which led back up to the open hatch. Decker wasn't certain who was next. He had sort of zoned out back in the hatch when directions and orders were being barked out. But someone would be coming down in a matter of seconds. He knew that much.

He looked over at the thick rope and noticed just the slightest of vibrations. Someone was on their way down. Decker stepped back. Odd as it may have sounded, and despite his large size and violent sports background, he found it rather creepy and unnerving being way down here amongst the tall bamboo trees all by himself. As he continued to stare straight ahead at the thick rope, he couldn't wait until whomever it was emerged and provided him with some much-needed company. He had already felt as though he had been down here for far too long, and it had probably only been a a few minutes at best.

Suddenly, Decker had the overwhelming urge that something had snuck up quickly from behind him. He flung himself around. Now he was staring straight ahead at a darkened row of bamboo trees. He couldn't see much beyond that.

Decker stared for a few more seconds before turning back toward the rope. He saw boots sliding down from some fifty feet above him, and before he even realized it, Finn Carter was unclipping himself from the rope. Finn was roughly the same height as Decker but outweighed the man by a good twenty pounds. Finn was also a native of England and had played on the same rugby team as Decker.

Together, both men stood still and silent as the rope once again shook and vibrated with life. Suddenly, Decker found himself spinning around once more to face the part of the forest that lay at their backs. Finn was immediately shocked by his partner's sudden skittish behavior.

"Deck, man, get a bloody grip on yourself," Finn said, staring at his partner with a confused look on his face.

Staring straight ahead with his rifle pointed toward the thick and entangled forest, Decker replied in a monotone fashion. "There's something off in the trees."

Finn smiled to himself. "This early on? Please. You're lettin' the jitters get the best of you. Now get it together."

Decker took another moment before he spun around once more and faced the rope.

"Here comes Daniels," Finn said staring straight up toward the black canopy.

Brig Daniels, the largest of the three men, came sliding on down the rope as if he weighed but a mere fraction of what he actually did. Quickly, he set foot on the forest floor and went about the task of unclipping himself. Once Brig Daniels was unclipped, he quickly stepped forward toward the other two men. He spoke into the microphone and together the three men watched as the thick black rope which had served as their elevator down into this pitch black world quickly ascended up into the limbs of the canopy before disappearing for good into the night sky.

Wasting no time, Finn pointed toward Decker with a big smile on his face. "Hey yo Brig, twinkle toes over here is already wiggin' out like he's seen a bloody ghost or something."

Brig held up a large and imposing hand. "You two don't even fuckin' start with rubbish like that, we got a lot a fuckin' work to do down here and not a lot of time. Now fuckin' get it together."

That was all that needed to be said. Both Finn and Decker knew their place, and here, amidst the endless sea of bamboo trees, there was one man and one man only in control, and his name was Brig Daniels. Like Finn and Decker, Brig had also been a rubgy player before a left foot injury forced himself into early retirement. At just shy of six feet in height, Brig more than made up for his lack of height by his overwhelmingly large physique. At two hundred and sixty pounds, Brig Daniels was an absolute bruiser in every sense of the word. His broad shoulders and well-defined arms only served to add to his imposing stature.

Brig took off his black hat for a moment and wiped at his clean-shaven head. Although it was now the middle of the night, he was dripping with perspiration. It was hot in this jungle, too damn hot, Brig thought to himself as he continued toweling off his head.

About six months ago, a covert internet operation based in Russia had managed to get wind of the documentary film crew's mission to come to this part of the world in search of the long thought to be extinct Gigantopithecus. They had managed to hack into the production company's email server and intercept key details about where they would be dropping the film crew. This operation dealt primarily in the black market, and had been salivating over how much a creature that had supposedly died one hundred thousand years ago would fetch in terms of a pure dollar amount. So they contacted Brig Daniels and his small three-man team.

The team's goal was simple. Find, capture, and prepare one of the gigantopithecus creatures for transport back to Russia. If they could in fact pull this seemingly impossible task off, the team of three would be paid handsomely for their efforts. And as Brig adjusted his gear that was already starting to feel as though it was weighing him down, he realized full well that they had one hell of an opportunity here. If they could just pull it off, the largest payday that any of them had ever seen awaited them.

Out of nowhere, Decker suddenly spun around once again, gun leveled out in front of him, staring off into the thick brush. Finn shot Brig a stare as they both rolled their eyes to one another. There certainly was one hell of an opportunity here, there was no denying that, but they had a lot of work to get done before they could even begin to entertain their huge potential payday.

31

Stacey Winston found himself pushing hard through rain-soaked vegetation in an effort to keep pace with the others. The director of this small documentary could barely see the silhouettes of Bob Hohrman or Diane Clor as they walked ahead of him. They walked on damp, spongy earth as they continued to snake their way through the tall, thin, green shoots of bamboo.

Meanwhile up ahead, Bob and Diane were leading the charge, doing their best to keep up the aggressive pace that they'd set. The two of them simply could not accept the fact that one of their teammates had been left alone to fend for himself in this brutal and at times unforgiving terrain. Now that night had officially fallen, their pace was even more feverish.

From behind at the end of the line, Stacey repeatedly found himself shouting for the two to be careful of the equipment, that if they kept maneuvering through the trees like this they ran the risk of damaging something, but as Stacey pushed harder through the wet vegetation, he knew that his pleas had fallen on deaf ears.

Stacey wondered hard if those two up ahead believed him or not. Did his story have plot holes in it? Did everything that he had told them make complete sense?

Were there gaping errors in the validity of what he had rehashed? As he crashed hard through another layer of vines, he had no clue what the two up ahead thought of him. Right now he had two concerns: to keep pace with both of them, and to most importantly not damage their precious equipment. To suffer mechanical problems way out here in the middle of fucking nowhere would be a monumental setback to their documentary film efforts at this point in time. And not seeing this project through to completion would put serious delay if he was ever truly going to break into Hollywood and be given the chance to direct his first full-length feature film. There was a lot riding on all of this. It felt like the weight of the world was bearing down on him if he was ever to truly make his ultimate goal happen one day.

For a brief second, Stacey felt his foot go down and into a squishy puddle of sticky mud. But he continued moving forward, continued plowing onward. After all, he had no choice. Stop, and he would be faced with the second issue of concern, which he knew was a big one as he ducked under another thick layering of vegetation. And that was the idea of being caught alone in this forest. To be trapped out here simply with oneself was a truly frightening proposition. He had seen the ungodly strength of the creature that had carried his fellow teammate away. Just thinking of encountering such a colossal beast in broad daylight was utterly terrifying, but the idea of encountering such a beast in this dark labrinyth of a world at night seemed downright nighmarish. Stacey pushed himself harder now, doing his best to keep pace with his teammates.

All of a sudden he felt his foot become entangled. Dropping his head toward the forest floor immediately, it was already too late. Stacey fell forward and literally face planted right there in the mud. The equipment had fallen somewhere to his right and now lay slumped over in wet vegetation.

"Shit," he cursed to himself.

Rather abruptly, he managed to push himself upright. Staring straight ahead at the darkened path that they had been blazing through, he saw the others. He saw the two lights from their headlamps dancing back and forth out in front of them, two thin beams of light penetrating the darkness that lay beyond. If it not for his own headlamp still going strong, Stacey Winston would have been plunged into immediate darkness. In fact, as he stared ahead toward the two, all he could make out were the dancing beams of light from their headlamps. Had they even noticed he was gone from the end of the line?

Pushing his hands down even further in the mud, Stacey resurrected to his feet an absolute mess. "Hey! Hey!"

He gathered himself for a second and then blasted the loudest roar possible. "Heeeeey!"

It took another second, but eventually he saw the dancing beams of light up ahead come to a stop. And then those same dancing beams of light turned around. It now appeared as though they were coming back for him. Meanwhile, Stacey went about gathering the equipment that still lay slumped over in the vegetation.

Once Stacey had fully gathered everything and had it securely back in his hands, the other two had returned.

Diane shot Stacey a mean glare while Bob appeared fidgety and nervous, tinkering with his headlamp. It was as if the other man was purposely avoiding making eye contact with Stacey. Whatever the reason, Stacey felt the obvious tension in the air.

As Stacey continued to just stand there, the front half of him completely covered in mud, he realized he had two options: stare at Bob who was making him nervous by just how jittery he appeared, or stare at Diane who was staring a hole straight through him. He opted for option number three. Rather, Stacey just stared off into the dark foliage that pressed tightly on them from all sides. Aside from the immediate light produced by their headlamps, the entire forest was cloaked in an inky, all-engulfing blackness all around them. This was not how things were supposed to go, meaning at this time of the night they should have been tucked away tightly in their tents instead of attempting to scour every inch of this forest. For whatever reason, the small documentary team had not equipped themselves with night vision goggles, and while they did have plenty of backup batteries to power their headlamps for days on end, the majority of the forest remained a dark and hidden secret to them.

Eventually, it was Stacey who decided to speak up. "We can't keep running around like this all night, y'all, just sayin'."

Bob's attention had been momentarily diverted by noise somewhere off to their left. Finally, the bald-headed man stared back at Stacey. "Look, one of our own is lost in this forest. Are we just going to abandon him to fend for himself out here? This should be priority number one right now."

Stacey let out a sigh and looked down at the ground. And then finally, the director looked up at Bob. Bob looked over at Diane who still had a stern look on her face.

"This had never been the intended plan," Stacey said. "To be out and about like this at night."

"Well, there's the shock of the century," Diane fired back. "It also wasn't the plan for someone to go missing now, was it? Ass fucking stupid statement if I've ever heard one."

"No," Stacey replied as he composed himself, "I mean wandering around like this. We're really not equipped to be doing this."

Diane appeared completely indifferent to what had just been said. Stacey tried a different approach this time. "Look Diane, all I meant was we don't have proper night vision goggles, we have absolutely no clue where we're headed or if we're even headed in the right direction, and it's getting quite late."

Diane folded her arms and turned and stared out into the forest, the beam from her headlamp boring a straight line of light into the darkness.

Stacey clapped his hands together, let out a breath, and stared down at the ground for a moment. Reaching up, he flicked his headlamp off with his right hand. When he raised his head, he was staring at both Diane and Bob. "Guys, listen to me. The footage I acquired back there when Clark and I got turned around is nothing short of incredible. In fact, I'm gonna go out on a limb and say it's the most breathtaking scientific footage ever shot. It's worth a fortune and we're all gonna make out like bandits because of it."

Stacey stopped talking and let his words hang in the air. He wanted to see how they would absorb what he had just said.

Diane was the first one to speak up. "What type of footage?"

Stacey stood straight-faced and looked her in the eyes. "Direct evidence of the creature. Gigantopithecus in the flesh and I got it captured on camera. But we can't stop now. We must pursue more breathtaking footage."

Stacey had expected more of a response from Diane, but instead the woman returned a look of indifference to him. He looked over at Bob, the sound engineer seeming as though he had barely heard the words that Stacey had just spoken.

Bob cleared his throat. "Stacey, I'm happy as hell for ya, I really am. I know how much this project means to you, but I really must stress that priority number one at this point be that we find our way back to Clark. Only when one of our own is back and accounted for should we continue on with the documentary."

Stacey looked back toward Diane. Still the woman did not have much of a response.

Stacey took in a deep breath and absorbed what Bob had said. "Okay then. First thing in the morning. As soon as the sun's up we resume our search, even head back to the clearing, start to retrace our initial steps from there. Leave no stone unturned."

Diane took a few more seconds as she stared off into the brush a bit longer before finally swinging her head back around. The light from her headlamp hit Stacey square in the eyes, causing the director to squint and put his hands up. Stacey immediately knew that although it had been a small gesture, Diane had done it on purpose.

Get a grip, Stacey said to himself. *Get a grip on yourself. You'll live.*

Stacey took a moment to rub his eyes.

Bob tilted his head to the left and let the light from his headlamp shine straight into a solid wall of bamboo.

"Okay," Bob said, clearing his throat and having a quick look back toward Stacey, and then a longer embrace with Diane. "First light sounds okay by me."

Diane nodded her head but still said nothing. She was poker-faced all the way. This time, however, she did not shine the light from the headlamp directly into Stacey's eyes. She remained quiet, staring off into the trees. Eventually, Diane brought her head back around and acknowledged the conversation that had just been spoken. "It's settled then. First light we head out."

There were no further words exchanged between the three. Both Diane and Bob turned themselves around and took off walking once again, the two lights from their headlamps dancing out in front of them illuminating the way. Beyond the reach of the headlamps, dark forest lay sprawled out ahead.

Suddenly, Bob turned around. "One more thing. Where we heading?"

Diane came to a stop. She turned around to face Stacey. Now both Diane and Bob were staring straight at the director. Stacey took a moment before he spoke. "Let's make our way back to the clearing. Set up camp there. That way at first light we can begin to retrace our steps starting at square one."

And with that, Bob and Diane turned and continued on their way. With the two out ahead and their headlamps still lighting the way, Stacey felt somewhat relieved that there had been no more questions regarding Clark's disappearance. It felt like a slight weight had momentarily been lifted from his shoulders. He was grateful for that.

• • •

From up ahead Bob and Diane were busy diligently making their way. They walked in silence, Diane's steps just a little bit quicker than Bob's. Although Diane had said very little just a few seconds ago, it did not mean she wasn't actively thinking about what Stacey Winston had just conveyed to them regarding the supposed award-winning footage he had recently acquired. The gears were most definitely churning inside Diane's head. But for the moment, she didn't feel that words were necessary. The heavy drone of insects was the only noise heard between the two as they continued onward in silence.

• • •

Meanwhile from back behind a bit, the next thought that came to Stacey Winston was about his footage. His thoughts gravitated in that direction as they continued onward toward the open clearing. The footage that he had shot and filmed was going to catapult him to another level. He knew this with relative certainty. Now all he wanted to do was get back to the safety and secrecy of his own private tent and have a look at the footage with his own eyes. He honestly couldn't wait. He had literally been brimming with excitement all afternoon now, and the possibility that this documentary could actually be a success put an added pep in his step.

Now they just had to find their way back to the clearing where they had eaten lunch earlier in the day. After that, it would be up to them to get their tents set up as quickly as possible. Guided only by their headlamps, the small documentary film team continued silently making their way through the forest.

32

Downs and Jeremiah returned back to camp just as the rain started to pick up once again. Beyond the outstretched limbs of the canopy, the clouds began to let loose. Everywhere around them, water was beginning to puddle up as a heavy rain pounded down upon the forest. Downs and Jeremiah were breathing heavily as their muddy trudge back to camp had finally come to an end.

Tori was the first one to approach the two men still struggling to recapture their breath.

Downs eyed her. "Anything?"

"No," she replied with a sigh. "No sign of the radio bag anywhere."

"Shit," Downs muttered to himself as he wiped water from his face and kicked at the muddy ground.

Tori had to shout now to be heard over the rain. "What about things on your end?"

Downs spoke loudly back to her. "Bear was gone."

Tori's eyebrows raised. "Really?"

Downs shook his head though as if she didn't quite understand. "Looked like somethin' *dragged* it away."

Burr's ears immediately perked up. "Say what?"

Jeremiah was still having trouble catching his breath. "He said that it appears as though something dragged our sun bear away."

By now the entire team had gathered around Downs and Jeremiah. The team had also started to put on their foul-weather gear. The rain was really starting to pick up now. They practically had to yell to one another to be heard.

"So you said it was gone," Burr said folding his large and imposing arms.

Downs nodded. "Yup. Did a quick investigation of the surrounding area. Found blood. Actually we found lots of it smeared across the vegetation. But no body."

Jeremiah jumped in. "We also found the vegetation to be flattened in the direction that it seemed as though the sun bear had been dragged off in."

"Any sign of the infant?" Tori asked.

Downs shook his head as he cleared his throat. "None."

Downs looked up. There appeared to be no let-up in the rain. "We wait out the weather. Eat. Hydrate. First sign of light we head out. Begin our search to track down one of these creatures."

Burr grumbled something to himself in only the manner that Burr Wellington seemed capable of. "I say we head out even earlier than first light, that small window that exists say thirty minutes before first light. Guarantee that we get a good jump on the day."

Downs nodded and as he looked at the rest of the team, each member nodded as well. "Done."

It was settled then. They would wake just before first light, or as Downs usually called it, the ass crack of dawn. But still he felt there was more. He hadn't said anything to the others yet; actually he wasn't certain if they had realized the growing problem yet or not either. But rather than speak, he decided it best for now just to keep it to himself. They had been extremely busy the last few hours and needed to regroup, regather themselves, and most importantly rest. They were going to need all the energy they could muster and then some.

But an odd thing happened when Downs turned in the direction of Max. He wasn't there. The zoologist was suddenly nowhere to be seen.

33

What Max Caldwell lacked in physical size and stature, he more than made up for with his excellent sense of hearing and smell. In fact, throughout the course of his entire life, he had always viewed both of them as his greatest assets. That is, aside from his highly functioning academic brain, of course.

But now the thirty year old zoologist found himself wading through waist-high, rain-soaked vegetation. And as Max continued on his way, he also realized that perhaps his skills for evading people had also improved over the years as well. Somewhere in the middle of Jeremiah and Downs' discussion back at camp, Max had found a way to sneak off without anyone noticing him.

But as Max continued plowing through the wet vegetation, he also realized that perhaps no one had noticed his leaving camp because Max Caldwell was a quiet and unassuming individual. Perhaps he needed to change that quality about himself, but Max had always been a quiet soul, an old soul, someone who sat back and formulated thoughts while others spoke. But something had clicked when Max was standing next to the others. He had heard noise, life. Actually, truth be told, he had been noticing that the forest had been alive with distinct noises all day. There had been the sound of branches breaking and leaves rustling from the far reaches of the jungle that he swore he had been hearing. And he decided that he needed to make a run for it, that the noise had finally reached a breaking point and he felt something had to be done. He needed to take action. It had been a rash act running off like that, but he had made the decision, and now he was completely isolated and on his own in the middle of the forest.

Now here he was, continuing to push his way through dense crowded foliage, guided only by his night vision goggles, while his air rifle was pressed out in front of him. Suddenly, Max stopped and peered to his left. He swung the air rifle around in the direction from where the sound had come. He listened and waited. All he heard for the moment though was the pattering of rain as it slapped down hard onto the surrounding foliage.

Way out here amongst the tall swaying stands of bamboo trees, the forest had a very unnerving silence to it as the trees continued to groan and rub against one another. Max wasn't certain how he felt about being out here all alone, but this was his idea after all so the zoologist knew that he had to own the moment. There was no turning back now.

Max continued on his way. It was incredible just how thick the jungle had become once he in fact left their small makeshift camp, with its flattened tents and tiny rectangular moat surrounding the perimeter of the camp. Suddenly and without warning, he lowered himself into a crouched position. Reaching out, he touched the two bamboo trees that shot straight up toward the night sky. They were thicker and more robust than he had given them credit for. Earlier in the day when the team had found themselves deep inside this forest, Max had seen hundreds of bamboo trees, and to the untrained eye they looked like tall, thin wispy things that shot straight up from all corners of the forest. But now that his hands were touching one of the trees, feeling it, rubbing it, actually experiencing it, he realized that they were far more robust and solid than he had given them credit. They had mass to them and a certain density that he wasn't quite prepared for. For a brief moment Max thought about the way in which the gigantopithecus had moved through the forest, tearing a path of destruction straight through these very same trees. What type of power was necessary to topple and break such trees over? For a second, Max shuddered to himself thinking about the brute, almost unattainable power of the species.

Suddenly, Max was broken from his thoughts. He had heard noise from somewhere out in front of him. Holding his breath, the zoologist strained with his ears to listen. It was no use though. Whatever the hell it was, it was in fact too far away to discern. But as Max scooted himself forward ever so slightly, he was surprised to see that he had reached a slight hillside downward. But he was still too far away. He needed to get closer.

Still wanting to tuck himself as low to the forest floor as possible, Max was just about ready to crawl forward when he immediately caught himself. Max Caldwell knew more than anyone just how much the jungle came alive at night, and coming alive meant a host of poisonous and potentially deadly snakes, spiders, scorpions, and a host of other creepy crawlers that he wanted absolutely no part of. The last thing he wanted to do was go crawling around way out here alone on the ground. So he stood back up, but not all the way. Now he was moving forward slowly, almost in a sort of crouched down, crablike walk.

Noise again stopped him dead in his tracks. Now he knew with certainty that there was movement coming from just a ways ahead and down the hillside. Max had no way of knowing for certain what was up ahead, but in the dim green lighting of the night vision goggles, it appeared as though the trees stopped and there was a sloping hillside that led downward at a sharp angle.

If there in fact was a hillside, he wondered for a moment what type of condition the hillside would be in from all the rain. And then suddenly like something out a science fiction movie, he saw light rising up from just ahead. He lifted his night vision goggles up. As he did so, he was instantly thrust into a dark and silent world. It was amazing just how quickly the transformation had happened. Traverse through this dense forest with night vision goggles on, and you're fine, lift those goggles up, and suddenly one finds himself sitting alone in complete pitch blackness. It was an amazing thing to behold.

As Max continued to stare out ahead, he wanted to make sure that what he was indeed seeing was real and not some trick by the goggles. As he stood there in near blackout conditions, he saw what his eyes had originally noticed just seconds prior. Several bright beams of light were dancing rhythmically back and forth, penetrating the darkness that was the bamboo forest.

He suddenly found himself feeling nervous and jittery. He pulled the night vision goggles back down over his eyes. Instantly he was greeted with a phosphorescent neon green world. Tall slender stalks of bamboo trees crowded in tightly around him as he slowly began creeping forward.

Now Max was close to the end of a thick stand of bamboo trees. After that, the forest floor appeared to give way to a sloping hillside. As he drew closer, he was able to see the bright lights rising up from the canyon below. They danced back and forth, criss-crossed, and shined straight up toward the top of the trees. Max paused for a moment, practically at the end of the row of trees that started the descent down the hill.

He grumbled to himself. "Oh, the hell with it."

And then he got down on his hands and knees and began crawling as low to the ground as he could. When Max finally got to that final row of bamboo, he saw what had been responsible for the lights as well as the disturbance.

Down below him, probably a good hundred feet or so, at the base of the muddy and rain-drenched hillside stood three men. Now he had totally abandoned his own advice as he lay quietly on his stomach. Completely leaving himself unprotected for the moment, he had momentarily stowed the air rifle at his side. He slid himself forward along the ground, slithering and pulling himself through the low-lying growth and mud with the use of his elbows. Finally,

Max had managed to drag his body to the edge of the hillside. Again, the dancing beams of light caught his eye. And then suddenly, one of the beams danced his way. It was shining right at him.

Immediately, Max lay his body down completely in the mud, face and all. He remained there for what must have been close to a minute before finally mustering the courage to look up. With mud lining the right side of his face and from the secrecy of the ridge some one hundred feet above, Max watched the three men below through the night vision goggles.

They wore army fatigue clothing. Max also took note that they were staring down at a small screen. Perhaps they were examining their coordinates or something. Who the hell really knew? It was almost impossible to tell such a detail from where he was situated.

And then suddenly one of them whipped out a flashlight and pointed it in his direction once again. Not moving a muscle he simply just lay there, having serious doubts about his location and whereabouts. For a brief moment, he wondered if this had been a mistake to come way out here by himself to investigate. Meanwhile down below, he was finally able to hear the sound of voices.

Words were shouted and commands were being given. And then almost as if on cue, the rain started to pick back up again. Within a matter of seconds, fat heavy raindrops began coming down hard. He looked around him, failing to realize his error until it was too late. Water was rapidly beginning to puddle up everywhere and before Max Caldwell could put any further thought into this, the entire hillside suddenly gave way.

34

Through the thick sheets of rain, two cold and steely eyes stared out from the dark foliage at the three soldiers who stood in the middle of the small clearing. It watched as the mud around the men started to puddle, quickly forming small shallow pools of dark, churned-up water. The forest had suddenly been thrust into another torrential downpour.

Then the creature cocked its head up and looked at the darkened sky. It waited, waited, and waited some more. And then suddenly, for the briefest of seconds, the sky above lit up in a brilliant, magnificent white light as lightning crackled and sizzled. When it ended, the creature lowered its head and returned its gaze toward the three men. And there it waited a few more seconds before finally mounting its attack.

• • •

Decker Johnson saw his partner's eyes go wide with horror before it was too late. Turning around quickly while attempting to shove his rifle out in front of him, all Decker could see was an immense, rain-soaked image with a mouth gaping wide as it roared. He went to level his gun, but it was too late.

The massive figure hit Decker with the impact of a train colliding with a small car. Decker was instantly thrown backward, his body splashing down hard into the mud. Meanwhile, his two partners had been completely caught off guard. Shots were fired immediately, but through the thick sheets of rain, it was tough to make out much of anything.

Finn Carter managed to get a shot off right into the creature's right shoulder. The gigantopithecus blasted a deep guttural roar. Brig scrambled to his feet but slipped in a shallow puddle of water himself as the rain continued to pound down on them. The creature bounded toward the smoking rifle and swatted the gun from the man's hand as if it were but a mere toy.

And there in the mud, amidst the pounding rain, lightning, and the battering wind gusts, the small band of three realized they were in way over their heads. But most importantly, they realized that at this moment, they should never have come.

The gigantopithecus let out another unearthly roar as it bounded forward toward the man on whom it had initially launched its initial attack. Wasting no time, it opened its mouth wide and bit right into Decker's left leg. Teeth punctured through flesh, bone, and tendons as the powerful jaw muscles did their thing. The man's screams, however, were completely drowned out by the pounding of the rain.

Finn sloshed forward through the mud, steadied himself, and fired. He had intended to put a bullet into the back of the towering beast. But in the madness of it all, his left foot slipped out from underneath him. The shot had been an errant one. The gigantopithecus spun around so quickly that it caught both remaining men completely by surprise. The creature let out a cavernous roar, a nightmarish sound to hear from such close proximity.

Quickly, the gigantopithecus bit down on the fallen man's other leg. Then it raced forward toward the head. Reaching out with an enormous hand, it grabbed Decker Johnson by the left shoulder, and dragged the screaming man through the rain and mud and off into the dark and entangled forest.

35

"He couldn't have gone very far," Downs shouted from up ahead.

The thirty-one year old San Francisco native and team leader of this small wing of members of the Society of Cryptozoological Agents continued pushing furiously through the drenched jungle. They were looking for Max Caldwell. One minute, the young zoologist had been in the middle of their makeshift camp, and the next he was nowhere to be seen.

As Downs continued slogging his way through the wet and soggy terrain, he found it an odd sensation. The air rifle was slung over his right shoulder while the Astra was now leveled out in front of him. He was a bit stunned that lately he found himself feeling more at ease with the revolver pressed out in front rather than the tranquilizer gun. The Astra itself was capable of stopping a charging rhino.

Suddenly though, Downs held up his right hand in a closed fist. The team came to a stop. It was still raining hard. Off to the right and through the night vision goggles, Downs saw a hillside which shot up at a steep angle.

About twelve feet up on that sloping hillside lay a cluster of bamboo trees slumped over a rather large boulder. Downs continued to hold his right fist in a closed position while moving forward. The rest of the team meanwhile stayed put and remained on guard.

Downs saw a small growing pool of water accumulating at the base of the hillside. It couldn't have been more than half a foot in depth at best and probably ten feet or so in diameter, but it was growing larger by the minute. Again, Downs' eyes shot back up toward the steep hillside. Through the night vision goggles, his eyes focused in on the several bamboo trees that lay broken. Or had they been uprooted? Standing at the edge of the ever expanding pond, it appeared as though the bamboo trees had in fact been uprooted, and by the way that they were stacked one atop the other and slumped over against another tree, it seemed as though they had been rather violently uprooted at that, torn straight from the ground.

Downs paused there for a moment, deep in thought. And just as he turned around to face the others, the rain started to come down even harder now.

• • •

Max Caldwell's eyes fluttered open as the rain pounded down hard onto his face. A few seconds passed before he finally came to. He was lying somewhere close to the base of the steep and muddy hillside from where he had just tumbled down out of control. But he was lying in dense vegetation. Had he not been lying in deep foliage, he would have no doubt been spotted.

Rather quickly, his mind registered what had just happened. The muddy ledge at the top of the hillside where he had been lying on his stomach had become fully saturated, and as a result, had suddenly given way. Managing to sit himself upright, he was now covered from head to toe in mud. Surprisingly though, the fall down the muddy yet soft hillside had yielded what appeared to be zero injuries, albeit a few cuts and scrapes here and there. Reaching back toward his right shoulder, Max suddenly realized that the air rifle was gone. Somewhere in that out-of-control tumbling descent downward, the gun had been lost. He'd been lucky he hadn't shot himself with a dart in the process. But now he was out here all alone with absolutely zero protection.

His eyes had frantically gone searching back on the mud hillside when suddenly he heard the forest crackle to life from somewhere behind him. Max turned around and immediately stood to his feet. Now he heard movement and the cracking of bamboo from somewhere out in the dark passages of the forest. Suddenly, an immense bellowing roar cried out, followed by the staccato of gun fire. But what was more alarming was the fact that it had come from close range.

And here at the bottom of the small hillside, absolutely covered in mud from head to toe, Max Caldwell realized he should have never abandoned the others. He should have never left the safety that only a large group can offer. He knew this better than anyone. After all, he was a zoologist who had both read and studied wildebeest migration on the African continent. When wildebeest come to a river crossing full of crocodiles, one of their own has to be sacrificed and taken by the crocs in order for the mass of the herd to continue on. But the key here is that there is safety in numbers. For a brief second he thought about the three-time NBA Champion Golden State Warriors slogan: *STRENGTH IN NUMBERS*. How true that statement was.

Another cavernous roar rang out. The rain had just started to pick back up once again when suddenly he turned and began moving back toward the hillside. Quickly, he noted how the whole hillside had turned into soft, squishy mud with small streams of water cascading down it every which way. The area just to the left offered him a better chance of being able to scamper his way back up the hillside. There were small shrubs and tall stands of bamboo to pull oneself up with, and that's just where he was headed.

Just as Max had begun ascending the steep hillside, his ears were assaulted again with the sharp staccato of gunfire. This was followed by one last deep and monstrous roar. He needed to quickly get back to the others. Safety in numbers.

• • •

Brig Daniels and Finn Carter stood breathing heavily in the middle of a dense stand of bamboo wondering just what in the hell they had gotten themselves into? Looking up toward the darkened sky, they knew that there would be no let-up in the rain. It didn't take a meteorologist to figure that out.

Together, the team of two had pursued the creature into the deeper passages of the jungle, but eventually the conditions as well as the confusion from being trapped inside the tall stands of bamboo had won out. And there they remained, breathing heavily while scanning with their rifles, both barrels still smoking.

"Fuck," Finn said, his voice having to talk louder than normal on account of the rain. "Did you see the way that thing moved?"

There was no reply from Brig though. The 5'10" two hundred sixty pound bruiser of a man was too busy thinking, calculating things, weighing their options.

"Well, I'll tell ya one thing," Finn said, still continuing to talk. "I think we got us a bloody battle on our hands."

Finn Carter appeared to be rattled, talking merely for the sake of talking, trying to fill the awkward space that existed between the two with words. Or perhaps his rambling had come from just having seen his teammate be dragged off screaming through the mud and into the trees.

Brig nodded his head quietly to himself, but again there was no reply from the man. He had seen the sheer size of the animal as well as the way that it had manhandled their partner, and in such abysmal conditions. They were on its terrain now, its home court. He couldn't even begin to fathom what the strength and sheer brute power of the creature would be in drier, easier-to-move conditions.

As Brig Daniels stood there grinding his teeth and chewing at his lower lip, a habit that his wife had worked tirelessly on ridding him of, he knew full well what they were up against. And now their numbers had been reduced to two. So far, things weren't looking good.

"What'll we do?" Finn asked as he now turned and faced in the direction of his partner.

Brig let out a deep breath as he stared up at the black sky. There was most definitely no break from the damn rain and the conditions around them were only getting worse by the second. The place was turning into a fucking bloody swamp right before their very eyes.

Finally, Brig spoke. "We go after the damn creature as planned."

He looked over at Finn. The way that his partner was holding his rifle made it seem as though he was ready to fire at anything that moved.

Trigger happy son of a bitch, Brig thought to himself.

Finally Brig spoke. "Remember, we need to capture one of these things alive, not dead."

Brig motioned with his hand to the tranquilizer guns holstered at both of their sides. When the correct moment presented itself, they needed to put several darts into one of these towering beasts in order to render them incapacitated. The bullets from their rifles were only supposed to be used for their own protection and to possibly hinder or slow one of these beasts as best as they could. Their Russian contacts were going to pay them top dollar for delivery of a live gigantopithecus.

Brig Daniels said no more as the rain continued to come down in thick sheets. He looked down at the mud quickly puddling at their feet. This forest had literally been transformed into a shallow swampland.

Things had become so bad that even Finn broke his gaze from the forest in order to have a quick peek at the conditions. This was getting uglier by the second.

• • •

Stacey Winston sat Indian style in the middle of his tent as the wind continued to whip the sides of it back and forth. Hunched over his laptop, he was now seeing the footage that he had shot earlier in the day uninterrupted for the first time. Stacey grabbed his chest for a moment and pulled his body back. The footage was beyond incredible—absolutely life-changing in every sense of the word. He paused the video and closed the laptop for a moment. It was stunning and had literally taken the wind from his lungs. For a moment, he struggled to recapture his breath. Meanwhile outside, the small tent continued to be battered by the powerful downpour, but surprisingly things were staying dry and comfortable inside. He was grateful for that.

Stacey looked to his right. Bob and Diane were holed up in the neighboring tent. He wondered for a moment how they felt about him. Did they buy the bullshit story he had given them earlier? He shrugged his shoulders. He couldn't control that right now. He knew that much at least. So Stacey put his attention back on the laptop once again and cracked it open.

Boy, it's really coming down out there.

Stacey hit the button and let the video play. The footage proved that the largest ape that ever lived was in fact very much still alive. But most important to Stacey was what the footage meant to him personally.

This content had the ability to officially put him on the map. With the successful completion of this documentary, he'd be at the helm of his first full-length feature film in no time. Fame and fortune would soon follow. It wouldn't be long now. He kept telling himself that over and over like a broken record, but it had been a record that he had been listening to for the better part of his adult life. He was ready for it to finally come true. He was ready to finally break out of mediocrity once and for all.

Beyond the glitz and glamour of Hollywood, suddenly a more serious question came to mind. How would Stacey get this footage out to the world without essentially incriminating himself in the process? After all, he had witnessed the bludgeoning death of one of his colleagues first hand and had done little to stop it. Well, that was partially true. He witnessed the man being dragged off. For a moment, he recalled the way that Clark's horrifying scream had cut off abruptly. That could only mean one thing. He had more than likely been killed out in the deep and entangled foliage.

But as Stacey un-paused the video, he realized the footage was something he had waited the better part of his adult life for. Hell, he probably had waited the majority of his entire lifetime for a moment like this. Call it luck, call it fate, this was Stacey Winston's moment, and he was fully intent on capitalizing on this moment. He wanted to parlay what would more than likely be fifteen minutes of fame into a lifetime of movie-making opportunities.

Stacey suddenly shut the laptop back down once again. He listened for a moment, pressing his ear up against the fabric that made up the side of the tent. He thought he had heard something, something beyond the pounding of the rain and the battering of the wind gusts.

With the laptop now closed shut, Stacey placed his ear back against the side of the tent and listened. He could feel the gentle vibrations of the fat raindrops as they thumped down hard against the tent. Stacey shook his head quietly to himself. Was he hearing things? How in the hell could he have thought he had heard something, when all his ears could process and make out was this godforsaken awful storm? As far as audible sounds went, there simply wasn't much room for anything else out there.

Stacey brought his ear away from the side of the tent and returned to the laptop once more. Just about ready to crack the computer back open, he again thought he heard the noise. Stacey paused right where he was. Now he was certain that the sound had stirred from just outside the tent. It most certainly hadn't come from the rain, and it damn well hadn't come from the bamboo trees rubbing and swaying against one another. It had come from something else.

Stacey felt his heart beating against his ribcage as he quietly turned the camera on. He placed it up against the side of the tent. Maybe he could even find a way to work in some nice audio to the documentary. The rain and the wind would add for some awesome effects at the beginning of this film.

Out of nowhere though, Stacey switched the camera off and quickly scooted himself back to the middle of the tent. Suddenly he felt scared. The hairs on the back of his neck now stood on end. Meanwhile outside, the rain continued to pound the small tent. Again, Stacey placed his ear up against the side of the tent and listened. It took a moment, but suddenly he heard it. Now he was certain that something was moving about outside. And judging by the sound of it, it sounded like something fairly large.

With his ear still up against the tent, Stacey yelled out to the others. "Guys, are you there?"

He waited. When no reply came from the neighboring tent, he tried once more, this time louder. "Guys, are you there?"

Nothing but the rain and wind greeted his ears though. And then he heard it again. This time it was much closer though. Stacey once again scooted himself away from the side of the tent, positioning his body in the dead center of the tent close to where the equipment lay. Now all he could do was wait, listen, and wonder just what in the hell was responsible for the noise outside.

36

Downs and the team had been searching for going on a good half an hour or so before the forest finally started to offer up some clues. Downs crouched next to a footprint in the mud that they had literally almost walked right on by. Now the others had gathered next to him. Whether out of old age or just pure stubbornness, Burr Wellington stood a ways behind the group, keeping watch, scanning the dark forest with his eyes. Thankfully, the rain had subsided. Now was the time when they were starting to feel the lingering effects of not having the ability to be in touch via the radios. But still, Downs wondered if the man was hurt and in need of their help. He wondered a lot of things to himself.

Burr stood with the air rifle secure in both hands, the Astra holstered at his side.

"This track is new," Josiah said, the paleontologist crouching down just to the left of Downs.

"So is this one," Tori said pointing.

From where Downs remained crouched, he managed to turn himself ninety degrees to his left. Now they were looking at another footprint off the mud trail and a few feet inside the vegetation line. Carefully, Downs brushed away several leaves. Tori pulled away what other forest matter had accumulated in and around the area. And before any of them realized it, they were staring at an enormous footprint. No one said a word. The footprint was most definitely the largest track that Downs had ever seen in person, and it was honestly something that Burr Wellington had spent the last three decades searching for.

"A living fossil," Josiah muttered to himself.

"Indeed," Burr said, the big man now hovering closely behind the group, staring down intensely at the massive footprint. "Would ya look at the size of that thing? Jesus Christ."

Downs laid his outstretched hand out toward the footprint. It was more than double the size of his outstretched hand.

"Just what in the hell are we up against?" Josiah muttered to himself.

Downs straightened himself. "I think it's quite obvious. We've seen the immense size of the creature, witnessed first hand its speed and strength, and now we're gettin' our first up close and personal view of just how enormous this animal truly is."

"I'm not certain I want to get much closer," Tori said, looking Downs' way. "I've got a second book to pen after all."

Downs smiled as he put a hand on her shoulder. "Definitely. Don't worry, we'll be home in no time and you can continue kicking ass in the publishing world. We'll find a way to get through this shit."

She smiled at him for a moment and then returned her gaze to the enormous footprint.

Suddenly, Burr shifted his enormous frame and turned himself around. Something was moving out there. The entire team had also heard it as they stood to their feet. With the air rifles raised, the team made a tight circular formation. Now they had eyes on every corner of the forest.

Whatever it was had come to a stop out there. Now there was only silence. With the rain having monentarily subsided, the forest now had a soft hum to it as the bamboo trees knocked against one another. The result of this was a relaxing, almost meditative sound that seemed to sweep through all corners of the forest as the trees continued to rock back and forth.

With his eyes still scanning, Downs picked up movement from off in the bamboo somewere. To Downs' left stood Tori, and to his right stood Jeremiah. Whatever was out there appeared now to be heading straight for Jeremiah.

"Hold your positions," Burr grumbled. "The attack often comes from the side you least expect."

"He's right," Downs fired back. "Hold tight."

Now it did appear with certainty that the noise was coming straight for Jeremiah. The forest was quickly converging upon the small team as things continued to bend and snap.

Still employing the service of the night vision goggles, Downs could see nothing but the neon green world and the tall stands of bamboo trees. Visually there was nothing more than that, but audibly the sounds coming straight for them were now louder than ever.

And then suddenly, everything died down. Downs turned his head ever so slightly toward the area of the forest that lay out in front of Jeremiah. But then rather quickly, he returned it straight ahead. Burr was right. Often times the attack came from the side that you least expected, the other notable sounds simply serving as the distraction, deterring the harsh reality of what was ultimately to come.

The silence must have lasted for another thirty seconds or so before noise stirred once again. But this time, the noise was not faint and distant. This time, it appeared to be coming from within fifty yards of where they stood.

Out amongst the entangled labyrinth of bamboo, something was moving rather quickly through the trees. The sounds of feet crunching down on leafy forest matter were almost upon the team when Downs noticed the slightest change. The noise that was making its way toward Jeremiah now appeared to be making a beeline straight for Downs.

Immediately, Downs began to unclip the Astra at his side. Burr's eyes flicked downward, the big man instantly taking note of this.

"Hold tight," Burr said. "She's almost upon us."

Downs hardly had time to level the Astra out in front of him before a shadowy figure emerged quickly.

"Don't shoot!" the voice cried, "don't freaking shoot!"

Downs felt his eyes go wide on him before barking out the next orders. "Lower your weapons!"

Before them stood a very wet, muddy, and disheveled Max Caldwell. The San Francisco zoologist looked as though he had literally been to hell and back. And for all intents and purposes, he had.

Downs faced the tranquilizer rifle down toward the ground as he spoke. "Max, what the fuck were you thinkin' runnin' off like that? Are you outta your mind? You could've been killed!"

There was no reply from Max; rather, he just kept moving forward, kept shuffling his way through the trees until finally he was standing an arms-length away from the team. Now the others had their first good look at him. Covered head to toe in mud, he was also bleeding from several locations. Immediately, Tori laid her pack down on the ground and began to pull out the first aid kit. Max's injuries were minor at best, but still she wanted to err on the side of caution. Minor gashes could turn into serious infections way out here in the fucking middle of nowhere. That's how it worked.

Meanwhile, Tori quickly went to work cleaning the zoologist up as best as she could. When all was done, and she had returned him to good working order, the zoologist was finally ready to speak.

37

The first words out of Max Caldwell's mouth were a befuddled mixture of stuttering, rambling, and what appeared to be utter confusion. At first, the zoologist made absolutely no sense whatsoever, but as he started to calm down, eventually a sense of normalcy had returned.

Downs stepped forward. He grabbed the frightened man by the shoulders and spoke directly at him. "Max, don't ever fuckin' do that again! Understood?"

In all the time that Max Caldwell had known Downs, he had never actually seen Bick Downs be so visibly forceful and aggressive to him, but he understood what was meant.

The team had stepped into an open area away from where they were originally in their tight circular formation. Now, with a bit more room to move about, Max decided it was time to speak.

"Bick, um, thanks for that," Max began. "What I did was both foolish and stupid and I shouldn't have done it."

Max looked over at Burr. The large man had the air rifle stowed at his side while he folded his large and imposing arms. With the night vision goggles on,

Burr looked like a combination of NFL linebacker meets cryptozoologist. Max was thankful to have such a hulking figure on his side.

Max continued. "Well, to be honest with you guys, I felt I had been hearing things all day. Strange sounds. A twig breaking here, a branch snapping there. Sounds that signaled that we weren't alone."

Josiah laughed. "Well, there's the shock of the century."

Max managed a smile. "But as I was saying, I began hearing distant sounds in the forest. Sounds that signaled the presence of other humans in this forest."

Downs nodded.

"The documentary film crew?" Burr asked from the back.

Max shook his head no.

"Maybe it is the film crew," Tori said. "I mean, after all, that's the reason we're all here. Why we've come all this way around the world."

Again, Max shook his head.

"Then who?" Jeremiah asked.

"Others," Max replied.

Downs didn't like where the conversation seemed to be heading. "Max, just what in the hell are you gettin' at?"

Max cleared his throat. "Not sure exactly, just that I made my way to a large hillside, crept close to the edge, and down below I saw what looked like a small team of military men."

Burr snorted in disapproval. "Military men, you say."

Max nodded. "Um, team of three dressed in all black, heavily armed. I heard the faint sound of rotor wash. Must've been dropped into this place via helicopter."

For a moment, not a word was said. Suddenly the forest had an eerie silence to it. Downs picked up on this. He quickly held up his hand in a closed fist. The team once again assembled into a tight circular formation. Now with their weapons raised, they watched, waited, and listened to the forest around them.

This time, it was Burr who had the pleasure of having the forest come alive right in front of him. There was an immense sound of bamboo being cracked and splintered.

"Jesus Christ," Burr shouted over the ruckus.

This was followed by a deep and unearthly roar, and then those sounds of distant cracking began moving toward the group at a more frantic pace.

"Look out!" Burr shouted at the last second.

Whatever it was had literally come out of nowhere. With no time to regather themselves, the team scattered in all directions. Now there was chaos everywhere. Voices shouted and screamed, and behind all of it was the sound of something massive as it moved about out in the trees.

Downs bounded quickly to his left. He did so just in time to catch a glimpse of an impossibly large creature as it bounded forward on all fours, tore up a handful of ferns in anger, and then beat aggressively on its wide chest while roaring before rearing up onto its back two legs.

Through the night vision goggles, Downs felt his eyes go wide on him as he tucked himself behind the base of a bamboo tree. Peeking his head out, he watched as Burr fired a dart into the immense, roaring beast. From where Downs stood, it was anyone's guess if the shot had actually been an accurate one or not.

Downs wasn't going to stand around and watch the action. Quickly, he began moving through the trees, dodging tall bamboo trees left and right. Now the gigantopithecus had turned its full attention to Burr. Lowering itself onto all fours, the massively-built creature let out another deep and ungodly roar from its chest cavity before taking off after the man.

"Burr, get the hell outta there!" Downs shouted. "Retreat!"

Managing to weave his way through the trees, Downs got himself to within fifty yards of the rampaging animal. He knew he was just out of range for the air rifle. But on the other hand, the Astra was still holstered at his side. Quickly, Downs pulled the revolver out and aimed. It was too chaotic though and the gigantopithecus was moving too fast through the trees, its huge body literally plowing a wake of destruction straight toward Burr Wellington.

Downs now found himself moving quickly through the trees in pursuit of both man and beast. Out of the corner of both eyes, he could see the silhouettes of his teammates running close, snaking their own paths through the seemingly endless maze of bamboo. Things were happening too fast at this point to officially make sense of who was doing what.

Downs continued onward. He managed to hurtle a rather large bamboo tree that had fallen and lay slumped over on the ground.

That was a close one.

Onward he ran. Up ahead he could still see Burr Wellington, the two hundred and fifty pound Washington native surprisingly navigating his way rather easily through the trees. That's not what had Downs worried as he continued though. What had him worried was that he had lost sight of the giganto-pithecus. The giant beast had momentarily disappeared back into the brush.

The sharp staccato of gunfire erupted on Downs' right side. The sheer barrage and intensity of it had startled the living shit out of him as it continued to ring out from somewhere in the dark passages of the forest.

"What the fuck," Downs mumbled as he kept his pace up.

More gunfire erupted from the deeper parts of the forest. It most definitely hadn't come from Burr or Downs. It sounded like high-powered assault rifles or something to that nature. There was nothing more that scared Bick Downs in this world than that of guns, but primarily the savage violence that often surrounded it. In the age of terrorism, mass shootings, and school shootings, Downs was constantly aware of how vulnerable an unarmed individual was in comparison to an individual armed with a high-powered assault rifle. But Downs wasn't exactly unarmed. He had the air rifle slung over his shoulder and the Astra now leveled out in front of him when he came to a full stop, breathing hard as his chest heaved in and out. Through the night vision goggles, he scanned in all directions. This time, the barrage of gunfire echoed from what appeared to be straight ahead. The sudden assault of bullets had come from the direction from where Burr had been chased off. Immediately, an uneasy feeling began to settle in Downs' stomach as the rest of the team quickly arrived at his side.

To the left of Downs emerged Jeremiah and Max, and on the right side came Tori and Josiah. Quickly, the team gathered tightly together, reunited once again as gunfire continued to go off.

Downs turned to Max. "How many did you say you saw in that team?"

Max held up three fingers.

Downs took a moment to process the information and then returned his gaze toward where Burr had run off.

"Do we think he made it?" Tori asked, her voice brimming with worry and concern.

Jeremiah fixed his gaze in the same direction as Downs. "Knowing the Burr Wellington that I know, I'd say he's fine. He's probably holed up somewhere right now behind a stand of bamboo trees. He'll be fine. But we need to get to him sooner rather than later."

Downs nodded. It all sounded fine and dandy, but the way that the gigantopithecus moved was something to behold. The speed, power, and ferocity with which the animal dominated and manhandled its way through this forest was not something that any of them had ever seen before. The animal seemed capable of tearing a path of destruction straight through the trees if it so desired.

Suddenly, noise from somewhere close by caught their attention. Meanwhile, more gunfire rang out from a little ways ahead. Downs turned and snapped his fingers. Jeremiah and Josiah knew instantly what was meant by the command.

As gunfire continued erupting, Downs, Tori, and Max maintained their positioning toward where the forest continued to crackle with life. With the possibility that the gigantopithecus was still close by, and the fact that unknown gunfire was going off, Downs was feeling increasingly uncomfortable about the growing situation. And with the whereabouts of Burr still unknown, that meant that Downs was the only one in possession of a lethal weapon at this point.

Now they had other parties on the scene, and at the moment that party most definitely had the upper hand. As Downs stood there, amidst the tall trees and the rain-soaked vegetation, he wondered how quickly they could get to Burr? As the sound of more gunfire continued to ring out from the dark parts of the forest, he realized that they didn't have a moment to spare.

38

Burr Wellington found himself wincing in quite a bit of pain and discomfort as he continued crawling on his hands and knees through the forest. Down here on the forest floor, things were quite a bit sharper, pricklier, and pointier than one would expect. Pain seared and burned from his midsection. As he looked down at his shirt, he could see the huge long diagonal tear in the fabric. It was a good-sized tear, probably somewhere in the neighborhood of six to seven inches in length. For a moment, he found himself thinking about the real problem that lay beneath that fabric. How badly was he injured? Burr winced through the burning pain as he continued crawling a few more feet. Then he came to a stop, rested his back up against a tree, and took a much-needed moment to catch his breath.

His head was spinning as he tried to take it all in. For a moment he thought about what he had just done not more than five minutes or so ago. Somewhere in the madness of getting cut and ripped wide open by a piece of sharp bamboo, he had passed by a tree that lay slumped over and broken, propped up on three other trees that grew in a tight configuration to one another.

At the base of those trees lay a thick clustering of heavy fern growth. Burr had quickly hidden his flare gun and a half a dozen or so extra flare gun cartridges in and amongst all that thick growth at the base of the trees and then staggered his way out of there. The heavy barrage of gunfire ringing throughout the forest had him on edge, and if for some reason or another he suddenly found himself overpowered and outmanned out here, at least he'd have a place to return to in order to once again potentially arm himself. He was giving himself a backup plan, a second option.

Now he continued to sit with his back up against a tree as he struggled to regain his breath. The air rifle was slung over his left shoulder and the Astra was at his side. Burr realized just how quiet the forest had grown as he began the painful process of lifting his shirt up. Gritting his teeth together and wincing through more pain, he lifted his shirt to have a look. Still wearing the night vision goggles, he could see a horizontal gash across what was essentially his abdomen. It didn't look as bad as he had initially thought and the blood had already caked around the wound, but still he needed to get cleaned up. But the team's official first aid pack was back with Tori. Hell, he didn't even have his own drinking water now that he thought about it. They had left so abruptly that his backpack was back at their makeshift camp.

Burr let out a groan as he looked down at his abdomen. The gash was roughly five inches in length, and probably a good inch or so in thickness. Over the years, Burr had gotten himself into some pretty serious injuries on account of his delving into the world of cryptozoology. But the one thing that he had learned time and time again while out in the field was to clean, disinfect, and properly bandage all wounds.

As a result, Burr always carried two band-aids and a tiny, travel-sized tube of Neosporin in his back right pocket. He wondered if in the madness of it all, those three items were still there. With more discomfort, Burr propped himself up and reached into his back right pocket. Yep, just as he had left it. He pulled out the small tube followed by the two band-aids.

He began to take in the forest for a moment. Just to his left was a rather long frond from a good-sized fern. With a little effort, he reached out with his left hand and pulled the green piece of vegetation back. The thing was teeming with moisture.

Burr scooted himself into position. More pain followed, but somehow he managed to get his shirt off. Then he took the shirt and began to take the delicate moisture that existed at the pointed downward edges of the frond and began working the water onto his shirt. Now Burr pulled his body back toward the base of the tree and began to take the damp shirt and wipe and clean around the edges of the wound.

He winced in pain as he did so. The wet shirt was doing its thing though. Burr now had the cut cleaned as best as he could muster out here. He opened the small tube of Neosporin and quickly began to spread the ointment over the wound. Burr kept repeating this until he finally had a nice, thin layer of ointment spread across the entire wound. Then Burr pulled out the first of the band-aids. He was determined to get himself cleaned up as best as he could out here.

He was just about to peel back the second band-aid when a snapping sound from somewhere close by stopped him dead in his tracks. Burr froze. Slowly, he unclipped the Astra from his side.

• • •

Brig Daniels and Finn Carter stood completely surrounded on all sides by dense, wet foliage. They were amazed at just how tight and constrictng their current surroundings had become. It was hard to say just how many rounds they had unloaded. The one thing they could say with certainty was that the short, yet intense barrage seemed like a mini-war to both men.

Brig broke out one of his Cuban cigars and now began chewing on the thing back and forth in his mouth. As he continued to chew on the thing, his mind started to wander. Perhaps they had unloaded too much of a barrage. After all, the mission objective was to capture one of these creatures alive, not dead. Although Brig would never let on to his partner Finn, perhaps even he too was feeling a bit scared considering what they had just seen happen to Decker Johnson. As his thoughts continued to consume him, Finn spoke up.

"What now?" Finn asked.

There was no reply from Brig. The man only replied when he had something to say. Talking merely for the sake of talking had never been his thing. Years of experience out in the field had also taught Brig Daniels not to rush to conclusions, to wait things out, and that patience wasn't necessarily a virtue but more of a necessity. The two of them had all the time in the world. If the creature had in fact been hit, then they needed to find their way to it ASAP and patch it up. If they could in fact pull this off and deem that the animal was in good working order, they would tranquilize it. However on the other hand, if the barrage of bullets had in fact killed the creature, then Brig quickly calculated they'd have to find themselves another specimen. Regardless of which scenario would in fact eventually come true, they had options.

Brig scanned their surroundings for a moment. He didn't care much for where they currently found themselves. Truth be told, he never really did. What the ex-professional rugby player cared about was not necessarily accepting missions, but more importantly executing and completing them. He liked the idea of seeing something through from beginning to completion. That's what he got a rise out of. That's what kept him coming back time and time again. The decent paydays that he'd received over the years didn't hurt either. Over the years, Brig had built himself a nice nest egg in the bank from missions such as the one he was currently undertaking.

Finn began pacing back and forth nervously now. His thoughts immediately went back toward their partner Decker Johnson. The last time either of them had seen the man, he was being dragged, screaming on his back through the mud and rain before disappearing into the deep dark vegetation.

It all seemed so distant and otherworldly, like that horrifying scene that had just played out in his head had been from some type of horror movie he had just seen. But it had happened, and now here they found themselves, halfway across the world, in the middle of some rain-drenched, humid, godforsaken jungle. Finn was well attuned to the fact that the hellholes of the world weren't the deserts or the oceans, or the frigid and frozen tundras of the Arctic; they were the jungles, the rainforests of the world. Places where leech-filled bogs were infinite, disfiguring diseases loomed, and millions upon millions of things merely wanted to feast on warm human flesh. Finn knew with certainty that the jungles of the world were where hell truly existed.

When the silence had finally won out between the two men, Finn decided to put an end to it. He spoke through gritted teeth. "And Decker, what about him?"

Brig took the cigar out of his mouth and took a deep breath in through his nose and let it out slowly through his mouth. Brig Danels was not one for idle chit-chat. When the man did speak, there was both sense and wisdom in his words, but more significantly, there was purpose and drive. But still, at this juncture in the game, Finn could have made do with any talk; the silence of the jungle was driving him mad. All around the two men was the constant drone and chattering of insects. To Finn, it was another painful reminder that they had been dropped smack dab into the middle of hell.

To Finn's surprise though, Brig spoke up. "We need to begin to accept that the worst has happened. Begin to make preparations for what is to come."

Finn felt his lower lip drop a bit. "Huh?"

Brig turned slowly and stared at his partner. To Finn, it felt as though the large, bald man was peering through his soul. "Look, we exhaust all resources. Go in search of Decker, just bloody saying at this point we need to be realistic as well. He may be a goner."

Finn nodded. For the most part, he held the same sentiment as Brig, but still, human nature was human nature, and he was holding out hope that their partner might still be alive somewhere in this godforsaken place. But it was a slim chance at best and he knew that. After all, they had both witnessed the size and strength of the creature that had dragged Decker off.

The sound of labored breathing from somewhere off to the left suddenly caught their attention. Immediately, they pressed forward, moving stealthily through the forest, snaking their way through the endless web of tall, slender bamboo trees. As they did so their feet crunched down on the forest floor matter. Neither man had ever seen anything like this place. It was a bit surreal to be moving through what seemed like a primeval landscape, a virgin world of forest seemingly untouched and unblemished by modern man's hand. Plant life was everywhere, flourishing, thriving.

Suddenly, Brig held up his right hand and formed a closed fist. Behind him, Finn came to a stop.

And there the two remained in silence for some thirty seconds before the sound of movement could be heard out from behind Finn. Finn felt the hairs on his arms stand on end. But as he stared over at at his partner, he could see the big man hadn't even so much as flinched at the sound. His attention was focused straight ahead toward a patch of waist-high vegetation.

Meanwhile, Finn had swung his neck around a few inches to have a look behind him. When he straightened himself and returned his gaze out ahead where Brig was staring, he heard the noise that had initially stopped them in the first place.

Truth be told, Brig Daniels honestly had no clue at this point just what in the hell lay in front of them, just that they had to keep moving forward, had to keep investigating the living hell out of this forest. Brig motioned with his hand and the two started up moving once again.

• • •

Burr Wellington slowly reached down with his right hand toward the Astra. Carefully, he unclipped the gun and had just pulled it ever so slightly from the holster when he realized his mistake. He was too late. With a rather frightened look on his face, the fifty-eight year old Burr Wellington saw two powerful figures emerge silently from the foliage.

"Don't!" a commanding voice said, the order coming from none other than Brig Daniels.

Burr felt his eyes go wide on him as he sat shirtless at the base of the bamboo tree. Meanwhile, a second large and imposing figure emerged from the dark foliage. Finn Carter trampled through the low-lying ferns and reached for Burr's revolver. Brig stepped forward and placed the barrel of his rifle inches from Burr's face. Burr may have been one stubborn son of a bitch, but he was certainly no fool. He also knew when he was outmanned, and right now he was most definitely outmanned. Two men both similar in weight to himself stood before him, and they were each heavily armed.

With a grumble and a shake of the head, Burr watched as Finn swooped down and took possession of both the air rifle and the Astra. In that moment, Burr Wellington knew that he had made a big, big mistake. His mistake was not necessarily letting his guard down, but putting himself in a defenseless position where he was vulnerable. And at the base of the bamboo tree, seated in the mud, injured across his abdomen, Burr was as vulnerable as a newborn straight out of the womb.

"Get up," Brig said as he forcefully jammed the barrel of the rifle into Burr's shoulder.

With a bit of struggle, Burr stood to his feet. As he did so, Finn came from behind and pulled the big man's hands behind his back. Quickly, he bound them together with a crude rope. Now standing on two feet, Burr wasn't necessarily accustomed to being around people who were equal in weight to him. And the two men who had now taken him captive were younger than he was, probably stronger, outnumbered him, and were armed to the hilt.

"Who are you?" Burr asked as he was now moving through the forest and walking with the two men. Finn Carter stood behind the bare chested man with the butt of his rifle jabbed into his lower back.

Burr had intended the question for Brig. Although Burr was now in serious trouble and most definitely feared gravely for his safety, he was still able to gather who was in charge here.

"Just keep moving," Brig spoke with the cigar still clenched firmly between his teeth, his voice showing not an ounce of care or concern whatsoever for the large man.

Burr didn't listen. "I'll ask again. Who are you?"

Finn was still behind Burr as they continued making their way through the forest. With the butt of his rifle, Finn Carter struck Burr square in the back. The fifty-eight year old Washington native took the hit, winced to himself, and continued marching forward silently through the jungle.

39

Quietly, Stacey Winston unzipped his tent and made his way out into the night air. He was instantly plunged into an inky black darkness that surrounded him on all sides. His feet squished down in the mud as he carefully went about the task of zipping the tent back up. He didn't want any water or moisture disturbing any of the precious camera and computer equipment inside, not to mention the myriad of insects. Once the tent was zipped up nice and tight, Stacey began the short walk over toward Bob and Diane's tent.

With each step, he could literally feel the damp and moist earth beneath him moving and shifting. No part of the forest seemed solid and firm anymore. Everything was now a dripping, soggy, and squishy mess as water teemed and puddled from what seemed like every corner of this place. At least for the moment, the rainstorm had subsided. It had only been about twenty feet or so between the tents, but through the mud, it felt like three times that. Stacey finally arrived at Bob and Diane's tent.

Rather than just barge right on in, Stacey opted for knocking on the back of the tent. Actually it was kind of weird, the idea of knocking on a tent. As he did so, his hand pushed inward into the nylon fabric, barely even producing an audible sound. "Guys, are y'all there?"

He stepped back for a moment and waited. When no response came, he found himself looking around, looking up at the forest canopy. For some odd reason, Stacey suddenly turned his headlamp off. The act was instantaneous, and he wasn't quite certain why he had done so in the first place. Perhaps it was the creative person in him, always wanting to see things from a new angle or different light if you will, or perhaps it was something that all kids wonder when they go to bed— do monsters really exist? Whatever the reason, the minute that he had made the decision to flick the headlamp off, he literally plunged himself into the blackness as dark jungle surrounded him on all sides. He stood there for a moment, soaking it all in, completely surrounded by utter darkness. Stacey couldn't even see his outstretched fingers in front of his face. Dark jungle pressed on him from all sides now.

He heard a soft hooting sound. It had come from somewhere close by. Then there was silence. He strained with his ears to listen. Again, the soft hooting sound called out. It seemed like it had come from up high in one of the trees. Perhaps it had been an owl or something. Whatever it was, Stacey suddenly flicked his headlamp back on. He felt much better about things now. There was something about the mere act of bringing light into the equation that had a profound warm and comforting effect on the human spirit.

And then Stacey realized that no response had come from the tent. This time, he'd be more direct.

Stacey made his way to the front entrance of the tent and tapped on the fabric with his knuckles. "Guys, are you there? It's me."

This time the response was immediate. From inside the tent, Stacey could hear a very worked up and frustrated person unzipping the thing. Stacey stepped back. Just as he did so, he saw Diane's head pop out. But she hadn't unzipped the tent all the way. Rather, she had only unzipped it enough so as to allow for her head to pop outside.

Now she glared back at him. "Listen, pal."

Despite their controversial back and forth relationship, Stacey was still somewhat caught off guard by the tone and ferocity in the woman's tone.

Diane continued. "Some of us are trying to get some much-needed shut eye over here. We heard you whispering earlier. Didn't feel like answering, so go back to your tent, tinker with your footage, take a fucking hike through the woods. Just don't bother my ass when I'm trying to get some much-needed beauty rest. Understood?"

And with that, Diane Clor pulled her head back inside the tent and zipped the thing up. Stacey stood half-stunned, half-frozen at what he had just experienced. Since when did she talk to him like that, with such ferocity and aggression? After all, he was the director of this project. For a moment, he thought about banging on the tent again to give her a piece of his mind. But then a warm and placid calmness washed over him. He didn't need her. Hell, he didn't even really need Bob for that matter. With the footage that had already been shot, he could simply get background footage at this point, add in some voiceovers once he got back in the studio, and bada bing bada boom, he'd have one helluva documentary. And then that would be it. It wouldn't be the longest documentary, but Stacey believed at this point in time that he could stretch the thing to one hour if he had to. He had no clue when the thing would air on T.V. or which channel would in fact pick it up, but with the footage that he had, the networks would be lining up to talk to him. He was certain. And following all of this would be the chance to direct his first full-length feature film. It wouldn't be long now. He just had to get through all this shit first.

Stacey took one last look at the tent and then stuck his middle finger out at it. How dare she speak to him like that! Again, he felt like ripping his way into the tent and giving Diane a piece of his mind. But he shook his head quietly to himself. He knew it ultimately served no purpose, served no benefit in moving the documentary forward. One day soon, when he found himself on the set of his first huge blockbuster movie, he'd have a good laugh about this very night. This he was certain of, and Stacey had already committed it to memory. Give it about five years or so, and he would have quite a laugh about this very night. But alas, he was getting quite ahead of himself. One thing at a time. Letting out a deep breath, he was just about to begin trudging through the mud back to his own tent.

When Stacey went to move, however, he found his feet were dug into the mud more than he had anticipated. Suddenly, he found himself listing to one side. Reaching out with his left hand, he thought he could stop the process. He was wrong. He toppled over onto his side and fell right where he was in the mud. His head collided with something hard and he blacked out.

• • •

Seated in a shallow puddle of water, Stacey Winston felt a sudden jolt to his body as he sat upright quickly. It had been the type of jolt you get when you are suddenly ripped from a dream or a nightmare and wake up too quickly. For a moment, he simply sat there, enshrouded on all sides by thick vegetation and dark jungle. His eyes continued to take it all in while his brain did his best to make sense of everything. Things seemed to be a jumbled and cloudy mess up there but slowly he started to feel the gears churning.

The first thought that came to him was a rather lazy one. He was seated alone in the pitch black surrounded on all sides by dark jungle. Reaching up to his forehead, he felt around with his hand. His headlamp appeared to have momentarily gone out on him. Oh fuck. With no light, he was completely and utterly without vision, enraptured in a world of inky blackness. Again he reached up with his right hand, his outstretched fingers making contact with the headlamp. He tapped several times at it. To his surprise, the light came back on. For a second, he'd thought the battery had gone out on him. He allowed himself to breathe a big sigh of relief. He absolutely could not fathom the idea of being trapped alone out here in pitch black surrounded on all sides by the tall trees.

For now though he had the light back on, and for that he was eternally grateful. He swiveled his head back and forth to gain a better semblance of just where in the hell he was. He was lying in a shallow pool of brackish colored water. Vegetation and ferns grew out of the small water source. As he looked around more, he was able to gather that he wasn't in a pond or a river system at all; he was merely in a large accumulation of water on account of the thunderstorm that had pounded the forest a short while ago. And then it hit him like a bolt of lightning. He remembered standing in front of Bob and Diane's tent. He remembered how Diane had conversed rudely to him. And then he remembered how he had gotten tangled up in the mud and fallen over. Suddenly, he felt a throbbing sensation on the side of his head.

Again he reached up and touched the side of his head. There was a large bump there. It hurt like hell and he had quite a headache going on, a real rager right between the eyes by the forehead. Letting out a quiet sigh, it all came rushing to him. He had fallen and knocked his head against something hard, possibly a large rock or rotted out tree stump. After that, he must have blacked out. But what confused him even more was the fact that he didn't appear to be back at their campsite. Where were the two tents? Had he, in a confused and delirious state, actually wandered right on out of their campsite and into the dense passages of the forest? As he continued scanning with his headlamp, seeing nothing but tall, slender bamboo trees with dense foliage at ground level, it certainly appeared as though that was the case.

Taking a moment he did his best to stand to his feet. It was a lot to take in. His heart was beating fast and the blood was already busy working its way to his brain. As he did so, water immediately began dripping from his backside. His entire backside as well as the back of his head was sopping wet with water.

Suddenly feeling a bit lightheaded, Stacey took in a deep breath of air as he scratched at his head. He remembered Diane's glare back when they were questioning him about Clark's disappearance. It had nearly bore a hole straight through him. He remembered the torrent of questions that had come his way. It seemed obvious that she didn't buy his story one bit, but at this point he had no clue of knowing whether that was true or not.

Again he felt an intense and throbbing pain from the side of his head. He reached up and placed his hand atop the massive bump. Slowly he dragged his fingers atop the bump. It hurt like a son of a bitch and was huge. It must have stretched several inches in length.

That was it then. He had gotten caught in the mud, fallen, hit his head on something hard, blacked out, and stumbled right out of their camp and back into the forest in a semi-delirious and confused state. When he finally awoke, he found himself in the middle of a puddle of water with a huge throbbing bump on the side of his head. He felt the bump with his fingers once again.

Without warning, he suddenly felt the hairs on the back of his neck stand up. He froze and listened. He thought he had heard a breathing sound from somewhere off in the dense brush. Meanwhile, the light from his headlamp was still shining a straight beam of light ahead into the black jungle. And then the breathing sound shifted. It now appeared to be on his left.

Instinctively, Stacey thought back to his colleague Clark from earlier in the day. He felt his body tense and tighten up on him. Where were the others?

Stacey continued to listen.

The forest around him lay silent except for a soft hooting sound from somewhere up high in the canopy. In fact, if it was not for the fact that he was in the middle of fucking nowhere in rural Vietnam, he would have found the soft hooting sound from high above rather soothing. It had an almost meditative feel to it, like the myriad of relaxation videos he'd found over the years on YouTube. Being a content creator, Stacey had been fascinated by those individuals who felt so compelled to go out into the wild places of the world and record sound. Stacey had seen dozens of these types of videos, videos where there was one hour of footage of trees blowing in the wind, or two hours of a tropical storm. The footage was simply captured by the content creator placing a camera in front of a meandering stream or behind a blowing tree limb in the forest, and from there it was simply about recording an hour or so of relaxing footage. It was then uploaded to the creator's official YouTube page where hopefully hundreds of thousands of people would see it.

Stacey found it odd that despite being surrounded by black jungle on all sides, that he could be racking his brain regarding YouTube and the idea of potentially earning money from creating content. He had long thought about the idea of earning some extra income by monetizing videos on YouTube. He would then take the money earned from Google AdSense and put it toward his independent film projects. The question that remained was: what would his channel be about? He had toyed around with different concepts over the years, but never actually settled on one. Probably the easiest idea was a behind-the-scenes look at making it in Hollywood. He had some good footage of him working on his first screenplay, actually having the courage to go out into the wild to film the screenplay, and even the editing and post production of his first short film. Perhaps he'd work on getting his channel up and running once he got home. That sounded like a good plan.

Again, the soft hooting from way up high in the canopy broke him from his thoughts. Stacey shook his head. What the hell was he thinking? Why would he waste his time with putting up his YouTube channel? He now had much bigger fish to fry in terms of getting this documentary officially made and distributed. Perhaps his mind was still cloudy and shaky on account of having monentarily blacked out. He knew that he'd have a hell of a time back in post production, but that was a problem for later. Sinking himself back into the moment, his ears searched quietly for the soft hooting sound, but now it was nowhere to be heard.

Craning his head back he looked up. The light from his headlamp shown straight into the dark and entangled canopy above him. He saw nothing and heard nothing. But then all of a sudden there was something else. He thought he heard the faintest of sounds moving off in the brush. As he continued to listen, he realized he had been wrong. Now there was nothing.

Stacey returned his head to a level position. Now, the light from his headlamp was illuminating the dark passages of the forest that lay beyond. For a moment, he thought about Bob and Diane. They obviously hadn't noticed that Stacey never made it safely back to his tent. And then Stacey shook his head. The hell with 'em. It wasn't so much that Stacey had a problem with Bob Hohrman. Actually it was the very opposite. Stacey found Bob to be quite pleasant, a very warm and good-natured soul. But as long as Bob was with Diane, then Bob Hohrman was officially dead to him.

"You're dead to me," Stacey mumbled to himself as a smile crept across his face.

Stacey was recalling the line from one of his favorite television shows Shark Tank, the line itself coming from the famous venture capitalist and entrepreneur Kevin O'Leary when he would say that to the would-be entrepreneurs on their way out of the studio after they had failed to successfully attract the interest of the shark investors.

Stacey smiled to himself once again thinking of the catchy phrase.

You're dead to me.

It was only four simple words, but it held such significant weight.

Suddenly, he picked up on a rank and musty odor. And then he heard noise, movement from somewhere off in the brush. Next his ears registered a soft wheezing sound. Again it had come from somewhere off in the brush, way out there in the darker parts of the forest.

And then suddenly something struck him lightly in the chest. Whatever it was quickly rolled down his shirt and plopped softly in the mud at his feet. Fumbling with his headlamp, it took him a moment or so before he was able to get the light to where it needed to be. He focused the beam of light at his feet. Moving it back and forth several inches, eventually he spotted it. There in the mud, no more than six inches from his left shoe lay something round and pinkish white in coloration. It took him a moment before it all came rushing to him. He was staring down at an eyeball. Continuing to shine the light on it, he could still see part of the white optic nerve attached at the back. Instantly, he felt his pulse quicken as his mind began to race on him. He was staring at a detached eyeball lying in the mud near his feet. But most importantly something had thrown the eyeball at him. Now he felt sheer and absolute terror coursing through his body. His heart was beating hard against his ribcage and he felt a spreading warmth in his pants. Looking down once more, he came to the realization that he had peed himself.

Again his ears picked up on the soft wheezing sound. Confused and bewildered, he spun around and in the process tripped on a root protruding out of the ground. As he fell backward he tried to brace with his hands, but instead of falling and hitting the ground something struck him hard from behind. He immediately felt the sensation of having the wind be taken from his lungs.

Stacey was thrown several feet. His body crashed through some low-lying ferns before slamming hard into the base of a bamboo tree. As his arms and legs unfurled from around the tree, his body slumped awkwardly down as he lay at the base. Moaning and disoriented, it felt like he had been struck by a small car. And then the smell hit him full on once again.

It was amazing just how quickly the awful scent had completely overtaken the area. It was a nauseating, pungent odor. Stacey rolled over, gasping in agony. Laying on his side and staring out across the jungle floor, he could see his headlamp lying face up in the shallow pool of water. The beaming light from the headlamp was shining straight up into the night sky. It was probably twenty feet from where he lay in agonizing pain at the base of a bamboo tree.

Groaning in agony, his mind began racing with worst case scenarios. And then he heard the sound of something heavy moving through the forest. Doing his best to force himself into an upright and seated position, he heard the sound of galloping followed by the trampling of vegetation from inside the crowded labyrinth of bamboo. Noise came up quickly on his right side. His body was racked in so much pain he was amazed that he was able to find the strength necessary to turn to the right and lift his body off the ground to have a look.

Again, Stacey eyed the ray of light from the headlamp beaming straight up into the sky, still lying in the shallow puddle of water. And then on the other side of that bright penetrating beam of light, his eyes locked in on an overwhelmingly large shape. It was moving toward him. The huge figure knuckled its way forward, stopping just short of the headlamp. And there it reared onto its two back legs, beat several times on its chest, and let out a deep cavernous roar.

Stacey felt the sickening feeling from deep within as his insides dropped. "Oh my God."

Noise from somewhere in the foliage on the left side of him suddenly materialized. He hardly had time to even muster a scream as something powerful clamped down onto his left leg. Stacey felt an enormous amount of pressure around his leg as he was dragged aggressively through the mud and low-lying vegetation.

He was barely able to make out another enormous figure now coming up on his left-hand side. Barreling forward, the monstrosity faded off into the background as he continued to be dragged through the foliage. Flailing wildly with both hands, he tried desperately to latch onto something. Anything. But he was being dragged too fast now and the vegetation was wet and slick. Next, he tried digging his hands into the mud. It was no use though as his fingernails scraped their way through soft mud while the rest of his body continued to crash through the thick underbrush.

Stacey Winston let out one last blood-curdling scream as he was dragged off into the dark jungle.

40

Quickly, Downs went about gathering the rest of the team into a tight huddle. His mind was still reeling with what had just happened. Burned into his memory like a smoldering ore was the huge hulking form of Burr Wellington as the man went bounding off into the trees, off into the deeper parts that they had yet to venture into. It was all still very vivid, very clear, and most importantly very real. And then there was the gigantopithecus. The image of its monstrous body pursuing Burr through the tight passages was enough to give even the heartiest of souls sweat-drenching nightmares for months.

The team now found themselves huddled closely together, each member doing their best to recapture their breath.

"What'll we do now?" Josiah asked.

Downs eyed each of them. They had all seen what they had seen. There was no doubt about it—they most certainly had a dog fight on their hands. But Downs was also worried about their own safety. How were they going to get out of this one? And then there was the lingering issue of how they were going to pull this mission off, to see the mission through from inception to completion? Question after question seemed to keep compounding one atop the other.

Downs looked over to Josiah, let out a sigh, and placed the barrel of the air rifle down toward the ground. "We need to get to Burr first. This should be priority number one. Everything else comes to a halt until we've got the big guy back."

"Fuck," Jeremiah said as he kicked at the dirt. "Fuck!"

Max Caldwell looked up at Jeremiah, knowing immediately what John Corstine's son was getting at. There was no doubt that collectively together as a team they were feeling the lingering effects of not having the ability to remain in constant radio communication with one another. Had the adult sun bear that stormed into their camp not grabbed the bag with the radios in it and deposited it somewhere deep in the forest, they could have remedied this situation a lot quicker. However, the cards had been dealt. They now had to confront this situation head on.

Downs looked at Max and nodded. "We're a team, and we're gonna figure this one out together. Gotta get by with just ourselves and our own senses now."

Tori decided it was time to speak up. "But we gotta be smart about how we approach this. First things first, we can't go stomping around this place shouting for Burr and making a ton of noise."

Jeremiah nodded. "Agreed. We need secrecy and stealth now. Essentially what is the heart and soul of this organization."

Downs turned and looked at Max. "We're gonna go in search of Burr, but we're gonna spot you from both sides while you search the ground below for details no matter how minute they may be. Got it?"

"Okay," Max said hesitantly. "Let's do this."

And then Downs turned toward Jeremiah. For a brief moment, the two stared at one another, their eyes doing the speaking for them. Words weren't necessary at this point. Both men nodded to one another.

Downs turned his attention momentarily back to the group. "We also got a rather large issue looming over us regarding the overall objective of this mission from here on out, but first we gotta get to Burr. We'll address the other issue later."

Heads nodded in approval as the team began to move out. As they did so, Downs knew in his heart of hearts that Burr would be okay. The big guy was resourceful. He was strong as an ox, and most importantly, determined. Burr Wellington was as determined as they came, and if there was anyone who possessed the ability to squirm his way out of whatever tough situation he may have found himself in, it was that man. But what loomed on Downs' mind as they started moving silently through the forest was the issue of what ultimately would become of this mission? There were decisions that would need to be made, and these decisions were going to have to be made very soon.

• • •

The team of five had been moving silently through the dark forest for going on ten minutes now. Downs was out in front leading the way. So far, they had managed to push silently through this green, buzzing, churning, and vibrant world. Now that they were well into the evening, the forest was bathed in the constant drone and hum of insect chatter. Mosquitoes buzzed and divebombed them repeatedly whenever progress became too slow and arduous. There was also the occasional croaking of frogs from the damper and wetter parts of the forest. All in all, the place was very much alive.

Downs held up his right hand in a closed fist. The team came to a stop. While Downs was out in front, Josiah was off to his left, Tori was to his right, and Jeremiah was taking up the rear. With each member guarding their own respective sides of the forest, this put Max in the middle of them all, giving the zoologist the chance to scour the ground quietly for any and all possible clues as to Burr's whereabouts.

Forming what was a rather crude rectangular formation, each team member continued to scour the forest with their air rifles. The only person not standing absolutely still was Max, the zoologist moving about diligently through the undergrowth. He paused for a moment, reached out with his right hand, and pushed the leafy vegetation toward him. Through the night vision goggles his eyes took in more of the under-growth.

Blood.

"Guys," Max whispered quietly. "You might, uh, wanna come have a look at this."

"We're not leavin' our posts, so just tell us." Josiah fired back.

On more of the outstretched leaves, Max saw quarter-sized splotches everywhere. "Looks like someone just moved through here bleeding pretty good."

"Someone or something?" Tori asked.

Max shook his head. "Hard to tell. Just by the looks of it though, lots and lots of blood."

Meanwhile up ahead, Downs could feel himself getting antsy and jittery. He didn't like the idea of one of their own being out here essentially with no backup or protection. They needed to keep going, keep pushing forward.

Downs maintained his grip on the Astra. Rather quickly, he took a quick peek back to Max. Max was still busy doing his thing so he decided to give the man a few more moments. As he turned his head back around, he could already see the direction that they'd be moving. Just off to his right, the undergrowth appeared trampled and pressed down. It was definitely possible that someone or something might have just passed through here, and rather recently by the looks of it. As Downs continued sweeping the area with his eyes, he believed it to be where Burr had run off to. The bamboo trees here grew exceptionally close. Downs believed with certainty that there was no way that something as large and imposing as a gigantopithecus could have rampaged through here without disturbing things. At this point it was just the undergrowth that was pressed down and flattened in the direction leading out and away from where the group stood.

Again, Downs glanced back to Max. They really needed to get going. Time was ticking.

All of a sudden, Downs heard the sound of feet crunching down on the leafy matter of the forest floor. He swung around and saw that it was Josiah.

The paleontologist calmly put his hand on Downs' shoulder and motioned with his head to their left.

Josiah spoke at barely a whisper. "Hey man, there's something moving off to the left."

Quietly, Downs snapped his fingers toward the rest of the group. Heads turned at once as Downs motioned with his hand. Slowly, the forest was starting to come alive on them. The sound of movement and things breaking and cracking rang out just to their left. The noise appeared to be heading straight for them.

Downs looked around. To their right about twenty feet away, the area was lush with ferns that must have neared four feet in height. Downs pointed toward the vegetation.

Immediately, the group began moving. Quickly, all five of them scurried toward the ferns, bent down, and pushed past the first few fronds before finally immersing themselves inside the dense growth. Now fully engulfed on all sides, they pulled themselves into a seated position, backs pressed tightly up against one another. The ferns were tall enough to conceal them now that they were all seated. Downs remained seated in the front, the revolver still clenched firmly in his hands.

Together, the team of five lay hidden in silence as they waited and listened. At first there was nothing, just the usual sounds of the forest. There was the occasional animal call here and there, the constant chatter of insects, and the soothing sound of bamboo trees knocking against one another from time to time.

From where Downs was seated, he could barely see out to the small open area that lay directly in front of them. He heard noise, although now it was difficult to tell from which direction. A few more seconds passed before it was evident that someone or something was now standing in the center of that small open area. As quietly as he could, Downs reached out with his left hand and ever so carefully pushed aside one of the fronds from the fern.

Downs froze in place right where he was, his left hand remaining glued to the frond as if it were a part of it. The others saw what Downs could see as well. Standing no more than fifty feet from where the team was crouched in hiding in and amongst the ferns stood two large shadowy figures. Immediately, Downs began sizing them up. Whoever the two men were, they were both extremely large. They must have been damn near the size of—

Burr Wellington.

Instantly, Downs thought back to Burr, wondering if the big man was indeed okay. These two men coupled with what else Downs knew resided in this forest had him on edge.

Downs was just about to gently release the delicate fern frond back to its original position. But instead of doing just that, he remained frozen as both men now started moving toward them.

41

Burr Wellington groaned in agony and felt like he was going to throw up all over himself. All he could manage though was some dry spit. Letting out a parched and heaving cough, he spit what saliva had built up in the back of his throat. He felt awful.

As he exhaled a deep breath, his brain registered two things. First, he was in extraordinary pain, and secondly, he was incredibly scared. There weren't many times in the 6'5", two hundred and fifty pound man's life that he had found himself scared, but now more than ever was one of those moments.

Burr was bare chested and seated on the ground with his back up against the base of a rather thick and sturdy bamboo tree. His wrists were tightly bound together as were his legs. There was also a rope that went around his midsection, securing his body to the base of the bamboo tree.

Burr groaned again as he managed to pull himself upright several inches. In doing so, his back scraped against the coarse bamboo. And then he looked down at his right forearm. Those bastards had cut him across his forearm. Burr suddenly looked down at the ground. Bleeding from the open knife would, Burr Wellington was continuing to lose blood. He was bleeding out. He had been left here to die. It was about as scary a thought as had ever come to him.

How in the world could this be happening? How could any of this be fucking happening? For a moment he lost himself completely in that thought. And whether out of blood loss or the sheer terror of it all, his thoughts completely took him now. His mind wandered back to his wife's losing battle with cancer. Over the years, the loneliness and isolation had been almost unbearable to him. He desperately wanted to see her again, but here at the base of the bamboo tree, he wasn't quite ready just yet to be reunited with her. He had more life in him, more adventures and travels to set out on.

And then he heard movement from somewhere close by. Immediately, his body tightened up on him. Burr froze as he strained with his ears and listened. It sounded like the noise had come from behind him.

Burr looked down at his empty holster. He couldn't believe the bastards had confiscated the Astra revolver as well as his tranquilizer air rifle. They had also taken his night vision goggles as well. Thankfully though, in this part of the forest, the canopy and crisscrossing limbs high above were rather open and his eyes had now fully acclimated to the night. He could see better than he would have thought, but it was still quite dark. Those fucking assholes. He would wring their necks if he ever got a hold of them.

Again, he heard the sound of crunching and movement from close by.

Even if he still had been in possession of his lethal weapon, he couldn't have used it. His wrists were bound. But then all of a sudden, he managed to move his midsection. The rope that held him fastened to the tree wasn't as tight as he had initially suspected. Perhaps there was just enough wiggle room to maneuver his way out of this situation.

Quickly though, Burr's eyes dropped back to his right forearm. He was still bleeding, the pain itself burned deep like a fiery knife. The pain along with the thought of his late wife only served to further fuel his pursuit to get out of this predicament.

As Burr continued to sit there, tied up and bleeding, it all quickly came rushing to the forefront. He hadn't been left to die. He had been left as a sacrifice.

• • •

From behind the thick covering of ferns, Downs watched as the two large men dressed in all black camo continued moving toward them. It was almost like it was in slow motion, almost like it wasn't happening at all. With their rifles out in front of them, the two silent figures continued moving forward.

Downs took a quiet breath in through his nose. He felt as though he was about to pass out. His trigger finger flexed and twitched ever so slightly. Downs was not a man of violence, nor was he a man that believed in lethal force or jumping the gun, but as he and the team sat crouched and hemmed in tightly amongst the vegetation, he had made the conscious decision that he was going to do what needed to be done.

Use force only when necessary, Downs thought to himself, uttering the very words that John Corstine had spoken upon his joining the Society of Cryptozoological Agents.

Those words were now more important than ever as the two men kept moving toward them. There was a silent and eerie nature about the way in which they moved, like ghosts passing silently through a darkened cemetery at night. It was almost as if they were floating. They both commanded and dominated the physical space in and around them.

Downs felt the tension in both his neck and back from having been held in such a constricting position for so long. Although he knew he shouldn't, he slid his butt back. He hadn't moved so much as an inch or so, when he must have placed his weight down atop a small twig or something. A slight cracking sound rang out from where Downs was seated. It had been the faintest of sounds, but it hadn't gone unnoticed.

Downs froze right where he was, cursing silently to himself for having been so stupid in the first place. Through the foliage, Downs watched as both men had come to a complete stop as well. But this time there was no scanning. Both sets of eyes remained transfixed straight ahead on the patch of vegetation that concealed the team.

With cautious yet aggressive steps, the two men in black once again started moving forward. As they neared to within twenty feet of the ferns, Downs now knew with certainty which option he would have to choose. The problem was he had never actually shot someone before.

Suddenly, Downs heard a sort of shuffling noise from somewhere behind him. Before he could even make sense of what was happening, something crashed down hard close to the two large men. And then almost as if on cue, a blood-curling cry rang out from somewhere close by. It had come from off in the dark foliage.

Quietly, Downs turned his head toward the disturbance. Quickly, the command was given and both men went stomping off in opposite directions. One went in search of the trampling sound while the other headed off toward where the scream had just rang out.

As Downs managed to turn himself around from inside the ferns, rain began to fall once again from the sky. The intensity of the rain now masked whatever noise they might be producing from inside the vegetation. He looked back to Max. He could see that the zoologist had a large rock in his right hand. Rather quickly, Downs put two and two together. That's what had caused the brief disturbance to both men. Max had thrown a rock to distract both huge men and now the zoologist had yet another large rock in his hand.

"Was that scream Burr?" Josiah asked grimly.

It was coming down hard now, the fat drops of rain slapping down noisily onto the foliage and surrounding leaves. Max let out a deep sigh, looking down at the revolver still firmly clenched in Downs' hands. "We, uh, outnumber them, but we're no match for their weaponry."

"Then we'll just have to outsmart 'em," Downs said. "C'mon."

42

As the rain continued to pound down hard atop the roof of their tent, Bob Hohrman and Diane Clor sat still and motionless in the middle. The wind was now whipping and beating back the sides of the tent as if it were pieces of flimsy laundry attached to a clothes line. Diane had not told Bob that while he had been sleeping, she had unzipped the tent just enough to witness Stacey fall and hit his head. She watched for a few moments longer before the director got up in a haze and stumbled right out of their camp and back into the surrounding brush. She also knew that he had not returned to his tent, which meant that the footage that he had filmed had been left unattended for the moment. Despite this, she felt it best not to convey these recent developments to Bob.

Bob cleared his throat and attempted to speak. But no words came though. Diane had set her headlamp down near the side of the tent. If it wasn't for the small light, the two would have essentially been seated in pitch black.

For another few seconds, a long and uncomfortable silence continued to fill the still air inside the tent. While they had no way of knowing how far the action that they heard a short while ago had come from, they had heard every bit of it—the sound of gunfire followed by a harrowing scream.

Now instead of Bob talking, it was Diane who spoke. Her voice was calm yet emphasized a sort of cold-hearted seriousness that Bob had not seen in all their time together out in the field. "We must finish this project. See it through to completion. But most importantly, we must pursue new and fresh footage of the creature."

Bob nodded quietly but did not speak.

Diane was now looking off into the distance, her eyes not wavering, not blinking. "We must make this the greatest film the world has ever seen. A modern day King Kong tale."

As Bob continued to look at his film colleague, there was a certain strangeness about her that he had never seen before, almost a sort of detached reptilian nature about it. Sure they were times when she spoke very bluntly to most around her, but this was something new, something otherworldly that he had failed to notice before. All of a sudden, she seemed very distant and removed, cold yet calculated, staring off toward the side of the tent, seeming like she was somewhere else entirely instead of seated in the middle of the tent with him.

Bob cleared his throat nervously. He straightened himself and found the necessary saliva to speak. "I'm not certain I'm comfortable with that given everything what's transpired. Besides, who do we think it was who just produced that scream?"

Diane turned and looked Bob straight in the eyes. "Bob, listen to me. We have the chance of a lifetime here, the find of a lifetime, and it's our moral right to bring this animal out into the light via our documentary. If we do this correctly, this will no doubt be life-changing stuff for all of us. Are you on board or not?"

Bob's response was immediate. He shook his head. "Diane, I'm not comfortable with any of this until we find Clark and his whereabouts. If we can pull this off, then sure, maybe we can return to work on this project, but safety should be our number one priority at this juncture."

Diane took a moment to herself to process Bob's words, to understand what they meant, but most importantly to understand where Bob currently stood in regard to the overall production of the documentary. She nodded quietly to herself

Diane turned and made direct eye contact with Bob. "Clark Geiger. Certainly that had to have been him. Clark. We need to go in search of him, but just you and I. He's still alive, I know it."

This time, Bob found Diane's stare not to be as unnerving as he had only seconds prior. Perhaps it had just been the unnatural lighting in the tent. They would go in search of Clark. But if they were to in fact still find him alive and well, they had their work cut out for them. They had no clue as to his whereabouts or where the scream had even originated from or who had been responsible for it.

"And what about Stacey?" Bob finally asked.

Diane shook her head. "The old director knows what we're up to. He's welcome to join us at any point."

Quickly, Diane began rummaging through her backpack, gathering up the belongings and loose items that were strewn across the floor of the tent. When she was done, she zipped her bag up tightly and looked up at Bob.

"Are we gonna go looking for him right now?" Bob asked.

Diane had a wide grin across her face. "You know it."

• • •

Stacey Winston's eyes fluttered open back and forth. He wasn't certain where he was. All he could make sense of was that he was being dragged downhill.

And then something off in the brush to his right went crashing on by him. Whatever it was had quickly come in and out of focus. Suddenly, he felt sick to his stomach. Again, the blurry image scurried noisily from somewhere close by in the foliage. Stacey could hear the crunch of the forest floor under its galloping limbs. Stacey felt a very unnerving feeling settling deep within his stomach. He knew what it was. It was roughly the size of an adult male silverback gorilla. If that in fact turned out to be true, then the thing responsible for the galloping in the brush to Stacey's side was probably around some four hundred pounds in weight. It was a big animal, no doubt.

Holy shit.

Terror suddenly washed over him as the director began to thrash his arms about, dragging them across roots, plants, anything he could get his hands on. But everything was slick and wet from the onslaught of the rain, and his hands couldn't find anything upon which to latch onto. Without the aid of night vision goggles, a headlamp, or even a flashlight for that matter, black jungle surrounded him on all sides.

Again his brain again registered that he was being dragged down a slight hillside. Somewhere beneath the terror coursing through his body, he felt pain, unbelievable pain everywhere. Forcing his eyes to look straight ahead through the inky darkness, he could barely see an overwhelmingly huge hulking figure out in front. He tried to listen in, see what it was, but all he could hear was his own panicked and labored breathing as he frantically tried to gain semblance of things.

And then in an instant, it all came rushing back to him. He remembered being ambushed by one of the creatures. He remembered the animal charging straight at him, teeth bared while roaring. And then he remembered the impact, that brutal moment of stark, blinding pain when he had been struck by the creature and knocked backward. After that, the rest was all a wash.

Again, noise scurried from somewhere close by. He turned but could make out nothing. His eyes shifted back to straight ahead. He was just barely able to make out the silhouette of the monstrous creature.

When Stacey turned his head back to the left, that's when the attack came. Charging in fast and aggressive, something latched onto his leg and bit down with incredible force. Teeth punctured through skin and muscle. Stacey screamed a guttural cry of terror as sharp teeth continued to pierce through him. Flailing his arms like a mad man, his body now felt torque and pressure from multiple angles. Part of him was now being dragged to the left, while the other half was still being pulled straight ahead. He now found himself caught in the middle of a primal tug-of-war.

This tug-of-war contest ensued for several more seconds before Stacey felt his right leg drop to the ground. And then suddenly, the large figure in front spun around so quickly it was startling. Moving about on four massive limbs it raced over toward the figure on Stacey's left side. He also felt his left leg suddenly be let go as well. Now Stacey lay in the mud, still completely surrounded by dark jungle on all sides as the sounds of a fierce battle ensued not more than fifteen feet from where he lay.

He couldn't make it out, but surely he had been dragged off by the gigantopithecus. That was obvious, that was clear, but what was the smaller shape that had come up on his left side and grabbed him by the left leg?

Stacey heard two fierce roars back and forth, followed by the unnerving sound of bodies colliding. Next, he heard limbs swatting each other, becoming entangled with one another. More swatting, more sounds of carnage, and more roaring ensued.

As the fight waged on, Stacey slowly began dragging himself through the mud. Little by little, inch by inch, he was putting distance in between himself and the ensuing battle. But as Stacey continued inching his way backward, the back side of him absolutely covered in stinking mud, he heard the distinct thud of a body as it collapsed and fell hard to the ground. Then silence.

Now breathing heavily, Stacey continued pulling himself backward through the mud. Despite his minimal progress, he was overwhelmed with an awful, reeking stench. And then that stench turned into a rage-filled roar as something enormous lowered itself. He felt hot breath from the big head now inches from his face. Lying on his back in the mud, surrounded by the eternal darkness that was the forest around him, Stacey Winston let loose a terrifying cry.

43

Downs and the team had just started moving silently through the forest, snaking their way quietly through the bamboo trees when they came to a complete stop. They paused. This time, the scream had come from what sounded like somewhere at their backs. Now they stood enshrouded in silence as a soft gentle breeze blew in and out of the tall and wispy trees.

Downs stole a glimpse back toward Max. Immediately, the zoologist pointed with his finger in the direction they were moving. Then Downs' eyes locked in with that of Josiah's. The paleontologist motioned in the same direction that Max had.

Downs gave them both a thumbs-up and just like that they were back moving, retracing the steps that the two men in black had just taken. Downs was out in front leading the way. He had given his air rifle to Josiah who now had two tranquilizer guns, one in each hand. Meanwhile, Downs continued to wield the only lethal weapon they were currently in possession of. At this point in time it was most definitely a precious commodity.

As they continued pushing deeper into the forest, all Downs could think about was the two large men they had just seen. Huge with powerful weaponry. Downs knew that whoever the two were, they would no doubt prove a force to be reckoned with. Could they overcome them? Quickly, Downs began running through things in his head. They were only two men, but they were two very large men. Next came the weaponry. Two assault rifles for certain with some type of powerful hand guns holstered at their sides. That alone gave them a significant advantage simply by the sheer firepower that they possessed. And God knows what else they had in their army fatigue vests and packs on their backs.

Downs looked at his own feet continuing to carry him as quietly as they could through the forest. How much noise were they making? He listened to the rest of the team close behind him. He could hardly hear a thing. The audible sound of their progress forward was minimized as they walked on damp, spongy earth. Everything was still quite wet and this in turn meant a relatively silent passage forward.

Downs held up a closed fist. The team came to a stop. Through the night vision goggles, Downs took in the bamboo forest bathed in its neon green color. From somewhere high above them, the soft hooting cry of an owl could be heard. And then from another corner of the forest, another call rang out. Looking up, he suddenly saw a dozen or so bats, their small leathery wings moving them quickly through the forest.

As the team continued to be engulfed by the sounds of the forest, again Downs felt the tension of this mission continuing to weigh on him. He let out a quiet sigh to himself. It was hard to fathom that Burr

Wellington was not at their side, at *his* side, providing not only mass and muscle, but a thick stubborn determination to see the mission through no matter what the challenges or obstacles. They simply had to get to him. No matter what the cost they needed him at their side once again.

Downs gave the high sign and they continued forward.

• • •

Taking up the rear of the group, Josiah Young had a tranquilizer gun holstered at his side, an air rifle slung over his left shoulder, and his original air rifle pressed out in front of him. Initially, when Downs had asked him to hold his air rifle, he thought about holding an air rifle in both hands. But rather quickly he shook that idea off, realizing that was not only egotistical, but downright dangerous as well. Holding two air rifles would make him awkward in a sense. Sure he'd essentially be able to shoot two targets at once, but he felt as though he'd be awkward and clumsy as well. In this particular circumstance, one was better than two.

Josiah smiled to himself for a moment with the thought of holding an air rifle in each hand, acting and behaving like many of the characters in his beloved HBO show Westworld. For a second he thought back to his DVR at home. He wanted to get back there, but more importantly, finally finish up his doctoral work in vertebrae paleontology at UC Berkeley. After that, he was hoping to have a career making rare guest appearances on channels like History Channel and Discovery and leading paleontological digs around the world. And there was also his secret book project that he had been working on for quite some time now. Although he hadn't told anyone, not even his good buddy Downs, Josiah had secretly been given an added boost of adrenaline when he saw the success that Tori had with her debut book on man's attempt to bring back the woolly mammoth. Perhaps he could have a similar level of success with his own project. Only time would tell though.

Josiah shook his head. For now it would all have to wait, all have to be put on the back burner. And while he found himself eager and antsy to get back home, he knew that he needed to focus. They all needed to focus for that matter.

• • •

Problem after problem kept rotating in Downs' head as they continued moving through the forest in silence. They were thankfully now moving through a part where the bamboo growth wasn't so heavy. Things had opened up a bit and weren't so constricting and claustrophobic.

For Downs though the questions kept rotating and swirling like a twister as they moved through low-lying vegetation now. Where had Burr Wellington run off? Was he injured and in need of help? Who were the two men whose trail they were currently tracing? And lastly, how would they fare with another encounter with one of the gigantopithecus? Not only that, but would they be able to take the creatures down, sedate, immobilize, and prepare them for transport back to the S.C.A.'s secret outpost in the wilds of Siberia?

For quite some time now, Downs had been mulling over this. It had been mounted squarely atop his shoulders. Given their situation and everything that had already transpired, maybe success on this mission needed to be redefined. By that, Downs was referring to the fact that they simply didn't have the ability to sedate and capture all the creatures. Maybe all they had to do was push these giant creatures back deeper into the hidden parts of the forest, far away from the prying eye of man. There was also the matter of getting hold of all cameras and equipment documenting the creature's existence. They needed to make certain that evidence via pictures and videos didn't make its way out into the rest of the world as well. Downs shook his head. Enough. It was true they needed to figure all this out, but for now it would all have to wait.

Suddenly, Downs noted just how quiet the forest had grown. There was an eerie silence to it. Even the soft breeze that had been passing through the trees had now ceased to blow. Now there was only silence and the thick humidity. Downs used his left hand to wipe away at a trickle of sweat running down his face. And then out of the corner of his left eye he spotted something. Downs whispered quietly to the others and motioned quickly for Max to come forward. The zoologist scurried his way to the front of the line. Immediately, he took note of what Downs was pointing at. As Max bent down to further investigate, Downs and the team stood on guard. Max was now crouched in the mud examining what appeared to be a tattered piece of clothing. Carefully, he reached out and pulled it from the small limb it had gotten torn and snagged on.

It looked like the sleeve from a t-shirt, but as Max continued to turn it over in his hands, he could see several dark splotches. It was blood. Quickly, his eyes made their way to the tree and beyond that, the surrounding vegetation. As Max continued following the various criss-crossing limbs and fronds from the low-lying fern growth, his eyes stumbled upon something. He froze right where he was, the tattered piece of clothing still in his hand.

Max Caldwell said absolutely nothing as two eyes stared back at him from probably a good twenty to twenty-five yards away. Deep and entangled amongst the thick limbs and foliage, he saw the silhouette of a rather large shape seated on its back haunches. The figure continued to stare silently at them. Max felt his body go icy cold on him. Suddenly, the muscles in his back and neck tightened up. Meanwhile, the scientific part of his brain was scrambling and working hard to make sense of what his eyes were seeing.

A juvenile, he thought silently to himself.

Surely, he must have known this from the start. Surely, they must have all known this. If you had an adult gigantopithecus, then it only made sense that there would be infants and juveniles running around these dark and isolated forests as well. Somewhere in that academic and scientific brain of his he must have known that this was an inevitability, but still it was hard to believe as the animal stared silently back at them. Here it was in the flesh, a juvenile gigantopithecus. Although nowhere near as massive and robust as the adults, the juvenile was still breathtakingly powerful and well-put together. It was quite the physical specimen.

Broad shoulders along with a powerful chest made up the overall physique of the animal. From where Max was situated, he could see the dome-shaped head starting to take shape. He remembered the coloration of the female, dark brown as the solid base, with stripes of black and a gray pattern on its front side. The juvenile was a light brown and had what appeared to be the start of patches of orange to reddish-brown on the front part of its body. Again Max looked back to the heavily muscled shoulders, the already well-defined and sculpted wide chest. With the way the young creature appeared to be built coupled with the coloration on the front, Max suspected it to be a male. But he had no way of knowing with certainty at this point if that was indeed a correct observation or not.

He also didn't know if the others had taken notice of the animal or not, so he just kept quiet to himself, kept absolutely still right where he was, crouching in the wet mud.

And then Max broke eye contact with the animal, not wanting to come off as a threat to the juvenile. But just before he had done so, he had carefully sized the animal up. Although his vision was partially obscured and he had to make estimates through the night vision goggles from roughly a distance of some twenty-five yards, he pegged the juvenile to roughly four hundred pounds in weight. It was a good sized animal by anyone's estimates. That thought alone was startling and only served to emphasize just how truly massive the adults were. It was hard to tell from his positioning how tall the creature was, but Max guesstimated it stood around five feet in height, half the height of the towering adults.

As quietly and calmly as he could, Max tapped Downs on the leg. Then Max looked up at his good friend while motioning the quiet sign to him. Downs looked to the area of the forest where Max was motioning his head. Downs saw nothing, looked down at Max, and then looked back toward where Max was still motioning with his head.

Again, nothing. Just an empty forest.

Finally, Max broke eye contact with Downs. As he set his eyes back toward the juvenile gigantopithecus, he was shocked to see that the young animal was suddenly nowhere to be seen. The animal appeared to have quietly disappeared back into the surrounding brush. For a moment, Max's eyes darted back and forth. Surely the creature couldn't have gone very far. But as the zoologist continued to frantically scour as much of the forest as he possibly could through the night vision goggles, his search turned up nothing. The juvenile had blended back into its habitat.

Max suddenly realized that his throat had run dry on him. He searched for whatever saliva he was able to muster in the back of his mouth. He now had a very, very bad feeling about things.

Oh shit, he thought to himself.

44

S lowly, Max stood to his feet and brushed himself off. Mud was caked on the front side of his pants. The zoologist spoke at just above a whisper into Downs' left ear. "No more than thirty seconds ago, I spotted a lone juvenile gigantopithecus eyeing us from not too far off in the foliage."

Downs felt his eyes bulge a bit, but still it was exactly as he had expected. After all, there wouldn't be much hope for the survival of even a small intact population of long thought to be extinct creatures if there were only adults running around. He was surprised they hadn't seen any signs of juveniles or infants earlier.

Quietly, Downs pointed toward the torn piece of t-shirt still lying in the mud. "And that?"

Max shrugged his shoulders as he looked down at the fabric. "Doesn't appear to be from Burr. Hard to say, possibly the documentary film crew."

By now, the others had moved in closer on their conversation. While still maintaining their watch of their respective parts of the forest, they spoke, although barely above a whisper.

"You say you spotted a juvenile?" Jeremiah asked through gritted teeth.

Max nodded. "Correct. The animal was, um, good-sized as well. I'd say roughly the size of an adult male silverback gorilla, give or take a few pounds."

"Holy shit," Josiah replied.

"And it just disappeared?" Tori asked.

Again, Max nodded. "Pretty quickly. The, ah, animal was here one minute, gone the next. Perfectly adept and capable in these thick passages as well. Very much at home here."

The entire time that this short conversation had been going on, Downs kept his eyes peeled. He wondered if they were making too much noise? And once again, his thoughts rotated back to that of Burr. That would have been priority number one, if it weren't for the fact that they were now close on the trail of two huge men dressed in black whom they knew nothing about. It all seemed a bit too much—the odds they were up against, the success of the overall mission. Everything, just everything seemed to be weighing down on him, weighing down on all of them for that matter. But still he kept his cool, kept his focus.

Again, Downs wiped at the side of his face with his shoulder. He was sweating bullets in this goddamn forest. For a moment, his thoughts gravitated back toward his dad and that meeting that he had several months ago where he sat in John Corstine's office and stared at a picture of Corstine and his father from over thirty years ago. He thought about what had been conveyed to him that grim and foggy San Francisco day, the fact that his dad and John Corstine had founded The Society of Cryptozoological Agents back in the early 1980's. Downs let that thought swirl for a moment in his head. He felt the tiniest of tears well up in the corner of his right eye.

Well, this one's for you, Dad, Downs thought to himself. *Let's make this shit a success.*

45

With her headlamp blazing the way out in front of them, Diane Clor lead the way. Meanwhile, Bob Hohrman followed closely behind. The two were moving quickly through the bamboo trees now. Meanwhile up ahead, Diane continued furiously moving through the vegetation, wondering if Bob even had a clue just where in the fuck they actually were. Bob Hohrman was a nice guy. Actually, he was an extremely nice guy, but he was exceptionally bad at directions. Diane had picked up on this early on in the expedition.

As she continued marching forward through the jungle, the beam of light from her headlamp kept bouncing back and forth out in the darkness that lay ahead. From time to time she thought about stopping to pursue more footage for the documentary, but she now knew with certainty Bob's stance on the matter. No more progress forward until they found the whereabouts of Clark Geiger.

The two walked in silence now, weaving their way through the dense tree growth. Diane kept her eyes straight ahead, but with her ears she listened intently to what was going on behind her. And at the moment she was not listening to the sudden quiet that had all of a sudden besieged the forest. She was listening closely to Bob who was still behind her doing his best to keep pace with her.

• • •

From deep inside the dark foliage, nestled amongst the tall and slender bamboo stalks, behind a thick and entangled mass of vegetation, an overwhelmingly large shape shifted its bulk from one side to the next. A huge hand reached out and pushed the limbs aside. Two eyes in two equally enormous eye sockets watched the two humans as they continued snaking their way through the dark forest.

Slowly, the large shadowy figure crept forward from its hiding and continued to watch as the two humans disappeared around a bend in the forest.

• • •

Diane came to a complete stop and looked around. From a few feet behind her, she could hear Bob as he also came to a stop. Together, the two stood surrounded on all sides by thick dark jungle, the only light coming from their two headlamps. Outside of the light from their headlamp, the darkness sat enshrouded amongst the trees.

Diane had slowed her breathing down to nothing now. She thought she had heard something. Next, she heard footsteps behind her moving forward. They were Bob's footsteps, but the minute that the man got closer, Diane took up walking again. Bob decided it best to say nothing, so they once again continued moving, their beams of light dancing out ahead continuing to penetrate the inky blackness that lay ahead.

And that's exactly how it went for the next several minutes or so. Not a word was said between the two as they continued to make their way silently through the forest. For quite some time now, it seemed as though they were walking on a trail of sorts, a rather pleasant and comfortable meandering trail back and forth that snaked and crisscrossed its way through the dense maze of bamboo trees. But Diane knew better. What they were on was essentially a game trail. This trail had been maintained by years and years of the animals of this forest repeatedly using it for both hunting and grazing. And right now, Diane was making full use of both its accessibility and ease as they continued onward through the trees.

There it is, Diane thought quietly to herself. *There it is.*

Up ahead, probably a good thirty-five yards away, was an area that she had spotted earlier in the day. Earlier this morning, when the men were busy getting their necessary footage and contributions to this documentary, Diane had managed to sneak away to this very same area on the game trail.

The area that she spotted just seconds ago was rapidly approaching, and surprisingly, she found her heart beating rather hard. She needed to stop for a moment, catch her breath, get her bearings straight, get some much-needed oxygen flowing into that brain of hers. Diane came to a halt in the middle of the game trail. Another few feet and Bob came to a stop as well.

"What is it?" Bob said as he got close to her. "Do you hear something? Is it Clark?"

Diane took in several deep breaths and slowly let them out through her nose.

Bob grabbed her gently by the shoulders now. But before doing so, he made sure to shine his headlamp in the opposite direction so as not to shine it directly in her eyes. "What is it?"

Diane took a moment, composed herself a bit more, and then looked up with a warm and beaming smile on her face. "Just needed to catch my breath. That's it. This humidity's getting the best of me. Not in my best physical shape these days, ya know."

Bob took his hands off her shoulders and placed them atop his hips. "Don't be so hard on yourself. None of us are."

She smiled back at him. "I think we need to conserve battery power. How about I hold yours for you? Give your forehead a break?"

Bob took a second. It was almost as if the man was weighing his options, pondering over the questions just asked. And then just like that, Bob Hohrman flicked his headlamp off, unhooked it from around his forehead and handed the thing over to Diane.

"Feel light as a feather now," Bob announced. "My neck's not in the best of shape these days either."

As Diane took hold of the headlamp and turned herself around, Bob's body was immediately plunged into darkness. It was okay though. She was probably right. His neck was rather stiff and sore, an ailment that had plagued him the majority of his entire adult life. But as they started moving once again, a simple thought started to rotate inside his head. And that was you didn't want to find yourself in this forest at night without the aid of some type of light. That's what Bob kept telling and reminding himself as they kept moving forward.

Quickly, Diane went to work slinging the head-lamp through her right arm. She was now carrying it like a purse. Meanwhile from behind, Bob was starting to feel the darkness of the forest closing in around him. It was amazing just how quickly that feeling came full circle. Remove light from the equation and it felt like the darkness had the ability to literally swallow you whole.

Bob looked ahead toward Diane. It seemed as though she had quickened her pace and was now moving considerably faster through the game trail. Bob did his best to keep up, but found himself struggling as the woman kept pulling further ahead.

"Hey, not so fast!" Bob laughed nervously. "Slow down! Not as young as I used to be."

Maybe the woman was in better shape than she gave herself credit for. But Diane didn't listen. She just kept moving faster and faster now through the game trail. They were quickly approaching what lay up ahead.

• • •

When Diane Clor had been a teenager and even into her early twenties, she had been fortunate enough to spend summers up at her aunt and uncle's cabin in Pollock Pines, California, a small community on the southern edge of Lake Tahoe. Their dinners were cooked exquisitely at night, the drink was always plentiful, and the company was always warm and pleasant. On occasion, however, they would go into the small town for dinner. They'd pile into one of their cars, drive down the windy road lined with towering pine trees on both sides, and make their way into town for a nice meal. Chinese or Mexican was always a solid bet and damn delicious too. Dinners were always great, but the real magic lay in the ride home. Diane would always be the designated driver. Her uncle was the drinker, never too much, but certainly never too little.

The drive home to the cabin from the restaurant was approximately twelve miles. It was a long drive through the windy trees on a tight and narrow two-lane road, so often this took in excess of twenty-five minutes. But on these magical drives home, Diane would purposely wait until their little car was surrounded on all sides by a long straightaway of road and tall pine trees that crowded in tightly on both sides of the road. And then with a quick flick of her hand she would turn the headlights off, plunging the car and all of them into absolute darkness. Each and every time she had done this, the result was instantaneous, sheer blackness on all sides and straight ahead. And what was even more terrifying was continuing on in the car at the same speed, not slowing one bit, and showing complete confidence in her understanding of the curves and bumps in the road. Diane had learned this trick from her uncle, and each and every time, it scared the living crap out of her, not to mention her aunt seated in the back seat. As terrifying as it was, it was also quite addicting. It was always like a gut check, a see-what-you're-made-of type of moment. See if you can drive the car safely forward for a few terrifying seconds using only sheer instinct.

Diane shook her head and brought herself back to the present. Up ahead, her headlamp illuminated what was quickly approaching. She took in another deep breath as she continued moving faster now. They were almost there. And with no further hesitation, she flicked her headlamp off, immediately plunging both her and Bob Hohrman into total darkness.

· · ·

From behind, Bob had felt the sudden jolt to his body. Removing light from the equation had been a real shock to the system. The shock itself had reminded him of jumping into the icy cold rivers in Yosemite National Park in his younger days with his parents and sister. It was that type of shock to the senses. Now there was only darkness.

What the hell?

Moving fast now, Bob continued onward a few more paces. And then something odd happened. He planted down with his right foot and suddenly felt the odd sensation of there being nothing there. And before he knew it, he felt himself falling. Next, he felt pain, a sharp and abrupt pain that rang out from his right ankle and radiated upward through the rest of his body. His body then crumbled and fell over to his side. In the process, he whacked his head hard as he slumped sideways and then flopped backward.

"Oh, fuck," Bob moaned in agony.

The back of his head hurt but the pain radiating from his right ankle was excruciating.

"Shit."

It took Bob a few moments to realize what had happened. He must have fallen in a ditch or something. One minute, he had been walking on solid ground, and the next he found himself tumbling downward. How far though? Meanwhile on top of him and all around he felt what appeared to be palm fronds and other sorts of matted vegetation. Had all this vegetation been lying over this hole?

Still racked in pain and in complete pitch black, Bob did his best to reach with his hand upward. He felt a combination of soil and roots, big roots criss-crossing in all directions. Bob Hohrman stood a good six feet tall and had a rather long arm reach. As he continued reaching, he could finally feel his hand patting down atop the game trail. So that was the answer. He had fallen in a hole that appeared to be some seven feet in depth, one that also appeared to have been covered over completely by a thick matting of vegetation.

Now Bob was moving his hand along the top of the path while the rest of his body was still trapped in the hole below. Suddenly, he didn't feel safe as an uneasy feeling quickly began to settle in his stomach. Immediately, he pulled his hand back and returned it to his side. Where was Diane? Surely any good and alert partner would have been at his aid in a matter of seconds. Had she not heard the noise that no doubt had been caused by all this ruckus? And she had the only working headlamp because she had taken his—

Bob froze as his body tightened up on him. Now injured and stuck in a hole below the actual trail, all of a sudden he had a very dark and unsettling feeling about things. He breathed and licked his lips. Suddenly, the back of his mouth felt very dry.

"Diane?" he called out, his voice not too loud, not too soft.

Rather, the tone of the call had been an inquisitive one.

With each passing second that Bob continued to stand trapped alone at the bottom of the hole in complete darkness, he felt his body slowly starting to comprehend the magnitude of it all.

"Diane, where are you?" Bob called out. "I need help! I'm at the bottom of a hole or some sort of depression, trapped and hurt."

But as the seconds stretched into minutes, slowly the grim reality of it all was starting to settle in. Surely this had been no accident. This had been done on purpose, with malicious intent. They never were going in search of Clark Geiger or Stacey for that matter. Diane Clor had meant all along for Bob Hohrman to fall in that hole.

• • •

Stacey Winston's eyes fluttered open back and forth as eternal darkness surrounded him on all sides. It was weird how things had taken on a rather detached and surreal feeling, like this wasn't happening to him at all, like this was happening to someone else entirely. Despite this surreal and detached feeling, he was still able to comprehend that he was lying on his back. That much was clear at least. Slowly, his hand crept up behind the right side of his body and he felt water. He now knew that he was lying in a shallow pool of water with mud that had caked and formed around the edges. Stacey's hand was now sitting atop the sticky muck that was the mud.

As he found the necessary strength to raise his head a bit, he saw the silhouette of two dark figures down around both his legs. And then his brain registered pain beyond belief. Stacey screamed out in sheer agony, a deep, guttural, primal scream of terror.

Stacey Winston was lying on the ground, in a shallow pool of mud and water, and had awoken to both of his legs being eaten. Again, he screamed a deep and wailing cry of primal terror from within. His lungs burned and wheezed from the intensity of the screams. Suddenly, he began flailing both arms, swinging them around like a man possessed. He tried pulling himself backward through the mud, but the two dark shadowy figures by his legs had him permanently pinned in place. With feverish grunts, they continued to go about their grim task of eating him.

Suddenly he picked up on something. He could hear the air wheezing in and out of the two juveniles' nostrils. It was a very unnerving sound to say the least. There were also feverish grunts and low growls that accompanied the breathing. And then there was tugging. Rather quickly, Stacey felt himself being pulled to the right as the juvenile gigantopithecus on his right side began pulling him with powerful jaw muscles. Momentarily caught off guard as well as overpowered, the dark silhouette of a shadow to his left suddenly began tugging as well.

And there it ensued, two animals, both the size of a modern-day silverback gorilla, began a tug-of-war contest with the lower half of his body. Stacey felt an enormous pressure mixed with torque as one leg was pulled one way, while the other was aggressively pulled the other. Suddenly, he felt himself being pulled to the left, the juvenile pulling him as if to claim him as its property.

In a strange almost detached part of his brain, Stacey still had a hard time comprehending that this was happening, that this is how it would end for him, at the hands of a creature or creatures that he had long gone in search of, creatures that were supposed to make him famous, put him on the map once and for all. Another moaning gasp of pain escaped his lips. He felt himself being tugged hard to the right now. It was clear that the juvenile on the right side of him was winning the battle.

Now the pain that the director was experiencing was replaced with that of sheer primal terror. Stacey began lashing out with his arms wherever he could. As he continued to be pulled, his arms still flailing wildly, his hands tried to latch down on whatever they could. He managed to place his right hand atop the frond of a rather large fern, but the vegetation was far too slick and wet at this point to actually grasp and his hand went sliding off.

He was dragged further. Rather violently, the right side of Stacey's body collided with the base of a bamboo tree. It was at this time that he also realized that the juvenile that had been so diligently tugging from the left had let go of him. From behind, Stacey began hearing the other one racing nearby in the foliage.

And then in a spectacular display of aggression, the juvenile that had let go of Stacey's leg bit down and attacked the other juvenile. Immediately, Stacey saw the animal that had been attacked spin around and roar in anger. There the two fought as they both reared up on their back two legs and bared their fangs while letting out moans of rage as they thumped aggressively on their wide chests.

Stacey quickly realized that this was his chance, his opportunity to put some distance between himself and this place. As the sounds of carnage continued to ring out from not more than fifteen feet from where he lay on his back in the mud, he somehow managed to roll over onto his side. Weak and delirious from blood loss, he still had the sensibility about him to crawl, and crawl is exactly just what he did.

As he crawled through the mud, his hands and kneecaps splashed through the shallow water as he frantically continued to pull his body away from the fighting juveniles. It was still pitch black, but thankfully his eyes had acclimated somewhat. Whatever pain he was previously racked in had been put on the backburner as he continued pulling his mangled body through the mud. He was now in all-out survival mode. Adrenaline mixed with sheer terror drove him forward at this point.

Frantically, Stacey searched for somewhere, any-where. There. Up ahead, some fifty feet away, he saw a thick stand of bamboo trees. If he could just get there, he'd be able to catch his breath, assess what to do next, and hopefully get back to the safety of Diane Clor and Bob Hohrman.

Still on his hands and knees, for the briefest of seconds Stacey forced his body back to have a look. A ways away from him, the two juveniles were still having it out, snarling, growling, beating on one another with their long and powerful limbs. Stacey lost himself for a brief moment in the savagery of the encounter, the primal nature of a small population of animals that had supposedly gone extinct a long, long time ago having somehow survived into current times. His mind shot back to his colleague and what had transpired earlier in the day. Clark Geiger. He shivered just thinking about the way in which the man had been dragged off and killed. That memory appeared burned into his subconscious.

Quickly, Stacey turned around and continued on his way. He was heading toward the thick stand of bamboo trees that he had spotted just up ahead. He wasn't certain why he was still crawling and if he could even walk, but he just continued doing what he was doing, pulling himself forward a foot or so at a time. That's how Stacey Winston had always operated in life—deal with one obstacle at a time, one day at a time. It had been the same with his scripts and film projects. When he was initially turned down by more than two dozen studios for his first screenplay, he simply took to Kickstarter and raised the necessary funds along with putting in some of his own money to complete his short film. That's how he had always operated day in and day out. And he would do the same here, one painful, fucking excruciating step through the mud at a time.

As Stacey continued pulling his body through the dense fern growth, he figured one day he'd have a hell of a back story that would go along with this Gigantopithecus Documentary. Hell of a back story. His face was now crashing through ferns as fronds brushed by him on both sides. As he continued pushing himself through the heavy growth, he could already picture the bonus extended edition of this documentary. There would be footage of him talking in front of the camera, talking about this near-death experience at the hands of these powerful creatures. It would make for great cinematic stuff. Great stuff indeed. And in yet another strange out-of-body experience, Stacey found himself eager to get back home to the states and begin the editing and post-production phase of this project. He was very much looking forward to that.

He heard intense, deep bellowing from somewhere behind him. He emerged out of the ferns and was now making a beeline straight for the thick stand of bamboo trees. Now the adrenaline was really flowing and Stacey felt as though he could actually stand. Pushing himself off the ground with his hands, he resurrected to his feet. His legs almost gave way the minute he placed his full weight on both of them. He wasn't certain what type of injuries he had suffered, just that the pain to both legs was like a fiery knife cutting deep into his skin. There was definitely no way he could stand, not even with all the adrenaline in the world, no way whatsoever. So he got back down on his hands and knees and continued crawling.

Again, sounds of immense bellowing roared from behind him. Quickly, he turned in that direction. He had managed to put a sizable distance between himself and the two combatants. He needed to put more distance between himself and the juveniles though. Stacey turned around and hadn't gone so much as a foot or so in the opposite direction before he flat-out collided with something. Whatever it was knocked him flat on his ass as if he had run into a brick wall. He keeled over onto his side.

For a moment he simply laid there. A few seconds passed before he realized that he was lying on his back on the hard ground once again. At first, he thought he had run into a tree, but that's when the smell came. It was a nauseating, pungent odor, absolutely unpleasant in every sense of the word. Next Stacey heard breathing. The realization that he had not run into a tree at all quickly came rushing to the forefront.

In the darkness, he attempted to force himself into an upright and seated position. As he did so though, something large and hairy reached out and knocked him backward. The back of his head hit the ground hard. He groaned as he winced in agony.

As his eyes flicked back and forth anxiously, eventually they settled in directly above him. He saw a large, domed-shaped head extend and lower itself. In the darkness, Stacey was still able to make out the large fierce eyes as they stared down at him.

From somewhere off in the distance, his ears could still hear the snarling cries of the juveniles. Now it was clear that one of the adults was hovering inches from his face. The impossibly large creature was straddling Stacey Winston's body, continuing to inspect the man as if he were a piece of meat, possibly perplexed at the sudden appearance of the small and puny human in its habitat.

Stacey felt his body tighten and freeze up. Was this really happening to him? The animal snorted through its nostrils, the warm fetid air hitting him square in the face. Yes. This was most certainly happening.

The natural gut reaction would have been to scream the most primal of all screams of terror that one could imagine, but Stacey couldn't find the necessary breath to do so. Instead, he attempted to pull himself backward, inch by inch, with no plan in sight, only to get himself away from the monstrosity currently crouching over him.

The gigantopithecus reached out with an enormous left limb and gently pulled Stacey back to where the gigantic creature had initially knocked him down. Now all Stacey could see above him was the enormous shadowy figure of the gigantopithecus. The creature was no longer standing on two legs; rather, it was resting on its four powerful limbs. Beneath it and trapped in the middle of those four pillar-sized limbs was the body of Stacey Winston.

Above him, Stacey could see nothing but the massive stomach of the creature. It looked like a giant boulder covered with long, flowing shaggy hair. Converging on all sides, the four gigantic limbs had formed a rather crude prison around the man, trapping him in with ultimately no escape. Now it truly felt as though everything was slowly closing in on him.

In one last delusional thought, Stacey still felt in his heart of hearts that he would find a way out of this, find a way to get back home, get back to the safety of the studio and tell the entire world about these terrifying creatures. Surely, there had to be a way out of this nightmare. Stacey saw the animal moving now. It was backing itself up, shifting its enormous girth as the pillar-sized limbs lumbered backward. He watched in stunned horror as the animal came to a stop, now resting on all fours directly in front of him. The animal lowered its domed-shaped head and let out a roar of rage. It had been a rumbling, monstrous sound to both hear and experience from such a close proximity. For a second, it appeared as though it had been intended for the two juveniles still having it out, still fighting. Stacey watched as the head of the creature lowered itself once again, stretched out, and bellowed another roar in protest in the direction of the two juveniles.

The result was instantaneous. The two combative youngsters came to an abrupt stop. Now the forest had suddenly been plunged into a deep silence.

The big head turned and stared back at Stacey as both human and animal were now entranced in a long and deep silence. Slowly, Stacey watched as the huge animal knuckled its way forward. The gigantopithecus was back straddling his body, the four limbs trapping the tiny human body inside its huge primal walls of fur. The creature lurched forward and pressed its weight down atop Stacey's chest with its right front limb. The big head lowered and roared a mere foot or so from the man's face. From up close like this the hot breath upon his face was like nothing he had ever experienced before. As the animal breathed above him, he heard the deep rumbling from within the great chest cavity.

With tears now streaming down both sides of his face, Stacey looked up at the monstrosity. He saw the domed-shaped head followed by the intense gaze from the big eyes. And then he saw the gums ripple back, exposing fangs and a mouth full of powerful oversized teeth. There was no time to scream, no time to panic as the big gaping mouth opened wide and closed down over Stacey Winston's panic-stricken face.

46

Downs continued fighting with every last ounce of strength to push his own physical exhaustion to the deepest, most inner parts of his body. This was certainly no time for a rest, especially not at this stage. The team had now been pushing through thick brush for going on damn near thirty minutes before things finally thinned and they now found themselves standing atop a slippery mud embankment that led down to a river. Upon first glance, the river system below appeared to be approximately fifty-five to sixty feet in width; the depth was unknown.

Each member of the team crowded in tightly around Downs. They extracted water bottles from their backpacks and attempted to keep hydrated. Max approached Downs and quietly placed his hand atop Downs' shoulder. "You know where there's water, you'll no doubt find predators."

Suddenly from behind them, they heard the familiar sounds of things cracking and snapping. Something was moving toward them. Quickly, the team formed a straight line, their bodies standing a mere foot or so away from the top of the mud embankment that led down to the water below.

Jeremiah was on the far right side of the line as he pointed with his air rifle. "It's comin' up on our right hand side."

Downs turned with the others. More breaking sounds ensued. Downs stepped a few feet to the left to give him some much-needed room to level the air rifle out in front of him. Now all the five of them could do was wait and listen.

Below and behind them, Downs could hear the soft gurgle of rushing water from the river. Something didn't seem right though. Suddenly, the noise from off in the foliage had ceased. And then as quickly as it had stopped, it picked back up once again. Moving through the forest and sounding like a small bulldozer, there was no doubt about it—something was indeed heading their way.

They held their ground firmly until finally, the sound was nearly upon them. At the last second, out of the corner of his eye Downs saw Jeremiah make a ninety degree turn to the right, swinging his air rifle around in front of him. And then Downs noticed it, too. Those sounds were not coming straight for them.

Through the phosphorescent green glow of the night vision goggles, Bick Downs watched as three dark shadowy figures emerged quickly from the thick growth, raced down the mud embankment, and plunged full bore into the river system below.

The minute that the explosion of noise had burst forth from the foliage, Downs had noticed immediately what it was. It was a family of three sun bears, a mother with her two infants. But the minute that the creatures had burst forth from the foliage, Downs noticed that this was most likely a different adult bear. This particular adult sun bear bore a large slashing scar down the side of its body. The animals had torn through the trees and down the mud bank almost as if something was chasing them, almost as if they were being pursued.

Downs stared back into the bamboo. He knew full well what could flush a full-grown adult sun bear and its young through the forest as if they were but mere field mice. With a quick flick of the eyes, Downs shot a glance back to the river below. He now had a good idea regarding the depth of the water on account of where it came up to on the adult sun bear. It was probably a good three feet in height. Meanwhile up river, the three bears could be seen pulling their wet and shaggy bodies from the water. They dragged themselves through the mud and began to make their way up the opposite mud bank on the other side of the river and back to the trees.

Downs had just tapped Jeremiah on the shoulder with his hand as two enormous rage-filled roars reverberated through the forest. Bursting through the foliage like two apex ambush predators, the team looked on in horror as the two adult gigantopithecus now stood at the edge of the muddy embankment, staring at the three fleeing inhabitants quickly scurrying their way up the opposite hillside.

One of the huge creatures rested on all fours while the other was hanging the bulk of itself over the embankment as it let out another deep and throaty roar. Meanwhile, across the other side of the river, the smaller of the two sun bear cubs came to a stop in the mud and turned its body around. Almost as if it were mocking the two huge hulking adults, it let out a series of high-pitched yapping cries. Both creatures reciprocated with deep and intense moaning roars.

The young sun bear let out a few more squealing yaps toward the two hulking figures still perched atop the mud embankment. The team watched as the bear then turned itself around in the mud. Now the animal was staring straight at them.

And then like something out of a slow-motion scene from a movie, Downs heard the two words he had feared all along.

"Oh, fuck," Josiah muttered.

The young sun-bear yapped loudly in the direction of the team, its head never wavering, its eyes transfixed now on the five humans. Over and over, the animal's vocal chords did their thing. And then Downs watched as the little creature turned itself around in the mud and headed up the embankment toward its family.

But it was too late. The damage had been done. From just a ways up ahead, two enormous heads housed atop two equally enormous bodies turned and shifted their bulk in the direction of the team.

With zero hesitation, the two massive creatures started to pursue the small band of humans. The two giants began snaking their way carefully along the top of the embankment. Things were moving fast as close to three thousand pounds of weight was now aggressively moving toward the team.

Downs' eyes shifted down to the water below.

"Let's go," Max said pointing down the embankment.

The team turned now and began making their way down the embankment. Progress down the hillside was both slow and cumbersome, the mud making them feel as if they were plowing their way through thick snow.

Downs had just pulled his left foot from the thick mud when he heard something falling behind him. From where he was, halfway down the mud embankment, he turned and saw that Josiah had fallen in the mud. The paleontologist lay twisted on his side, clutching at his right ankle.

Quickly, Downs glanced back up to where the two creatures stood. The two animals stood perched some twenty-five feet above on the enmbankment from where Josiah lay grabbing at his ankle. There the enormous animals stood, resting on all fours, giant furry mountains of both muscle and mass.

Josiah waved Downs to continue on toward the water.

"Go!" Josiah shouted. "Go, man! I'm fine."

Downs gave his good friend one last look, turned, and then continued on down toward the river. A little ways down below him, he saw the figure of Tori as her body splashed down noisily into the water. Now Downs could see the rest of the team as they began to scamper their way up the other side of the embankment. And then a thought quickly entered Downs' mind. This was Vietnam. Water sources here were home to crocodiles. Quickly, he did his best to scan the surface of the water. Off to the right, a little bit away from where the bears entered, the water appeared to be a bit deeper as it pooled and swirled with the current. As Downs continued scanning, he could have sworn he saw a set of eyes resting just above the water line. He strained a bit further with his eyes. And there, toward the deeper part of the river, near the roots of a tree that grew down and into the water, Downs spotted a pair of eyes moving silently toward them. It was a crocodile.

And then from behind, Downs heard noise. It was Josiah.

"Go, man!" Josiah shouted. "C'mon, let's go."

"Croc!" Downs shouted all of a sudden pointing to his right.

Josiah was moving fast now as he plunged down and into the water. Whatever pain the paleontologist seemed to have been previously racked in appeared to be all over. Downs watched his good friend quickly plow his way through the middle of the river. In no time, Josiah could be found traipsing through the middle of the river and then scrambling up the mud bank on the opposite side. Quickly, Downs made his way into the water. Turning to the right, he saw the pair of eyes continuing to move swiftly toward him. He needed to move faster, and that's just what he did as water began splashing on either side of him.

Meanwhile above him, Downs could hear the others shouting to him, shouting for him to make his way up the mud embankment, to hurry as fast as he could. Downs heard more undecipherable shouting. Looking to his right, the eyes of the croc were still moving toward him, the majority of the body hidden and submerged beneath the water. He was giving it everything he had now, his legs pushing him forward as he plowed through the flowing water

Again, more shouting from above ensued. Downs had just pulled his body free from the water, when suddenly a fierce set of jaws rose above the waterline and lashed out at him. He scampered his way up the mud bank. And there in the mud, Downs flung himself around. He saw the ferocious head of the croc at the edge of the water and then watched as the large animal pulled the rest of its thirteen foot long body from the water. With surprising speed the crocodile sprung to life and began charging through the mud. With its mouth open and letting out a loud hissing sound, the croc charged. Downs, seeing this, turned and began racing his own way up the hillside. He pushed harder until finally he had reached his team. A quick turn back and he could see the croc; the large animal had made its way halfway through the mud up the hillside, but had not pursued any further than that. Rather it just remained there, the big head followed by the powerful tail. Its jaws were slightly agape and there was a low hissing sound still emanating from its jaws. Now the team stood a safe distance away from the croc. They also now stood on the opposite side of the two gigantopithecus.

"What the hell took you so long?" Josaih said as he came and put a hand on Downs' shoulder.

Downs looked his good friend in the eyes. "You okay?"

Josiah nodded. "Yeah, just rolled the old ankle a bit. Just like when we used to play pickup basketball as kids. I'll live, though."

Quickly, Downs turned his attention back to the river. Scanning the surface of the water, the croc appeared to have disappeared back into the river. Next he heard noise. Movement from atop the opposite side of the river caught his attention. He looked out across the river. He saw the tail end of the two adult gigantopithecus. The two massive creatures were making their way back into the trees. Downs watched the huge wide rumps of the apes as they retreated back into the dense coverering of bamboo. Now the only noise came from the soft gurgle of water from the river below. All was quiet once again.

47

B rig Daniels and Finn Carter slowed a bit as they pushed through the last layer of thick bamboo and entered another small clearing of sorts. The clearing couldn't have been more than fifty yards across and featured a dozen or so palm trees in the twenty-five to thirty foot tall range. Below those palm trees, ferns grew in thick patches and clusters.

Together, both men did a quick visual sweep of the area.

Finn swung to his right and was surprised for a moment to see a downed palm tree, its roots completely exposed and dangling in the air. For a second, he wondered what could've taken the tree down. Could it have been diseased? He shook his head. No. It was far too healthy a tree to have succumbed to a disease. Surely that couldn't have been the culprit.

Suddenly, a cracking sound from off in the brush stopped both men dead in their tracks. The noise had come from the far end of the clearing in a part where no palm trees grew and the bamboo trees acted literally as a solid barrier between the rest of the forest and the small open clearing. And in fact, as Finn continued to look around, he truly saw the clearing for what it was. While there was no doubt that a certain beauty and serenity existed inside the very confines of this particular clearing, the outer ring was what was most unnerving about the setting.

Slowly, Finn's eyes began sweeping from left to right. What he saw was the reality that the bamboo trees had this place completed surrounded. One minute you could be walking about an evenly-spaced clearing, and the next you could find yourself walking through extremely thick and dense bamboo growth. The transition between the clearing and the rest of the forest was that abrupt. And what really had him on edge was the fact that every which way you turned, you were surrounded by a solid layer of trees, an immense and almost impenetrable barrier. It felt like the clearing was on full display to the rest of the forest, and that there were more than likely eyes staring at them from inside the dark and entangled forest. They were no doubt being watched. He could feel it inside him.

He shuddered at the thought. Finn had just taken a step to his right, when again the sound of something moving out at the far end of the clearing caught their attention.

Finn came to a complete stop. Out of the corner of his eye, he noticed that Brig had taken notice as well.

Silence followed. Only the rustling of the bamboo trees back and forth could be heard.

Finn could hear his heart beating, and for a second he thought that the rest of the forest could hear it too. He didn't like that one bit and for the next few seconds he focused intently on controlling his breathing, trying to slow his body down. There was no doubt he was having a hard time. Out of the corner of his left eye, he looked over at his partner Brig. Brig stood confident and still, a statue of physical prowess in every sense with the cigar still clenched firmly between his teeth. He had been gnawing on that thing for quite some time now.

Still watching the man from the corner of his left eye, Finn watched as Brig continued to work that cigar back and forth in his mouth for all it was worth. Perhaps he was feeling the pressure as well. Or perhaps he just liked to chew on big tobacco leaves.

If he is feeling it, he certainly doesn't show it, Finn thought to himself as he turned his view straight ahead of them. But when he did so, this time he saw something. Faint and from the distance of some one hundred and fifty feet, something immense stared back at him. It took a moment but eventually the realization came full circle. It was one of the gigantopithecus. The animal was showing no signs of aggression though. Rather, it stood still as a statue, resting confidently on the knuckles of one of its huge arms.

"What'll we-"

"Quiet," Brig breathed as he raised his tranquilizer gun.

And then suddenly, noise from somewhere off to their left could be heard. Rather quickly, something was making its way through the forest, out and away and on the right-hand side of the lone gigantopithecus.

Quickly, Finn's eyes shot back toward the lone creature still staring at them from the edge of the clearing. As the noise continued from inside the forest, Finn watched as the enormous giant didn't budge.

Was this a coordinated attack? Possibly a diversion of sorts?

Finn didn't know. All he knew with certainty was that something was moving aggressively through the brush just to the left of where they stood. Quickly, he turned to have a look. Whatever was moving through the brush had now reached what appeared to be the midway point of the clearing. Finn and Brig were also situated in about the middle of the clearing as well.

Without putting any further thought into it, Finn turned his body and aimed. However, he noticed that Brig hadn't budged. The big man had never stopped facing forward, facing the giant that still sat at the far end of the clearing staring silently back at them. Brig now had the tranquilizer gun pressed out in front of him.

"Fuck it," Finn mumbled to himself as he stepped a few paces away from his partner and waited.

And there, Finn remained with his rifle aimed squarely at a thick gathering of trees that stood at just about the midway point of the clearing. When the animal inside the dense brush passed by that middle portion and continued onward, Finn immediately knew something was up. With his eyes, he followed the cracking and snapping of bamboo from inside the brush as it continued making its way out and away from them.

"What the fuck," Finn mumbled to himself.

Now he knew with certainty that something was going down as he watched with horror as the thing didn't stop; rather, it appeared to be making its way around the outer edges of the dense trees that bordered the clearing. Again, Finn flung his body around. He saw Brig and beyond that, the huge gigantopithecus still resting calmly at the far end of the clearing, when he was struck hard from behind. Finn felt the air taken from his lungs as he was pushed backward. Just before he hit the ground, his finger pressed down on the trigger, the rifle firing straight up into the air just before it went sailing out of his hands.

He hit the ground hard with an awkward thud. Now lying in the dirt with the wind having been taken from his lungs, Finn tried desperately to turn himself around. Already racked in a considerable amount of pain, he managed to stagger to his feet, but as he did so, a huge shadowy figure launched itself at him. A powerful set of jaws opened wide and bit down with crushing force onto his right shoulder blade. Teeth punctured through skin and bone as he felt a hot, searing pain dig into him. His body was jerked back and forth, tossed side to side like a ragdoll, before finally being released and thrown through the air.

Finn slammed down hard into the dirt about fifteen feet from where he had originally been attacked. Now he was lying on his back, pain radiating everywhere as both his mind and eyes did their best to take it all in. Where the fuck was his rifle? He had lost his grip on the damn thing. Summoning the strength, he pushed himself upright with his left arm, when suddenly he felt an odd sensation of dead weight. He turned his head to the right and saw his right arm was dislocated. When Finn turned himself back around to his left, he heard an unearthly roar, smelled a overwhelming stench, and saw a mouth full of powerful teeth coming straight at him.

The gigantopithecus blared loudly in Finn's face, pushing the man over easily with the bulk of its snout. Finn was knocked backward as he fell in a shallow pool of water. Landing hard on his tailbone, he tried to right himself, but as he did so, he was greeted with unbearable pain as the creature quickly spun around and bit down with crushing force upon his left foot.

Finn screamed again as the animal bit down and twisted on the ankle as bones and tendons were undoubtedly snapped and broken. In a moment of stark, surreal pain, Finn yanked his head to the left. He could no longer see Brig, and as he looked further, the lone gigantopithecus at the far end of the clearing was gone as well. Where the hell was his partner?

Movement off somewhere to his right suddenly caught him by surprise. He heard the sound of something as it went galloping right on by him, but it was too quick to see just what it had been. He heard the spat of gunfire, but again couldn't tell where the sound was coming from.

Finn yelled a primal scream of terror as the gigantopithecus bit down on his right foot. The ex-rugby player now found himself bathed in a solid wall of pain beyond measure.

Feeling as though he was on the verge of unconsciousness, his eyes rolled back into his skull and his head flopped hard against the ground. He was in the process of being dragged through the dirt when suddenly his eyes fluttered open.

He heard the sound of something galloping close by again. With his head being scraped along the ground, his eyes searched back and forth for the culprit of the galloping sound. Surprisingly, through all of this, his night vision goggles had managed to stay intact. He was being dragged faster now as his body went sloshing through another wet and muddy puddle. Next he heard gunfire, lots of it. What the hell had taken his partner so long? Either Brig was coming to his aid or the man had his own shit to deal with. Finn had no clue which one it was. All he knew was that a staccato of gunfire was ringing out from somewhere within the clearing.

Finn had just attempted to raise his neck up to see when suddenly something dashed in on his right side and took a bite out of the flesh of his neck. He screamed. The burning pain was intense, and he now had an open and bleeding wound on the back of his neck to deal with as well. Mustering every last bit of strength he could, Finn managed to see the backside of the latest culprit.

A juvenile, he thought, his mind spinning with both terror and delusion.

The last thing that Finn's mind registered was the fact that this had all been a coordinated attack. The two huge lumbering adults had used the juvenile to create a diversion while the two larger animals came in shortly afterward to do the heavy lifting. Sixty-five million years ago, packs of Tyrannosaurs would have essentially utilized the same strategy to take down their dinosaurian prey—the lumbering adults taking up the rear while the speedy youngsters raced out ahead to rip and tear chunks of flesh out of their prey.

Hunting as a pack, Finn thought to himself.

And then suddenly, lying in his own pool of blood, darkness took Finn Carter.

• • •

Bick Downs and his team stood for a moment enshrouded in silence as the last of the gunfire rang out from somewhere close by. Still standing on the opposite side of the river system, Downs clutched the Astra in his hands for all it was worth. It was all they had in terms of a lethal weapon, its stock having gone up considerably over the last few hours with the disappearance of Burr. They simply had to find their way back to the big man.

Downs' head shot up quickly as he looked out toward the opposite embankment. All was quiet with no visible signs of the two gigantopithecus. The giant animals had retreated back into the forest a short while ago. Even the family of sun bears was nowhere to be seen. Now, only the soft gurgle of water from the river system down below could be heard. Josiah was at the end of the line, and rather quickly, he gathered the others. They had now formed a tight small circle around Downs.

Downs took a moment to regather himself, get his mind and body straight. "We're all a team here right? We gotta live and die with these decisions."

Jeremiah nodded. "Bick's right."

"Live and die with what decisions?" Josiah asked with a smile.

"Well, for starters, we got a lot to deal with right now. We're potentially being hunted by two enormous creatures long thought to be extinct. We've lost a member of our team. We have gunfire going off all around us, and we're supposed to be here to capture, sedate, and transport a gigantopithecus to the S.C.A.'s reserve in the wilds of Siberia."

Not a word was said. Downs was right. It was most definitely a lot to take in. Actually, it was a shit ton to take in. Downs looked back across the river to the other embankment for a moment. Meanwhile, Tori stepped aside and set her gaze up upon the river as well.

"I wonder how far the water runs in each direction?" Tori asked.

Downs eyed her for a moment. Instantly he knew what she was getting at.

"Because, ah," Max said, "we have a natural barrier between us and the two creatures so long as we are on the other side of this river."

Downs glanced over toward the opposite embankment again. "Definitely would appear so."

"And when we're on the same side as them?" Josiah asked.

Downs shook his head. "Well then, all bets are off. Game on."

"Shit outta luck is more like it," Josiah replied.

For a moment, Downs scanned up and down the river as far as the night vision goggles would allow. Both parts went on for about fifty yards or so before the bends and turns in the river twisted off and into the vegetation. It was hard to tell just how far this natural barrier extended in both directions. It was anyone's guess.

There was absolutely one hundred percent no doubt that Downs was worried about the safety and well-being of Burr Wellington. That was a given. That was the easy part. The problem resided in the fact that they had so much on their plates right now, not to mention their own safety and well-being to look out for as well. It seemed to be one thing after the other, one giant clusterfuck that seemed to be compounding rather aggressively each hour.

Downs exhaled a long and drawn-out sigh. "Look, we all knew the risks comin' into this mission."

Again, Downs looked back to the river. Still no sign of the creatures. "We have a lot of shit to do, have no clue how long this barrier extends in either direction, and the list goes on and on."

"So what are you sayin', man?" Josiah asked.

Downs eyed each of them. "We can't go searchin' for Burr. At least not right now. We have absolutely no clue where he is. We need to start addressing the problems currently at hand. One by one. Then once we've addressed each of those problems we'll circle back to him."

Downs cleared his throat. "Problem numero uno is just who in the fuck is responsible for all this gunfire. We need to see what we're up against, who we're dealin' with. Understood?"

Downs took a moment, gathered himself. "Second problem revolves around the fact that there isn't just one gigantopithecus. We know there appears to be at least two adults, a juvenile, and potentially more."

"We definitely don't have the capability to sedate and prepare two full-grown gigantopithecus for transport," Jeremiah chimed in.

"You can say that again," Tori said. "Those things are as big as a small car."

Downs continued. "I think what we should do here is this. We first need to get to the heart of what this organization is about, and that is keeping long thought to be extinct species away from the prying eyes of the world. Let's cut right to it. Maybe success on this mission means simply pushing these creatures into the deeper parts of the forest, and most importantly above all else, keeping and making sure they remain a secret from prying eyes. Not allowing whoever it is that's in this forest with us to get word out and spread knowledge of both their existence as well as their whereabouts."

Jeremiah continued to nod his head in approval. So too did Max Caldwell.

"So we're all in agreement then," Downs said. "The objective of the mission has changed. We're no longer trackin' down an animal, sedating, and then calling in the air team. We're makin' the executive decision that from this point forward, it'll be up to us to make sure these animals remain a secret, to push the animals into the deeper uncharted parts of this forest. That'll be the primary goal, to simply maintain their secrecy. But before we do that, we gotta find out who's in this forest with us, but most importantly how we can defeat them and remove any and all evidence via cameras, phones, etc."

Max stepped aside and looked back down the mud embankment toward the water. "And, uh, in order to achieve this objective, we need to cross the river once again and head back that way, back toward where all the gunfire came from."

Downs took a quick scan back to the river, his eyes looking for visible signs of any potential crocs. He knew that despite the night vision goggles, all he would be able to see at best would be glimmering eyes staring back at them. As he continued to scan though, he saw nothing. Whether on land or on water, this place seemed to be one potentially lethal obstacle after another.

And then with a sigh, Downs nodded and looked toward the others. Taking one final glance at everyone, he looked over to Max. "Alright, let's do this then."

And with that, the team turned and began heading down the mud embankment toward the water.

48

In the very early morning light, Burr Wellington came to the realization that the rope that the two military men had fastened around his waist was not as tight and constricting as he had initially suspected. He now believed that he had the small window of wiggle room necessary to begin working the rope up and down on a sharp knot protruding out of the back of the bamboo tree. That's exactly what he began doing. First he started slowly and deliberately. Then Burr began to work the rope up and down vigorously, rubbing the rope against the knot on the back of the tree and pushing forward with his full weight for all it was worth. A short while later, the rope eventually gave way and Burr slumped forward. He now found himself a free man. Semi-delirious from blood loss, he stood to his feet and tried to gather himself. He was still bound around both his wrists and ankles. Wasting no time, Burr was able to hop his way through the low-lying vegetation until he stumbled upon a large rock. From there he began to rub and cut the rope around his wrists on the sharp part of the rock. The rope was no match for the rock's sharp edge. Once Burr had managed to get the rope arounds his wrists off, he went to work untying the rope around his ankles. Next he quickly went about locating his shirt that lay in the vegetation and immediately tied a tourniquet above where the two men had cut him and left him to bleed out. Once he had managed to stem the bleeding, he was able to get his bearings straight. With a little bit of work and a struggle, he was able to get himself back to where he had initially hid his flare gun in a gathering of wet ferns. He secured it in his back pocket and then continued on his way.

• • •

A short while later, Burr found himself hemmed in closely by vegetation as noise approached him. He jammed his hand into the brush and tore away at a loose piece of bamboo. Thankfully, the bleeding in his right forearm had dried and caked over somewhat. He was grateful for that. He didn't fancy dying out here in the middle of nowhere.

Now he was surrounded by dense brush with the Orion flare gun and extra flare cartridges tucked inside his back pocket. He managed to get hold of a piece of bamboo that had to be damn near seven feet in length. With not a moment to spare, he turned and jammed it into the attacker as the animal rushed forward, mouth agape and blasting a hot breath of musty stench his way.

Although the bamboo was not necessarily as sharp as he would have liked, it did have somewhat of a natural pointed and jagged edge simply by the way it had been torn off. The attacker, a one hundred and fifty pound, five foot long sun bear, howled in anger as Burr once again jammed the bamboo into the side of the animal. The small yet aggressive sun bear let out a moaning growl of pain, took a few steps back, lowered its head, and then roared as it charged once again.

"Jesus Christ!" Burr shouted as he jumped to the side, plunging the bamboo into the backside of the bear as the animal raced on by him.

Burr was both intrigued and terrified at the same time. The sheer ferocity and aggression with which this small species of bear possessed was utterly remarkable. How could such a relatively small bear be so goddamn aggressive? Perhaps living in this forest with a small population of gigantopithecus still in existence had forced such a drastic change in both its behavior and nature. This is what it had taken in order for the species to survive. Burr didn't know the answer. All he knew was that he had his hands full as the bear ran for about ten feet and then turned itself around. It shook its body, took a moment to gather itself, and then lowered its neck out and bellowed another moaning roar.

The sun bear charged once again. Burr looked down at the piece of bamboo still clutched firmly in his bloody hands. If he could only buy himself a small window of time, he could sharpen the damn thing and make a sort of makeshift spear, but Burr quickly realized he wasn't going to get such a break. At the last second, he flung his body to the right, once again jabbing the bamboo into the neck of the enraged creature. This time, he had stuck the animal good. Surprisingly though, the small yet rotund girth of the sun bear had knocked Burr off his feet. He tumbled and fell to the ground. Landing awkwardly, the piece of bamboo slipped out of his hands and momentarily disappeared.

The minute that Burr found himself lying on his ass on the ground, scrambling, and desperately trying to get back to his feet, the sun bear came charging in. Baring teeth with its mouth wide open, the small but extremely powerful animal began scratching, clawing, and biting at Burr wherever it could. The one hundred and fifty pound animal's attack had now reached its pinnacle. The only choice the big man had was to cover his head into a ball as the attack continued. Burr felt the hot panting breath of the animal against his skin as the thing continued to claw, bite, and scratch him all over.

Now a sense of disorientation set in as the bear kicked and scratched at Burr with the long and curved claws from its front two limbs. Still lying on the ground in a tight ball, Burr somehow managed to kick the back leg of the bear. It did nothing though and only served to further enrage the bear as the attack continued.

The only thing he could do now was to roll himself from his right side to his left. Burr somehow managed to do just that, his hands and arms covering his head as best they could as the attack waged on. It hadn't done much. Now the sun bear was simply biting, scratching, and clawing at the left side of his body.

And then suddenly in the madness of it all, Burr realized that he had closed his eyes shut. He opened them, saw the two back legs of the creature, and with his right foot delivered as swift a kick to the animal's hindquarters as he could muster.

For a split second, Burr thought that the kick hadn't done a damn thing. But then he watched as the animal lifted its hind leg and moved several feet to the left.

Burr noticed something. But then the animal moved back to where it had originally been, and whatever Burr had seen was now blocked by fur and muscle. Again, Burr kicked out with his left leg, this time harder. Burr knew he had struck the animal hard in the hind limb this time because the bear pulled back for a moment and let out a loud and piercing yelp of a cry. The minute that the animal had dislodged itself from him, Burr launched his attack. He delivered a swift kick with his size fifteen boots to its back left leg. The result was an animal yelping in pain, but more importantly, an animal that was slowly starting to back up.

This small window of separation gave Burr all the distance he needed. Quickly, the big man rose to his feet. The sun bear meanwhile came charging in. This time Burr sent his huge fist slamming straight into the head of the bear. He heard the dull thud as the knuckles of his fist collided with dense bone. He had given it everything he had.

The sun bear lowered its head for a moment. It let out a low moaning sound as it backed itself up several feet.

Immediately, Burr turned and began searching through the ferns for what he had seen only seconds prior when he was lying on the ground being attacked. At first, he saw nothing, but then he spotted it. About fifteen feet from where he was lay a rock roughly the size of a football. Burr stumbled forward. With a grunt, he picked up the fifteen to twenty pound rock and turned to face his attacker. Now he had the rock firmly in his grasp. It was a good-sized rock by anyone's estimates. And there in the low-lying ferns, bleeding and covered in bite and scratch marks, Burr Wellington stood staring back at the sun bear.

The sun bear stood some twenty-five feet away from him. The animal straightened its head out and blasted out another roar. The minute the animal took up charging, so too did Burr.

Burr sprinted forward. He ran through the low growing ferns and back onto the dirt. And there, the two combatants met in spectacular fashion. The sun bear let out one final bellowing roar as it was finally upon the Washington native. Burr used both hands to grip the rock like a baseball bat and with everything he had smashed it right into the side of the roaring bear's face.

The bear continued on its way as Burr lost his grip on the rock and went running and trampling once again through low-lying vegetation. Burr came to a stop and flung himself around. The rock was now some ten feet away from him lying in the dirt. He looked back toward the bear. The fierce one hundred and fifty pound predator made one last attempt to turn itself around before finally, its body weight won out and it collapsed under its own weight. And there the animal lay.

Burr made a beeline straight for the rock. He knew what needed to be done. He located the rock, picked it up, and then made his way toward the fallen animal.

When Burr arrived, he found the sun bear lying on its side. He approached the backside of the animal with caution, making his way to the head of the animal.

Instantly, he noticed the blood quickly spreading beneath the mass of the bear.

"Blunt force trauma to the head," Burr muttered to himself. "Helluva way to go."

He saw the mouth open, the thick tongue slathering back and forth. The bear looked like a dog panting for water. What had once been fear quickly shifted to that of empathy on Burr Wellington's part. Burr felt a tremendous sadness as the sun bear now lay dying on its side in a growing pool of blood. But it had to be done. It was either the bear or Burr at this point.

Burr looked down at the large rock still firmly in his grasp. Then his eyes shifted toward the bear. His feet were probably a good five feet away from the head of the animal. He was still playing it safe, steering clear, not taking any chances getting too close to those aggressive snapping jaws. Upon seeing him, the bear managed to lift its head several inches off the ground before letting it flop back down with a heavy thud.

Burr could see that the animal was struggling, its breathing coming in low and ragged gasps. The growing pool of blood beneath the mass of the animal now supported the notion that it was bleeding out, literally dying right there before him. Again, he looked down at the rock. There was nothing more on this earth that Burr hated to see than that of an animal in distress. He got down on his hands and knees and scooted himself forward. He was now no more than two feet from the head of the animal, just at the edge of the growing pool of blood. The bear simply couldn't go on like this. Burr took in a deep breath of air through his nose and let it out through his mouth, steadied himself, and quietly raised the rock above his head. And then with every last ounce of strength he could muster, Burr Wellington sent the rock crashing straight down through the skull of the animal.

• • •

Diane Clor had been hastily making her way through the forest as the early morning sunlight continued filtering down through the canopy from high above. Bits and pieces of light streamed in wherever there was space and an opening in the canopy. Suddenly though, she forced herself to a stop. She reached in the side pouch of her backpack and drank thirstily from her water bottle. Diane could tell that morning was slowly approaching. With that in mind, she flicked off her headlamp. Now the forest had taken on a dark grey color to it, a silent green world waiting patiently to start another warm and humid day.

Finishing her water, she stuffed the bottle back into her pouch and continued on her way. She had been busy traversing her way rapidly down the same trail that she and Bob Hohrman had previously traversed.

Meanwhile, on both sides of her, the jungle lay for the most part silent and still. She kept her eyes glued to the trail though, moving forward, moving with both a sense of determination and purpose. She was already starting to go over things in her head that she was going to do once she got back to camp.

Diane hadn't taken more than ten steps when suddenly, the image of Bob Hohrman popped into her head. The thought hadn't exactly come out of left field. After all, it had probably only been twenty or so odd minutes ago that she had left the man injured and at the bottom of a ditch. But despite the fact that it had been as recent as twenty odd minutes or so ago, she thought she had put that behind her, had compartmentalized and moved on. After all, that's what she had done for the past fifteen years. When her first husband had died suddenly after eighteen years of marriage, she put it behind her and moved on. When she finally managed to get engaged two years later, only to be stood up at the altar, she moved on. When the guy she had been dating as recently as six months ago all of a sudden said he couldn't continue, Diane moved on. The simple fact was for the past fifteen years, Diane Clor had been putting things behind her, putting things quickly in her rear view mirror, and moving on with her life. It's what she had done, to compartmentalize things, walk away, and just move on.

But now here in the middle of fucking nowhere in Vietnam, something was tugging at her, constantly nagging at her side. She tried to continue making her way back to the camp, but she couldn't. Weighing her down like an eight hundred pound gorilla sitting squarely atop her shoulders was Bob Hohrman and what he potentially represented. She took a deep breath. Suddenly she felt light-headed. What had she done to him? He didn't deserve that. It was just that he happened to be in the wrong place at the wrong time, and that he essentially stood in her way of acquiring more footage, the type of footage that Stacey Winston had spoken of. Despite the want and need to make this documentary a monumental success no matter the cost, she still felt a sense of tremendous guilt for what had transpired in regards to Bob.

"There's still time," she said aloud to herself.

And with that, Diane turned herself around and began heading back toward where she had left Bob. She was walking fast now. She had only left him twenty minutes or so ago. She would help him out, deal with whatever minor injury or injuries he had sustained, and figure out the rest from there.

She didn't have everything worked out, but she knew she needed to get to him. The thought of what resided in this forest quickened her pace now.

Nothing was going to stop her. As she continued plowing her way through the game trail back to Bob, she wondered how he would fit in with her plan of getting more gigantopithecus footage. She was confident she'd be able to get Bob to rethink things in regard to continuing on with this documentary.

She shook her head. One thing at a time, one thing at a time. Handle the first thing and move on from there. And the first order of business right now was to get back to the hole to make sure he was still there.

Now she was getting close. She slowed a bit, prepped her mind, tried to give herself a moment to recapture her thoughts, regain clarity if you will. She was making the right choice. She knew this. The only question that remained was how would Bob react? She honestly didn't know and had no way of knowing but was sure that one thing and one thing only would save the day. And that was money. Money trumps all. Always has and always will. She'd find a way to get him more of a cut. After all, he had a wife and kids, and a wife and kids cost money. Money always trumped all. She'd find her way to work her magic in regard to that issue.

Now she was really close. She came to another stop and heard herself breathing. She was nervous. Her heart was racing.

Breathe, she told herself. *It hasn't been that long. Just walk right up to him and lend a helping hand.*

That was it. Without putting any further thought into this, she continued moving forward. Diane had always been a firm believer that too often, humans over complicated things. Life was simple, and more often than not the solutions to problems were even simpler. She had already rehearsed the scene in her head. She'd walk right up to the hole, Bob would still be at the bottom, she would extend a hand down toward him and help him back up to the trail. It was as simple as that. Once that was done, and Bob's injuries were addressed, everything else would fall into place regarding the continuation of the documentary. Diane was certain of this.

With a renewed pep in her step, she suddenly came to a screeching halt. Some five feet away from her was a long streak of blood. As she followed it with her eyes along the ground, she saw that that the trail of blood went abruptly off the game trail and made its way into the dense foliage. She shuddered to herself as she continued moving forward.

Diane now had a really bad feeling about things as she continued creeping forward one step at a time. She neared the hole. She was still a few feet away from it, not quite able to peer down into it. She stopped moving.

"Bob, are you there?" she whispered.

The forest had grown incredibly quiet.

Her heart was pounding hard against her ribcage as she waited for a response. When none came, she swallowed the saliva that had built up in the back of her throat and stepped forward another yard or so. Now she could see down into the hole on the far end. No sign of Bob. She moved forward and then stopped again. The only place the man could be now was up against the part of the hole that she couldn't see down into, right up against the dirt wall itself. Suddenly she found herself not wanting to go any further.

Again, she called out, her voice barely above a whisper. "Bob, are you there? It's me, Diane."

For a moment she felt foolish. Why the hell would she announce herself by name? Who the hell else would it be, walking and stumbling around in the wee hours of the jungle morning? Whatever she was thinking, it honestly didn't matter.

Now her heart was really thumping and she had a pounding migraine to add to the list as well. Slowly, she moved forward the last few feet. Wasting no more time, she lowered her head and looked down. Nothing but dirt and some detached palm fronds lay at the bottom of the hole. Immediately, she looked up and drew in a deep breath. It felt like the wind had been taken from her lungs. Her worst nightmare had in fact been confirmed. Bob was gone.

Suddenly, she heard movement off in the brush to her left. She froze in place for a moment before slowly turning in that direction. She found herself hoping that it was Bob, that perhaps the guy had scrambled his way out of the hole and then went wandering off into the brush. However, she found nothing but swaying stands of bamboo.

Now that she had fully turned her body, she started to see what looked like blood. Quickly, she looked back to the hole. She was surprised she had missed it before, but on the side of the hole that lay close to the vegetation where she had just heard the noise, she saw blood, lots of it. Slowly, Diane's eyes began to take it all in.

There was blood that led up the dirt wall from the hole back up to the game trail. At the top of the hole, there was also a small pool of blood. And then from there, there were drops and splotches of blood that veered off into the vegetation. After that, everything disappeared off into the brush.

Diane looked back toward the hole and then swiveled her head to the left and took in the bamboo trees. How had it come to this? How had things gotten so completely out of control? She heard movement again from somewhere off in the brush. By now, her senses were tripping out on her. Again, movement stirred. But this time it had come from much closer, possibly as close as twenty-five yards. Suddenly, all that feeling of guilt toward what had happened to Bob disappeared. Now all she felt was fear, fear for her own safety and well-being. She wanted to get away from this place, to put it far behind in her rear view mirror. To do exactly what she had planned on doing the first time around, to continue the documentary, and most importantly, to go about acquiring new breathtaking footage.

Again, she heard more movement from off in the brush. She found herself wondering if it was Bob, or if it was something else, something far, far worse. Whatever it was, Diane now felt she had reached her breaking point.

Fuck this.

And with that, Diane Clor took off running back toward her tent, back to safety.

• • •

Bob Hohrman's bloodied left arm forced its way through the brush as limbs and branches tore and scraped at him. The forest was fighting back. He came to a stop. He was bleeding all over, and his right ankle was severely sprained if not worse. He hunched over for a moment, taking in where he was. Bob leaned himself up against two thin bamboo shoots that grew in close proximity to one another. Now propping his body up against the two trees while still breathing heavily, Bob was able to fully take stock of what had just happened.

Surely he had not fallen in some random ditch in the middle of the game trail. He had been led there on purpose. But most importantly, he had been led there by Diane.

But why? It didn't make any sense. Why would Diane go forth such a horrific act? It made absolutely no sense whatsoever. At least that's how he saw it.

Unless, Bob thought to himself. *Unless.*

His thoughts quickly reverted back to the sharp sounds of gunfire that had gone off from somewhere in the forest a short while ago. Was Diane somehow linked to that? Bob thought about it for a moment. He simply didn't know. Again in his mind, he could still hear the sound of gunfire. He shuddered. If there was one thing that scared Bob Hohrman more on this earth than anything, it was that of guns. It was as frightening a proposition as one could ever hope to have to endure.

Quickly, Bob turned himself around. He was hemmed in closely now by tall bamboo on all sides of him. For the second time now in less than a minute, Bob felt his body shudder. But this time, it wasn't on account of guns, it was because of what he knew was essentially out in this forest with him.

He knew what resided in the deep dark passages of the forest, and it downright chilled him to the core. Despite the fear running through him, Bob took a step away from where he had been propping his body up against the tree. The minute that his right ankle took his full body weight, he knew he wouldn't be able to go more than a dozen or so paces. In fact, how he even got himself out of the hole and to where he currently found himself could be considered a small miracle in its own right. But in all seriousness, Bob couldn't walk. He was stuck right where he was. Leaning himself up against the bulk of the tree once again, Bob's thoughts now began to consume him. How could Diane have been capable of this? How could she have done this to him? She had essentially led him into what should have been his tomb. But Bob couldn't and would't let that happen. As a former cancer survivor, the will to live was as strong as anything. Just as he had beaten cancer a decade prior, he knew he would prevail. He would beat this, defy the odds, and most importantly, find a way to get home safely to his wife and two kids.

Bob needed to figure a way out of this living nightmare, and he needed to come up with something fast. For if he didn't come up with something soon, he ran the risk of this area, packed tightly with its tall thin bamboo trees, turning into his final resting place, his coffin for all of eternity.

49

Bick Downs held up a closed fist. The team behind him came to a stop. Before Downs lowered himself to have a look at the track in the mud, he pulled his night vision goggles off and reached around and stuffed them in his backpack. The others also did the same.

Morning had finally come to the bamboo forest. And with it, that meant that the night vision goggles were no longer needed. Although in most parts of the forest, things were always a perpetual dim grey color, Downs could now see bits and pieces of light as they streamed in via the openings in the canopy from high above.

Downs crouched where he was. The others held their positions in line. In the mud below Downs was the print from what appeared to be a rather large boot. Immediately, Downs worked out in his head that it had not come from Burr Wellington. It wasn't big enough. Downs put his own size twelve next to it to get a sense of scale for the track. The print in the mud was just about the same size. Downs knew that depending on the shoe, Burr wore either a size fifteen or sixteen. The track in the mud did not appear to have come from

Burr Wellington. Downs suspected that the track had more than likely come from the men whom the team saw was responsible for all the gunfire.

But just who were those men? They had obviously come for one of the creatures, if not more. As Downs continued crouching while staring down at the footprint, his mind continued to run through everything that they were up against.

Suddenly he felt hungry. Actually, he felt really hungry as his stomach rumbled. It had that hollow empty feeling to it. Of course, spending the entire night awake didn't help either. Quickly, Downs turned and faced the others. "I think we need to take a short break. Get some food in us."

As Downs looked a bit closer, what he saw were tired, spent, and hungry faces. They needed to get some food in them, some sustenance. As the team came in close together, Jeremiah pointed to the footprint in the mud. "I'm assuming that's not Burr."

Downs shook his head no. "Judging by the size and pattern of the tread, I suspect it has to be from the two guys we saw in dark camo outfits."

Downs reached into his bag and pulled out one of the premade sandwiches and a Powerbar. This wasn't going to be comfortable, but then again, this terrain was anything but comfortable. Quickly, Downs began unwrapping the sandwich as he had holstered the revolver at his side. Meanwhile, the air rifle was propped up against a bamboo tree to his left. Everyone else got the hint and followed Downs' lead.

Downs took a bite of the sandwich. Turkey and cheese with lettuce never tasted so good. Several bites later, the sandwich was gone. Next he went to town on the Powerbar. As he took his first bite into it, Josiah wandered over to him.

Downs nodded to him. "What's up?"

Josiah smiled. "Not much man."

Downs quickly looked at his good friend and then back toward the others. Their faces and body expressions said it all. People were tired. They couldn't go on wandering aimlessly like this forever. Downs took a few more bites before finally speaking through a mouthful of energy bar. "I think we need to get back to camp. Assess things from there. Besides, we can't be leavin' any of our tents or stuff here. Leave no trace behind. No direct evidence that we were ever even here."

Immediately, Max's head popped up. Downs watched as the zoologist pulled a compass from his back pocket. "Before we left, I took detailed coordinates of the camp."

"Good shit, Max," Josiah said to him.

Tori smiled at Max. "Do you think you can get us back?"

Max nodded. "Should get us back within the general vicinity. From there we'll hopefully stumble right out into the open and be back at the camp."

"Okay, it's settled then," Downs said. "Let's head out, get our asses back to camp. From there, we'll work out our next move."

Downs finished the last of the energy bar and took one last swig of water before finally heading out.

• • •

Twenty to twenty-five minutes or so later, the team stumbled through the last layer of vegetation before emerging out into a small open clearing. Before them lay their camp, or at least what was left of it.

"Holy shit," Josiah said.

Tori's eyes quickly took it all in. "Jesus."

Before them lay the tattered and ruined remains of their camp. With their air rifles raised, they carefully proceeded forward.

Downs both saw and heard the soft gurgle of water just to their left. It was coming from the stream. Next his eyes locked in on the tiny makeshift moat that they had built to surround their camp. It now lay completely dry. As he began making his way toward it, he saw Max moving out ahead.

Quickly, Max bent down to have a look. The small moat was bone dry.

Downs followed the moat with his eyes as the others continued to make their way further into the camp. Downs crouched next to Max.

"This moat," Max said as he placed his hand inside the empty dirt walls, "acted as a form of protection. Wasn't certain but it appears even these huge primates exhibit the same natural aversion to water that modern-day gorillas do. With the water gone, they, uh, stormed the castle. No barrier to entry."

Downs was just about to stand to his feet when suddenly Max grabbed him by the leg.

"Look," the zoologist whispered.

Slowly, Downs raised his head. He saw it. Out about fifty yards or so, a head had materialized from way out in the foliage.

"A juvenile," Downs whispered

"Exactly," Max muttered back.

Meanwhile, the rest of the team continued moving about through the camp. Downs watched as the juvenile's head immediately shot toward the moving humans. The animal shifted its weight. Downs could not see the lower part of the juvenile's body, the vegetation was too thick way out there. He could only see the upper half, primarily that of the head. The animal let out soft grunting sounds as it moved itself several feet to the left.

Downs watched as the rest of the team eventually took notice. Each member immediately froze in place. They had all now heard it. The juvenile gigantopithecus also froze. It turned back in the direction of Downs and Max.

Still with the air rifle slung around his right shoulder, Downs gently strummed the trigger with his finger. The head of the juvenile remained steady and attentive, not budging, not moving an inch, the eyes everpresent and watchful.

Meanwhile, Downs continued to strum the trigger of the air rifle. Even from a distance, he noted the muscular physique of the animal, the wide chest, the powerful limbs, the beginning of what would one day be the pronounced dome-shaped head.

Downs tilted his head ever so slightly toward Max, the entire time continuing to make eye contact with the juvenile off in the foliage.

"Now what?" Downs whispered to Max.

"You know," Max whispered back out of the side of his mouth. "You know that we shouldn't be making eye contact in the first place. Comes off as a threat. But…"

"But what," Downs said.

Max continued whispering. "But the animal doesn't appear to be threatened or agitated, so just keep still."

Downs decided to try something. Slowly he reached to unhook the air rifle from around his shoulder. The result was instantaneous. The sudden movement in turn triggered movement from way out in the foliage.

Max had immediately taken note of the change in the animal's behavior and appearance. From his crouched position, he looked back up at Downs. Downs shrugged his shoulders and gave a smirk. Meanwhile, Max returned a look that basically conveyed one thing. Don't fucking do that again.

Downs returned his eyes to the juvenile. The animal remained frozen, hemmed in closely by thick vegetation. Only the head was still visible. Downs looked back to the rest of the team. They were each frozen in their own positions amidst the crumpled and tattered remains of their small camp.

Downs looked back to the juvenile. The animal continued to stare silently back at them.

• • •

Burr Wellington pushed through a thick layer of jungle before finally spilling out into an open clearing. And thank God for it. As if the brutal injuries he had suffered while being kidnapped and strapped to a bamboo tree weren't enough, now he had dozens upon dozens of cuts and scrapes along the open areas of his body. The forest was winning.

Moving forward, he stepped out into the early morning light as the sun continued streaming down onto the clearing. As Burr had a quick look around, he estimated the clearing to be roughly the size of a regulation basketball court. The problem at this point though was that he had absolutely no clue where he was in relation to Downs and the others. He had gotten all twisted up. And it wasn't that difficult to do just that. With every corner of the forest seemingly looking alike, the idea of getting completely turned around was a very realistic problem. All Burr knew with certainty was that this clearing at least offered up the chance to take a mental breather, to catch his breath and step out of the nightmarish maze of wall-to-wall bamboo growth. For the past thirty minutes or so, it felt like the trees had been constantly pushing against him. The forest and the stranglehold of vegetation that resided within it had taken on a very claustrophobic feeling.

Burr took several deep breaths and stared up at the sky. He wondered how the others were doing. He wondered where they were? He wondered where *he* was? He found it beyond words just how frustrating it was that out of all those questions he had just asked himself, he knew the answers to none of them.

All Burr really knew with absolutely certainty was that he was standing in an open clearing with bright, beaming rays of sunshine streaming down. Dense stands of tall bamboo trees surrounded the clearing on all sides, blowing and swaying occasionally whenever there was a breeze big enough to do so.

Burr took in another deep breath and focused his gaze on the tall swaying stands of trees. Still bare-chested, he was scared and he knew it. He had no clue how he would get back to the others. He had no clue if the two large men who took him captive would return for him. Things had gone terribly awry. Burr had always prided himself on his sense of direction. It had always aided him time and time again in the many Sasquatch and Bigfoot trackings that he had undertaken in the state of Washington over the years. But now here in the middle of this clearing, Burr was having a difficult time understanding just where he was in relation to the rest of the team. He knew where the sun was, and therefore knew which direction east and west was. But after that, he didn't know much. He had gotten himself far too turned around back in the forest. Now it was all about damage control, trying to find a way safely back to the others.

Burr reached into his back pocket. He felt somewhat naked without his air rifle and most importantly his Astra revolver. It had been a shock to the system when both weapons had been confiscated by those two overgrown gargantuans. Those fuckin' bastards. But Burr Wellington was quite a resourceful man. Just minutes before Burr had arrived at the base of the bamboo tree, he had managed to discretely drop his flare gun from his back pocket into the deep vegetation close to where he had been seated. When he had managed to escape and free himself from the bamboo tree, he was able to find and locate the flare gun where he had tossed it. And now, as Burr stood in the open clearing, he realized it had most definitely been worth it. He should have dropped the Astra instead, but hey it was better than nothing at this point. Simple as it was, it was worth its weight in gold now. He stood a good chance that he just might be able to signal his team with it. But he also knew that shooting a flare up and into the sky would also alert the military men as to his presence. He was fully aware of this. The flare gun also offered a slight chance of protecting himself if needed. It was most definitely better than nothing and he was grateful to still be in possession of it.

He looked down at the small black and orange plastic gun. Without giving any further thought to it, Burr pointed the flare gun toward the sky and fired.

50

Diane Clor tripped and fell on the trail as the early morning light continued streaming down through the openings in the canopy high above. She had landed awkwardly on the hard dirt, breaking her fall thankfully with her outstretched hands. Now she sort of wiggled and massaged her wrists in the air for a moment. Both of them had taken the full brunt of the impact with the fall. Rather quickly, she turned around and saw the culprit. It was another one of those bastard roots that lay exposed. The fucking place was loaded with them, and she immediately found herself looking forward to putting this place in her rearview mirror. She was really looking forward to that moment.

Diane swore silently as she continued dusting herself off. Having a look back down the game trail toward where she had just come, she shuddered to herself with several thoughts. Had Bob Hohrman actually pulled himself free of the hole or had something reached down and yanked him out of there? She shuddered again with the thought of either scenario. If something had indeed reached down and pulled him out of the hole, then by now he was most likely a goner. But if Bob had climbed out of the hole on his own power, then he most definitely wouldn't be in the best of moods. Diane felt a knot forming in the pit of her stomach. It seemed that both options were equally awful.

Quickly, she shook her head and continued onward.

New beginnings, she thought to herself, and she wasn't going to give another thought to this. *New beginnings.*

As Diane continued to make her way down the game trail, ferns that grew to just about her kneecaps bordered the path on both sides of her. Beyond the ferns, the tall bamboo trees grew straight as an arrow up toward the sky.

Suddenly she looked off to her left. She thought she had both seen and heard something. But when she set her gaze back straight ahead, again she realized she had taken her eyes off the path. She tripped and fell once more. What the fuck? Was she losing her mind? This time though, there was no pausing on the ground, no taking things in. She needed to be on her way and this damn game trail was already proving to be trickier than it looked. She had had enough.

But this time, when she pushed herself up and stood to her feet, she suddenly heard something rushing through the underbrush toward her. Whatever it was had literally come out of nowhere. As she resurrected and stood to her full height, the sound abruptly came to a stop.

And there she stood, mired in silence as a soft breeze blew through the trees. Quickly, she scanned with her eyes for a fleeting second before suddenly taking off like a bat out of hell back to the camp.

• • •

Twenty-five minutes or so later, Diane Clor arrived back at camp. Her hair was displaced and disheveled, her clothes matted and soaked with perspiration, her skin had beads of sweat on it, her pulse was beating through her head, and her thoughts were running rampant.

She quickly scanned and took in the small area. It looked like a hurricane had ripped through here. Both tents were flattened and oddly there were half a dozen or so bamboo trees that had been uprooted and lay scattered about on the ground. As Diane moved closer toward the two downed tents, she saw heaps and piles of uprooted vegetation, and lots and lots of ferns scattered about everywhere. She wondered if the storm and rains from earlier could have done this or had it been something else?

She had a bad feeling about things as she kept moving forward though. On her right was her and Bob's tent. She forced herself not to think about the man and kept herself moving. She was now making a beeline straight for Stacey Winston's tent. After all, that's where she planned on recovering all the computer and camera equipment that contained the firsthand footage chronicling once and for all the existence of the gigantopithecus species.

Stepping over a dozen or so uprooted ferns and heaping piles of vegetation, she began to take in the condition of the tent. It was shredded on all sides and had a long slash that ran down the side of the tent. Diane took a deep gulp as she bent down to have a better look at the flattened tent.

Please be here, please be here, please be here.

With her hands trembling, she fumbled for the zipper to the tent. As her hands made contact, she went to task unzipping it. Now inside, her hands took a moment before they felt down upon the camera equipment as well as Stacey's laptop.

"Yes," she mumbled aloud. "Yes. Yes. Praise the Lord."

For a moment, she paused in celebration. It felt like she had won the small-time lottery. Diane pulled both cameras out that Stacey had filmed with. She took hold of the larger of the two and turned it on. With a few more clicks, she saw the coveted footage that Stacey had brought them all this way for.

Diane put the camera down on the ground and took a moment as she let out a long and drawn-out sigh. She was exhausted beyond belief, but the footage that she held in her hands was literally going to change her life. After all she had been through in her life, after all she had persevered through, she was now charging full-steam ahead. No ceiling, no limitations, about to break through toward the stars. Diane was about to live the dreams she always hoped she would achieve.

She would dedicate the beginning of the documentary to the lives lost on this expedition. She began to play the video again and watched on the screen. Now she saw Stacey perched on the edge of the hillside, standing in front of the camera for a moment as he set the tripod down in the wet mud and began to set up his shot. Then the director went behind the camera and began panning back and forth, zooming in and zooming out. At first, she saw nothing but dense brush and criss-crossing vegetation.

Finally things came into focus. Diane felt her eyes bulge a bit as she watched the camera pan one last final time and then zoom in. The lens locked in on a blurry figure at the bottom of the hillside. It took her a moment but eventually her mind put two and two together and she saw the figure in its entirety. It was Clark Geiger.

Diane felt her heart really thumping now as she pulled away for a moment. Then she watched as the camera zoomed in and focused on the subject. Clark Geiger was lying on his back in the mud, attempting with all his might to pull himself backward. It wasn't clear how he had gotten way down there at the bottom of the canyon in the first place. All that was clear was that by his limited range of mobility, the man was no doubt severely injured.

Diane watched as the camera continued to focus in on the injured man lying in the mud at the bottom of the rain-drenched hillside. As she continued to watch the video, suddenly the sounds of cracking and snapping from inside the forest could be heard. It took a moment for the camera to catch up, but when it did, Diane watched as an enormous dark figure silently emerged from the forest. The hulking form of an animal now hovered closely to Clark. Quickly, the camera zoomed in on a muscularly-built mountain of fur. In fact, the image was so big that it momentarily blocked out the entire screen. Diane watched as Stacey countered by zooming out with the camera before finally coming back into focus. And when the camera finally did come back into focus, Diane watched in horror as the adult gigantopithecus bit down viciously on one of Clark's ankles. And then the huge monstrosity spun around and bit down with crushing force on the man's shoulder. Diane continued watching as the big animal lowered its head and bellowed an immense roar. The sound rumbled through the forest. And then Clark let out a blood-curdling cry of his own as the creature dragged him off and into the deep brush. Both disappeared and then all was quiet. The video cut off the moment there was nothing left to film.

Diane quickly shut the computer down and sat upright. Her heart was racing, her breath coming in ragged breaths, and she suddenly found herself with a pounding headache. It took her brain a few seconds to comprehend what it had just witnessed. Stacey Winston, the leader and director of this documentary, had literally just left the man to fend for himself. He had let Clark Geiger die. Straight up, that was the reality of the situation. He had literally filmed and documented what was a man's demise.

Diane was seated Indian style in front of the crumpled tent, still busy trying to absorb it all, still busy trying to make sense of the enormity and gravity of the situation.

• • •

A deep silence had filled the camp as the team had been working diligently for several minutes now to put their tents away and remove all possible evidence of their stay here. Meanwhile all around them in the surrounding brush and foliage, a deep silence had suddenly besieged the forest. All was deathly quiet. Even the usual steady drone of insect chatter had ceased.

Now each of them hoisted their bags on their backs and looked around. The only visible evidence that they had been here came in the form of their small rectangular-shaped moat.

"It's not going to return," Tori whispered to no one in particular.

Downs knew she was correct. The juvenile giganto-pithecus had disappeared back into the brush. Downs was just about to move forward when suddenly he felt the odd sensation that something was behind them. Quickly, he threw himself around, the Astra leveled out in front of him. The rest of the team also flung their bodies around. And together, the five humans saw a very large man dressed in head-to-toe camo gear with a cigar gritted between his teeth and a rifle leveled out in front of him.

"Drop it, all of you," the large man said.

But it was too late. Bick Downs had already sprung into action. The big man dressed in head-to-toe camo gear keeled over in agony as blood began to pour from a bullet wound to his right leg. The team watched as the man stumbled forward and then fell to the ground. Bick Downs had shot him.

Tori turned and saw Downs holding the revolver.

"Get the weapon," Downs ordered.

And with that, the team moved forward. Josiah scooped down and with a bit of a struggle managed to wrestle the rifle from the large man. The man was not to be denied though as he grabbed at a knife stowed at his side and stabbed at Josiah's leg. The paleontologist screamed as he fell over in agony to the ground, the knife having just barely grazed through the fabric of his pants.

Out of the corner of Downs' right eye, he could see Tori as she rushed to Josiah's aid as the paleontologist fell to the ground. But all Downs could really see was the assault rifle as it too hit the ground with a heavy clank.

Downs sprinted forward. Just as he did so, he could see the big man whom he had shot in the leg reach out to grab him. Downs jumped high into the air, narrowly avoiding the large man's outstretched hands. When Downs landed on the ground, he spun, delivered a swift kick to the man's rib cage and scooped the rifle off the ground. Now Downs was in possession of the rifle. Downs had never actually held such a weapon, and the rifle felt cold and heavy in his grasp as he stared down at the man on the ground.

"Who the hell are you?" Downs demanded as he pointed the barrel of the rifle at the man.

The man, however, still clenching a cigar firmly between his teeth, grumbled to himself as he keeled over and began to have a look at the bullet wound to his right leg. Up on his right thigh, a small hole in his pants could be seen, and now that small hole had started to pump a steady stream of blood through the fabric of his pants.

"Who are you?" Downs asked again, this time with more force.

By now, Jeremiah Corstine had come round to his side. Downs handed the assault rifle over to Jeremiah. Now Downs stood several arms-lengths away from the bleeding man with the only the small yet sleek Astra revolver in his grasp.

"I'll ask again," Downs said. "Who are you? We can help you. You need help. We can get you bandaged up."

"Fuck off," the man said.

Suddenly from all around them, the forest started coming to life. Downs heard limbs and branches as they cracked and snapped. And then all of a sudden, everything stopped. Now there was a deep silence once again. Five seconds became ten, ten became fifteen, fifteen became twenty, and then suddenly the noise had once again returned. Now deep sounds of movement from within the forest could be heard. It sure as hell sounded as though the forest was converging upon them.

"We have to go," Downs said.

Now the sounds of things being broken and battered had returned as they grew rather loud. Max Caldwell sprung forward and sprinted over to Downs. When the zoologist got to Downs, he pointed at their backs. Quickly, Downs made the decision. That's where they would head. Without letting his eyes off the man on the ground, Downs motioned for the others to turn and head in that direction. The team did so, following Max Caldwell off into the brush. Now only Downs remained. Once again, he carefully approached the man. The sounds of things crashing and breaking were now louder than ever. It had gotten extremely loud as Downs neared the man on the ground. He was bleeding but he had already torn a section of his shirt off and had a makeshift tourniquet around the bullet wound.

"You need our help," Downs said, his eyes scanning.

Things were close now as the trees shook, vibrated, and swayed from all around.

"Come with us," Downs said. "We can help you. We can get you fixed up."

The man said nothing. Rather, he merely continued applying pressure to his wound. Then he looked up at Downs and extended the middle finger. Downs took one last look at the man, and then quickly began backtracking toward the thick vegetation behind him. Maintaining eye contact with the man the entire time, when his backside finally collided with one of the bamboo trees, he turned and disappeared off into the vegetation.

51

In order to keep pace, the slighty larger of the two juveniles launched its body up and over a shallow puddle of mud, splashing down sloppily on the other side on its four limbs before giving up chase once again. Meanwhile out in front of it, its speedier sibling moved stealthily though the trees while maintaining something firmly grasped in its jaws. Again, the juvenile from behind pushed harder, its body slamming and forcing its way through the tight bamboo growth. It crashed through a layer of thick undergrowth before exploding out on the other side. Now the forest thinned a bit and the animal could really push itself. Galloping on all fours, its nearly four hundred pound body was driven by one thing and one thing only at this point. And that was hunger.

With its sights set on feeding, it focused on the wide rump of its speedier sibling as both juveniles raced toward the open clearing that lay straight ahead. The juvenile out in front reached the clearing first, the second one arriving some ten seconds later. Now the latter of the two watched as the first one began circling, almost pacing back and forth, its kill still firmly clutched in its jaws.

The juvenile continued pacing back and forth before finally settling on a particular area in the clearing. Releasing its jaw muscles, its prey slumped awkwardly to the ground. And there the animal stood, resting on all fours, guarding its precious kill as the mass of its body hovered over the dead meat.

Meanwhile, the second juvenile began racing back and forth, at times going on its back two legs and beating aggressively on its chest. Next, the juvenile began an odd display of moving sideways in strange, crab-like movements. This lasted for a minute or so before eventually the animal began racing through the clearing now, tearing at vegetation where it could, before discarding and moving on to fresh patches of vegetation. In a matter of minutes, the clearing was littered with heaps of uprooted vegetation everywhere.

The slightly smaller juvenile, still guarding its kill, lowered its head, opened its mouth, and began to feed on the meat. Blood now ran down both sides of its mouth as the second juvenile gigantopithecus approached with caution.

The second juvenile continued moving forward, cautious, weary of its every step. When it neared to within an arm's-length of the feeding juvenile, it came to a stop. It paused there for a moment, watching its mate as it made feverish work of the kill. And then the second juvenile suddenly pushed its way forward, lowered its head, and began to feed. The feeding juvenile paid no attention to the other animal whatsoever. Now both animals fed on the carcass. Blood dripped from the lower part of their jaws and onto the ground beneath them.

Feverish snorts and grunts ensued as the two continued to feed. And then suddenly, the cracking of bamboo trees could be heard. An overwhelmingly large shape bulled its way into the clearing and began heading straight toward the feeding youngsters. The huge hulking shape now leaned on the knuckles of one arm and watched the two for a moment.

And then it bellowed an immense and deep roar. The rumbling sound dominated the clearing. The response was immediate. Both juveniles raised their heads and stared back at the enormous creature. With their snouts red with blood and bits and pieces of ragged flesh hanging from their lower jaws, slowly and quietly both animals began to back up from the kill.

The male gigantopithecus, still leaning on the knuckles of one of its huge front forelimbs, stood in the middle of the clearing. Now the immense creature began moving forward, its colossal bulk shifting from side to side. As the huge creature drew nearer, the two juveniles continued to retreat.

The giant adult now stood some ten feet from the edge of the kill. Resting on all fours with its enormous head towering above the ground, the massive creature suddenly rose onto its back two legs and beat aggressively with flat palms on its wide chest. More chest pounding ensued, followed by another immense bellowing roar. The animal then dropped to all fours, lowered its head, and proceeded to feed.

• • •

Bob Hohrman stood absolutely frozen in place. He was hugging his body tightly with his arms wrapped around one of the tall and slender bamboo trees. For going on the past five mintues or so, he hadn't budged so much as an inch. His arms and wrists were now scratched and bleeding as a result.

Slowly, Bob forced himself to breathe. He had no choice. The air was wet and humid, and as he still clung to the tree it felt like he was breathing through a sponge. He couldn't get a good, fulfilling breath. It reminded him of those times during the winter when he'd get a bad chest cold which in turn would trigger his asthma. It was those times of the year when he would lie awake in bed at night, not able to get to sleep simply because he couldn't get a deep breath of air. Now in the jungles of Vietnam, the humidity was very much making him feel the same way.

Breathe, Bob, breathe, he told himself.

And just like that, his hands and arms unfurled from around the tree and he carefully took a step back. Now that he had backed himself up, he suddenly felt the ability to produce a deep and fulfilling breath again. For that, he was grateful. Bob sucked in a few warm and humid breaths before he thought about what to do next.

The oxygen flowing through his body in turn triggered his brain to start thinking and processing once again. And that in turn triggered other things. He couldn't believe what he had just seen and witnessed. Bob had been wandering aimlessly through the trees when suddenly he had stopped dead in his tracks. Actually, it was more like he was forced to stop dead in his tracks. Completely caught off guard and out in the open, he frantically searched for a place to hide. Out here, it honestly felt like there was nowhere to go. So as the sounds of things charging toward him at a quick pace kept drawing closer and closer, Bob had no choice but to just cling tightly to one of the trees that was closest to him. And that's exactly what he did.

Bob had clung tightly to that bamboo tree like flies on shit as the sounds of things tearing through the forest neared. Whatever it was had literally come out of nowhere and completely surprised him. Hoping and praying that he was somewhat concealed and hidden, he caught the tail end of the two juveniles as they had literally gone racing on right by him. The two creatures had come as close as twenty feet to where Bob clung tightly to the bamboo tree. The speed at which they navigated through this maze of trees was startling, but what was even more startling was what the first of the juveniles had been clutching tightly in its mouth.

Although it had been a little difficult to make out through the endless maze of trees, Bob could have sworn that the first animal was clutching a lower torso in its mouth. He could still see it vividly in his mind, and what was even more unnerving was the fact that it appeared to have been the lower torso of a human body. The powerful jaw muscles and teeth had been sunk into the torso, while the two legs flopped back and forth on both sides. Bob could still see it burned and etched into his memory bank. He shook his head and let out a deep breath. All of a sudden, he was feeling short of breath and lightheaded once again. Bob propped himself up on a neighboring tree. His mind continued to play back what he had just seen, the images coming like the frames and shots of a movie.

Following the two juveniles, he remembered next hearing something heavy coming his way, something that caused the trees to break and bend in its presence, something that literally seemed to cause a minor disturbance to the very ground itself. Some twenty seconds or so after the speedy youngsters had raced right on by him, Bob heard a terrifying unearthly roar. This was followed by the sound of things being smashed and broken as something quickly approached. Another deep rumbling roar heralded the arrival of one of the adult gigantopithecus as the huge animal tore a swath of destruction straight through the trees.

Bob had waited until the bulk of animal had passed by him before extending his neck out as far as it would go. He caught the tail end of the animal's wide rump. The animal was massive, absolutely massive in every sense of the word.

"Holy shit," he mumbled, recounting the whole situation.

He had just seen the speed of the juveniles a short while ago, he had seen the brute size of the adults, and here he was with not a damn thing to protect himself. How could they have been so stupid as to come out here unarmed? But as Bob thought about it more, who could blame them? They didn't actually think they'd find what they'd set out to look for. Bob thought they would be making one of those cheap documentaries that he'd seen time and time again on television about The Loch Ness Monster or other Bigfoot related documentaries. One of those documentaries where there's always evidence, they always have someone citing they saw it, but every picture or video is blurred so as to have a hard time making it out. That was the type of documentary that Bob thought they'd be making way out here, something that was essentially nothing more than a cheap trick. But as he continued to stand enshrouded amongst the bamboo trees as sweat rolled down his forehead, he realized that they had been wrong. Hard as it was to imagine and comprehend, they had been dead wrong and it was a mistake to have ever come here.

52

Downs and his team had turned themselves around. Several hundred feet into their journey through the brush away from the rushing sounds of movement back where they had just come from, they now oddly found themselves traversing their way back toward the clearing. But this time they weren't merely heading straight back the same way they had exited, they were heading off a ways to the right, making their way back to the clearing at a slight angle.

Meanwhile, the light sky high above the out-stretched limbs of the canopy continued to take shape. Despite the fact that the morning was now in full effect, it was still rather dim underneath the cover of the trees. It always was for the most part. That was the true nature of this place. The team moved quietly now as they snaked their way through the tall, thin trees.

A silence now stretched around each and every member of the team. Downs had convinced them only a short while ago that they needed to get back to the clearing, that whomever was sharing this forest with them, if they were in the vicinity, would be having a look as well. Now they were close. Downs raised a closed fist into the air. The group came to a stop. Downs pointed up ahead.

Probably some twenty feet away, they could see that the trees thinned and gave way to the clearing. Downs looked back at the others quickly. Nothing needed to be said amongst any of them. He couldn't be certain exactly what they would find once they in fact had a visual back into the clearing, but he knew one thing for certain—he had just shot and injured a man in the leg. It was as serious an act as he had ever done before in his entire lifetime. In that split second, he had shot the man, thinking about nothing more than protecting the safety and overall well-being of his teammates. But also in that moment, he had quickly sized the man up. Whoever he was, he was a powerful man indeed, and Downs suspected by now that the man had gotten up off the ground and was now moving about somewhere in this forest with them. Downs kept the Astra pressed out in front of him. They couldn't be certain if the man was armed besides the rifle that they had quickly confiscated from him. It had all happened so quickly that there had not been time to do a quick pat down of the man, to do the necessary due diligence that should have been followed. But what was done was done now.

As the team neared the last of the trees before the clearing, Downs motioned for them to lower themselves. They did just that, sinking their bodies down and into the foliage as best as they could. Now they moved forward those last dozen or so feet until they came upon a thick layer of waist-high growth. Downs let out a deep breath, steadied himself, and then peered through the vegetation and back out into the clearing.

• • •

Brig Daniels had managed to pull his bleeding body from the open clearing and into the dense forest as the sounds of hungry animals began to cry out in the distance. He took a moment to get his bearings straight and take stock of what had just happened. And what had just happened was that he had just been fucking shot in the leg. He had acted quickly though, tearing the bottom part of his shirt off in order to tie a makeshift tourniquet above the gushing wound. Now it was soaked through with blood. Quickly, he went to work tearing off more of his shirt. He didn't have a second to spare. Brig had just managed to tear a section off when suddenly he heard a cavernous roar, a deep and terrifying guttural sound that seemed like something that had come from the primal past of eons ago. It sounded close by. The noise stopped him right where he was.

He was lying on his back on the ground, surrounded on all sides by thin bamboo trees. With his ears primed, he waited and listened. Quickly, he shoved aside all thoughts of what had happened to his men. Point blank, they had been decimated, and while they started as a unit of three, he now realized they would end as one. And as Brig went about the task of replacing the old, blood-soaked sleeve with that of the new one, he now realized he had a new objective. Not only was he going to get out of here alive with one of the creatures in his possession, he was going to make that bastard who had shot him in the leg pay dearly. He now had a score to settle. Brig tightened the tourniquet one last time as another immense roar rang out from somewhere close by. He knew what was out there, what was waiting for him.

Grinning and bearing through the pain of being shot, Brig managed to stand to his feet. One thing that remained entirely true was that when push came to shove, Brig Daniels was as tough as nails. He wasn't going to let a bullet stop him. No sir. No way. He would prevail in this situation. First though, he had to stop the small band of humans that he had just encountered.

• • •

From the edge of the forest, Downs quietly brought his monocular up to his right eye and peered through it. It wasn't easy at first, but as he adjusted the tiny lens things quickly came into focus. He saw the two juveniles, both equally enormous in their own right, a dozen feet away from where the main kill lay on the ground. The two creatures were now watching the adult gigantopithecus as it fed on the torso.

Suddenly, the two juveniles began pacing back and forth. It was clear they were hungry, but as Downs continued looking through the monocular, it was also clear that they weren't at the top of the pecking order. There was a social hierarchy here, meaning the biggest fed first, the smaller fed on what was left—essentially the scraps.

Downs zoomed out for a moment. All he could see was the backside of a giant mountain of fur. It was one of the adults. Its head was lowered and feeding. Next Downs did his best to focus in on the ground. Still peering through the monocular, Downs could see the back two legs. They were as big as small tree trunks. And then he saw it. Between the two huge, pillar-sized legs, Downs could see what looked like the lower torso of a human. He could see the legs, could see the half-eaten foot as it lay limply at its side.

Downs pulled away for a moment. His heart was pounding against his ribcage. Next to him, Tori had taken notice.

She mouthed the words: *You okay?*

He nodded and returned to the monocular. He began looking around. Where was the second adult gigantopithecus? Downs knew that there were at least two of these monstrosities roaming these forests, and the fact that the other one was nowhere to be seen had him concerned and on edge.

Still peering through the monocular, Downs focused his attention back on the two juveniles. They were busy play-swatting and nipping at one another. Next, he looked back to the adult. From where Downs was positioned, it looked like there wasn't much left to the lower torso. But as Downs swung the monocular around, something stopped him dead in his tracks. Tori grabbed his left shoulder at the exact same moment. She had seen it as well.

Across the clearing from where they were situated, probably a good one hundred and fifty to two hundred feet away, a woman sat entrenched in and amongst the trees. It almost looked like she was sitting lazily in the city park on a Sunday afternoon just taking in the sun and nice weather. Downs zoomed in. She was a middle-aged woman, no older than fifty. White. Caucasian. He could see that much. And now that he looked at it, she appeared to be standing, not sitting. She was standing in amongst a patch of chest-high vegetation while several slender bamboo trees grew directly in front of her. But for the most part, her head and neck were the only things visible.

Downs tapped Tori on the leg with his left hand. She knew what it meant. Quietly, she tapped the person next to her, and so on, and so on. They needed to all be alerted that the three feeding animals in the middle of the clearing weren't the only ones present. Downs pulled back for a moment, looked around. They also had a large man whom he had just shot and wounded that was unaccounted for. There was that big issue to look out for as well. Downs brought the monocular back to his right eye. Quickly, he made sure he had a good visual of the clearing. He saw the feeding adult and noticed that it wouldn't be much longer now. There wasn't much left to the torso. The two juveniles were still play-fighting a safe distance away from the feeding adult. Then Downs swung to the right. It took a moment to locate the woman, but Downs quickly spotted her once again. Whoever she was, she appeared to have changed positions. And then Downs spotted something—no doubt, the real reason she was a few feet inside the forest in the first place. Downs saw a rather expensive-looking camera mounted atop a tripod. The woman was now behind it, filming, manning it as if she were directing a scene in a big budget movie.

"We gotta get the camera," Downs whispered ever so gently.

Still situated next to him, Tori nodded. "We will."

Downs had just gone about repositioning himself, when suddenly from somewhere behind, deep and entangled amongst the bamboo, a terrifying sound could be heard.

53

Deep and intense cracking sounds from inside the foliage began to ring out at their backside. On his far left, Downs could hear Jeremiah Corstine's voice.

"Go," Jeremiah said. "Go."

With little to no choice, the team rose from their crouched positions, unhooked their bodies from inside the dense patchwork of vegetation, and pushed through the final layer of bamboo trees. They spilled out into the clearing. Now without the cover of the trees and the dense vegetation that had previously surrounded them, they lay completely exposed and on full display for all. Immediately, Downs' eyes shifted back to the feeding adult. It had hardly taken notice of their presence in the clearing as it continued to devour the last of the torso.

"We got company!" Josiah shouted, pointing.

As Downs' eyes continued moving, he could see that they had been spotted by the juveniles. The two ravenous creatures could now be seen moving rather quickly through the clearing, hugging tightly to the tree line. Downs found it downright chilling the cold-hearted way in which they moved forward. The team was now being hunted.

"We've got company there, too," Tori shouted pointing.

From back inside the forest where they had been crouched and hiding, the tops of the trees now shook back and forth furiously. Deep, immense, cracking sounds continued. Then there was a momentary silence. Downs looked back to the two juveniles. They were still stalking the team, still hugging tightly to the trees that bordered the clearing. And then as Downs spun around one last time, he witnessed a huge explosion and heard a monstrous roar as one of the adult gigantopithecus came charging out into the clearing. Now out in the open, Downs could see that it was the larger of the two adults. At just over sixteen hundred pounds in weight, and a little over ten feet in height, the massive male rose onto its back two legs and beat aggressively on its wide chest with the flat palms of its hands. Then it roared triumphantly. The bellowing cry dominated the small clearing. It was a terrifying, otherworldly sound—a sound that had come from the animal's massive chest cavity. Downs watched as the huge animal dropped to all fours. And there it stood like some type of prehistoric statue, an ancient relic of the past, yet something that was still very much alive.

Downs turned his attention back to the feeding female at the far end of the clearing. As he did so, another huge roar rang out from the animal. The torso was all but scraps and bones now as a thick cloud of flies had started to converge upon the mess. Downs shifted toward the middle of the clearing. The two juveniles were still hugging tightly to the trees, their bodies just having passed the middle of the clearing.

They were slowly closing in on the team. Suddenly, Downs looked for the lady, the woman whom he had seen filming in and amongst the trees. He saw nothing but bamboo. Where the hell had she gone? Another colossal roar and Downs realized that was now the least of their worries. Downs turned and together the team watched as the massive male was now moving toward them.

• • •

Brig Daniels adjusted himself from inside the foliage. He was standing in and amongst a thick stand of trees, a good ten feet away from where the actual clearing began. He had been watching the brewing scene out in the clearing for several minutes now. Raising the pistol, it was a bit tight where he was. This damn forest was always pushing in on you, trying to suffocate you to death in its terrible green embrace. Despite being hemmed in tightly by vegetation, he had managed to find a clear and unobstructed shot back toward the team. If he wanted, he could easily kill each and every one of them. It would be simple. It would be clean. Head shots to all of them. There would be chaos for a brief few seconds, people bleeding, people screaming, but eventually when they found out where the shots were coming from it would be over for all of them. He studied the team closely for another few seconds. Next, he saw the two juveniles who were still moving forward, still stalking their prey silently like raptors.

Perhaps he didn't have to take out the team by his own hand. Perhaps he didn't have to have that stain on his conscience. God knows in this line of work he already had enough bad memories and experiences that would break a normal man. Brig Daniels was not a murderer, but he was cold and emotionless. They had started this mission with three men, and now only one remained. One man that was currently wounded, but still it was a tough man at that. At just shy of six feet in height and some two hundred and sixty pounds, Brig was built rock solid like a tank. It would take more than a bullet to the leg to stop him. Quickly, he looked back out onto the clearing. Things were happening fast now. The small team was slowly being converged upon.

Next, Brig set his gaze upon the massive male gigantopithecus. The huge animal was still moving forward toward the team. That was his meal ticket. If he could just somehow manage to sedate and immobilize the creature with his tranquilizer gun, render the huge creature unconscious for just long enough so as to set up a rendeszvous date with his contacts, he would be more than on his way. It would give Brig a small window of time to prepare the huge beast for transport up and out of this area and back to where his contacts were located in Russia. Then he could sit back and await the payday of all paydays. His mind wandered for a moment thinking about how much such an animal would fetch on the black market. He knew modern-day silverback gorillas fetched nearly four hundred thousand dollars. *Four hundred thousand dollars.* It was an ungodly sum of money by anyone's estimates. The creature in the clearing weighed four times what a gorilla weighed and was double the height, absolutely immense in every sense of the word. What was it worth in terms of a pure dollar amount? His mouth was salivating wondering just how much money such an animal would command on the black market, not to mention an animal that had literally come from another time and place in earth's history.

Brig was now hell-bent on showing the rest of the world what would literally be marketed as a modern day KING KONG. Come and see the beast from another time. He could already see it now, already see the flurry of media attention and social media buzz that the animal would garner. From inside the concealment of the foliage, Brig Daniels took dead aim and fired.

• • •

Things were happening fast now for the team. At their backs, the two juveniles were still stalking them, while at the opposite end of the clearing, the other huge adult sent its two pillar-sized forearms slamming hard down into the dirt, sending up a large plume of dust in the process. The animal growled and then roared.

Suddenly, above all of the noise and chaos, a sharp and distinct cracking sound rang out from somewhere inside the concealment of the trees. It took Downs a moment before he spun and realized that the huge male gigantopithecus had been shot. A small trail of blood on its upper right forearm could be seen starting to form and then trickle down its thick matting of fur.

The animal roared either out of pain or anger, or possibly both. And then suddenly, another sharp cracking sound rang out from deep inside the foliage. This time, the animal appeared to not have been struck at all. Rather, the bullet from the shot landed several feet in front of the huge creature's front limbs as dirt kicked up into the air. The big male, wasting no time, gathered its two forearms together and then sent them slamming down hard into the ground. Lowering its huge head, it bellowed a moaning roar. The cry reverberated across the open clearing. It had been a terrifying, rumbling, guttural sound, a cry that had been ripped straight from the prehistoric past.

The gigantopithecus, not knowing that the gun shot had come from deep inside the bamboo trees, turned and faced the only humans currently standing in the middle of the clearing. The animal blasted another roar, sent both forearms slamming down into the ground, and then charged.

"Holy fuck!" Josiah cried out.

They were about to be steamrolled. Immediately, Downs knew that someone was firing at the giganto-pithecus from inside the foliage. As the huge monstrosity bounded toward them on all fours, they quickly had to figure something out.

"At our backs!" Downs yelled.

Josiah Young turned, faced the oncoming attackers, and fired. The tranquilizer dart from the air rifle struck one of the oncoming juveniles in the muscle of its shoulder. Downs turned himself around and now saw the feathered dart now protruding out of the muscularly-built creature. And then Downs watched in stunned horror as the other juvenile approached the animal and tore the dart out with its right hand. Now, the one that had torn the dart out was racing toward the group on three limbs with the dart raised high above its head. Downs was shocked at the level of intelligence.

Madness ensued now as the huge lumbering adult continued racing forward toward the small band of humans. The creatures were quickly converging upon the team. In the midst of it all, Downs had figured things out. Someone was most definitely firing shots at the gigantopithecus from just inside the confines of the trees. But what stuck out was the fact that none of them had been shot. Had that individual wanted to kill each of them with his own hand, he could have easily done so. Rather, the bullets appeared to have been fired as a means to rile up and infuriate this small family of prehistoric beasts. It had been meant as a means to officially put Downs and his team on the extinct list once and for all.

54

Diane Clor was still wedged tightly in and amongst the trees. Her feet were standing in a soggy puddle of standing water and mud. But she didn't care one bit. The footage she had already filmed was going to change her life. It had been meant to change Stacey Winston's life, but now it was going to change hers. She would be an instant multi-millionaire. She was confident of that. It may not happen over night, but she was certain that it was an economic certainty. And who in their right mind wouldn't want to bank a few million? She'd worry about what to do with the money once she was in fact in possession of it. She was already toying with a few different options. Perhaps she'd finally get to buy that dream home she'd always envisioned, or possibly buy a small apartment building as an investment that would give her consistent cash flow for the rest of her life. Or perhaps she'd invest the majority of it in low-fee index funds. She shook her head. Again, that was a problem for later. And it would be a great problem to have. It was one that she most definitely welcomed.

Hastily, she collapsed the legs of the tripod and began moving quickly through the trees now. The camera was still screwed on tightly to the top of the tripod, but Diane was careful to make sure it was shielded and protected as she continued navigating her way through the trees. The camera and the footage it contained was about as important as anything she'd ever guarded before in her entire life. She was making her way from the clearing, but things were thick in here as she continued forward.

Diane could hear what was taking place back in the clearing and she had just filmed much of that action. That was all in the past now as she continued making a beeline through trees. Actually, it was more like dodging and weaving. These fucking bamboo trees grew everywhere. She glanced quickly to her left and caught the tail end of the adult female gigantopithecus as it lumbered toward the five humans. She shuddered thinking of the horrors that awaited them. Suddenly, she came to an abrupt halt. Although she had only run a hundred feet or so through the trees, she was breathing hard. Diane knew she was out of shape, and she also knew she'd worry about getting her ass back in good working order once she arrived back in the States and banked those millions that she knew awaited her. With money would in turn come good health, peace, prosperity, and the overwhelming reality that the money would once and for all truly allow her to pursue her own passions and pursuits for the rest of her life. It was about as deep a concept as she could ever hope to ponder.

She turned around. From where she was standing, she didn't have as clear a view back to the clearing as she once did, but she most definitely could hear what was going on. The small band of humans were being hunted, and she could very easily head back to where she was, set the legs of the tripod down, and resume filming. She thought about that for a second, the potential carnage flashing before her eyes like the scenes of a movie.

"No," she whispered aloud.

She shook her head. No. She didn't want that on her conscience, and she already felt as though she had taken enough calculated risks. She had already seen what Stacey Winston had filmed and documented, and it would be up to her in post-production whether or not she wanted to show that gruesome footage or not. She wasn't certain just yet. She also knew she was toying with the idea of throwing Stacey Winston under the bus, to blame it entirely on him, which in fact was true. After all, it was he who had filmed the demise of Clark Geiger. That was a fact. That was the truth.

Menacing growls followed by a monstrous bellowing roar reminded her as to what was still taking place back out in the clearing. She needed to get out of here, and quickly. She had enough footage.

With the legs of the tripod tucked neatly under her right arm now, Diane began moving quickly through the trees once again. The sound of something off to the right suddenly caught her attention. Instinctively, her head twitched in that direction. It had been the sound of something cracking and breaking way out there in the foliage. She kept moving though. She had only let her eyes stray for a second, but that was all it took. Diane's left arm scraped against one of the trees. It took several more seconds before her brain finally registered an intense burning sensation. She had been cut pretty good along her arm and was now bleeding.

She came to a stop and set the tripod down. At long last, the heavy thing was finally starting to weigh her down. Looking down at her arm, she could see that she had torn a large hole in her left shirt sleeve. She grimaced in pain as she looked inside. The bastard tree had ripped a nice gash that must have been damn near three inches in length across her skin. She swore silently to herself as her arm was bleeding like hell now. To have an injury like this at this stage of the game.

"Fuck," she cursed once more to herself.

If you gave it the chance, this forest could tear you to pieces, tear you a new one. Now she felt as though the forest was fighting back, rearing its teeth as well as its claws. Looking around for a second and feeling like she was running out of time, she simply put her right hand over the gash. Again, she grimaced with pain as the cut continued to pump with blood. She held her hand there for thirty seconds or so. When she pulled it away, her hand looked like something out of a slasher film. It was covered in blood. Quickly, Diane looked around. She really needed to get going. She heard another deep cavernous roar. This was followed by the sound of gunfire.

That was enough for her. With the bottom of her shirt, she did her best to pull the fabric up to the gushing wound in an attempt to stop the bleeding as best as she could. Quickly, she pulled away. The blood had soaked right through the fabric. For now, she felt as though she had no choice. She would have to get cleaned up once she arrived back at camp. Diane looked down at her hand and smeared the blood across the pant leg. Now she was really a mess. She grabbed hold of the tripod and camera in the foliage and continued on her way. As she increased her speed from that of a brisk walk to that of a light trot, she knew her arm was in need of bandaging. But it would have to wait, it really would. If she continued moving at this pace, it wouldn't be long now before she arrived back at camp.

The sound of things cracking and breaking from out in the foliage rang out once again. But this time, it had come from straight ahead of her. It was hard to tell how far, just that it appeared to have come from in front on the intended path that would take her back to the camp. Diane came to a stop. She was breathing hard now, her cut still gushing and pumping crimson red blood. Her eyes scanned frantically. She couldn't seem much of anything. Suddenly, she felt the hairs on her arm stand on end. She knew she wasn't alone. With the legs of the tripod now as her only form of defense, she pressed the thing out in front of her. Now all she could do was wait and listen as she continued to bleed out.

$$\bullet \ \bullet \ \bullet$$

Downs ordered the team into a tight circular formation with their backs pressed up against one another. The team now had every inch of the clearing covered. Downs was staring straight ahead as the giant male kept coming forward, walking on all fours like some type of oversized tank that didn't have a care in the world. Meanwhile, Downs knew that the accompanying female was bounding toward them on his right, and behind Downs, the two juveniles were still advancing silently toward the group near the tree line at the edge of the clearing.

Downs spun himself around, not necessarily to assess the situation, but to confirm it. A quick two second scan and he had done just that. He turned around and faced the giant male still advancing toward them. Leveling the Astra out in front of him, he knew the revolver had the capability to stop a charging rhino. White rhinos tipped the scales at 5,100 pounds, black rhinos at anywhere between 1,800 – 3,100 pounds. Downs knew he could stop the animal if he had to. As he continued to watch its progress forward, he saw the huge dome-shaped head, the limbs as wide as small tree trunks, the powerful hands and feet, and the mouth lined with the teeth of an animal that had been forced to adapt.

Suddenly, Downs saw dirt kick up close to the left leg of the huge male. It took a moment but eventually he realized that a bullet had hit the dirt in front of the animal. The creature was still being shot at. The gigantopithecus stopped advancing and reared back onto its two limbs. From there it thumped several times on its chest, lowered itself, and bellowed a rage-filled roar directed solely at the team.

They were running out of both time and options as the big male continued moving quickly toward them. Something needed to be done. With no other option, Downs pointed the Astra toward the sky and fired. A sharp cracking sound followed as Downs lowered the gun and then pointed the barrel in the direction of the male. The animal appeared to show no signs of slowing though. And then out of the corner of his right eye,

Downs saw Jeremiah Corstine raise the assault rifle toward the sky. John Corstine's son fired off several rounds before lowering the weapon. The result was instantaneous. In a world where dominance usually won out, there appeared to be something bigger and badder on the block. Movement in the clearing stopped at once. Now there was a heavy silence as the rain suddenly began to fall.

· · ·

Burr Wellington had heard it all, each and every round that had been fired. Although he had no way of knowing how far in fact the gunfire had come from, he had a good idea of the general direction. That was all he needed. He glanced down at the flare gun. It was certainly better than nothing.

All he really knew with certainty was that the sound of all that gunfire made him nervous. His teammates needed him. But they were more than just his teammates. They were his friends and he desperately wanted and needed to get back to them. At least that way, together they could face what they all knew resided in this forest.

Crouching down, he quickly tightened his shoelaces. Standing back up, he tucked the flare gun into his belt. It was going to be a long and rain-drenched walk back. The skies had once again let loose, unleashing a torrent of water down upon the forest.

· · ·

The rain continued to fall hard, thick fat raindrops that splattered upon impact. And had it not been for the rain, a deep and unnerving silence would have dominated the clearing. But now all Downs and his team could hear was the pounding of the rain coming down in unrelenting sheets. Quickly, the clearing was turning into a sloppy and muddy mess. The trees that bordered the clearing on all sides were swaying back and forth at a good rate now.

The team still maintained their backs to one another, essentially having eyes on all sides of the clearing. Downs eyed the approaching juveniles. For some reason or another they had halted their progress forward. Downs continued to eye them, their shaggy fur now slicked back with water. It gave them an even more ferocious and menacing appearance. Downs turned to his right. The huge female had also come to a stop. There she remained, breathing heavily while resting on all fours. She was breathtakingly huge, although she was still smaller than the huge male that lay ahead. The huge male was also resting on all fours, hair slicked back and wet, a menacing grin cast upon its face.

"Everybody, get eyes on them!" Downs shouted.

He had to yell just to be heard over the rain. It was slapping down noisily all around them now. Downs turned and faced in the direction of Jeremiah Corstine. The man had the assault rifle pressed out toward both the two juveniles as well as the huge female. Downs knew that was the real reason why these creatures had stopped. But it wouldn't last forever.

Downs turned in the direction of the juveniles. All of a sudden one of the animals came to a stop, turned itself around, and faced in the direction of the bamboo forest. That was all it took as the other one out in front also stopped and turned itself around. Through the thick sheets of rain, Downs watched as the two now stared at the solid wall of bamboo trees.

Downs spun back around. Another gunshot from back in the brush rang out. It had been an errant shot. The bullet had hit the mud several feet in front of the animal, splashing up a spray of mud. But it appeared to have been purposely placed there, meant to infuriate and rile up these creatures. The huge animal shifted its bulk, roared, and stared in the direction of the swaying bamboo trees.

Through the rain, Downs could hear Jeremiah shout. "I got eyes over here!"

Downs didn't budge though. Rather he kept his eyes on the big male. It had finally taken notice, finally appeared to have figured things out a bit. The male gigantopithecus let out one final cavernous roar before it took off in the direction of where the gun shots had rang out from. Through the dismal conditions, Downs watched the rain-drenched, wide rump of the creature eventually get smaller and smaller as it pushed its unstoppable mass through the muddy clearing.

Now Downs turned his attention back to the opposite end of the clearing toward the remaining female.

"In a straight line!" Downs shouted. "Now!"

Quickly, the team shuffled their way through the mud and assembled into a straight line. Now they had eyes on the female while staring in the direction where the two juveniles stood.

Downs watched as the huge head of the female swung in the direction of the juveniles. They were still standing and waiting, hair slicked back, fierce growls plastered upon their faces, just at the edge of the trees that bordered the clearing. And then through the rain, the female let out a monstrous roar, took one last look at the humans, and then took off bounding after the big male.

The animal made its way toward the foliage on the opposite side of the clearing from the juveniles and then banked hard to the left. The wide rump disappeared off into the rain.

All that was left now were the two youngsters. They turned, sniffed at the air, and then just like that, plunged through the treeline and disappeared. Immediately, Downs pointed and shouted. He suspected that the animals must have taken off after the woman with the camera, the camera that held the visible evidence as to their existence.

Through the rain, Downs shouted and pointed to where the juveniles had just disappeared to. "We follow them."

55

Diane Clor continued pushing her way frantically through the forest. She was running as hard as she could through the trees. The ground was a spongy and muddy mess. Now there was only her and the sound of the rain as it hit the surrounding foliage. Onward she ran though, afraid to look back, afraid to take her eyes off anywhere but straight ahead. Several times she thought she had lost her way, gotten turned around, but thankfully she had managed to figure it out. Now she believed with relative certainty that she was on her way and would be back to camp in under five minutes.

Suddenly from up ahead, amidst the soaked bamboo and knee-high growth, she thought she had spotted something. It was like a jolt to the system. Diane thought she had seen Bob Hohrman. And the man had just been standing there, both arms hanging limply at his side, bleeding from multiple locations, a lifeless expression plastered sullenly across his face, looking as though he was literally a vertical corpse. He was covered head to toe in blood. There had also been a huge gash that ran down his forehead and a thick trail of blood streaming down one side of his face. His tongue hung slack out of the corner of his mouth as if he were a dog panting for water. It was honestly the most horrific image she had ever seen before.

Diane came to an abrupt stop. It was like she had seen a ghost, something ripped from her worst nightmares. When she focused her attention back on the spot through the trees where she thought she had seen him standing, she saw nothing but wet bamboo trees. Now there was a heavy silence, the rain no longer coming down relentlessly. It was now coming down gently, the noise at the ground level coming from the soft pitter patter of rain landing ever so gently atop the surrounding foliage.

Diane could have sworn she had seen the corpse of Bob Hohrman, but she obviously hadn't. It had all been a figment of her imagination. At least that's what she thought. Now she just needed a moment to catch her breath. That was it, just a moment, but try as she might she wasn't able to get the image of Bob out of her head. His face was bloodied, his arms looked incapable of movement, and there was a look of utter discomfort but mostly terror plastered squarely across his face. There had been an eerie presence about the way in which he had just been standing there, nestled in and amongst the tall bamboo trees like he had literally risen from the bowels of hell itself. Diane shook her head. She really needed to get it together. Her mind was playing tricks on her. Pushing the image to the farthest reaches of her brain, she started moving once again.

She glanced down quickly at where she had been cut. She needed to get back to camp and get patched up. Suddenly, she heard movement and felt the presence of something else in this forest with her. This time, however, she didn't stop. She was absolutely hell-bent on making it all the way back to camp.

Suddenly the noise and cracking inside the forest appeared much closer, possibly some ten to fifteen feet or so to her right. She wasn't stopping though. She had pushed through another ten feet or so of jungle when the attack finally came. Coming up on her right side and moving quickly, Diane realized it before it was too late. A large shape suddenly emerged. She was blindsided and tackled to the ground. The moment of impact was stunning as the wind was taken from her lungs and she was thrown through the air. Diane lost sense of everything as her backside collided hard with a nearby tree.

When she finally came to, she found herself lying on the wet ground, dizzy, confused, and most importantly, terrified. Forcing herself upright with a grunt, it felt like she had been struck by a small car. She heard movement from all around, but the fall had left her monentarily out of it. As the endless array of trees from all around her slowly came back into focus, she was again hit hard from behind. This time the pain in her back was searing. She keeled over and began to cough. It took only a few seconds for her to realize she was coughing blood. Now she began to panic. Noise was all around her, yet she still couldn't make sense of any of it. Still seated, she managed to turn her neck. Where was the tripod and the camera? At this stage in the game, that camera and the footage it contained was simply invaluable. To her surprise, she found the legs of the tripod not more than seven feet or so from where she lay.

Again, she hunched over and coughed more blood. Her head and ears were ringing. Somehow she found the strength necessary to stand to her feet. As she did so, she immediately scooped the tripod up off the ground. With the precious camera now hovering close to her stomach, she pressed the legs of the tripod out in front of her. The protection that the legs of the tripod offered up was all she had now.

The forest cracked with life somewhere on her left side. Wasting no time, Diane turned and swung the tripod like a baseball bat. The legs of the tripod collided with outstretched arms and a mouth full of hungry teeth. The juvenile gigantopithecus, perhaps shocked by the woman's brazen attempt at self-defense, quickly backed away.

Now Diane stood amidst the trees with the legs of the tripod still pressed out in front of her. She looked like a woman out of options. She spat blood. She had never coughed up blood before in her entire life. She wasn't certain if she was still bleeding out of her left arm or not; all she knew was that right now, at this moment, she felt no pain. The energy coursing through her was like a shot of adrenaline to the bloodstream. But perhaps, it just might save her life.

With the legs of the tripod still pressed out in front of her, Diane raised it above her head and let out a primal scream. She found herself shocked at the level of intensity of the scream. She didn't know she had that in her. It had been a deep primal scream of rage, the place that exists in us all that at times can give a mother the power to lift a two ton car off of her child. Diane now felt as though she was wielding that very same power. Trying to make herself out to be as big as possible, she raised the tripod above her head and let out another scream. It felt good, intoxicating, and for a second she found herself liking the power. Perhaps she could fend them off this way. She did a quick 360 degree sweep, attempting to take in as much of the forest as she could. With the clearing no longer at her back, she was essentially surrounded on all sides by thick jungle. Continuing her sweep, she saw nothing.

But as she returned herself to her original position, her eyes finally caught movement. In a flash, she saw the wide rump of one of the juveniles moving fast on her right-hand side. Again, Diane raised the tripod and blasted a roar as loud as she could muster. She waited. She saw the backside of one of the juveniles again. But this time the animal appeared to be retreating. Had it actually worked? She waited and listened a few seconds longer, and then Diane deemed that this was her chance. She began moving at once. Rather quickly, her brisk walk turned into that of running. Diane Clor now found herself moving quickly through the trees, tripod clutched tightly under her right arm, the will to live now stronger than ever. With the adrenaline still flowing through her body like some type of drug, she continued on her way back to camp.

• • •

The two juveniles pushed further into the dense foliage, crouched their wet muscular bodies down beneath the vegetation line, and let out soft exhaling snorts through their flattened nostrils. There, hidden amongst the trees, they waited patiently. Being ambush predators had taught them as such.

From behind a mass of vines, limbs, leaves, and verdant vegetation, the two watched the woman as she hastily made her way through the trees and disappeared around a bend. The two creatures lurched forward. Now out in the open, their mouths opened and their gums rippled back. And then with two fierce growls, the two juveniles took off in hot pursuit of their prey.

• • •

Diane Clor returned to camp a sweaty and bleeding mess. Breathing hard, she still felt very little pain. Her adrenaline wouldn't allow for it. She felt somewhat triumphant, like she had cheated death in a way. She was hell-bent on surviving through this nightmare and living to tell the tale now more than ever. As she left behind the cover of the forest and now stood in the small sun-filled clearing, she frantically took in the whole scene. The tents still lay a crumpled ruined mess in the middle. Rather awkwardly, she stumbled forward, her eyes locking in the on the tent in which she needed to get to. It had been the tent that she and Bob had occupied.

Diane looked down at her watch. She had approximately forty-five minutes before the helicopter was supposed to pick them all up. Still continuing stumbling in the direction of the tent, her mind suddenly began to wander. There would be questions asked of her, lots of questions. Suddenly she stopped and held her body upright. After all, it wasn't she who had killed Clark Geiger. By now, she assumed that Stacey Winston was a goner as well. Moving forward, she stopped once again. The only one left was Bob Hohrman. But as she thought about it more, she made the quick conclusion that Bob had more than likely suffered the same fate as Clark Geiger. She nodded her head. That was her story. That was exactly what she would tell the pilot. They had all gotten separated and she was the only one who made it back to the pilot. After that, it'd be up to him if they wanted to launch a search party to go in search of the missing members.

Putting no further thought into it she continued onward. Now at the tent, she quickly located her backpack. It wouldn't be long now. She'd rub some alcohol across all wounds and cuts, put some antibiotic ointment on it, bandage up, then grab her bag, camera, and all computer equipment. Then she'd begin to figure out the coordinates back to the rendevous point. From there, all she had to do was wait for the helicopter. She was really looking forward to putting this lush green world behind her. After that, it would be off to the studio to begin post production on this documentary.

Diane had just screwed the cap off the alcohol bottle when a snort and a grunt from somewhere behind told her she wasn't alone. Immediately, she felt her body stiffen. An icy cold sensation shot through her blood at once. Slowly, she forced herself to turn around. Her heart was pounding.

Standing at the far edge of the clearing, probably a good forty to fifty feet away from her, was one of the juveniles. There the animal stood in silence, resting on four limbs, frozen like a wet, ferocious statue. Diane reached for her only form of protection. When her hands finally made contact with the legs of the tripod, she quietly turned it around. Now that the camera was close to her stomach, she carefully went about unscrewing the camera from atop the tripod. Her goal was to remove the camera, zip it up nice and tightly in her backpack, and then defend herself with the heavy legs of the tripod as she had done before. As crazy as it sounded, the imminent danger at the far end of the clearing still seemed distant and otherworldly, like it really wasn't happening to her at all. Diane still had time to process the fact that she wanted to make damn sure that the precious camera was snug and safe before she went about the task of fending these nasty things off with the legs of the tripod.

Despite being fully confident with her strategy, she suddenly felt a bit nervous. Perhaps she was slowly coming down from her adrenaline high. But she still believed she would prevail. Diane had successfully managed to fend one of them off a short while ago, and she would do so again. She wondered if this was the same animal that had attacked her.

Diane fumbled with her hands for the camera. The entire time she began to unscrew it from atop the tripod, her eyes never left the juvenile still standing silently at the far end of the clearing. Once she had finally managed to get the camera unscrewed, she felt with her hands to the backpack. Again her eyes never left the juvenile.

Once her outstretched hands reached the backpack, she quickly went to town reeling it in. Now she had it open and in a matter of seconds she had successfully zipped the camera in nice and tight inside. Mission accomplished. She had done exactly what she wanted. Now she just needed to fend these things off.

Wait a minute, she thought to herself in a moment of panic. *Things. Multiple.*

She focused her eyes on the far end of the clearing. The lone juvenile was still resting quietly on four limbs. But where was the other one? Where was its sibling?

A loud roar somewhere off to her right suddenly erupted out of nowhere. Diane barely had time to raise the legs of the tripod in defense before she was knocked hard to the ground by the second individual. It had all happened in a blur, but in doing so, the juvenile had managed to bite down on her neck. She screamed in pain as her body was knocked backward. Landing awkwardly against the hard ground, Diane flopped about helplessly for a few seconds. As she scrambled about, she heard movement closing in on her.

Somehow she managed to push herself upright. Frantically, she scanned back and forth. Where the hell was the tripod?

She heard another roar and saw one of the animals bounding toward her. Out of options, she searched helplessly for something, anything. Her eyes locked in on the tent behind her. And then her eyes registered something even more specific. Diane quickly went to work pulling up one of the spikes that held the tent in place. She had just managed to pull the thing free from the ground when the attacker was upon her.

Diane turned just in time to see two outstretched arms with a hungry mouth full of teeth catapulting itself toward her. Diane stood, jumped to her right, and stabbed the stake into the muscular backside of the roaring juvenile. The four hundred pound creature howled in pain.

Diane pulled herself back now and watched as the animal landed nimbly on four limbs. The stake came away bloodied and she found her eyes searching furiously for the second juvenile. A few more seconds passed before she found it. Coming up sharply on her left, another attack was being mounted.

Diane remembered the advice that had been conveyed to her time and time again back on her local hiking path at home. If you ever happen to find yourself encountering a mountain lion, make yourself appear larger than you are and scream and make a lot of noise. Do whatever you have to do, but most certainly do not turn and run. Diane did just that. She raced forward with her arms outstretched while flailing her arms and screaming at the top of her lungs. Still with the bloody stake in her right hand, she swiped in the air as the juvenile drew nearer.

The creature let out an immense roar, but this time instead of attacking, it peeled off hard to its right. Diane continued screaming and flailing her arms as the fleeing creature hugged tightly to the trees that grew along the edge of the clearing.

Again, she felt the same adrenaline coursing through her body that she had experienced earlier in the forest. It had literally been a life-preserving energy, and once again she found herself wielding its power. Diane screamed—a deep guttural cry of rage that burned deep into her lungs.

She spun around. In doing so, she spotted the legs of the tripod. They were only some ten feet away from her, but before she could reach for them she needed to do a quick visual. The original juvenile that she had just stabbed had retreated about thirty feet but was now moving quickly toward her. Diane went to lunge for the legs to the tripod but it was too late. The animal was upon her with a loud and commanding roar. In lunging for the tripod, Diane had momentarily lowered her head. When she looked back up, she saw a blur of a large figure that collided with her and knocked her hard to the ground.

Diane was thrown backward as her head hit the ground hard. Now she lay helplessly on her back. Quickly, she forced herself into an upright position. To her surprise, she still held the bloodied stake in her right hand. And she needed it. Diane saw a large mouth open wide. Suddenly, she felt hot panting breath upon her skin. And then she felt searing pain that literally took her breath away. Before she realized it, the creature had sunk its teeth deep into her neck. Incapable of screaming, Diane did the only thing she could. With everything she had, she stabbed the bloodied stake into the thick muscular back of the juvenile. Pushing with all her might, she could feel the animal's powerful back muscles as she struggled to push the stake in further. The animal was made up of tightly coiled muscles, an evolutionary powerhouse of God's creation.

Diane had just begun to retract the stake when she suddenly felt a warmth quickly spreading down her shoulders and spine. It was blood, her own blood.

Now she was beginning to panic. And then just like that, the juvenile pulled back and let go of her.

Diane felt her body sort of flop forward. Again, she felt the spreading warmth as it continued making its way down her shoulders and spine. She knew she was bleeding significantly yet oddly, she felt no pain.

And then in a strange, surreal, out-of-body experience, Diane felt her legs propel her body upward. She powerfully resurrected to her feet and let out a primal scream. With the bloody stake still in her right hand, she bounded forward, quickly scooping the tripod off the ground. Then she spun around and faced her attacker.

In a flash, she saw the juvenile propel itself forward, limbs outstretched, teeth bared as it blared a menacing roar. She batted the thing hard in the face with the legs of the tripod. As the animal darted hard to her left, she managed to get in one final swipe with the tripod. She jammed the legs of the tripod as hard as she could into the midsection of the animal. There was no sound from the animal though, no conveyance of pain, just the fact that it was now moving fast to get away from the enraged woman. What had once been a fearsome creature now resembled a scared kitty cat.

The juvenile raced out toward the fallen tents as Diane spun around. The second attack by the other juvenile followed the first by only a matter of seconds. Diane, having little time to process much of anything, stabbed the stake into the thick and muscular neck of the creature. She pushed hard through both fur and muscle. This time, however, there was a loud and resounding howl of pain. Diane retracted the stake as the creature planted four limbs in the mud and went whimpering away to the far end of the clearing.

Now Diane took a step back, assessed the situation, and tried to figure out what her next move should be. Off to her right, she could see the juvenile giganto-pithecus that she had just stabbed in the neck. The animal could be seen traveling close to the trees before disappearing off into the bamboo.

She turned to the left. She could see its mate standing atop the fallen tents in the middle of the clearing. And then her eyes looked down to the ground. She could see her backpack, and in that backpack she knew had both the camera and the footage that was going to make her a very wealthy woman not to mention a famous one. The animal stepped back, shifting its large mass. The back left limb of the animal was now dangerously close to the backpack. She couldn't run the risk of the creature crushing her precious footage. Then all would truly be lost.

Putting no further thought into it, Diane rushed forward with the tripod raised in her left hand. In her right hand, she still held the bloody stake. Diane let out a terrifyingly loud roar as she bounded in the direction of the remaining juvenile. The creature took one look at the furious human coming its way and then quickly turned and darted for the safety of the trees. Diane watched the animal's wide and powerfully-built rump as the creature made its way toward the stands of bamboo. And then the animal plunged head first through the bamboo and disappeared.

Now Diane found herself running hard. She could see the precious backpack still lying atop the downed tent right where she had left it. All she had to do was get there, secure the backpack, and then begin hiking her way through the forest to the next open clearing where the helicopter would meet her. At this point, she wasn't too worried about the juveniles. Hopefully they had learned their lesson, and if they hadn't, then she'd be plenty fine reminding them of the finer points of both the legs of the tripod as well as the bloodied stake. In fact, as she neared to within ten feet of the tent, she quickly eyed all the stakes that they had used to hold both tents in place. She could pull out several of them, just in case she had to teach more than one lesson. Allowing a slight smile to creep across her face, she realized she just might actually make it. And to her, that was about as good a feeling as she could have imagined.

• • •

Diane Clor felt a sudden jolt to her body followed by a sharp tug. It took her a few seconds to realize where she was, to process what in fact had just happened. Her head shot upright. She could tell immediately that she had an absolute rager of a headache. And then she felt a dull sensation from the lower part of her body. As she looked down toward her feet, at first she had a hard time processing it. Diane Clor awoke to her left leg being eaten. She saw pink muscle exposed. And then she saw the powerful jaw muscles of the juvenile gigantopithecus as it continued to chew at what was essentially her thigh.

And then it all came rushing to her like an oncoming tidal wave about to make landfall. She had blacked out somewhere in the process of being attacked.

She had hit her head hard on the ground when she had been knocked backward by one of the juveniles. The result was that she must have lost consciousness. She had never actually risen to her feet, never fended the two juveniles off with the stake and the tripod while in the clearing. The attack by one of the juveniles had rendered her unconscious for a short period of time, although it was impossible to tell how long she had been out. Now after all that was processed, pain suddenly registered loud and clear. Diane screamed at the top of her lungs as immeasurable pain burned deep into her leg as the muscle from her thigh lay open and exposed. It was like nothing she had ever experienced before, absolutely pure horror.

Frantically, her eyes darted back and forth, searching, scanning the area. She was lying in a growing pool of her own blood, literally bleeding to death while slowly being eaten alive. Summoning what strength she had left, Diane grabbed hold of the ground around her and managed to pull her body back upward. Miraculously, she had managed to free her leg from the jaws of the juvenile gigantopithecus. With a loud snort and grunt, Diane watched as the animal lifted its head and glared at her. She saw ragged flesh in the creature's mouth, a face that was reddened from the blood, and a mean and cold-hearted emotionless stare.

Diane kept pulling herself backward. Suddenly, she remembered the stake and the legs of the tripod. Perhaps she could make her way to the tent, pull a stake out, and defend herself as she had dreamt she had done. She began searching with her eyes. She found nothing though. Now she just kept pulling herself backward as the bulk of her body slid right on through the large, slick pool of blood.

With wide eyes Diane watched as the creature let out a low growl. She saw the lower part of the jaw open, exposing the already well-developed canine teeth. With a loud snorting sound, the creature bounded forward. It was at her legs in a tenth of a second. And then before she could do anything, the creature was once again upon her. It came around to the right side of her body, lashed out, and bit down onto her windpipe. Immediately, Diane felt the crushing power of the jaw muscles and the hot panting breath upon her skin as the creature sunk its teeth further into her windpipe. Diane's eyes went wide with horror as they rolled back into her head. Her face was now smashed right up against the fur of the juvenile. She could smell the pungent unpleasant odor of the animal. And then suddenly, it all ended. The juvenile let go and her neck and head flopped backward and clunked hard against the ground.

For a moment, she just lay there, completely helpless and at the mercy of her environment. Somehow she was able to lift her head slightly to witness the retreating juvenile as it made its way toward the trees that bordered the clearing. Diane watched for a few more seconds before gravity finally won out and she could no longer support the weight of her head. Again her head fell back and clunked hard against the dirt. There she lay, bleeding to death and injured beyond belief in the middle of the clearing. Somewhere in the outer reaches of her brain, beyond the insane pain of it all, beyond the vast amounts of blood that she was rapidly losing, she couldn't help but think back to the camera with the footage of the creatures wrapped nicely in her backpack. There was no doubt that camera was worth a small fortune. But beyond the small fortune was the chance for her to actually do something with her life, to actually see her goals and dreams through to fruition. She had to get back to it, she simply had to get it back. At all costs, she had to find a way out of this living nightmare.

Summoning every last bit of strength she could muster, Diane started pulling her body back once again. She had pulled herself back a foot or two when suddenly, the back of her head bumped into something hard and solid. She noticed a strange sensation on the skin at the back of her neck. Still losing blood at a rapid rate, it appeared as though her mind was starting to fail her. She reached around with her hand and touched her neck. She felt hair—tough, course, and fibrous hair. And then she noticed a slight tickling sensation to the back of her neck. Reaching around with her hand once more, she suddenly realized there was lots of hair back there. And then the smell hit her square in the face. All at once, her senses were hit with a nauseatingly bad, suffocating smell. A pungent odor that reeked of blood and meat, death itself. Next, Diane felt the immediate sensation of terror, sheer and absolute terror coursing through her body.

The suffocating stench burned deep into her nostrils. And then Diane heard breathing, the type of deep and immense breathing that could only have come from an enormous chest cavity. Still looking up at the sky and nearly on the verge of unconsciousness, Diane spotted something.

Staring down at her with its two front limbs planted firmly into the ground was the female gigantopithecus. The massive creature let out a low, rumbling sound from its giant chest cavity. Now up close like this, the true size and scale of the creature was terrifying. Tears began to well up in her eyes. Suddenly, she felt her head and neck lifted effortlessly from the ground. In an upright and seated position, all she could do was stare up at the enormous creature that held her. And then she saw the huge gaping mouth open wide, revealing the oversized canine teeth at the front of the mouth, and felt the hot panting breath upon the skin of her face. Diane Clor managed one last gut-wrenching, gurgled cry as the cavernous mouth opened wide and closed down tightly over her head.

56

T he sound of a single shot from what appeared to be a handgun rang out loud and clear on the far side of the clearing as Downs and the team ran. Heads instinctively turned, but Downs simply motioned for them to continue on their way. They didn't have a moment to spare. They were now in hot pursuit of whoever that lady was who had been filming from the other end of the clearing. Downs felt his heart pounding as they covered the last part of the muddy clearing and plunged full force through the trees, instantly immersing themselves back inside the wet and teeming embrace of the bamboo forest. It was early morning now, the humidity quickly on the rise as they plowed their way through the wet vegetation.

Downs found himself in the back, while Jeremiah Corstine was up ahead leading the way. Downs felt slightly better about their current position. He was in possession of the Astra in the back of the line, while Jeremiah had acquired the semi-automatic assault rifle. They now had more lethal force than ever if the moment called for it. Downs shook his head. The whereabouts of Burr Wellington were still unknown. For now, they simply had to get that camera back at all costs. And that's exactly what they were going in pursuit of.

With Jeremiah up ahead leading the way, Downs was now able to take in the blood. He could see trails of it on the forest floor and in the surrounding vegetation. Someone or something had bled considerably through here. Still, they continued onward. The adult female and male gigantopithecus appeared to have pursued the large military man that Downs had shot in the leg, while the juvenile creatures had gone after the woman who had been filming on the opposite side of the clearing.

The team was moving at a brisk trot now through the tall thin trees, the clearing having fully disappeared behind them. Meanwhile all around them, signs of blood loss were everywhere.

Focus. Stay the course, Downs thought as they continued pushing forward. *Stay the course. One thing at a time.*

• • •

Brig Daniels spun through the trees, raised his pistol, and then backed himself up against a thick stand of bamboo trees. He was working hard to have as many eyes on the forest as possible, with no potential blind spots. With the stand of bamboo now firmly at his back, he believed he had done just that. Now all he could do was wait, listen, and most importantly be ready.

With a grimace of pain, he looked down at where he had been shot. Shaking his head, he swore silently to himself. The torn piece of clothing that he had used as a makeshift tourniquet was now all but soaked through. He was most definitely in need of medical attention and he really needed to tie on a new tourniquet. But despite the growing and insurmountable odds, Brig still felt as though he could pull it off. Again, he looked down at where he had been shot. He'd replace the tattered, blood-soaked piece of clothing right here and now. It would only take a second or two. Brig knew that wasn't the truth, but that's what he told himself. He just needed to tear himself a new piece of clothing. He'd worry about the details that would follow after he'd done that.

All of a sudden, Brig heard the forest come alive on him. An enormous, angry roar filled the air. And then he watched in partial disbelief as several bamboo trees were broken and bent back. He continued watching as the forest gave way to the colossal male gigantopithecus. The huge creature was literally tearing a path straight through it. Again the massive male roared. Brig watched as it reared up onto its back two legs and beat aggressively on its wide and muscular chest.

Despite being an overwhelmingly large man himself, he suddenly felt timid, scared, and silly all at once. Silly like they should have never entered this forest, silly like they should have never come to this place. And that was saying a lot. There were few times in Brig Daniel's lifetime where he felt scared. But now was most definitely one of them.

He watched as two bamboo trees were knocked over and fell to the ground. The creature charged forward. Brig wasted no time. He fired a shot with his pistol straight into the right forearm of the huge beast.

He needed to worry about his safety first at this point. If he could just wound and partially slow the animal, he'd then worry about tranquilizing and sedating the huge beast.

The male roared, grabbed the base of a rather large bamboo tree, and tore the damn thing from the ground, roots and all. And then in one swift move, it flung the tree in Brig's direction.

Brig quickly dropped to the ground. The act of aggression by the largest ape the world has ever known had caught him completely by surprise. He hadn't seen that coming, and in doing so his finger had pressed down on the trigger. The gun went off just as Brig's body crashed down hard onto the ground. Meanwhile, somewhere behind him, the bamboo tree that had been flung crashed noisily into the rest of the forest. Quickly, Brig regathered himself. Now the male stood some forty feet away from him as it rested on all fours.

More noise followed. Brig heard movement from somewhere off to the right in the foliage. His right eye twitched in that direction while still maintaining partial eye contact with the large male. Brig watched in horror as the forest shook to his right and the large female emerged from the heavy growth. And there the animal stood, the front of its face stained red with blood as Brig took the scene in its full entirety. The male on his left rose onto its back two legs and beat on its chest. This was followed by a deep and throaty roar. The female did the same.

Despite the growing severity of his own situation, Brig still believed he had a plan that could be executed. He had an interest in taking out the big male, and that's exactly what he planned on doing. He was also counting on the fact that once the male was down and wounded, it would cause the female to retract and head deeper into the forest. Take down the bigger more imposing game, and the lesser ones would retreat. That was the plan. At least that was his hope.

As Brig stepped to his right and prepared to fire another shot, he realized he had been wrong. He had grossly underestimated these creatures. The female, seeing that her mate had been shot, took off after Brig. Rampaging forward, it batted down several of the tall, thin bamboo trees that stood in its way in order to get to the bleeding man.

Brig turned and fired at the female. He had shot the creature somewhere in the underbelly region. Despite taking the hit by the bullet, the rampaging creature was quickly upon him. With a powerful right limb, it swatted and knocked the pistol from Brig's hand. The power with which the creature had batted the weapon out of his hand made the pistol seem as though it were a plastic toy gun. But there was no time to process the pain as the female went charging right through him. At the last second, Brig managed to unsheath the knife at his belt with his left hand. With everything he had, he plunged the dagger to the hilt into the back of the rampaging female. The female retaliated by backhanding the two hundred and sixty pound man. Brig felt an immensely powerful forearm collide with the side of his stomach. The blow was so powerful, it knocked him off his feet. It felt like he had been struck by a small car.

Now down on the ground, Brig quickly began scrambling about in an attempt to locate the pistol. It lay some ten feet away. He had just managed to secure the weapon and sheath the knife at his side when suddenly he felt the ground shake and an immense shape materialized behind him. Brig felt terrifying pain as the huge male opened wide and bit down on his shoulder. The huge mouth lined with oversized canines bit through his chest as well as part of his back. As the animal sunk its teeth further into him, Brig felt crushing pain as those same very teeth bit through bone and muscle. Surprisingly, Brig was still able to raise the pistol in his left hand. Now up close next to the huge animal, one side of Brig's body was smashed and pressed right up into the fur of the animal, while the left side of him remained opened and free. All he could hope to do now was shoot the big animal point blank in the head.

Just as he leveled the pistol, the lone female emerged, baring fierce teeth accompanied by a monstrous roar. The enraged female bit down atop his hand. Powerful jaw muscles crushed through bones and tendons as the animal tore the gun away. In doing so, it tore Brig's left hand off. Now all that remained was a bloody ragged stump as a blood-curdling scream of insane terror escaped Brig Daniels' mouth. The big male released him and he fell forward and face planted right there into the ground. Flopping around awkwardly for a few seconds, Brig managed to push himself upright with the aid of his right hand. His eyes flared wide with horror as he saw what the animal had done. He saw the ragged mangled flesh just at his wrist, an absolute bloody mess. His body had gone into a partial state of shock. He was now bleeding from multiple areas.

Pushing himself upright, Brig scrambled and tried to locate the gun. But in the madness of it all, he had become turned around and now the gun was nowhere to be seen. Brig tore away at one of the juvenile bamboo trees. He had done so just in time to witness the enormous male moving in his direction. The huge beast let out a cavernous roar as it raised one of its massive limbs. Despite his injuries, Brig managed to fling his body and narrowily avoid the mass of the animal as it passed right on by him. Again he looked down at the bloody stump. He knew he was losing too much blood. He needed to put a stop to it or it would be all over for him. Brig had just begun tearing at his shirt when suddenly the female came out of nowhere. The animal knocked him flat on his ass and then continued onward.

Blood flowed from the mangled stump as he flailed awkwardly around on the ground, his limbs thrashing about in his own growing pool of blood. Brig didn't have a moment to spare, so he immediately began taking off his shirt. He needed to wrap it around the bloodied stump. Somewhere in the madness of it all, he heard another deep and throaty roar. He didn't know if it had come from the male or the female, just that it had come from somewhere close by. The bottom of his shirt got caught on his head and then suddenly, he felt an enormous crushing force that crashed down upon his chest.

Brig had been knocked over on his side. Now he was racked in pain beyond comprehension, but somehow, someway he was still able to get his damn shirt off. Despite the surreal nature of it all, he still had the wherewithal about him to quickly wrap the fabric around the gushing stump. Being in the armed forces for years, he had seen his fair share of leg and arm amputees, even had a few close friends die in the line of battle, but he never envisioned having one of those atrocities happen to himself. And here he was, lying on the ground deep in the middle of fucking nowhere in Vietnam bleeding to death, scrambling for his very existence.

Suddenly, something bit down on his back. Brig felt powerful jaw muscles and oversized teeth clamp down on him, piercing through his skin, muscle, and bone. His two hundred and sixty pound bleeding frame was lifted up and off the ground. Brig tried desperately to fight off the enormous male as it continued to bite down on him. Now Brig was hovering in the air, several feet off the ground. For one of the first times in his life, he felt that he was truly in over his head. He heard movement from somewhere close by. It had to be the big female, but at this point he couldn't see her, couldn't make out much of anything for that matter.

And then all of a sudden, Brig was dropped and let go. He hit the ground hard and fell forward on his face. But the large man was not to be denied. With the shirt that covered the bloody stump on the left arm now soaked all the way through with blood, Brig managed to push himself over and onto his back. He knew he needed to propel himself back upright to his feet.

He was in the process of pushing his body up when something enormous suddenly toppled him over. Again, he was knocked backward on his ass. And then suddenly, a massive limb pressed him back down to the ground. He felt the wind taken from his lungs as the creature pushed down on his chest with crushing force. He was pinned down by one of the massive limbs from the big male.

Next, Brig saw the big dome-shaped head followed by the large eyes. The animal pressed down harder on him as it extended itself and leaned in closer toward him. Now up close, Brig watched as the gums rippled into a fierce grin. His eyes took in the oversized canine teeth. And then the big mouth opened wide and the fearsome creature blared loudly into his face. At this close proximity, it had been a terrifying, earth-shattering sound. Brig felt the hot panting breath of the animal upon him, the unpleasant stench that was this animal. Another loud roar followed and then suddenly, the huge creature straightened itself. The male giganto-pithecus released itself momentarily from the man and backed its body up. And there it stood on all fours, towering triumphantly over the forest floor. This was its forest, its domain, there was no mistaking that. Noise cracked from somewhere nearby.

Brig managed to cock his head at an angle. Near a thick stand of bamboo, he watched as the female gigantopithecus emerged slowly. The animal came to a stop, rested itself on all fours, and turned its head in the direction of the male. The big male went up onto its back two legs, beat loudly on its chest, and roared. The female followed suit.

The two creatures then turned and faced the man lying on his back and bleeding to death. Slowly, they began closing in on him. Suddenly, Brig began to cough blood. He was teetering on the edge of unconsciousness. With a wet, gurgled cry of sheer terror, Brig Daniels screamed at the top of his lungs as the two creatures converged upon him.

• • •

Bob Hohrman pushed aside what fear still resided in him and just kept making his way through the forest. The monotony of seeing green bamboo tree after green bamboo tree was really starting to weigh on him, but he just had to keep pushing, otherwise he'd never make it out of this nightmare of a place. He looked down at his watch for a moment which in turn caused him to trip on something. This damn place was loaded with potential hazards. And then Bob heard a distinct hissing sound. He froze in place right where he was. Immediately, he felt his pulse rate elevate.

Bob knew instantly that he had stumbled upon a snake. The problem was that there was far too much going on in this damn jungle to make sense of things. And then he spotted the thing. Probably several arms-lengths away from where he stood, a neon green banded body also stood frozen in place. A few more tense seconds passed before Bob eventually saw the coils of the snake unfurl themselves, and before he realized it, the snake was on the move, disappearing and blending back into the surrounding leafy foliage.

Bob breathed a momentary sigh of relief. He had been grateful for the hissing warning that the snake had given him. Although he had no way of knowing with absolute certainty what species of snake it was, he was most positive that it was poisonous. After all, most of the things in this goddamn place appeared to be.

Rather quickly, Bob was on the move once again. He felt confident that he was moving in the right direction of their makeshift camp. But this entire time, he kept experiencing a nauseating feeling from deep within. The helicopter would be here soon. He felt absolutely sick to his stomach about the whole situation. Regardless, he needed to gather his belongings, but he also needed to keep a look out for Diane. She could no longer be trusted and he wondered if she was dangerous at this point.

And once that had been achieved, he planned on making his way back to the exact hillside where they had been dropped off. That was the so-called rendezvous point. The only person who had ever spoken of the rendezvous point was none other than Diane Clor. Diane fucking Clor. That thought alone made Bob sick to his stomach. The woman who had literally left him to die at the bottom of a hole was the one who had been solely responsible for arranging the transportation logistics that was supposed to get them out of here and home safely. But some of them weren't going home. At this point, Bob had no clue if Diane, Stacey, or Clark were in fact still alive; all he knew with relative certainty was that he had to get to the rendezvous point.

Bob needed to make it out with his life. After all, he had a wife and kids to get home to. He had beaten cancer several years back and was determined not to let this bamboo forest be his final resting place. He had been through far too much already in his life to just lie down and give up. With thoughts of his family and all that he had achieved and beaten so far in his life, Bob's pace quickened.

Now he was moving quickly through the trees, diligently making his way back toward their makeshift camp. In his right hand, he carried a six foot piece of bamboo that he had managed to break off from one of the smaller bamboo trees. It just so happened that by the manner in which he had broken it off, the front of it was torn in a rather sharp and jagged edge. Now he held tightly his only form of protection he had as he continued moving. Bob's senses eventually picked up on the fact that all sounds around him had suddenly died down. In what seemed like a matter of seconds, the forest had been plunged into a deep silence. It was quite the shift to go from the constant drone and buzz of insect chatter to suddenly hearing nothing at all. That could only mean one thing. Bob wasn't alone. Quickly, he came to a stop, lowered the bamboo spear out in front of him, and scanned with his eyes. He knew he potentially had two things to worry about: fending off one of these creatures, and possibly having to fend off Diane herself.

Bob heard shuffling from somewhere off in the brush close by. He turned and saw nothing but bamboo trees. Now the noise appeared to be coming up from his left side. He turned his body, again pointing the bamboo spear toward where he thought the sound had originated from. And there he remained, his muscles taut with tension, the forest reluctant to give up its clues.

A few more seconds passed before suddenly, something came up quickly from behind him. He tried to fling himself around, but it was already too late. Whatever it was had completely engulfed him.

57

Downs pushed ahead to the front of the line as the sight of an open clearing was fast approaching. It was just past the next thick stand of bamboo trees, probably a good one hundred feet from where the team was. They were moving quickly through the forest now. The minute Downs left his positioning at the back of the line, Josiah immediately took up defending and guarding the rear.

Now Downs was walking close to Max; the thirty year old zoologist had been busy the entire time guiding them by following the trail of blood. Actually, it had been much easier than originally expected. The team had been following a serious trail of blood the entire time. There had been blood smeared across the low-lying vegetation as well as the ground itself. They needed to keep their wits about them. With this much physical blood in such close proximity to them at all times, it could only mean one thing: predators wouldn't be too far behind.

"Looks like it's just up ahead," Downs whispered.

"Do we think the film team stayed here in this clearing?" Josiah asked.

Downs nodded yes.

"And what about the, uh, military guy we had the run in with?" Max asked.

"Hard to tell if they're working together or not," Tori replied.

Downs nodded. "I agree. Tough to tell if the woman who we spotted filmin' is workin' with that special forces guy or not."

"It's possible that special forces guy has the fight of his life on his hands right about now." Jeremiah said.

Heads turned toward John Corstine's son.

"Shots were fired back in the clearing," Jeremiah continued. "That in turn attracted the attention of both adult creatures. Whoever that guy is, he now has his hands full with the full brunt of both of those creatures coming down hard on him."

Again Downs nodded as he turned his attention back to the clearing. He still couldn't see much of anything; most of his view was obstructed by the sheer density of the bamboo growth, but what he could see was sunshine beaming down into the clearing. Morning in Vietnam was now in full swing. The humidity was rapidly rising toward its usual midday brutal levels. Downs pulled his canteen from his backpack in order to drink. The others did the same as well.

Downs wiped his mouth and stuffed the canteen back in his bag. "Be on guard. We gotta assume at this point she's armed. But she also appears to be seriously injured. We need to get in, secure that camera and all other equipment which might have documented evidence of the creatures, offer her our assistance in getting out of this place, and we'll take care of the rest of the details from there."

By taking care of the rest of the details, Downs meant that the S.C.A would potentially offer her money and a non-disclosure agreement to keep her mouth shut about what existed in this forest. And over the years, the Society of Cryptozoological Agents had been very good at getting people to keep their mouths shut simply by shelling out lots of money. It seemed to work time and time again. Downs believed they'd be able to do the same here.

"Alright," Downs said. "Let's keep movin'."

They continued toward the open clearing. As they neared, Downs saw more beams of sunshine beaming down on the open clearing. But there was also a smell, a downright pungent and awful odor that seemed to waft all the way from the clearing and into the trees. Finally, the team stepped through the trees and out into the clearing. The sun beamed brightly on them now.

Downs pointed toward the fallen tents. "Over there."

But then there was something else. It was the steady yet thick sound of buzzing. Heads turned and swung in unison just to the left of where the downed tents lay. As they moved close they could see that the thick buzzing mass was in fact one big, dense cloud of flies. The constant drone of hundreds if not thousands of flies rang out. It was a solid hovering mass of black.

Before them lay the half-eaten remains of a human. As Downs' eyes continued to take it all in, he could see that it sure as hell appeared to be the remains of the woman he had spotted a short while ago. As they drew nearer, the smell only intensified and the buzzing mass of flies grew louder. Downs snapped his fingers. And just like that he and Tori took off, making a beeline straight for the crumpled tents that lay in the dead center of the clearing. The rest of the team headed to investigate the body.

This time, it was Tori who was moving quickly toward the tent. Downs had a hard time keeping pace with the newly minted bestselling author.

"It has to be there," Downs said.

"Let's freaking hope so," Tori replied from up ahead.

When they got there, they found that what they had thought was one big tent was in fact two tents that lay sprawled out across one another. Tori arrived at the tents first. Downs watched as she bent down and within a matter of seconds had what looked to be the camera that they had been after.

Tori handed the camera to Downs. But he didn't take hold of it. Rather, he looked back to the rest of his teammates who now hovered over the dead body. Downs then turned and looked back to the rather expensive-looking camera that Tori held in her hands. Suddenly, a distinct noise from somewhere behind them could be heard, reminding Downs that this was far from over.

58

Bob Hohrman both felt and heard something come up quickly from behind. With no time to turn, he suddenly found himself in the tight embrace of something powerful. He felt an immense squeezing sensation around his body, and felt hot breath upon the right side of his face. And then just like that, he was released from the suffocating embrace that had momentarily engulfed him.

It took his eyes a few seconds, but eventually Bob saw a rather large looking man standing before him.

"You're lucky I didn't snap your neck like a chicken, son," the voice said.

The man standing before Bob was none other than Burr Wellington. Bob took a moment, brushed himself off, and felt around his neck for the strong stranglehold that had previously gripped it.

Bob was quite flustered to say the least. "Who, who are you?"

Burr grinned and breathed in the air. "Someone that's alive."

Burr continued breathing in the humid morning jungle air as if it were his first time experiencing oxygen.

"Listen, son," Burr continued. "Here with a small team. Our mission was to locate, sedate, and transport one of the adult gigantopithecus to an undisclosed location."

"Oh, I see," Bob said as he rolled his eyes. "So you're here like the others. To exploit and profit from these scientific wonders."

Burr shook his head and spit on the ground at his feet. "See son, that's where you got it all wrong. We're here to serve and protect, to keep what's previously been secret, a secret. And we like to keep it that way."

Bob shook his head. "I'm not following. I don't get it."

Burr shook his head again and propped his large body up against an adjacent bamboo tree. "Follow me and you'll find out."

• • •

From where Downs stood next to Tori amidst the crumpled tents, he watched as a lone juvenile gigantopithecus emerged silently from the trees. But the creature didn't stop there. Rather aggressively, it kept moving forward.

Next, Downs heard a sharp whistling sound. He saw that it had come from Jeremiah Corstine. On the opposite side of the clearing stood the second of the two juveniles. Downs could only hope and pray that they would only have to contend with these two young and aggressive creatures currently patrolling this part of the forest.

Quickly, Downs took hold of the camera from Tori. Next he grabbed the laptop as she handed it to him.

Securing both of them in his backpack he quickly turned around and faced her. "I'll spot you. You thoroughly search both these tents. Make sure there aren't any more cameras, laptops, phones, or tablets lying around. We take anything and everything that might be evidence of the creature's existence."

Quickly, Tori crouched down and began sifting through the tents. Meanwhile, Downs turned back around, his revolver leveled out in front of him. Out of both corners of his eyes, he saw the two young creatures quickly converging upon them.

"What'll we do now?" Josiah shouted from over near the rotting remains of Diane Clor.

"Hold your ground," Downs fired back.

Downs looked to his left. The juvenile on that side of them was now within twenty five yards. A quick look to his right and he could see that the other juvenile had also worked its way closer. The last thing Downs wanted to do at this moment was to kill one of these magnificent creatures. Raising the revolver as the two approaching youngsters drew nearer, Downs fired a shot straight up into the air. He had hoped that the distinct sound of the gun going off would deter the two animals, but as the two creatures continued moving forward, he realized it hadn't worked.

Downs grabbed hold of Tori and the two butted their backs up against one another. Downs watched as the rest of his team began to fan out as they continued to watch one of the lone juveniles approaching them. Downs turned. He and Tori now had their own problems to deal with as one of the four hundred pound juveniles continued to pursue them.

"Fuck!" Downs cursed.

"What is it?" Tori asked back through gritted teeth.

"We don't wanna have to kill one of these animals. Defeats the whole purpose of our mission."

Tori took several steps back. She was now standing shoulder to shoulder with Downs as the two faced the oncoming attacker. "Well, we might have to. At this point it seems like it's us or them."

Downs raised the revolver and fired several feet into the dirt in front of the juvenile. The bullet sprayed dirt into the air, which in turn caused the animal to rear up aggressively onto its back two legs. The juvenile gigantopithecus lowered itself onto all fours and quickly bounded off to its right. Meanwhile, Downs sprung forward, holstered the revolver at his side, and grabbed hold of the air rifle from around his left shoulder. Downs took aim, steadied himself, and squeezed the trigger. From a distance of some forty-five feet, Downs pinned the animal with a dart on its back left hind leg.

It wasn't certain whether or not the animal had even taken notice, but now Downs and Tori could see the bright pink feathered dart protruding out of the animal's fur. All that was certain was that the bounding animal appeared to now be heading straight for Jeremiah and the others.

"You've got company on your right side!" Downs shouted to the group.

Both he and Tori quickly stepped away from the crumpled remains of the two fallen tents. Downs and Tori found themselves running full sprint toward the rotting remains of Diane Clor.

Up ahead, Downs could see his good buddy Josiah.

"You've got company on your left as well!" Josiah shouted.

Downs and Tori turned just in time to witness an enormous figure burst forward in an eruption of leaves and limbs. The monstrosity sent its two front limbs slamming straight down into the dirt. It was the large female. The two came to a stop. They were breathing hard and now situated in the middle of the clearing.

"Oh, shit!" Tori yelled.

The large female gigantopithecus now stood in between Downs and Tori as well as the others. Meanwhile, a little ways behind the twelve hundred pound animal, the two juveniles were quickly converging upon the rest of the team.

Downs watched as the large, dome-shaped head peered down at them. Although not as bulky as the heavier male, the female gigantopithecus was still quite an impressive creature to say the least. The imposing animal stood resting the front part of its body on the knuckles of its front limbs.

Downs and Tori stood absolutely still. And then Downs watched as the gums of the adult rippled back, exposing an arsenal of teeth that both of them wanted absolutely no part of. The giant animal let out a deep, rumbling, cavernous roar. From such a close distance, the roar had been a horrifying thing to experience, the sound rumbling from deep within the great chest cavity. It was a cry that seemed to have its origins based in another time in earth's history, something from the savage primordial past.

The creature was so big that it in fact blocked Downs' view back to the rest of the team. He scooted himself to the right, saw around the enormous silhouette of the animal, saw past the huge tree-sized limbs. He noted instantly that Jeremiah and the others had their hands full as the two juveniles were slowly closing in on them from both sides.

Meanwhile to his right, Tori had her own air rifle leveled out in front of her, the tranquilizer gun seeming pathetically small in the presence of the huge and imposing creature. Quickly, Downs lowered his gaze to his own backside. He saw the bright orange flare gun holstered. It momentarily reminded him that Burr Wellington's whereabouts were still unknown.

The female roared from its position in between Downs and Tori and the rest of the team. The huge creature raised its two front arms and sent them slamming down hard into the dirt. Downs' eyes shot back to Jeremiah and the others. The two juveniles had now drawn to within fifteen feet of them.

And then suddenly Downs thought he heard noise. He listened closer, his eyes never wavering from the unfolding scene before him. Again, he strained with his ears to listen. There it was again. It was faint, but it was most definitely there. Downs heard the very distant thumping sounds of the rotors from what appeared to be a helicopter. The sound was drawing closer and closer.

And then time seemed to stand still as Downs stepped to his right, putting some separation in between Tori and himself. At the other end of the clearing, he spotted Jeremiah Corstine. Jeremiah had spotted him too. Quickly, the two nodded to one another. Downs unholstered the flare gun from his back side and raised it in the air. Meanwhile, on the other end of the clearing, Jeremiah took hold of the assault rifle. And then together as one, both men fired straight up into the sky.

• • •

Burr Wellington's large outstretched hands reached out and grabbed Bob Hohrman by the back of the shoulders. Bob had been busy for several minutes now leading the two men through the forest back to the camp where the documentary film team had originally set up camp. Now the two men stood in silence as the bamboo trees swayed and groaned all around them.

"Did you hear that?" Burr said, his large hands still resting atop Bob's shoulders.

Bob shook his head, staring straight ahead. "No. No, I didn't."

Burr looked straight up toward the top of the canopy. It was quite crowded up there. The canopy was thick and blotted out most of the sky. "Well, I did. And that sounded like a chopper to me. Our ticket outta here."

Bob was visibly exhausted, injured, tired, and weak. It felt like they had been out here for weeks on end. As Burr finally took his hands off the back of Bob's shoulders, the man was grateful for that. He wasn't quite certain how he felt about this large man whom he had just met and knew literally nothing about being in such close proximity to him. But that was the least of Bob's worries. Now it was simply about life and death, getting the hell out of here alive. That was all that mattered now as all other worries were cast aside. He wanted to get back to his family. He wanted to get back to his life.

Bob was just about to say something when once again Burr quieted him. The two stood mired in silence. They waited and listened. It was faint and distant, but this time the sound appeared to have come from a much closer distance.

"I hear it," Bob suddenly whispered.

"We're getting the fuck outta here," Burr replied back. "Let's go. That's gotta be our chopper."

Bob's eyes shot up toward the top of the canopy. It was tough to make out much of anything up there. All they could do at this point was basically use their ears.

Burr took a few steps away from Bob. Again, he tried his best to gain a vantage point back up to the sky. But the canopy was just too damn thick in this part of the forest. It was a criss-crossed, entangled, and jumbled mess way up there. What this ultimately meant was that neither Burr nor Bob had seen the bright orange flare that Bick Downs had just shot up into the sky.

Burr returned to Bob's side and there the two listened for a few seconds longer. They could no longer hear the faint yet distant sound of the chopper. Instead, all that registered was the constant buzz and drone of insects from all around. The humidity was growing with each passing second, as was the need to leave this place and put it far behind in their rear view mirror.

Bob patted quietly on his chest. "Let's get back to our camp. We made camp in a rather wide open clearing. Should be able to have a better view of what's going on up in the sky once we're smack dab in the middle of that clearing."

Although he still felt very uneasy about potentially encountering Diane Clor back at camp, he knew that was their best and only option at this point. Besides, he now had acquired quite a bit of additional muscle if he did indeed encounter her.

Burr slapped a large hand down atop Bob's shoulder. "Best damn thing you said all morning, son. Lead the way."

• • •

The pilot of the yellow and black B14 helicopter had been seeing the agonizing monotony of the top of the green forest canopy below for quite some time now. The green vegetation line stretched as far as the eye could see in all directions. A short while earlier, he had been treated to the real beauty that this trip had to offer up. He had been treated to none other than Vietnam's coastline.

Flying low in relation to the water, the pilot had seen blue turquoise waters and beautiful geologic designs in the form of chunks of land that formed small mini islands in the picturesque water. For a brief while, the pilot had been so enamored with what he was seeing that for a moment he had forgotten the real reason why the B14 had been summoned in the first place. He had been summoned by John Corstine and he was here to pick up Bick Downs and the rest of the Society of Cryptozoological Agents. That was the plan.

The pilot blinked and brought himself back to the present. He simply couldn't get the beauty of Vietnam's coastline off his brain. It was burned into his subconscious and as soon as the mission's objective was complete, he vowed to return. How he yearned to take a swim in the tropical waters that this Southeast Asian country had to offer.

Now the pilot found himself flying high above the endless sea of green bamboo trees below. It had all happened rather quickly. One minute he had been flying, his eyes locked in on the rather monotonous solid green below, when out of nowhere, a bright orange flare had shot straight up into the sky from the green canopy below. The glowing orange ball burned and sizzled its way up into the sky before finally burning off. Now all that remained was a thin, wispy trail of smoke.

The pilot veered to the right. That's exactly where he was heading now. That's where he would find them.

59

For a precious few seconds, there had been absolute silence in the clearing. The monstrous vocalizations by the female gigantopithecus had died down and the advancing juveniles had halted their progress as well. Downs looked up to the sky momentarily. He could see the fading trail of smoke from the flare that he had shot quickly disintegrating into thin air. But that was not what had stopped these enormous primates.

Downs shot a quick glare toward Jeremiah. The man was still in possession of the assault rifle, and it was the sound of the assault rifle releasing several rounds into the air which had more than likely quieted everyone. The immense sound produced by the rifle was what had frightened them. In a world where vocalizations are meant as a way to challenge rivals, the assault rifle had proven for a precious few seconds that there was something bigger and badder on the block. But as the silence continued to stretch, the animals now appeared hesitant, unsure of themselves. However, when the dominating sound of the assault rifle did not return, the creatures slowly started to come back to life.

Downs quickly pointed to his right. Both he and Tori were now on the move, moving away from the flattened tents in the middle of the clearing and toward the two advancing youngsters. But no sooner had they made their way some twenty-five feet or so out and away from the tents, the female gigantopithecus was once again on the move as well. The huge creature lurched forward and began tearing its way toward the two humans.

Downs turned just in time to see the huge female come to an abrupt stop, raise both arms into the air, and beat aggressively on its chest. An intense bellowing roar followed. Now it was pretty clear what the female was doing. She stood in between the two humans and her young. She was protecting them.

• • •

Josiah Young felt a shot of adrenaline straight to his bloodstream. If a twelve hundred pound rampaging primate with its two infants isn't enough to get your blood flowing, then nothing in this world would.

Josiah pushed off with his feet and propelled his body forward. Up ahead, he could see the enormous backside of the female gigantopithecus. The massive creature had its back to them and faced in the direction of Downs and Tori. Josiah got to a position, steadied himself, and fired a dart straight into the wide rump of the animal. He had pinned a dart on the creature's right buttocks, the small dart quickly burrowing its way into the thick matting of fur before disappearing altogether.

As Josiah retreated back to the others, he had no way of knowing if the liquid contents inside the dart was slowly working or if it had simply served to enrage the huge animal. He managed to get back to the others just as the enormous creature turned and faced them. Planting both arms down into the ground, it again bellowed an earth-shattering roar.

• • •

Downs saw his opportunity. Quickly, he reached into his bag for another dart. Getting down on one knee, he steadied himself. Just about to squeeze the trigger on his air rifle, he watched as a green feathered dart suddenly materialized on the opposite butt cheek. Turning, he saw that it was Tori who had fired the dart into the animal.

Downs stood to his feet. "Nice fuckin' shot."

She smiled and stood. "Can't let you boys have all the fun."

Now the female gigantopithecus was truly enraged. Abandoning its post where it had been standing, the twelve hundred pound creature turned and began pursuing Downs and Tori once again. Quickly, Downs scanned the clearing. He had lost visual of the two juveniles.

"Where're the juveniles?" Downs shouted.

He watched as the rest of the team spun momentarily and scanned. But Downs and Tori couldn't stick around to find out where the two juveniles were. The female rampaged forward and bellowed a moaning roar toward the two fleeing humans. Now Downs and Tori were fleeing, unsure as to what their next move should be. Quickly, he looked down at the Astra revolver still holstered at his right side. The flare gun was holstered at his backside.

"Perhaps now's as good a time as any to use the Astra!" Tori shouted, breathing hard.

Downs scanned frantically with his eyes. And then suddenly, out of the corner of his right eye, he saw something charging and moving fast. It was one of the juveniles.

"We've got company on our right!" he shouted.

As they continued running, he lowered the air rifle and fired a dart at the attacking youngster. But they were moving too fast and the dart sailed right on by the four hundred pound, muscularly-built creature.

Still running, Downs could now hear the huge female behind them giving chase as its tree-sized limbs thundered across the dirt of the clearing. And then suddenly from above, they heard a new sound.

"The chopper!" Downs yelled, pointing.

Somewhere in the far reaches of Downs' brain, he knew that the helicopter had come a bit early and this was their ticket out of this place. Downs stopped momentarily where he was and craned his neck up toward the sky. Trying desperately to get his bearings straight on where the chopper was, he saw nothing, only heard the faint yet distinct sound from the rotors.

"Bick!" Tori shouted just as Downs brought his head back to level.

He watched as Tori lowered herself and fired a dart into one of the oncoming juveniles. It had been a clean shot, the dart pinning the screaming youngster somewhere on its burly neck. The animal veered hard to its right.

Downs turned and watched as the juvenile was now quickly approaching Jeremiah and the others. This time, each member of that small team stood with their air rifles raised in the direction of the oncoming attacker, except Jeremiah that was. John Corstine's son stood with the rifle raised and ready to fire.

Downs could sense the frustration in Jeremiah's hands. He was battling the same internal struggle as he was, as he once again unclipped the Astra and held it at his side. They were trying with everything they had to not kill one of these creatures, to not unleash a barrage of bullets on these prehistoric wonders. But at the same time, they were trying not to get killed either. It was a delicate balancing act to say the least.

Downs stood next to Tori.

"Get at my back!" he shouted.

She did just that. Downs felt her back slide up against his. He faced in the direction of the opposite side of the clearing just as he heard the sound of something coming forward. There was a momentary pause just before a giant figure came bursting forward in an enormous explosion of limbs and branches from inside the forest out into the light of the clearing.

A massive, deep, and throaty roar heralded the arrival of the big male. The huge creature immediately took up chase, charging toward Downs and Tori, showing no sign of fear whatsoever, no backing down. From where Downs stood, he watched as the big cavernous mouth opened wide. Ropes of saliva flew from both sides of the creature's mouth as it bounded forward. And then the huge male came to a screeching halt, reared onto its back two legs, and thumped its huge chest several times.

Downs sprung forward, got himself into position some thirty-five yards away, and fired a dart. He pinned the male somewhere in its massive gut region. Quickly, the animal dropped to all fours and roared in the direction of Downs. And then to Downs' surprise, the creature reached down with its right hand and plucked the dart from its chest. It discarded the dart and then began rampaging forward.

To Downs, it felt like a small car was thundering their way as the big male once again roared. Next, a sharp piercing whistle rang out. Downs spun and saw that it had come from Jeremiah Corstine. Jeremiah pointed out toward somewhere at the edge of the clearing toward the tall stands of bamboo. As Downs did his best to follow, he saw the two juveniles were nowhere to be seen.

Then he shifted his attention back to the big male. Downs' eyes set in on the edge of the clearing some thirty to forty yards behind the male. Materializing out of the trees came the two juveniles. The minute their powerful limbs set foot in the clearing, they immediately gave up chase. The two animals immediately gave chase as they aimed to catch up with the sixteen hundred pound behemoth pounding toward Downs and Tori.

Quickly, Downs grabbed Tori by the hand as they began backtracking. Moving backward now at a quicker pace, out of the corner of his right eye, Downs could see the rest of the group was also moving in to join them.

"Where's the female?" Tori shouted as they continued backtracking.

Max Caldwell yelled back as they were practically all together now. "It disappeared back into the forest!"

"Get together!" Downs ordered.

As a tight and cohesive unit, the team made a solid wall against the oncoming attackers. Quickly, Downs barked out the next order. "Josiah, you watch our backs and sides!"

"Done!" Josiah said as he stepped aside.

"Now what?" Tori screamed as the creatures closed to within one hundred feet of them.

Downs looked out to the edge of their line. Jeremiah stood there with the powerful assault rifle still in hand. Then he returned his gaze to the oncoming attackers. The juveniles had just about caught up to the huge male as Downs quickly pulled the flare gun from his backside. Holding the flare gun in his left hand while bringing the Astra up in his right, he now held both of them out in front of him, pressing the smaller orange plastic emergency gun up against the larger revolver. Now both guns were raised and pointed at the family of three.

Downs waited until finally both juveniles ran on either side of the large male. Then he got got down on one knee, steadied himself, and fired the flare gun.

A sharp, sizzling sound resonated as the gun went off. The tiny spark struck the big male square in the chest, the huge beast coming to a stop as it roared in pain while rearing back on its two enormous legs. The initial impact of the flare sent small sparks which shot out on both sides of the creature, which in turn caused the two juveniles to come to a screeching halt as tiny sparks rained down around them.

Bellowing cries of rage could be heard as Downs loaded another cartridge into the flare gun. Again he raised both the flare gun and the Astra together. He fired a second flare into the shoulder of the juvenile on their left. The animal howled in pain as it sizzled and burned a small hole through its fur. But when Downs turned to fire into the lone juvenile on their right, he found the animal charging and advancing forward at a faster pace now. Downs fired a flare at the fast approaching juvenile. The shot had not been accurate and he missed.

Slowly, the group began backing up.

"We may have to fuckin' shoot them," Jeremiah said.

"That's, uh, not the point of why we're out here," Max said to the group.

Josiah shook his head, his own air rifle pointed straight at the oncoming attackers. "Yeah, well neither's getting fuckin' eaten either!"

"Quiet," Jeremiah Corstine shouted to all of them.

From somewhere above, the team could hear the rotors from a helicopter growing nearer. Still though, it was hard to make sense of which direction the damn thing was coming from. Quickly, Downs holstered the flare gun at his backside. Now with the air rifle slung over his left shoulder, he maintained a firm grasp on the Astra.

The team watched as the big male gitantopithecus once again thumped its massive chest. Meanwhile, the juvenile that had been shot by the flare also appeared to be in a bit of discomfort. This left the remaining juvenile that hadn't been shot. The creature was now galloping toward them.

Together as one, the team kept backtracking as well.

"We got eyes on the back of us?" Downs called out as they kept moving backward.

"Roger that," Josiah replied.

To Downs, it felt like the creatures were leading them into an ambush. With the female nowhere to be seen, it left quite a formidable and sizable animal hidden in and amongst the dense bamboo. Still, the team continued moving backward. Downs was just about to do a quick visual with Josiah. He was the only one in the group who had his back to them so as to have eyes at their backs. Suddenly, the juvenile gigantopithecus on the right of them took a more aggressive approach.

"Should we fire?" Tori asked.

Downs quickly scanned. Again, he heard the faint yet distinct sounds of the rotors from the helicopter drawing nearer.

"Yeah," Downs ordered. "Fire the tranquilizers."

But before they could do anything further, a sizzling, white spark struck the oncoming juvenile. The animal howled a moaning cry as it reared up onto its back two legs and bellowed. As it dropped to all fours, it was once again hit with another hot spark of white that struck it somewhere in the neck.

Downs quickly put two and two together. The only other person that had a flare gun was-

A bare-chested and bloodied Burr Wellington stepped out of the trees and into the clearing, the six foot five inch, two hundred and fifty pound man stood close to where the fallen tents lay. Quickly, he began moving forward.

Downs spotted it immediately and shouted. "Burr, freeze!"

But the big man was not to be denied. Downs and the others watched as Burr's hulking figure could be seen making his way, hugging close to the tree line as he was quickly advancing toward the adult gigantopithecus and two juveniles. And then Downs saw another figure emerge from the trees. Running rather fast, whoever the man was quickly caught up to Burr.

"Hold tight!" Downs ordered to the team as he moved forward.

Another quick scan and he could now see both men snaking their way close to the trees on the right. The ferocity and manner in which Burr moved didn't surprise Downs one bit. Again, Downs' eyes locked in on the flare gun locked firmly in Burr's grip. The man was now busy quickly loading another flare.

On the one hand, Downs was completely ecstatic to see that Burr was alive and well, but he now wondered if the big man had fallen completely off his rocker. Burr Wellington was now moving like a man possessed, one that seemed fully committed to what appeared to be a suicide mission. Going at the big male gigantopithecus and two juveniles with nothing more than a flare gun seemed every bit the word crazy.

Downs continued moving forward. Jeremiah Corstine had suddenly joined his side. Now the two men moved forward with their weapons. Meanwhile behind them, the remaining three members of the team stood with their backs pressed up against one another on guard.

Quickly, Downs could see that the family of three creatures had taken notice. Burr and whoever it was trailing close behind him had officially been spotted.

Again, Downs yelled out to Burr. "Burr, freeze!"

But by now Burr Wellington was far too committed to the cause to abandon ship.

From where the two stood, this time it was Jeremiah who yelled out to Burr. "Burr, freeze! That's an order!"

Downs shook his head. "There's no stopping him now. We have to shoot the animals. Seems like no other choice."

Jeremiah nodded. "Agreed."

Together, the two men continued moving forward. Quickly, the young juvenile gigantopithecus on the right side of the two men immediately began pursuing Burr Wellington and his mate instead. Burr wasted no time though as he fired a flare straight into the upper breast bone of the oncoming attacker. The bright, white spark struck the animal hard, momentarily knocking it backward.

Now as Downs and Jeremiah continued moving forward, Downs picked up on the fact that the man who was crouched in hiding behind Burr now appeared confused as to his next move. Burr, however, was not hanging around to find out more about the man's confusion. The big man moved forward aggressively. He quickly approached the juvenile that he had just shot with the flare gun. The juvenile was visibly rattled and roared at the man as it started to pace back and forth. Downs noticed that the flare had injured it more than he had originally anticipated. This time, it had singed and burned a small wound into the long course fur of the animal.

Burr came to a quick stop. Downs heard it, too. The helicopter was close now. Over at the far end of the clearing, the tall stands of bamboo were starting to be beaten back. With eyes flaring wide with determination, Burr finally shouted and acknowledged his teammates. "Fucking move! Get the bloody hell outta here! Go!"

And with that, Burr waved his arms frantically to Downs and Jeremiah. He motioned rapidly for them to retreat to the other side of the clearing as the roaring sound of the helicopter continued drawing nearer. All of Burr's waving had finally won out as he managed to attract the attention of the big male. The huge creature lowered itself, dropped to all fours, opened its gaping mouth, and blasted a deafening roar. Even with the approaching helicopter, the big male's roar had still been a terrifying sound.

Burr was moving swiftly now.

Meanwhile, Downs turned and motioned for the man who had been clinging tightly to Burr to head on over their way. The man froze, total deer in the headlights. As Downs kept motioning swiftly with his arms, the reality of the situation must have eventually hit the man full bore. With unsure legs he began moving toward Downs and Jeremiah. No sooner than he had taken five steps forward, the man was tackled hard to the ground.

Downs flung himself around and witnessed Burr fire another flare straight into the chest of the massive male. The male lifted itself from all fours, beat aggressively on its chest, and took the full impact of the brightly glowing flare as it struck it hard. And then it roared a blood-curdling roar that rumbled from the massive chest cavity.

Downs yelled back to Jeremiah. The noise from the chopper was growing closer now. "Help Burr! I got this over here."

And with that, Downs took off toward the fallen man who had just been tackled. His eyes quickly took in the situation. The juvenile that Burr had shot with the flare gun had pinned the man to the ground like a rag doll. Now with effortless power, the creature bit down as the jaws held the man firmly in place. As Downs drew nearer, he could hear a low growl emanating from the creature's mouth. It was hard to make sense of things now as limbs were intertwined, human and animal combined to form a ball. All that was truly distinguishable was the fact that the four hundred pound juvenile was crushing the man, pinning and holding his left shoulder in place with its powerful jaw muscles.

Downs leveled his revolver out in front of him. When he neared to within ten feet, he took aim and fired. Downs placed a bullet into the muscular right thigh of the juvenile. In a matter of seconds blood began to flow from the gunshot wound. The creature released its jaws from around Bob Hohrman's shoulder and let out a shrieking howl of pain. In doing so, that gave Downs the confidence he needed to get in there and do the necessary work. Downs burst foward, dropped to his knees, and began removing the powerful animal from atop the man. Even for someone as strong as Bick Downs, the dead weight of the creature was almost unmanageable. Despite this, Downs summoned every last bit of strength he could muster. Eventually, he felt the weight of the animal slip free from the man below. The problem was that this in turn freed the jaws of the juvenile. As the head slid downward toward the growing pool of blood beneath its body, the jaws snapped down hard on Downs' left arm. The crushing pain was immediate as teeth bit down on bone and skin. With his right hand, Downs sent the butt of the revolver slamming straight into the skull of the creature. The blunt force from the blow was enough to knock the wounded juvenile backward as its muscular body slid downward and fell to the ground.

Downs went to work helping the man to his feet. "You okay?"

The deafening roar of the helicopter was literally right above them now.

"Yeah!" Bob Hohrman shouted back to him as he stood to his feet, visibly shaken by what had just happened.

Downs could tell by the way that the man's shoulder hung limply at his side that it was more than likely dislocated. Downs grabbed him by the other shoulder. He yelled at the man and pointed now. "Head over there!"

Downs sent Bob toward the remaining team members. He then spun around and faced what was continuing to transpire.

From a distance of some twenty feet, he watched as Burr fired a flare straight into the massive chest of the male gigantopithecus. The animal roared another one of its monstrous and cavernous roars.

Quickly, Downs' eyes flicked to the left. He saw the young juvenile standing there at the feet of the towering ten foot tall beast as the big male now stood on its back two legs. And then Downs saw the big male begin knuckling its way toward Burr.

Downs realized he had lost visual on the remaining juvenile. Downs turned. He saw the remaining juvenile hastily making its way toward its fallen mate. With zero hesitation, Downs began moving at once toward Burr Wellington. As he drew nearer, he could now smell the musty stench of the big male. The smell of the large animal had completely overtaken the clearing.

"Burr, get back here!" Downs shouted.

This time, to Downs' surprise, Burr took one last look at the charging gigantopithecus and then quickly turned and fled himself. Burr high-tailed it back to where Downs was.

"Good to see you, son!" Burr shouted as he reached Downs.

"Definitely good to see ya, big guy. Get behind me!" Downs yelled back.

As the sixteen hundred pound creature continued charging forward, Downs watched as the huge beast opened its cavernous mouth, bared its teeth, and blared another menacing roar. He saw the copious ropes of saliva flinging from both sides of its mouth. Burr now stood at Downs' right shoulder, holding the flare gun in his right hand.

Downs held off until he felt he could wait no longer. He steadied himself, took aim, and squeezed the trigger on the revolver. He fired a shot straight into the left shoulder of the big male. The sound of the gun going off was muffled by the roar from the chopper high above. The gun had done exactly what it had been designed to do. It stopped the charging sixteen hundred pound creature. The male gigantopithecus howled in pain, reared back, and let out another chilling roar, a primal cry that rumbled across the clearing.

Quickly, Downs pulled Burr back with him. "Let's get the hell outta here!"

"Sounds like a plan, son!" Burr yelled back.

And together, the two turned and began racing back toward the rest of the team. As they ran, Downs tried to make out the exact location of the helicopter high above, but they were moving quickly now and things were happening too fast. All that could be processed with certainty was that the helicopter was damn close. They had almost reached the rest of the team when Downs stopped momentarily. He flung his body back around.

His eyes went wide on him with what he was seeing. A man bloodied, battered, beaten, and with only one hand emerged from the trees and out into the clearing. Downs watched for another precious few seconds before finally turning and sprinting back to join up with the rest of the team.

• • •

In a state of consciousness that fell somewhere in between delirium and death, Brig Daniels pushed his way through the jungle until finally spilling out into the clearing. Now he stood out in the open as the sun illuminated the bloody mess that was himself. He was bleeding everywhere and had cuts and scrapes on every part of open skin. His pants, shirt, and vest were tattered and torn. The mangled and bloody stump where his left hand used to be served as a reminder of what had been taken from him. Now he was hell-bent on killing this beast rather than capturing and transporting it. It had all changed in a matter of seconds, and whether out of sheer blood loss or not thinking clearly at all, revenge burned deep inside him now. It was all that was pushing him at this stage as he stumbled forward.

Thinking that he was in a clear state of mind but far from it, he quietly unsheathed the blade at his side. His eyes locked in on his target, hate and revenge hard on his mind. The big male had its back to him. Now he began moving quickly through the clearing. He had probably only gone several feet or so before finally, that brisk pace turned into that of an all-out sprint. With the dagger firmly secured in his right hand, Brig summoned every last bit of strength as he sprinted toward the big male.

It was the oddest of sensations running with only one hand. It felt distant and otherworldly. Quickly though, he got his body up to speed and prepared himself for what was to come. Somewhere in the madness of it all, he had to know it was a suicide mission, that the odds were so severely stacked against him that he could actually pull this off. Now with his body fully committed, he planted his right foot down hard on the dirt and propelled his body up.

Brig leaped, his broken and battered body lifting up into the air as he landed atop the back of the male gigantopithecus. Just seconds prior to the man's brazen attempt, the huge creature had lifted itself from the ground as it reared back onto its back two limbs. And there Brig perched for the briefest of moments, high atop the shaggy mountain of fur that was the back of the big male gigantopithecus. Wasting no time, he drew the dagger back and plunged it full force into the animal's thick and muscular shoulder. The beast screamed a deep and guttural cry of rage as the blade pushed through both fur and muscle. Using every last ounce of energy he had, he pushed the dagger until it could go no further. As gravity finally won out and he could hold out no longer, he somehow managed to retract the bloody dagger just as his body fell backward toward the ground.

* * *

Downs and the rest of the team stood both stunned and shocked at what they had just seen. Even if they had wanted to, there was no way they could have gotten to the man's side to aid him. Things had literally transpired in a matter of seconds. Downs stepped forward. He watched as the huge male lowered itself, spun quickly, and then blared a monstrous roar in the direction of the bleeding man who now lay on the ground. He watched as the juveniles quickly sprung forward into action. The man had just attempted to lift himself from the ground when he was tackled by one of the powerful juveniles. A shrill scream of terror echoed loudly across the clearing as the attacking youngster bit down on the man's right elbow. The powerful jaw muscles bit down and forced Brig to relinquish his grip on the dagger. Now with no weapon in hand, bleeding, and missing one hand, that's when the real attack came.

The two youngsters converged upon the fallen man. Suddenly, Downs looked up. And then he flung himself around. It was the first time he could actually see the helicopter as it now hovered at the far end of the clearing.

"Let's go!" Downs shouted to the team over the blare of the noise from the rotors.

The last thing that Bick Downs saw as he turned himself around one last time was the huge male pinning its right forearm down atop the man's heaving chest. Slowly, the towering beast pressed down, crushing the man's ribcage with each inch of pressure exerted. Meanwhile, the two juveniles quickly went to work tearing ragged chunks of flesh from wherever they could. Downs took another second before finally turning himself around and racing with the others toward the helicopter.

60

U p ahead at the far end of the clearing, the team watched as a ladder unfurled itself from the back hatch of the helicopter. Now they could see it. With an actual end goal in sight, each and every one of them pushed themselves harder. As Downs ran, he managed to crane his neck back one last time. All he could make out was the feet of the man and the silhouette of three huge figures as they continued to consume him. It was a grizzly sight as the legs shook back and forth as the creatures fed on him.

Downs turned his neck around and focused in on the rope ladder as it now hovered just above the ground. They were so close to officially extricating themselves from this situation. This was their time, their time to get out of here safely once and for all.

Downs holstered the Astra at his side as he ran. No sooner than he had done just that, he realized his mistake. An enormous, rage-filled roar shook and rumbled the trees and vegetation that lay just beyond the ladder. The team watched a spectacular explosion of leaves and foliage as the female gigantopithecus came rampaging through the low-lying vegetation. The large animal tore and broke off a thin bamboo tree as it continued bounding forward.

As the huge female emerged from the last of the vegetation and officially entered the clearing, it now had a thin bamboo tree about a dozen feet or so in length secured tightly in its right hand. The animal roared loudly as it charged into the clearing, wielding the tree like a baseball bat in one hand while galloping on its three powerful limbs.

Meanwhile, the rope ladder from the helicopter continued to hover and dangle several feet above the ground. Downs grabbed the ladder quickly and looked around. The roar from the chopper above was deafening now.

Downs turned and looked at Tori. He grabbed her by the shoulders and shouted to her. "Go! Climb up!"

She shook her head. "No way!"

Downs screamed back. "You gotta go!"

"Not 'til you leave!"

"Fuck," Downs replied. "Well, someone's gotta go up!"

Downs spun around, his eyes flaring with intensity. The female gigantopithecus was now within fifty feet of them as it continued to charge. Downs grabbed the first body he could. It was Max Caldwell. The zoologist looked as though he wanted to say something, but Downs quickly began pushing him up the ladder. As Max began climbing the rungs of the ladder, Downs turned toward the others.

"Who's next?" Downs shouted.

Josiah came forward.

"Go!" Downs shouted as he pushed the paleontologist toward the swaying ladder.

"You sure, man?" Josiah shouted back.

"Just fuckin' go! We gotta get outta here." Downs yelled.

As Josiah began to climb, Downs quickly pushed Burr Wellington in the direction of the ladder. The big man began climbing the second there was enough space to do so. Meanwhile, the rotor wash from the chopper above continued to drown out all other sounds.

Downs looked straight up. Max was almost at the open hatch. And then Downs swung and turned in the direction of the three other creatures.

Tori's voice suddenly rang loud and clear above it all. "We got company!"

Downs turned and saw that the female was now within twenty feet of them, roaring while the bamboo tree was still clutched tightly in its enormous right hand. He looked at Jeremiah. But just as he did so, Tori grabbed hold of the assault rifle and yanked it clean from the man's hands. Downs looked him square in the eyes and shouted. "Go!"

Jeremiah did not counter. Downs had just begun sprinting and making his way away from the rope when suddenly he heard the assault rifle go off. Tori now had possession of the weapon. The newly-minted bestselling author unloaded a barrage of bullets at the feet of the charging beast. Downs watched as the dirt from the clearing sprayed and rose up all around the gigantopithecus. The momentary barrage of bullets had slowed the animal somewhat but the twelve hundred pound animal still came steamrolling forward, heading straight for the ladder.

Both Downs and Tori quickly hurried themselves backward as the ladder rose higher into the sky. The female roared as it hurled the bamboo tree at the rising ladder. The top of the tree caught the bottom rung of the ladder, but that was it as the pilot took the aircraft higher into the sky now.

Downs and Tori pulled themselves a ways back now. Rather quickly, they found themselves engulfed in a thick, buzzing mass. A brief look back and Downs could see that they were close to the half-eaten remains of Diane Clor. Thick hordes of flies buzzed in and around them now, completely surrounding them on all sides with their sheer numbers.

Together, the two watched as the twelve foot tall piece of bamboo fell from the sky. The sound of it crashing down hard onto the clearing was nearly all but muffled by the rotor wash from high above. And there the helicopter remained, hovering in the middle of the clearing as Downs and Tori turned and faced the female gigantopithecus.

61

"Now what?" Tori screamed into Downs' ear.

He yelled back at her. "Was hoping you had a plan!"

Downs quickly looked around and assessed the situation. He looked back to the two juveniles and the big male. In the madness of it all, the feeding frenzy hadn't taken further notice as to the two humans still standing in the clearing. They were busy going to town, tearing pieces of meat off and feeding on the man who had made the brazen attack on the big male giganto-pithecus.

To Downs' surprise, when he turned, the female gigantopithecus lifted the bamboo tree off the ground, faced them, and immediately began to charge. Together the small team of two saw the twelve hundred pound creature rampaging forward now, its three powerful limbs carrying it across the clearing while it brandished the tree once again in its right hand. This was one determined primate.

The creature's eyes flared brightly with intensity now as the big mouth opened wide and the massive creature bellowed a monstrous, gaping roar. Reaching out with his right hand, Downs backed the two of them up. They were within six feet or so of the mangled and partially-eaten woman. And in doing so, they had now become completely engulfed in the thick, black, swarming mass of flies.

• • •

The huge female gigantopithecus came to an aggressive stop. With a snort and a grunt, it reared up onto its back two legs. Still holding the bamboo tree in its right hand, from its full height of just shy of ten feet, it scanned and watched with big eyes. The creature had seen the two humans disappear just seconds prior. It scanned for another few moments before lowering itself back down and roaring.

• • •

Downs and Tori had momentarily been thrown into a chaotic, buzzing, churning, vibrating, and pulsating world of blackness. Downs found himself completely unprepared for the scope of just how loud and intense the buzzing roar that thousands upon thousands of flies had the ability to produce. Now inside this dense black thumping cloud of flies, it was hard to speak, hard to do much of anything. A short distance behind them, the nauseating smell of rotting flesh from the half-eaten corpse assailed their nostrils.

Downs opened his mouth and went to speak, but when he did so he found that several flies had found their way inside. He started coughing, gagging on the small, black, buzzing annoyances. Tori had a hard time hearing the man coughing and gagging beside her.

Barely able to open her eyes, when she finally did see Downs struggling, she knew immediately what it was. Almost as if he was choking on a piece of food, she pounded on his back with her right hand. She did so for another second or two before finally Downs gave her the thumbs up.

Now Downs stood upright, straightening himself to his full height of 6'3 inches. Wasting no more time, he yelled into Tori's left ear. "Take the animal out with two shots! One from me. One from you. Both of us aim for the huge chest. Got no choice now."

She yelled back into his ear. "Completely agree!"

The duo took another second or two, the shifting black mass of flies almost resembling an entity itself as they crisscrossed through the air in all directions. It was now time to put their plan into action. They stepped forward several feet through the black mass of flies and back out into the open.

• • •

A sense of disorientation set in momentarily as Downs and Tori stepped out of the center of the massive swarming black cloud. Now with that behind them, Downs again heard the roaring blaze of the helicopter from high above. As he looked up, for a moment, he could have sworn he saw a figure emerge out of the open hatch and begin climbing back down the ladder. He turned away though. The minute he did so, his eyes locked onto the female gigantopithecus. The large animal stood still and motionless about thirty feet away from them.

When the two humans finally raised their weapons, the female charged. The huge mouth opened wide which in turn summoned a monstrous sound as the animal exploded forward. The female raised the tree in its right hand and began bounding on three limbs toward the humans.

Downs steadied himself, released a small breath of air, and fired. It was confusing to tell what had in fact happened next. He heard the sound of Tori's assault rifle going off. Downs watched as the female gigantopithecus' right breast now pulsed with blood from the gun shot. That had been Tori's shot.

Next, a rage-filled roar rang out as the creature had been struck by Downs' shot into the wide chest. Despite the fact that the animal had been hit, it still managed to extend its huge head out and bellow another moaning roar. The animal continued to charge.

"Wait!" Downs yelled. "At the last second, you head to the right, I go left!"

Another bellowing roar filled the air and the animal was upon them. As planned, Downs darted to the left, Tori to the right. As Downs threw his body to the left, he managed to look back toward the rampaging female. The large animal with all its forward-moving momentum could not stop itself at this point and went charging headfirst straight into the swarming black cloud of flies.

Downs saw Tori out of the corner of his eye now. He could still hear the constant booming roar of the helicopter from high above. He turned in that direction, remembering that he thought he had seen someone seconds prior to the female charging. As the chopper drew nearer, he now realized he had. It took a few seconds, but from where Downs stood, he saw Burr Wellington hanging halfway down the ladder. And then Downs saw one of the air rifles in Burr's hands.

Downs looked up at the ladder which still hung from the chopper. Straight below the bottom of the ladder, Downs could see the big male gigantopithecus as it lifted its head from Brig Daniels' kill site and glared straight at Downs and Tori. The two humans had now officially been spotted. Downs watched as both juveniles immediately fanned out wide on either side of the big male.

Again, Downs lifted his head back up. He watched as Burr fired a tranquilizer dart aimed at the back of the male gigantopithecus. The shot was an errant one though, the dart disappearing into the clearing. The huge animal roared as it glared up at the helicopter, more specifically at the man perched halfway down the ladder who had attempted to shoot it.

Downs lowered his gaze to Tori. The entire time, she had not taken her eyes off the female that was still enshrouded amongst the thick cloud of flies. But before Downs looked back toward the female, he set his gaze on the approaching juveniles.

Now he could hear Tori shouting. He turned and saw the huge female still standing amongst the thick cloud of flies staring menacingly back at them. He could see the big, domed head and the fierce eyes staring back at them through the black mass.

Downs turned to Tori and shouted. "Let's go!"

He pointed toward the helicopter which was now heading toward them. Downs and Tori took off moving in the opposite direction just as the female gigantopithecus came bursting out of the cloud of flies roaring triumphantly.

Now the two were running hard. Downs craned his neck for a moment, made visual with Burr, and watched as the big man was getting himself into position for another shot.

Next Downs spotted the two juveniles. Now he and Tori came to a stop. Breathing hard, they now stood in the dead center of the clearing with their backs up against one another. With their weapons pressed out in front of them, they stood and faced the oncoming attack.

• • •

Burr Wellington felt the ache and pain in the fingers and palm of his right hand starting to win out. He wasn't certain how much longer he could hold on. For going on a solid two minutes now, he had been perched precariously, hanging at the bottom of the ladder, holding on for dear life with his right hand while maintaining his grip on the air rifle with his left hand. His first shot had missed. But now he was working hard to get himself into position for a second shot and then a third. His intent was to put a tranquilizer dart into the back of the big male, hopefully in a matter of time sending the creature into a catatonic state as the liquid contents inside the dart worked its way through the huge animal's bloodstream.

But now there were other issues to worry about. From up high like this, Burr had a bird's eye view down toward the unfolding scene below. He watched as the big male roared once more toward him before finally dropping to all fours. Now back down on the ground, it immediately shifted its focus toward Downs and Tori. Next, Burr saw the two juveniles fanning wide, approaching the situation with caution, yet still advancing forward, stalking their prey like raptors would have done millions upon millions of years ago.

From up high like this, things felt a bit surreal and detached for Burr, like he was watching the moving pieces to a real life-and-death chess game. The roar of the helicopter still continued to drown out everything. But still he knew his two teammates needed him. Suddenly, Burr craned his neck back up toward the top of the ladder. He saw two heads peering out of the hatch staring down at him. It was Jeremiah and Josiah.

Burr motioned with the air rifle for the helicopter to keep moving. He watched as Jeremiah's head suddenly disappeared back into the hatch, and then just like that, the helicopter was on the move once again.

• • •

Downs heard and literally felt the powerful thumping sensation of the rotor wash from high above. The helicopter was once again headed their way. But at this point, shit was too real, too serious to take one's eyes off the brewing situation that existed at ground level. It felt as though the entire clearing was converging upon them. And as Downs continued to take it all in, he knew that observation was indeed an accurate one.

Still butted up against each other, Downs was forced to yell to Tori.

"I got eyes on the female and two juveniles!" Downs shouted.

She yelled back. "And I got visual on the big male!"

Downs saw the female gigantopithecus. Now that it was back out in the open, he was able to make out both bleeding wounds to its chest. The animal suddenly appeared hesitant, unsure of itself, hampered by the two bullets that it had taken. The huge creature was still advancing, but only walking forward on its knuckles, moving in essentially the same manner as one would expect a modern-day silverback gorilla to move. Downs suspected it wouldn't be long now before the beast in fact collapsed.

The big male and the two juveniles, however, were not moving in unsure manners. The two juveniles were still fanned out wide, stalking their prey silently yet aggressively from both sides. Meanwhile, the big male was bounding forward, each huge limb helping to aid the sixteen hundred pound creature's assault.

Now Downs shifted his attention to the male gigantopithecus and the one juvenile stalking them from the far left.

The roar of the helicopter was still above them. Downs turned his head and shouted into Tori's ear. "You got eyes on the other juvenile!"

She yelled back. "Roger that!"

Downs took in a deep breath. Now the chopper was flying low behind the male gigantopithecus. Downs could see the ladder still dangling downward. Quickly, he looked from the bottom of the rope to the top. No sign of Burr.

Despite the deafening roar of the rotor wash from high above, Downs heard an immense sound from the ground level on the clearing. Downs brought his head down and saw the big male moving quickly toward them. Again, the huge mouth opened wide and the creature let out a monstrous, thundering roar.

And then suddenly, Downs saw an odd sight. A little bit behind the male gigantopithecus, behind its four massive pillar-sized limbs, Downs saw the silhouette of a human moving quickly across the clearing. For a second, he thought it was the fallen soldier with only one hand. But as he continued to watch, Downs saw that it was Burr Wellington. The big two hundred and fifty pound Washington native was moving fast now. Downs watched as Burr neared to within ten yards or so of the backside of the big male. As he watched Burr bring himself to a stop, he thought he noticed the slightest of limps in the man's step. Burr Wellington appeared to be injured. Downs wasn't certain how he had gotten back down to the clearing. It appeared Burr had been forced to jump from the ladder. Whatever the scenario, he now found himself slightly hampered behind the big male.

Downs shouted over to Burr. But it was too late. Burr steadied himself and fired a dart into the backside of the male. The big male instantly took notice. It unleashed a monstrous roar and flung its sixteen hundred pound mass around, pounding its two front forelimbs into the ground as it lurched forward.

Downs watched as the massive creature now began moving toward Burr. Wasting no time, he turned to

Tori and pulled the assault rifle from her hands. In place of it, he gave her the Astra. "Trade ya."

Before she could even respond, the two had taken off and were on the move once again. Downs raced forward, making his way to the left side of the rampaging male as the huge animal continued its assault on Burr. Out of his left eye, he could see the approaching juvenile, the one on the right was blocked out by the huge body of the male.

Downs pushed his legs harder now as he edged past Tori. She was fast, damn fast, but Downs was in top gear now, hauling ass in an attempt to get himself into position. The big male turned the second Downs arrived on its left hand side. Downs watched as the large, domed-shaped head stared down at him as the creature continued thundering forward. Just as it did so, Downs aimed the assault rifle and unleashed a torrent of bullets into the dirt just at the animal's huge limbs.

The sudden barrage of bullets did nothing though as the massive creature galloped onward. Downs however managed to edge himself slightly ahead of the giant beast. Turning himself around, Downs was now backtracking across the clearing while staring back at the big male. Again, he unleashed a spray of bullets into the dirt just a few feet ahead of the creature. This time, the result Downs had been hoping for was achieved.

The male gigantopithecus came to a complete stop and reared up onto its back two powerful legs. The animal let out a monstrous cry. And then it lowered itself onto all fours and veered hard to the right.

Downs continued moving forward. Up ahead, he could see Burr. The big man wasn't stopping either.

Downs motioned for Burr to stop, but there was no stop in the big man's step now.

Downs took one more look Burr's way. And then he spotted it. Downs pulled the flare gun holstered at his back, steadied himself, and fired. The bright orange ball of fire pinned the juvenile that had been pursuing Burr Wellington somewhere on its neck. The screaming juvenile was instantly knocked backward.

Downs flung himself around. Where in the hell was Tori? It took a moment, but eventually he found her. She was running off just to the right of the male gigantopithecus. But as Downs continued scanning, he could see that she too was being pursued by one of the juveniles.

"Oh, fuck!" Downs mumbled to himself.

Rather than race out in front of the massive male, Downs ducked in closely behind it, literally following within yards of the thundering footsteps of the huge beast.

Downs turned his full attention back to Tori. He both heard and caught the tail end of the big male as it let out another cavernous roar. And then it turned and headed in Burr's direction, appearing hell-bent on ending the Washington native.

Downs peeled hard to the right, reaching into his back pocket and reloading a flare cartridge into the flare gun. He saw Tori, and about a good fifty feet behind her, he spotted the other juvenile. Downs raced forward, shouting. The helicopter was literally right above them now so his words were drowned out. Tori managed to see him. He quickly motioned for her to continue on.

Downs eyed his target and got himself into position. The minute that he had been spotted by the attacking juvenile, the animal changed its course of direction. The youngster let out a rage-filled roar as it charged toward Downs. Feeling the energy welling up from within, Downs blasted a roar of his own. Now the energy was absolutely coursing through him, flowing through every ounce of his body. He felt completely overcome with rage now, wrapped tightly in its warm and powerful embrace. And then for the briefest of seconds time stood still. All the other sights and sounds of the clearing faded off into the background.

Downs watched as the juvenile quickly closed the distance from fifty to within twenty feet. Again the animal let out another cry. Now Downs' senses went into hypersensitive mode. He saw the animal and watched as the mouth opened wide and blasted another roar. Keeping up his speed, he let out a primal scream of his own.

Downs waited. The two combatants were now some ten feet apart. He had waited long enough. He saw the creature raise its forelimb high and into the air. The mouth baring teeth opened wide once again. At the last second, Downs raised the flare gun, took aim, and fired straight into the mouth of the charging beast. The flare from the gun had struck the animal square in the back of the throat, momentarily lighting up the gaping black hole. That was all Downs could see though as he flung his body to the right and went tumbling off into the dirt. He tumbled end over end until finally coming to a stop. Quickly, he holstered the flare gun at his side while taking possession of the assault rifle in both hands.

Downs could hear the roaring sound of the helicopter still high above. He rapidly pushed himself upright and stood to his feet.

He saw the juvenile that he had shot with the flare gun. The animal was limping, letting out deep, course, gagging coughs. And then just like that, the animal collapsed. Was it dead? Downs didn't have time to find out.

Quickly, he began scanning while moving forward. No sooner than he had spotted Tori, he heard the sound of the Astra going off. He turned and saw the smoking barrel pointed in the direction of the big male. Tori had shot at the ground just in front of the huge creature's limbs. This had caused the animal to come to a momentary stop. Had she not, the rampaging animal would have more than likely put an end to Burr Wellington. Now as the huge animal turned and roared in her direction, Downs watched as Burr was busy making his way quickly around the backside of the immense creature.

The big male shifted its massive girth and spun around in the direction of Burr. But the man was now nowhere to be seen. Immediately, the male giganto-pithecus turned in the direction of Tori. Now Burr and Tori were bolting toward Downs. A short distance behind them, the big male began to take thundering steps on all fours in pursuit of them.

Downs turned. Near the edge of the trees, he spotted the juvenile that he had shot in the back of the throat lying on its side. There was minimal movement in the animal. Downs turned and saw Tori and Burr sprinting back toward him. A short distance behind them, the big male was still pursuing. Downs continued scanning. The original juvenile was quickly closing the gap on the right side of the male gigantopithecus now.

Downs spun around. Behind him, he watched as the ladder dangled some six or seven feet off the ground as the helicopter hovered there. This was their chance, it was now or never. Leave now, or run the risk of meeting their maker in this clearing. He didn't fancy that one bit.

Downs shouted and waved them on with his arms, urging them to move faster now. He knew he could be to the ladder in a matter of seconds and climbing the rungs to safety if he so chose to, but he couldn't leave them. He needed to get everyone aboard safely and then he'd worry about himself last. That was the main objective now.

Out of the corner of his right eye, he spotted the female gigantopithecus. The huge beast had lumbered its way into the center of the clearing now, raised both front forelimbs high into the air, and sent them crashing down hard into the dirt. It let out one last bellowing cry as it extended its head and neck outward and then collapsed right there under its own weight. Now he focused his attention back on the big male and attacking juvenile. And then suddenly, he realized that the dying cries of the female gigantopithecus had not gone unnoticed. Slowly, the male gigantopithecus brought its huge girth to a stop and looked over toward its fallen mate. Sixteen hundred pounds of muscle and mass took off thundering across the clearing in pursuit of the female as the huge beast let out a roaring cry. In the chaos of it all, the juvenile gigantopithecus had also come to a stop as well. The young four hundred pound animal appeared unsure of itself.

Now Downs was encouraging Tori and Burr to cover the last bit of the distance. Pushing off with his feet, he raced out to greet them.

"C'mon!" Downs shouted. "Now's our chance! Let's get the hell outta here."

Looking Burr straight in the eyes, he spoke to him. "You shouldn't fuckin' be down here, big guy!"

Burr smiled a wide grin as he yelled back. "Like to live dangerous, son! Now bloody move!"

Downs pushed Tori and Burr past him and in the direction of the ladder. The minute that Downs looked back toward the juvenile, he watched as the frozen animal suddenly sprung to life. Now the four hundred pound creature was headed straight for them, galloping on four powerful limbs, striding aggressively across the clearing. Downs turned and began hauling ass toward the ladder.

He could see up ahead some seventy to eighty feet away that Tori was the first one to reach the ladder. She turned and faced in the direction of Burr, but the big man frantically waved her on. Quickly, she began climbing the rungs of the ladder. Burr turned back toward Downs, but Downs waved him on as well.

The Washington native quickly began climbing up the ladder. This left only Downs as he neared to within forty feet of the ladder.

• • •

The male gigantopithecus arrived at its fallen mate's side. It peered down at the bleeding animal's stained fur. The twelve hundred pound creature had collapsed on its right side. Now a growing pool of blood had slowly puddled beneath its body. The big male moved forward, extended its left front limb, and gently nudged the massive gut of the fallen creature. No movement, no response. Following this stark realization, the huge male lifted itself onto its back two legs, beat aggressively on its wide chest, and bellowed an earth-shattering roar.

• • •

Downs closed to within fifteen feet of the ladder. He could feel the ladder in his grasp, feel it in his fingertips, feel his feet climbing the rungs to safety. For the past dozen feet or so, he had been diligently rehearsing his every move. What would he do when he got there, how fast would he be able to execute each step? He was literally an arms-length away from the ladder when he heard a stiff growl from behind. He knew he was too late.

Downs didn't stop though. He continued running for the ladder, ran past it several feet, and then quickly spun his body back around. Six feet away from the ladder stood the juvenile. Now the dangling ladder stood in between the two now. Up close like this, Downs was able to fully appreciate the muscular physique of the young animal. Heavily built around the chest, forearms, and neck region, Downs watched as the gums rippled back, exposing a mouth full of teeth. Without any further warning, the juvenile charged. Its four hundred pound mass collided with the rungs of the ladder. The charging animal knocked the ladder back, which in turn hit Downs. The impact was stunning and knocked him to the ground. With the rotor wash from the helicopter still dominating high above, Downs quickly rose to his feet.

The second he stood, he found the juvenile gigantopithecus momentarily caught up and entangled in the ladder. Downs wasted no time. Blasting a roar of his own, he rushed forward. Turning the assault rifle over in his hands, he struck the juvenile square in the side of its jaw with the butt of the rifle. The impact was powerful enough to momentarily knock the large animal back. But the powerfully-built creature was not to be denied. With a commanding roar, it once again lunged forward toward the ladder.

Downs was already busy climbing the first two rungs when the creature grabbed hold of his right leg and began pulling him down. Downs held on with everything he had, but the power with which the animal had grabbed him was too much. Downs fell back toward the ground.

His backside took the blow square on as he hit the ground hard. The fall from the ladder had momentarily taken the wind from his lungs. But he couldn't allow it to go any further than that. He stood and squared up. His eyes locked in on a fuming face as the juvenile bared its teeth, blared loudly, and charged straight at him. Throwing his body hard to the right, Downs watched as the mass of the animal passed by him. As it did so, again he slammed the butt of the rifle into the back of the creature's skull. Meanwhile, the ladder began to move slowly as it started swaying back and forth. Downs allowed himself a moment to gaze up. He saw faces peering down through the open hatch, but that was it. Just below the open hatch, he saw the figure of someone hanging from the ladder with a tranquilizer rifle pointed downward. But there was too much going on at ground level to extend the view any further than that.

Downs turned and made sure he had visual of the juvenile. The animal spun sharply and turned itself around. And there it remained for a moment as it rested on all fours. Downs watched as the gums rippled back into a sinister grin.

Then Downs saw an even more pressing issue from behind the juvenile. His eyes stretched toward the middle of the clearing. The big male had spotted Downs once again. The huge animal now appeared to be taking a renewed interest in the 6'3" two hundred pound man. He watched in horror as the immense creature lowered its neck and bellowed a moaning roar in his direction. And then the massively built creature took off. The roaring beast was now heading straight for the ladder.

Downs locked back in on the juvenile. The animal now stood some ten feet from him. The juvenile began moving forward, but this time it was more deliberate, more calculated. Like a lion stalking prey on the Serengeti of Africa, the creature moved forward silently and stealthily. Downs squared up. The assault rifle was firmly in his hands. He thought about firing into the ground at the animal's feet, but with the sheer magnitude of the chopper still hovering loudly above them, he feared the sound made by the rifle would fall on deaf ears.

Now the juvenile began moving at a quicker pace. Downs shot forward. The ladder was practically in his grasp, but he had underestimated the speed of the juvenile. The four hundred pound creature burst forward in a flash. Downs braced for the impact. As his hands made contact with the rungs of the ladder, he watched as the juvenile gigantopithecus stopped momentarily, reared up onto its back two legs, and let out a furious roar. Downs knew instantly what had happened. The animal had been shot in the back with a dart. This momentary distraction gave Downs all the window he needed. He wasn't hanging around to find out what was going to happen next down here. The time to leave was long overdue.

Quickly, he began climbing the ladder. When the approaching youngster neared to a close enough distance, Downs countered with a swift kick to the side of its face. The aggressive act momentarily stunned the creature. This gave Downs the time he needed for the helicopter to pull higher into the sky. But all of them had underestimated the speed of the big male. Blasting a triumphant roar, the male gigantopithecus reached up with a powerful hand and grabbed hold of the bottom of the dangling ladder.

Downs was perched jut a few feet above the huge leathery hand of the creature. Pulling back, the brute strength of the creature was not to be denied. The big male had now brought the chopper to a halt as the aircraft struggled to lift higher into the sky. From where Downs remained perched, he peered down at the huge, enraged beast. He saw the massive dome-shaped head followed by the dark black, oversized, flappy cheek pads known as flanges on both sides of the giant's face. Downs locked in on the big eyes. He gazed into the huge, gaping black hole and saw the huge teeth and the saliva. To move any closer would be certain death. As the animal blasted another primal roar, it sent a wave of hot breath with it.

Again, Downs could feel the chopper struggling to lift up into the sky. Once again though, he felt the big male pulling them back with sheer brute strength. Downs watched as the huge male gripped down with two hands atop the bottom rung of the ladder. With what appeared to be ungodly strength, the male gigantopithecus was now pulling the helicopter down. Little by little, inch by inch, they had reached a standstill.

Quickly, Downs began moving down the ladder. His eyes momentarily locked in on the huge eyes of the big male. The enraged animal began pulling harder, trying to literally pull the chopper down from the sky. Downs moved faster now, his eyes intently focused on the creature's huge hands still gripping down tightly around the bottom rung of the ladder. As Downs neared, he was instantly greeted with a wave of hot breath accompanied by the overwhelming stench of the animal. Another step closer and he now found himself perched precariously just above the huge hands. He watched as the large, domed head craned its way back even further. And then the huge mouth opened wide and Downs felt the hot, panting breath of the animal. Up close and personal like this, for the first time Downs got a true sense for the scale of this beast. The head was absolutely enormous, possibly twice the size of an adult male silverback gorilla. It was as frightening an animal as he had ever encountered in the wild.

Still perched on the second rung of the ladder, just above the huge leathery hands of the animal, Downs watched as the mouth opened wide and blasted another roar of hot stinking breath his way. Downs had no choice. Giving no further thought to it, he lowered himself into position, and then with everything he had, sent his full two hundred pound body slamming down hard as he stomped both feet down upon the beast's left hand. Downs was amazed at how solid the massive fingers felt under his feet. As he stood there atop the gigantic knuckles and fingers of the animal's left hand, at first he felt he had achieved nothing. And then he suddenly felt movement beneath him. Then to his surprise, he felt the animal pull back with its left hand. From way up close like this, Downs watched and felt the animal as it blasted a roar of rage. But Downs was not to be denied. Still holding on with his hands to the rung of the ladder just above him, he again hoisted his mass up into the air. Using every last ounce of strength and energy he could summon, he sent both feet plunging down upon the animal's final and remaining hand. The male gigantopithecus let out a deep and cavernous roar. The lone right hand slowly fell away. But then suddenly out of the corner of Downs' right eye, he saw something large moving fast toward him. It was the big male's left hand. Downs grabbed hold of the rungs above him and hoisted his body into the air as the huge five fingers closed down on nothing but thin air.

He watched as the huge leathery hand with its equally massive fingers closed shut. For a brief moment, as Downs hung with his legs lifted up toward his chest, he felt the enormous burn and strain in his core. He thought about the crushing power of those hands as they closed shut. Had his leg in fact been there, he would have found himself in a powerful vice-like grip right about now, literally being crushed into oblivion. Instead, he felt the burn and pain in his abs as he continued to hold his legs extended up toward his chest. And then to his surprise, he saw one last attempt by the animal to get to him. A huge leathery hand stretched wide attempted to grab his right foot. Downs countered with a swift kick to the hand. And that was all it took. He watched as the huge hand was pulled backward.

Immediately, Downs felt the helicopter rising up and into the sky. Wasting no more time, he turned and began climbing the lower rungs of the ladder. Looking down momentarily to the clearing, he could see the remaining juvenile and the big male as they took off together in hot pursuit of the flying craft.

Downs watched them galloping possibly a good twenty to twenty five feet below as he held on tightly. It was an exhilarating sensation to feel the warm air upon his skin and his face. To see and experience the jungle like this even for the briefest of moments made him feel truly grateful to be alive. Looking down, he continued to observe the two pursuing creatures in the clearing, the speedier and quicker juvenile out in front while the massive, slower male took up the rear.

Again Downs felt the helicopter pulling higher into the sky now. He looked up the ladder and saw faces peering out the open hatch waving and yelling for him to hurry. He took one last look back toward the clearing, watched the two creatures below still giving chase, and then began climbing the remaining rungs. Focusing all his attention and energy now on the task at hand, he carefully began ascending up the ladder as the wind continued to whip all around him. Nearing the halfway point up the ladder, he could see that they were nearly at the end of the open clearing. A solid wall of green bamboo trees awaited them beyond that. The helicopter rose higher into the sky now. Downs was climbing quickly as he neared the top. When he finally arrived at the open hatch, there were hands there to greet him and pull him inside. For a brief few seconds, he sort of pulled the rest of his body inside by snake crawling on his stomach. Two powerful hands carefully helped him to his feet. It was Josiah.

Josiah gave him a thumbs up.

It was a lot to take in. The whole team was there, and each and every one of them was ready to head home. They were bloodied, battered, beaten, injured, and dehydrated. The list went on and on, but most important was the fact that they had made it and were here. They had thankfully arrived in one piece. Downs looked over to Burr. He had to yell to be heard. "That was batshit crazy what you did comin' down there like that, big guy!"

Burr yelled back from his seated position. "I like to live dangerously Downs, always have, always will! And I'd do it again!"

Downs smiled and laughed. "I know you would! But I definitely appreciated it!"

Suddenly, Max Caldwell got up and out of his seat. With shaky legs, the zoologist made his way over to the open hatch and carefully peered down. They were flying over the tops of the bamboo trees now; a beautiful and pristine green blanket of forest canopy stretched out in all directions below them. But a ways back, Max spotted something. He motioned for Downs.

By the time Downs made his way to the open hatch, the others had joined in as well. Downs made his way carefully to Max's side and peered out. Max pointed to an area about a quarter of a mile back. It took Downs a few extra seconds to spot it, but eventually he noticed it.

Downs pointed with his right arm while the bulk of his body hugged tightly to the rest of the open hatch. The tops of the bamboo trees were shaking and swaying back and forth now. As they watched further, it appeared as though something was following them. There was no doubt it had to be the big male accompanied by the juvenile. Down on the forest floor, the massive sixteen hundred pound creature appeared to be causing a wake of destruction headed in the general direction of the helicopter, following the team as they flew out of here. The team watched for a few more seconds, the wind whipping furiously all around them before finally Downs motioned for them all to have a seat.

The helicopter veered hard to the left. Each and every member of the team walked on somewhat unstable legs as they crossed the middle part of the helicopter and made their way back to their seats. Downs was the last one to sit down. He lowered his head while letting out a deep sigh. Quickly, he buckled himself in and looked up. Tori was staring back at him. She too seemed tired as hell. With both hands, she raised her backpack up and motioned to him. It was the bag that contained the cameras as well as computer equipment documenting the existence of the small family of gigantopithecus. There were even two cell phones in there accompanied by an iPad. Downs nodded back to her. Even if he had wanted to, he was far too tired at this point to even manufacture a smile. It just wasn't going to happen. And then Downs leaned his head back against the headrest and let his eyes fall shut.

EPILOGUE

In the end, Bick Downs and the Society of Cryptozoological Agents had managed to find success with their mission to Vietnam. The team had done what had been asked of them by Society President John Corstine while at the same time upholding the standards set in place by the organization. Force was only to be used when all other options had been exhausted. Their lives had potentially been in danger and there had been no other option but to use the lethal means necessary.

The team headed by Bick Downs had entered the rugged and untamed wilderness of rural Vietnam and stopped the human interests hell-bent on showcasing the remarkable yet still intact small population of gigantopithecus species to the rest of the world. The goal had been the same as always—to keep the prehistoric wonders of the world a secret from the prying eyes of humanity. And while the overall objective may have changed mid-mission, namely they did not in fact capture and transport the giganto-pithecus to their remote location in Siberia, Downs and his team had managed to thwart all human efforts to bring and expose these creatures to the world. That was something that the team could be proud of, and they most definitely were.

Upon arrival back in San Francisco, Downs delivered the documentary film crew's computer equipment, video cameras, two cell phones, one iPad, and all other potential footage that had the ability to be leaked and spread to the far corners of the globe to John Corstine's office. The footage was reviewed, analyzed, and ultimately destroyed. Death by incineration was the chosen route of erasing all possible evidence suggesting that a small population of giant primates had in fact managed to survive into the present day.

The small, privately-owned company behind the funding of the documentary film team headed by Stacey Winston launched a formal investigation as to why four fully capable and adept adults were dropped into the teeming bamboo forests of Vietnam only to have one return home. Pieces of tattered clothing, their downed tents, and a few other random tripods and boom mics here and there were all that was found. The bodies of Stacey Winston, Diane Clor, and Clark Geiger were never officially recovered. For a period of several months, Bob Hohrman was questioned and under brief investigation, but he was eventually found not guilty in regards to the disappearance of the others. His story was as follows: they had entered the jungle in attempt to create a short documentary about the possible existence of the largest ape the world has ever known. One afternoon, around midday, they had found themselves in the company of a series of strange sounds from deep inside the forest. Being the professionals that they all were, they took off in hot pursuit of what had been responsible for the sounds. In that mad dash to go after the prized footage, they had all gotten separated in their frenzied pursuit to get footage of the unknown sounds. They were never reunited again and Bob spent the next forty-eight hours alone wandering aimlessly through the bamboo forest before eventually being rescued by a lone helicopter doing survey work of Vietnam's bamboo forests. Bob Hohrman eventually signed a non-disclosure agreement by The Society of Cryptozoological Agents to keep quiet with regards to what he had witnessed and was paid a moderately sized amount of money valued in the high five figures. With a little bit of wrestling back and forth, Bob eventually accepted the money he was offered. He had two teenagers after all that would need their college educations to be funded.

In regards to Brig Daniels, Finn Carter, and Decker Johnson, their bodies were never found. Because of the covert nature of their work and the contacts that they had associated with on the dark web, each of the three men had never spoken of their current assignment to family or friends. Consequently, no one knew of their trip to Vietnam. They are still considered missing.

As far as the Society of Cryptozoological Agents went, Burr Wellington returned home to the state of Washington. Having finally seen and experienced the living Bigfoot up close and personal in the flesh, he gave up his own personal search for signs of Sasquatch in his native Washington. Rather, he decided he would take a nice two week vacation with just him and his two dogs to Arizona for a little rest and relaxation. Tori Nguyen returned home to the San Francisco Bay Area and continued to aid her elderly parents with their Vietnamese restaurant as well as resumed work on her follow-up to her debut bestselling book. Although it took a bit longer than she would have liked, eventually the payday that she had been patiently waiting for finally came in. She was offered an advance in the amount of $450,000 from Random House. It was a giant chunk of change by anyone's estimates and served to do the one main thing that had been on her agenda for quite some time now, and that was to allow her parents to retire once and for all from their restaurant. She sent them on a one-month cruise around the world with the money as well as ultimately gifted the rest of the entire advance to them. Tori eventually hired a manager of the restaurant to assist her during those long days of writing when she could not be physically present.

Max Caldwell returned home to the San Francisco Zoo's Zoology Department. Josiah Young returned to UC Berkeley to finish up work on his doctoral degree in Vertebrae Paleontology. As he prepared to graduate, he was also busy writing and seeking approval to fund his first dig for dinosaur bones in the Sahara Desert. The best news of his short-lived career came when he received written notice that he had been approved to receive the necessary grant money in order to fund the dig. The timing couldn't have come at a more opportune time for him.

Jeremiah Corstine returned home to Maui where he was responsible for managing his father John Corstine's vast real estate empire. As always, both he and his father continued to monitor the gigantopithecus situation in

Vietnam remotely. Lastly, Bick Downs returned home to his beloved San Francisco, to the Potrero Hill neighborhood of the city where he ran his locally owned and operated action sports store. Now that the store had actually begun to turn a profit, Downs was able to shift part of his attention to working on what he was hoping would be his first short film: a documentary based on Tori Nguyen's bestselling book about man's obsessive attempts to resurrect the ancient woolly mammoth.

Each member of the team quietly awaits their next assignment from John Corstine.

• • •

TWO MONTHS LATER

Twenty-two year old YouTuber Grant Jones readjusted his positioning behind the camera and checked the legs of the tripod once again. He stepped back a few paces. All appeared to be in good working order. Now he took a moment to fully soak in and appreciate just where he was. He was smack dab in the middle of a lush bamboo forest somewhere in Northern Vietnam. All around, tall thin bamboo trees surrounded him. They grew straight as an arrow toward the entangled canopy high above and blocked out most of the light.

It seemed to be fate, almost his destiny if you will. A good buddy of his had a friend who was fired by the very same production company that had sent Stacey Winston and a team of three others into the teeming bamboo forests of Vietnam to search for the largest primate that has ever existed. That friend had relayed two messages Grant's way. The first one being that an expedition in search of the unknown had been launched, and secondly and most importantly, only one out of the four from that team had returned home alive. Grant had considered it to be a godsend that his good buddy had gotten this news to him. It seemed like it was all coming together for him, like things were finally going to work out. He had just graduated from the University of California, Riverside with a degree in business. And for going on the past several months, Grant had felt on top of the world, like he had literally just mountain climbed straight up the face of Half Dome in Yosemite National Park. And this was only the beginning of things to come. There were more mountains to climb. Hell, he felt he could literally get to the top of Mt. Everest. If he could just eke it out, claw, scrape, and fight his way to one million subscribers, then he'd get to ten million subscribers one day. Then he'd literally be a bonafide rock star with the earning potential of seven figures a year. He let out a deep breath. One thing at a time. First things first, he needed to ensure that his trip to Vietnam was well worth the expense and that he got some amazing original content for his channel. He planned to be uploading his latest video exactly this time tomorrow. The video was going to be about the potential that Gigantopithecus could in fact still be alive in these parts, but a good part of his new video would be dedicated to the fact that a film crew of four had come here while only one person made it home.

He had set up his YouTube channel over two years ago. At first it had started as nothing more than a hobby, a time-consuming hobby that kept Grant up into the wee hours of the night in order to produce three videos per week, but within six months he had hit one hundred thousand subscribers. With that, for the first time, Grant Jones saw the true power of social media and being a so-called social media influencer. He had made up his mind halfway through his senior year at UC Riverside that upon graduation, he would forgo looking for a corporate career and pursue YouTube fulltime. And so far, as Grant looked up to the bamboo canopy high above, he had been making a modest living for the last six months. Most importantly, he'd been surviving and was able to pay his rent and bills from his YouTube earnings. He was surviving solely from what most would consider to be a foolish endeavor.

Grant's channel had been dedicated to exposing and uncovering the great mysteries and secrets of the world. He was scheduled to go to Roswell, New Mexico sometime late next month, and even had a trip already lined up for Loch Ness in Scotland next summer. There was a lot going on for him in terms of the mysteries of the world and he hoped it would just keep continuing. Once he indeed hit a million subscribers, he was fully planning on making a good living, a damn good living to put it bluntly. Online fame and fortune in the form of becoming a small-time social media influencer wasn't long now. He was confident of this. He just needed to keep producing content.

Suddenly, a noise from out in the trees caught Grant's attention. He looked around, fully absorbing the tall bamboo trees that grew all around him. He listened for a few more seconds before finally returning his attention back to the camera still mounted atop his brand new tripod. The tripod had come last week in the mail from Amazon, and he had found himself tremendsously excited to finally get to use it out in the field.

Again, Grant thought he'd heard something. He froze right where he was. For a second, he felt his pulse increase, but quickly his brain took over. He wasn't going to let his mind freak him out. He had content to film and produce. He waited for another full minute before things returned to normal.

Reaching down to his backpack, he grabbed his water bottle. He drank thirstily from it in several aggressive gulps. Setting the water bottle down next to the bag, he grabbed hold of an item. In his left hand, he held what appeared to be the tattered and torn portion of a t-shirt.

Not more than ten minutes ago, Grant had been standing in front of his fancy HD camera speaking directly into it. He spoke of how through his day trip up and down the sloping hillsides, he had retrieved a piece of a tattered shirt and the top portion of a boom mic. Grant was convinced he had retrieved direct evidence that the small documentary film team had encountered a living, breathing Gigantopithecus. The entire time he had been filming and speaking directly into the camera, he was picturing the comment section of this video. He could already imagine the comments once the video was uploaded. He would see comments talking about BigFoot, Sasquatch, and potentially the legend of the Chinese Yeren. All good stuff. He couldn't wait to upload this video and showcase to all of his subscribers that he had found direct evidence that the small documentary film team that had entered these isolated forests had in fact encountered and suffered casualties at the hands of what more than likely was several members of the Gigantopithecus species.

A distinct cracking sound from somewhere close by broke Grant from his thoughts. He looked up. Without taking his eyes off from the area where the sound had just come from, he leaned down and set the piece of shirt and broken boom mic down near his bag. As he raised his head back up, his eyes caught his camera for a second. On the screen, the symbol for low battery was now flashing. He knew it wouldn't be long now before the camera shut off entirely.

Grant set his gaze back on a distinct row of bamboo trees that grew several yards in front from where he stood. Now all was quiet. To his left, his ears picked up on the sound of several of the bamboo trees as they knocked gently against one another. A quick glance back to his camera and he could see that the thing had officially shut down on him, the screen now replaced with solid black.

More sounds of cracking could be heard from off in the brush. But when Grant brought his eyes away from the camera and back to the forest straight ahead, this time he heard more noise. He heard movement to his right, off to his left, and from somewhere behind him.

Holy fuck, he thought to himself in a moment of panic.

Now noise appeared to surround him on all sides. As he listened closer, he realized just what it was. It was the sound of bamboo being splintered and broken, but by what was the question.

The sound of trees cracking was now accompanied by what sounded like leaves under foot. The forest was being trampled and broken, but what was most unnerving was the fact that it all appeared to be working its way toward him. Now the forest had truly come alive. Despite the wave of terror that had quickly risen up from within him, his eyes glanced back to his camera. The screen was still black. He eyed his backpack. He didn't have time to put the spare battery in. Grant looked up. Just as he did so, he heard noise at his back once again. He spun around. Now the panic and terror in him was real. The world started to spin as his heart pounded hard against his ribcage. He spun to his left as more noise continued to ring out.

And then quickly, everything died down. The forest now lay completely silent. Grant stood there breathing hard, his heart still pounding like mad. The silence stretched for what seemed like an eternity before he heard more noise. An immense rumbling and cavernous roar rang out from somewhere off in the trees straight ahead. No sooner than it had ended, another deep moaning roar came at his back. Suddenly, it all came rushing to him. He felt stupid, the absurdity of ever coming to this place. His insides felt as though they had been reduced to jello, his legs were shaky and wobbly, and his bladder was threatening to unload literally at any second. And then swiftly, with the dead camera still mounted firmly atop the tripod and the backpack accompanied by the torn piece of t-shirt still lying on the ground at his feet, Grant Jones watched as four impossibly huge creatures emerged from the trees, stepped out into the open, and quickly began to converge upon him.

Bick Downs will return in

BOOK FOUR

To read more in the Bick Downs series,
see the following

PREHISTORIC
HYBRID

To read other standalone thrillers, see the following

THE ICE GORILLA

WALKING WITH
ZOMBIES

SILVERBACK

Manufactured by Amazon.ca
Bolton, ON